SHERLOCK HOLM
21st CENT

By

Magda Jozs

This book would not have been possible without the narratives provided by Dr. John H. Watson MD, his daughter, Joan Watson Hudson and Sherlock Holmes Lestrade.

This book is available in all online bookstores in print format and in eBook format end of December or purchase via the author's website at:

www.read4life.com

Copyright © September 2000
All rights reserved
First Edition

Published by Create Space independent publishing

ISBN: 978 1503218 550

Other books by this Author:

SHERLOCK HOLMES BOOKS
Sherlock Holmes on the Wild Frontier
Return to the Wild Frontier.
The Private Diaries of Dr. Watson
Sherlock Holmes and the Femme Fatales
Sherlock Holmes in the 21st Century
The Great Detective – His further Adventures.

NURSING THRILLERS
Night Moves
God's Disciple

ANDROMEDA FOX SERIES
1. Death Bringer
2. Art for Art's Sake
3. A Friend in Need
4. Kidnapped

NEPTUNE KING SERIES
1 Introducing Neptune King.
2. The Casebook of Neptune King.
3. The Adventures of Neptune King.
4. The Revenge of Neptune king.
5. The Exploits of Neptune King.
6. The Marriage of Neptune King.
7. Neptune King Investigates.
8. Neptune King Down Under.
9. A Surprise for Neptune King.
10. The Friends of Neptune King.
11. Neptune King and the Newly Weds.
12. Neptune King and the Psychic Witness
13. The Bizarre Cases of Neptune King.
14. The Singular Cases of Neptune King.
15. The Challenges of Neptune King.
16. Neptune King and the Counterfeiters.
17. Neptune King of Baker Street.
18. Dosvidonia, Neptune King.
19. The Enemies of Neptune King.
20. The Charity Cases of Neptune King.
21. The Deductions of Neptune King.
22. Neptune King and the Lunatic Asylum.
23. Neptune King and the Gallant Thief
24. Neptune King and the Missing People.
25. The Miscellaneous Cases of Neptune King

MISCELLANEOUS TITLES
Natural Progression
Tall Tales and Other Stories

CONTENTS

BOOK ONE

SHERLOCK HOLMES IN THE 21ST CENTURY

Narrative by Dr. John H. Watson

AUTHOR'S NOTE

While this book may not be suitable for die hard Holmes fans who only like stories that strictly follow the canon, if you have read my other stories, you will know that I like to put the boys in situations outside their comfort zones. Naturally, as always, they triumph over everything. If you have read and liked my other stories, then I hope you will like this one also. Just as I like Westerns, I also like science fiction, and as I've already put our heroes in a western setting, it was only natural that they would dabble in science fiction. I had a lot of fun writing it, so I trust you will derive as much enjoyment reading it.

PS: While as a rule I use British spelling in my books, which often confuses some American readers, this time I have attempted to use American spelling. Please forgive me if an occasional British word has slipped in. ☺

Read and enjoy

Magda Jozsa

CHAPTER ONE

In my long association with Sherlock Holmes I don't believe we ever encountered a more remarkable situation than that which started on that fine summer evening of May 10th 1890.

Holmes and I had just finished a pleasant dinner at Simpson's. Due to the mildness of the evening we decided to stroll home and enjoy the night air. As we sauntered along Baker Street about one block from our lodgings, Holmes suddenly stopped and darted down a side alley. I followed him curiously, wondering what had caught his attention.

At the end of the alley was a strange hazy fog, yet the air was clear everywhere else. Holmes stopped in front of it.

"What do you make of that, Watson?' he said, looking at the cloud with interest.

"Is it emanating from a vent?" I queried.

"No, I don't believe so." Holmes reached out a hand, touching the fog. His hand seemed to disappear, but was still attached when he pulled it out.

"Curious," he said looking at his hand. "It has a strange pins and needles type feeling. Not wholly unpleasant though."

I too reached out a hand curiously. He was right. My skin seemed to prickle. "What is it, Holmes?"

"I'm not sure, some natural phenomenon I suppose." He took a step forward, and then another and disappeared into the cloud.

"Holmes!" I cried out in shock, for he seemed to have vanished. The cloud began to dissipate. I leapt forward into the cloud before it disappeared completely. When I landed I stumbled on the floor of the alley. I straightened up and looked wildly around. With relief I spied Holmes at the end of the alley. I hurried forward calling out, "Holmes!"

He turned, and there was a strange expression on his face. "You shouldn't have followed me, Watson," he said.

"What! Why?" I asked, moving closer.

His reply was to step aside and let me see what he was looking at.

It was the streetscape of Baker Street, but looking nothing like the street we had just left moments before. There were strange horseless vehicles moving along the road. People were walking along the pavement, but they were dressed strangely. Men went about in public in shirtsleeves, or worse – in what appeared to be undershirts, and good Lord! Some of the women appeared to be in their underclothes. One rather attractive young woman passed us wearing what appeared to be a short half-length slip and some sort of corset top. I couldn't understand what had happened. Had the whole world gone mad? I put this question to Holmes.

"I don't think so, Watson. Unless I am greatly mistaken, we are no longer in our own time." Holmes took off his top hat and evening frock coat, and removed his tie and collar, opening the top buttons. "Do the same, Watson," he instructed. "We will be less conspicuous like this."

I did as ordered. We stepped out into Baker Street. There was a news vendor nearby.

Holmes picked up a copy of The Times, and showed it to me.

I read the date—10th of May, 2000. "My God, Holmes!" I gasped.

The vendor was looking at us suspiciously. "Do you want it or wot?" he said in his heavy cockney accent.

"Er, yes," said Holmes. "How much?"

"One fifty."

"One pound fifty for a newspaper?" I asked, shocked. That was a month's wages!

"I sure as hell don't mean one shillin'," he replied.

Holmes gave him the paper back. "Perhaps some other time." He grabbed my arm and pulled me away. "Come on, Watson."

When we moved away, I turned to Holmes. "Ye Gods, Holmes. We're one hundred and ten years into the future."

Holmes smiled. "Fascinating isn't it?"

"Fascinating! Are you mad? How are we going to exist in this world? We have no money. I am sure Queen Victoria is no longer on the coins. And even if she was, I only have around fifteen pounds on me. At these prices it is not going to last long."

"Ever practical Watson," he said. "However, I think we are slightly better off than you imagine. Admittedly tonight we may have to spend the night in the park, but our situation should improve come tomorrow. In the meantime, our bellies are full; the weather is fine, let us check out what the future holds for us."

"You are taking it very calmly, Holmes. Have you given any thought to how we are going to return to our own time?"

"No. Simply because I am not sure how we ended up here."

That did nothing to reassure me. If Holmes was baffled, what hope did I have in figuring it out?

We walked along Baker Street, our eyes wide with interest. Holmes missed nothing, taking in every sight. My own misgivings eased as I took in the many fascinating things. The street lights were powered by electricity, which was still a relatively new invention in our own time. The vehicles along the road were both noisy and smelly, not to mention dangerous. Holmes attempted to cross the road, but was nearly flattened by one huge black vehicle with TAXI written on its roof. It made loud blaring noises similar to a foghorn to warn Holmes out of the way. On the corner there were coloured lights. I noticed that when it turned red the vehicles stopped and the people were able to cross the road. We followed the crowd.

Once across the road, Holmes said, "I wonder if 221 still exists?"

It didn't appear to. We walked up and down the street until we came to a shop that was still open. The writing on the window proclaimed it to be The Sherlock Holmes Memorabilia Shop.

Holmes flashed me a grin. "Are you game, Watson?"

I returned his smile. We entered the shop. There were books—books with a collection of my stories in them. There were quite a few I was not even familiar with. Holmes picked up one entitled *His Last Bow*.

"At least we know we will get home, Watson," he said.

"How do you figure that?"

"If we didn't, you wouldn't be writing about my retirement. We would have ceased to exist in our own time."

Now that did relieve me. He was right. Those stories that I didn't recognize, they were still to happen. If we were trapped in the future then they would never have been written. I looked about the shop with interest. There were posters of some fellow named Basil Rathbone, dressed in Holmes' deerstalker hat and inverness cape, and another rather ugly chap named Jeremy Brett, also dressed as Holmes. These were apparently actors who have portrayed Holmes in films—whatever a film was. There were postcards and cups, and little statues of Holmes, myself, Inspector Lestrade and even Moriarty.

Holmes studied the figurine of his brother Mycroft and chuckled.

There were magazines featuring articles about Holmes, and numerous books about Holmes purporting to come from me but written by other authors. Obviously these were all fiction.

When we left the shop, Holmes said, "It would seem, Watson, that you have immortalized me in your stories. It is rather flattering to know that one is not forgotten after one's death. Perhaps I have judged your writings too harshly in the past."

Further along the street was the Sherlock Holmes pub, and there was even a pharmacist bearing his name. Near Baker Street station was a fellow handing out leaflets advertising the Sherlock Holmes museum, dressed in a deerstalker and inverness. Holmes took one of the leaflets, still smiling broadly. No doubt all this adoration was inflating his ego.

We had nearly reached the end of Baker Street when a sign caught his eye. He cut across oncoming traffic at great risk to life and limb, and like a fool I followed. There was an old house with a sign proclaiming it to be Hudson's room and board.

"It's an omen, Watson," he said, indicating the smaller sign beneath it.

"Vacancy," I read.

As Homes approached the front door, I hesitated. "We don't have any money, Holmes," I reminded him.

"We will have, don't worry." He knocked on the door as I joined him on the front step.

The door was open by a blonde woman in her early thirties. She was rather attractive of face and significantly attractive of form. She was wearing a tight fitting short green dress that emphasized every curve and showed off her legs most admirably. She looked over Holmes first, and then turned her appraisal to me. She smiled invitingly at me.

"We would like to inquire about your vacancy," said Holmes

"Upstairs flat, two bedrooms, a sitting room and a bathroom," she replied.

"May we see it?" asked Holmes

"Sure." She stood aside to let us enter, smiling at me again.

Holmes was quick to note her interest. As she led the way upstairs, he whispered to me, "Charm her, Watson."

The rooms were neat and pleasantly furnished. There was a strange flat black screen panel in the corner. I did not know its purpose. She showed us the bedrooms; both were spacious with double beds, large wardrobes and heaters of some sort.

"Very nice," I said. "How much?"

"One hundred and fifty a week—each. That includes meals." Before I could react to such an exorbitant sum, Holmes replied:

"That is fine. We'd like to take these rooms."

"Righto, three hundred down now and you can move in," she said.

"Ah yes," said Holmes, sighing. "Slight problem with that, you see John and I were robbed this evening in the underground. We don't actually have any money on us, not until we can visit the bank tomorrow."

She looked at us suspiciously.

"We're just newly arrived in London, having been abroad for several years. Not only have we lost our wallets, but our luggage as well. I have to say London has certainly changed since we were last here."

"Yes, it was really quite dreadful," I said taking up the tale and looking at her pleadingly. "Of course it is only a temporary setback, but as things stand, we do not have a roof over our heads tonight."

She looked at us, at me especially. "Well, call me a big softie, but you boys don't seem the conman type. I guess I'm willing to trust you for one night, but I'll want that rent by tomorrow afternoon, or out you go."

I smiled at her. "Thank you, you are a true lady. By the way what did you say your name was?"

"I didn't' say. I'm Mrs Wiona Hudson. I'm a widow," she said.

I exchanged looks with Holmes. She certainly didn't look like the Mrs Hudson we were familiar with.

"My name is John Watson," I began, introducing myself, "and this is…"

Holmes interrupted, "Holmes, Samuel Holmes."

"Holmes and Watson!" she laughed with delight. "Isn't that a coincidence? Must be fate."

When she left us we selected which bedrooms we wanted and then checked out our new quarters. Holmes seemed fascinated by the black panel.

"We can hardly visit the bank tomorrow, Holmes. Just how do you plan on getting money to pay for this place, or for anything else for that matter?"

"You forget, Watson, we are one hundred and ten years beyond our time. The notes and coins we have in our pockets are collector's items, which we will sell tomorrow at a rare coin and stamp shop. I saw one in Baker Street as we were walking along it. Plus I have this." He turned and exhibited his emerald tie pin—a present from Queen Victoria for services rendered.

"Not only is this stone worth a considerable sum, but the historical value is immeasurable. We should return a tidy profit—certainly enough to live on until we can figure out a way of going home."

I heaved a sigh of relief. I hadn't thought about our money increasing in value. Certainly anything over a hundred years old was usually considered antique. "I have my watch," I added. "That might be worth something too."

Holmes nodded. He examined the flat panel and then picked up a small long object and pressed a button on it. The panel suddenly came to life with sound and moving pictures.

"Good Lord!" I gasped. "What is that?"

"Some kind of advanced kaleidoscope," replied Holmes looking at the coloured realistic pictures with interest. It appeared to be some kind of medical drama, with doctors performing miraculous surgery. It all seemed rather far-fetched to me, but Holmes pointed out that it was probably an accurate representation, as medicine has advanced along with everything else.

"Just as well you didn't introduce yourself as a doctor," he added. "Your knowledge is no longer current, so you would be unable to practice."

"What about you, what could you do in this century?"

"I could be a musician, an actor, a labourer, a seaman what have you. I have played all those parts in the past."

He was right of course. Versatility was one of his main traits. For myself I wondered what sort of things I could do. Heavy labour was out—despite my age, I found it too strenuous for my wounded shoulder. If the drama on the screen was any indication, my medical knowledge was practically medieval. I could write. I suppose I could get a job as a writer of sorts, or perhaps in a shop, certainly I had fewer options than Holmes. Then again given what high esteem Holmes was still held in even in this day, perhaps I could write fictitious Holmes stories and make a living that way. Other people seemed to be cashing in on his name, so why shouldn't I? I could probably make a jolly good living out of it. I consoled myself with the thought that this existence was only temporary, that somehow we would find a way to return to our own century.

It was around eleven pm when I retired and fell into a deep dreamless sleep. Holmes stayed up watching the panel. When I went to bed there was a police drama on. I heard Holmes laughing as they muddled their way through clues he found absurdly obvious. If that was the best they could do, perhaps he could resume his own profession.

CHAPTER TWO

The next morning after a breakfast of eggs on toast and coffee, we left our new lodgings and made our way to the rare coin shop. The owner was a wizened old man, who became quite excited when Holmes showed him his coins and five pound notes. It seemed a penny with Queen Victoria on it was worth quite a bit. He offered to buy the coins, but said his business wasn't so brisk that he could also afford the notes. He suggested we take them and the antique emerald pin to Sotheby's for appraisal and auction. That we were likely to get more for them that way. Holmes sold him two pounds worth of coins for some four hundred modern day pounds. At least we had the rent for a week.

Our next destination was Sotheby's. The appraiser was interested in the notes and the remainder of coins from my pockets. When he saw the emerald pin it was his turn to become excited. According to him the pin was priceless as there was an engraving on the back from Queen Victoria. He offered to include it in the auctions being held that very day as a special item.

Holmes agreed.

We gave him our new address and he promised he'd be in touch the next day.

After we left, I said, "Holmes, maybe you shouldn't sell the pin. After all it was a personal gift to you."

"You know how I feel about such trinkets. We can derive much more use from it this way."

At an open market we purchased some clean clothes and underwear. Their quality was inferior to our usual garments, but they were cheap. We also purchased razors, unlike any I had ever seen before, as we were both sporting day old beards not having been able to shave this morning.

Holmes was in fine spirits, seeming to enjoy strolling about this new London. It was a hundred times more populated than it had been in our day, and I was getting used to the skimpy clothes the women wore, why, some even wore trousers!

I have to admit to certain confusion at times. It was not always easy to differentiate between male and female. I splashed out and bought a newspaper but I dropped it and a young woman with long brown hair stepped on it. Her back was to me, and she seemed unaware of what she was standing on.

"Excuse me, Miss, you're standing on my paper," I said.

The 'Miss' turned around and glared at me from behind a bushy beard!

"Oh, I'm terribly sorry, sir," I gasped in surprise. He took his foot off my paper though, which I quickly retrieved. As we moved away, I complained, "How can anyone tell what anyone is in this day and age. Short haired women in trousers, men with long hair…"

"Men in dresses," added Holmes nodding towards a 'woman' coming along the street. He certainly looked like a woman, but Holmes' eagle eye had noticed the prominent Adam's apple at his throat which indicated his true sex, despite all the powder and rogue and female clothing.

"Good Lord!"

"This is an interesting time period, Watson. Really it is quite amazing. Those vehicles are called cars, by the way, and that picture panel in our room is called a television."

Holmes' viewing of the panel had obviously been educational as well as entertaining. I resolved to pay more attention to it.

We wandered the streets most of the day, our interest and wonder overruling the weariness of our feet. Eventually we found ourselves in the East End. Some things never changed, this was still the rough part of town. The people here were less prosperous than others we had seen, although class distinctions did not seem to be as apparent as it was in our day.

Feeling somewhat footsore, I entreated Holmes to take a break. He agreed and we made our way to a small pub for a drink and a rest. The clientele were a rather rough looking lot, which didn't seem to faze Holmes, but I kept a wary hand on the rent money. The barmaid, dressed in leathers with rings through her nose, ears and eyebrow plunked two beers in front of us, which we took to a table. I gratefully sat down.

We had almost finished our drinks, when a gang of young ruffians entered. I am afraid my jaw dropped in amazement. They too were dressed in leather trousers, and leather vests adorned with chains and silver studs. They had multiple rings through ears, eyebrows, lips and noses, but the most noticeable thing about them was their hair. They wore a Mohawk Indian style of cut with their hair spiked up and multicoloured in purple, green, orange and red—in fact they sort of looked like a gang of coloured roosters.

"Are they circus performers?" I asked Holmes. Unfortunately I said that much louder than I intended.

One of the young men with red and orange spiked hair glared at me and strode over with his multicoloured friends following along behind. "'Ere, are you callin' us clowns?" he demanded.

"No, certainly not. I meant no offense. I was just asking my friend here what your occupation was."

"Tryin' to be smart are ya?" To my dismay he slipped on a pair of brass knuckle dusters. This did not bode well for us.

"He didn't call you clowns, but I did," replied Holmes tactlessly. "Anyone that would deliberately wander the streets in such outlandish garb is just begging to be laughed at. As to occupation, Watson, they have none, as no employer in his right mind would take on such petty thugs."

A rumble of anger went through the group.

Holmes glared back at the orange haired leader.

I expected violence to erupt at any minute, but to my surprise, orange hair merely shrugged. "Come on lads, these toffs ain't worth skinnin' our knuckles on." He then sauntered away.

It seemed that no matter what century Holmes was in, he still retained his ability to cow petty criminals with just a look. His courage was such that he did not fear bully gangs, but then, he always was heedless of his own danger.

The barmaid came over to collect our mugs. She leant down provocatively over Holmes, giving him an unlimited view of her cleavage and said, "I like the way you handled them punks, Honey. Just don't turn your back on them; they'd as soon stab you as look at you." She handed him a slip of paper and gave him a wink. "Gimme a call sometime."

We took that as our cue to leave. Outside, Holmes looked at the paper which contained the name Wendy and a string of numbers beneath it.

"Was that woman propositioning you, Holmes?"

"I believe so. Have you noticed that the women are quite forward in this century?"

"Indeed I have," I agreed thinking of our landlady—Mrs Hudson the second.

As we made our way along the street, Holmes said softly, "Don't look now, but we are being followed."

It was with an effort that I refrained from turning around. "The punks, Holmes?"

"Yes. Quick, this way!" He dashed sideways into an alley, and then turned left again. "I know a short cut away from here."

I followed him. We ran around another corner only to come to a sudden halt—the alley end was blocked by an eight foot high brick wall.

"Shit!" swore Holmes as he skidded to a stop.

I looked at him in surprise.

"Er…I heard it on the television. It seemed appropriate for this occasion," he explained.

"It is indeed. I guess that wall wasn't there in 1890?"

"You guess right."

"What do we do now?"

Holmes glanced quickly around the alley, and then strode over to a pile of rubbish. He pulled forth an old broom handle and a plank. He handed me the plank. "Face the front of the alley and uh, look tough."

At that moment, the group of eight punks raced around the corner and into the alley. It was their turn to skid to a halt. For there Holmes and I stood, legs spread, calmly thumping our pieces of wood into our hands, glaring at them.

Holmes took a couple of steps forward and said, in his most precise voice: "What kept you? We've been waiting for you."

The punks looked at us, at our apparent confidence, and then to the accompaniment of obscene language, they turned and fled. I was amazed.

"Bluff, Watson. However, we also better make tracks before it occurs to them that they outnumber us and we don't stand a chance in a concentrated attack."

I discarded my plank and we hurried off. We made our way quickly to the nearest underground and from there back to Baker Street.

On the train, Holmes said, "It is fortunate that they were bullies that only hunt in packs. There's not a brain amongst the lot of them."

I agreed, thinking it was very fortunate, for we would certainly have gotten the worse of any set to. I heaved a sigh of relief. I couldn't wait to get home and soak my feet in the tub and relax. Even Holmes was looking tired by the time we arrived home to 317 Baker Street. I paid Mrs Hudson the three hundred pounds and received a receipt. She was delighted that her trust was not misplaced.

The only thing which marred Holmes' enjoyment of this century was the fact that we could not find a tobacconist. We eventually ended up purchasing pre-packaged cigarettes which were rather weak and flavorless compared to what we were used to. It seems that smoking is banned in most public places in this century, it being considered an unhealthy disgusting habit that caused lung cancer. Holmes was appalled at such a state of affairs.

*****

It was much later in the afternoon; we had both bathed and changed and were relaxing with our weak cigarettes when Mrs Hudson knocked on the door.

"Mr Holmes," she called out. "There is an Inspector Lestrade here to see you."

Holmes and I exchanged glances of astonishment. How could this be?

CHAPTER THREE

Inspector Lestrade entered the room and we both shot to our feet. She was an attractive brunette of some four and thirty years, dressed in an elegant suit, which emphasized her well-knit figure and shapely long legs (the skirt ending above her knees). She held an open wallet which revealed a badge and announced herself. "Inspector Georgina Lestrade of New Scotland Yard."

"How do you do, I'm Sherlock Holmes and this is Dr. Watson."

"Oh, very funny. I'm sick of that tired old joke. I suppose the landlady is Mrs Hudson?"

"Actually, she is," replied Holmes with a faint smile."

"I am here on official business," she said. She took out a notebook. "Did you or did you not visit Sotheby's today with a request to have a large collection of old notes auctioned?"

"Yes we did."

"Where did you come by the money?"

"Why? Has there been a theft of someone's private collection?" returned Holmes.

She looked at him suspiciously. "Yes. Your notes have been impounded and the serial numbers are being checked against those that were stolen."

As we seemed unconcerned, she asked again, "Where did you come by the money?"

"We had it in our pockets," replied Holmes. I could see him looking the young lady over with interest. "Please have a seat, Inspector Lestrade; actually I'm glad you are here. Watson and I are somewhat out of place here and would value some assistance. Your great grandfather and I were close acquaintances."

"Oh, you're not still pretending to be Sherlock Holmes. Anyway, what makes you think that I am in anyway related to the Lestrade of those old Sherlock Holmes stories? It's not that uncommon a name."

"Your tie pin. It's a family heirloom. You inherited it from your father, and he from his grandfather, George Lestrade, who in turn received it from me on Christmas day 1880. There is an inscription on the back—*Observe and deduce, Holmes*. I gave it to him when he was promoted to Inspector. He called it his good luck piece.

Her eyes were on Holmes now. She didn't want to believe what she was hearing. "How do you know about that inscription? No one but the family knows."

"I told you. I gave it to him."

"That's impossible. It would make you one hundred and fifty years old."

"One hundred and forty-six actually," he corrected.

"Well when you're that old, what's a few years," she returned sarcastically.

"I know it is difficult to believe, but I am Sherlock Holmes and this is Dr. John Watson. Yesterday, somehow, we were transported to your century. The reason we had so many antique notes, was because it is every day currency to us and all we had on us. To exist in this time period we had to sell it for more current bills."

She looked him over, taking in everything about his appearance, concentrating on his hands and his eyes. She paid particular attention to his shoes, and then glanced across at the hooks on the back of the door from which our frock coats and top hats hung. She frowned and paid closer attention to the coats.

"I grant that the shoes and costumes appear authentic, but that can be purchased. I'm not sure how you knew about the inscription on the pin. Your grammar is correct and old worldly as are your manners, but again that could just be good acting. Who was Norton Villers?' she asked, changing tack suddenly.

"Norton Villers was the name of the man who murdered Bishop Edgeware. It is I who helped Senior Sergeant George Lestrade capture him. It is how Lestrade received his promotion to Inspector."

She stared at Holmes for a long moment. "That was never in the papers and never written about. Sherlock Holmes' involvement was kept secret. Only the Lestrade family knew about it."

"And Sherlock Holmes," pointed out Holmes gently.

"It's so unreal! How could you be sitting here?" She shook her head, and then a smile suddenly crossed her face. "You were wounded in that affair. You should still carry a scar. If the scar is there I am prepared to believe you are who you say you are."

Holmes looked uncomfortable, whilst I looked on with curiosity. The affair that they were talking about happened before I met Holmes.

"I would prefer to just tell you where the scar is rather than show it," he said.

"I would rather see it—seeing is believing. If you want any help from me..." she left the sentence unfinished.

Holmes stood up and began to undo his trousers.

My eyebrows shot up. *Where on earth was his injury?*

He turned his back on our visitor and dropped his trousers partially.

She came forward and pulled his underwear down to reveal his left buttock, across which was an old scar. To my amusement and Holmes' embarrassment, she gave his buttock a pat and said, "Nice buns."

He hastily pulled up his trousers, his face crimson.

"Even if I doubted the scar," she said with a grin, "Your embarrassment proves to me that you're not from this century. Guys nowadays aren't so bashful."

"If that's the case, why did you want to see it?" I asked curiously.

"I've just made history. I'm the first woman to pat Sherlock's butt!" She grinned at me.

I put a hand up to conceal my own smile. Holmes was right. The women of this century were very forward indeed.

"Do you believe me now?' asked Holmes turning around, buttoned up and respectable once more, although his face was still flushed.

"I guess. You said you don't know how you came to be here. I don't believe that; you must have some idea. Something must have happened prior to your transportation, or were you beamed up by the starship Enterprise and beamed down again?"

"Pardon?" Holmes looked at her blankly.

"Never mind. What happened prior to your arrival in this century?"

Holmes described the fog that we walked into and our experiences since.

She shook her head in disbelief. "I can't believe you walked into the Purple Elephant down at the East end and walked out again in one piece. That is the roughest place in London. No tourist has ever survived a visit there without being robbed, bashed or mutilated.

Holmes pulled a paper from his pocket and handed it to her. "The barmaid Wendy witnessed a little altercation we had with some…punks I think they're called. Unless I am greatly mistaken these characters are the ones responsible for the violence at that place. Give her a call."

At that moment Mrs Hudson arrived. "How many for dinner?" she asked.

"Will you join us, Inspector?" I asked.

Georgina nodded. After Mrs Hudson left, Georgina said, "Actually what you are describing is not all that odd. I've heard of it happening before."

"People have been transported through time?" I asked incredulously.

"Sure. Happens quite often. Most accounts are of people going back in time. I haven't heard of anyone coming from the past to the future, but it stands to reason that if you can go one way, you should be able to go the other."

"What sort of things have you heard?" asked Holmes, leaning forward in his seat with interest.

"They're called doorways or windows. Over the years there have been reports of people going into a shop and when they left, they stepped into a different streetscape. In fact, about six months ago there was this American tourist, who went into an old curiosity shop, he opened the door to leave, but stopped in shock because instead of cars there were horse and carriages. He took a step backward in his surprise. When he worked up the nerve to walk forward again, the street had changed back to normal. Scientists say that he was looking through a window to the past. What saved him was that he didn't step into it, if he had he would more than likely have been trapped there."

"But where do these windows come from?" I asked.

"The theory is that the past, present and future exists simultaneously, but in different dimensions so that they are not visible to each other. These windows occasionally give us glimpses into another dimension. I think I've read about that fog thing too. People stepping into a fog and disappearing—the fogs are doorways. You must have come through a doorway."

"So all we have to do is find another doorway," mused Holmes.

"Yes. Only that's not quite so easy. They're floaters. They don't stay in the same place. If they did, scientists would be studying them by now and time travel would become a reality. But with an unstable doorway, no one is willing to take the risk of jumping through and perhaps being stuck in another time."

"No one except Homes," I muttered.

She flashed me a sympathetic smile, whilst he ignored me.

"If we did find a doorway or a window, we could jump through and cross back over into our own time?" asked Holmes.

"Theoretically, only there is no guarantee that you would be in your own time. It could be a few years before or after, or even a few centuries before. Read a story once of a lady that was looking at the monuments of Vikings in an old church. She disappeared and then the history books recorded the rise to power of one particular Viking who had taken on a 'foreigner' as a wife. The Viking who became the leader was the one whose monument she was studying before she disappeared. We know who the brains behind that partnership was, don't we?" she added with a smile.

CHAPTER FOUR

Over Mrs Hudson's excellent dinner, we chatted. Georgina spoke about her great grandfather, whom she never knew personally, but who was considered quite a hero in the family because of the many stories he handed down about his experiences with Holmes. She smiled at Holmes and said, "To hear his version of events, it sounds like he mostly helped you solve your cases, but now after meeting you, I wonder…"

Holmes smiled at her in return. "That doesn't really surprise me. Still, Lestrade always was a good fellow, and he has helped me out on occasion. He is always quick to follow instructions. I think that is his most redeeming characteristic."

She mentioned how her own father was a Chief Superintendent at Scotland Yard and that she was the youngest female detective to be made Inspector. She proved to be an intelligent woman, very observant and though I hate to say it, far superior to her great grandfather, whom we knew so well.

"Miss Georgina," I said, "can I ask you why, when you studied Holmes before to determine if he was lying or not, you paid so much attention to his hands, face and feet?"

Holmes looked at her with interest although I had a feeling he already knew the answer.

"Hold out your hands, Sherlock," she requested with an easy familiarity that we were unaccustomed to, but which, I noticed seemed to be the norm in this century. Shop attendants introduced themselves by their Christian names; people greeted each other familiarly on introduction. It was unusual and unheard of in our day, but it certainly made the atmosphere seem friendly and intimate.

Holmes did as she requested, whilst she indicated the various points of significance for my information.

"Firstly, anyone can see that here is a man that dabbles with chemicals from the various stains on his hands. Then, notice the calluses here on his left hand from playing a stringed instrument. My first thought was a guitar, but his right hand doesn't have shortened nails, which he would require to hold a pick, or extra-long nails to use those instead of a pick. Therefore, logically, he plays a stringed instrument with a bow.

Everyone knows Sherlock Holmes plays a violin, so I looked for a corresponding depression on his neck from frequent contact with the end of the violin and wallah—there it is." She pointed to a faint mark on Holmes' neck.

"His shoes, as are yours, are interesting as they are also period pieces, but well-worn down at the heel which means you have worn them for a considerable time, which is not consistent with a couple of fellows merely dressing up and pretending to be from the past."

Holmes nodded approvingly at her deductions and I had to admit I was impressed as well.

"And my eyes," asked Holmes. "What did they tell you?"

"That they really are grey. I've never seen grey eyes before. That fits Dr. Watson's description of you. What's more, they are not artificially coloured with the use of contact lenses."

"Contact lenses?" Holmes looked at her in askance.

"Little pieces of glass that sit on the eye ball itself. They can either be prescription lenses to improve eye sight, or coloured to change the colour of your eyes. You'd love them; they'd be great for disguises."

"Actually we do have something like that in our time, invented by a German, but they are not called contact lenses," said Holmes.

"Your deductive reasoning is far superior to your ancestor's," I said.

"I learned from the master," she said looking at Holmes. "Did you know that as students, we are expected to study your methods? In fact you are considered the father of scientific crime detection. A lot of what we do nowadays was pioneered by you, Sherlock. You're my hero."

Holmes looked a little uncomfortable at her open and sincere praise.

"Well I am glad to see that all my work has not been in vain," he finally responded.

"It certainly hasn't. God, I'd love to take you to work and introduce you. You'd be a big hit."

"Yes," I said. "It seems strange that Holmes is so popular in this century—even more so than in his own time."

"Everyone loves Sherlock and you too, Doctor," she said. "You should see the Americans. They can't get enough of him."

"Why?"

"There is something elusive, impressive, and romantic about Holmes that excites the imagination. You could have any woman you wanted, Sherlock; they'd be swooning at your feet. His abilities capture the imagination…actually it's hard to explain. I guess he's just a legend."

"Getting back to the topic at hand," said Holmes clearing his throat to change this uncomfortable subject. "We should consider how we are to go about finding a way home."

"How could we possibly find a way to predict where a doorway will appear?" I asked.

"I suggest we research the incidents reported and check out the places where a time portal appeared. Obviously we will need to collate data of times and places and make our plans accordingly. Perhaps they are more prevalent at certain times of the year, and in certain places. The more data we gather the more likely we are to improve our chances."

Georgina nodded. "Good idea. If one place shows up repeatedly, then odds are that it will turn up again."

"Where would we go to obtain this information?" I asked.

"The internet would be the best bet," she said.

"The what?" asked Holmes. Although he appeared interested and eager to learn new things, I knew that it galled him to be so ignorant of every day commonplace things that people of this century took for granted. He had always prided himself on his knowledge.

"The internet. You can access information world-wide via a machine called a computer," she answered.

"Really? Where would I find such a machine?"

"Most anywhere. Nearly every person has one. However, perhaps you'd better come to the Yard. I can show you how to use it. It's really quite easy once you get the hang of it."

"Thank you," replied Holmes. "I'll do that."

She glanced at her watch. "I'd better call it a night. Just one question, Sherlock."

"Yes?"

"Why do you keep staring at my legs?"

"They're nice legs," was his most unexpected response.

She chuckled. “Hmm, I don’t know about you; can you be trusted I wonder? After all, you come from an era where men get excited from just seeing an ankle. The whole leg must be a real turn on.”

“It is not an unpleasant sight,” returned Holmes.

“Indeed it isn’t,” I agreed wholeheartedly, to be rewarded with another chuckle. We stood up when she did, and Holmes escorted her to the door, holding it open for her. She found that action amusing also. When she left and he closed the door, I said,

“I must say, Holmes, she’s a considerable improvement on the Lestrade we know.”

“Mmm,” he murmured thoughtfully.

CHAPTER FIVE

Next morning after breakfast, we made our way to New Scotland Yard. It was located next door to the old one. We were escorted to Georgina's office by a young policeman dressed in a smart uniform.

She smiled a greeting to us. "You can use Samson's desk, Sherlock. He won't be in today."

On the desk was a strange machine consisting of several boxes, the largest being similar to the television in our rooms, yet different. Georgina quickly described the working parts and named each piece. She showed Holmes how to 'access' the internet. He took to it quite quickly—I never knew he could type, but apparently he could, for he had no trouble with the keyboard. Within half an hour he was marveling over the wealth of information it contained.

"This is incredible, Watson!" he enthused, like a schoolboy with a new toy. "Imagine what I could do with something like this in my time!"

"Not a lot," grinned Georgina. "It needs to be connected to other computers around the world. It doesn't work very well on its own."

"It is still an amazing piece of machinery." He continued to search the 'web' as Georgina called it until he located what he was looking for.

"Is there any way of keeping this information for later perusal?" asked Holmes.

Georgina looked up from her own desk where she had been busy typing into her computer. "Just press print—a hard copy will come out of that other machine over there—the printer."

Holmes smiled delightedly.

I have to admit, I was rather bored.

"Watson, you don't have to stay here if you'd rather not. Actually, I wonder if you would mind going to Sotheby's and finding out if they sold any of our items. We only have twenty pounds left from yesterday."

"Of course, Holmes," I replied, glad to have something useful to do.

Holmes fished some money from his pocket and handed it to me, adding, "Take the money, just in case you see a tobacconist."

"There's one down in High Street," offered Georgina with a knowing smile.

"I take it the police returned our money to Sotheby's when they were through checking it?" said Holmes.

"Of course."

"I'll meet you back here later, Holmes," I said moving to the door.

It didn't take me long to find my way to the famous auction house. The gentleman we spoke to the previous day was pleased to see me.

"Mr Watson, I am glad you've come. I meant to ring you but you never left a phone number. We sold the stickpin and the money."

"That's very good to hear, sir. Did you get a reasonable price?" I asked.

"I think you will be pleased with it." He hurried to his desk and removed a cheque, handing it over to me. Holmes and I were hoping for at least five thousand pounds, considering its age and all.

I glanced at the cheque and I must say I received something of a shock. "By Jove!"

"Yes, you see it was the personal engraving from Queen Victoria which pushed the price up. I take it you are satisfied, sir?' asked the auctioneer.

"Three hundred and fifty thousand pounds!" I gasped, my eyes bulging as I looked at the cheque. "Uh, yes, I am very satisfied."

"How would you like the proceeds for the old notes—cash or cheque?"

"Cash please," I responded, slowly recovering my wits. This had to be a lot of money even in this day and age of high expenses. I put the cheque carefully away in my wallet. He then handed me a rather large wad of cash. I smiled delightedly. Now Holmes and I could really go shopping and buy some decent clothes, after all we needed more items than we purchased the previous day.

Outside Sotheby's I caught a taxi—these vehicles are what apparently replaced the hansom cab in this motorized age—to High Street, to the tobacconists and bought over a hundred pounds worth of their strongest tobacco and pipes for Holmes and myself. Neither of us having been carrying one when we went out for that fateful dinner at Simpson's. I then caught another taxi back to Scotland Yard. Happily I made my way back to Georgina's office, stopping outside its door for a moment and frowning as I heard strange sounds emanating from it. I opened the door and stepped inside.

Holmes was still sitting at the computer, making all sorts of weird noises with his attention focused on the screen. Georgina seated at her desk was making similar sounds. Apart from the fact that they were sitting at opposite desks, they seemed to be in a battle or a contest of some sort. Holmes didn't even look up as I entered and I moved over to him to see what he was doing.

The screen was alive with colour and there were little people running around battling monsters and firing weapons. Holmes finally acknowledged my arrival with a brief comment. "Computer games."

"Hah!" cried Georgina as the cartoon character that I suppose represented Holmes was shot and collapsed.

"Damn it!" cried Holmes.

"Holmes," I reproved gently. The exposure in this lax and amoral environment seemed to be permeating Holmes. That he would swear in front of a lady was unthinkable. He would never have done it in our own time.

Georgina laughed. "Don't feel too bad, Sherlock, after all you only just learnt how to use the computer today, and you did give me run for my money."

"Watson," said Holmes. "Take a look at what I found." He pressed a few keys and was soon in a screen labeled A&E mysteries.com. "There are some people here from other countries writing about us. There's a story here about you being a fairy—a mage, Watson. I printed it out for you to read later, it's rather amusing. And there's another called Cheap Flat by someone named Violet Smith—that's a coincidence isn't it—her name I mean, after all we had a client by that name. And this one, called Cat is a prolific writer. She has written quite a few stories about us, although some are a bit farfetched. I rather liked this one too," he added, holding up a page headed Galloping Gators. "It's a farce, but amusing. You know it's amazing how many people attempt to sound like you in their writings. You should be flattered, Watson."

"I suppose," I said. "But considering that they are stories about you…"

Holmes merely chuckled. "I can see by your expression and that large packet of tobacco that you have good news for me," he said.

"I'll say, Holmes!" I put the packet down and pulled my wallet out. "We collected two thousand pounds for the notes, and wait to you see what the pin sold for!" I pulled the cheque out with a flourish and handed it to him. Even the normally inscrutable Holmes was moved by the amount.

"Is this correct?"

"Indeed it is." I returned, smiling broadly.

Georgina left her desk and came over, reading over Holmes' shoulder. She whistled. "Wow! You guys are rich!"

"So this is considered a lot of money, even in this day?" asked Holmes.

"I'll say!" she agreed. "What did you sell—the crown jewels?"

"A crown jewel," replied Holmes. "A stickpin."

"Oh, not the emerald stickpin given to you by Queen Victoria herself?"

"Yes, that's the one."

"What a shame," she said. "Still, at least it has come useful. You won't have to worry about expenses at any rate."

"About this cheque," I said, "how can we cash it? It's not much use to us in this form."

"You'll have to open a bank account," explained Georgina.

"No problem. That should be easy enough to do," said Holmes, returning the cheque to me.

"Er, actually not quite that easy. You need identification nowadays to open an account, including your tax file number."

"Then we have a problem."

She bit her lip for a minute. "Maybe not. Perhaps if I went with you and vouched for you. I could sort of give the impression that you work for the government. We can only try I guess."

Fortunately for us, Georgina was having what she called a 'paper day' at work. A day in which she caught up on all the associated paperwork that when with charging a criminal. So she was free to come to the bank with us.

At the main branch of the Bank of England, she showed her badge and introduced us to the manager. With some creative narration on her part, he agreed to set up an account for us without the required identification. It took about half an hour to finalize all the formalities. He promised that we would be able to access the account by the end of the week once the cheque cleared, plus our new cards would be ready. We refrained from asking what he meant by cards, as we did not want to appear ignorant. Needless to say, that once we left the premises we queried Georgina.

Instead of explaining, she took a small card from her purse and showed us how to withdraw money from a machine in the wall with it.

"Amazing!" I said, and I was most definitely amazed.

"When we get our money, I'd like to buy a computer," said Holmes. "Can I do that?"

"With that kind of money you could buy a thousand computers," she replied.

It was lunch time, so Georgina took as to a place called MacDonald's® for lunch. According to Georgina it was called a 'fast food joint' which apparently was the most common sort of eatery in this century. I don't know that I was that favourably impressed. Certainly it was clean enough, but it seemed to lack that personal touch. The food was fried, and whilst it was edible, it wasn't really up to the standard of fare that Holmes and I were accustomed.

"When we get our money, Georgina," I said. "We will take you out to the finest restaurant in London to show you our appreciation for your help."

She smiled. "Thanks, John, I'd like that. Will you invite Wiona, too?"

"Er...she's our landlady."

Georgina frowned. "There is something I should point out. I know in your time land ladies and the like were considered to be in the servant class, but not in this time. In fact, if we were to be class conscious, Mrs Hudson would rank higher than you, as she is actually a property owner, whilst you are just tenants. Class nowadays seems to be reflected more by assets than by birth."

"I'm sorry," I apologized humbly, having been well and truly put in my place. "It is hard to change the habits and mannerisms of a lifetime."

"It's all right. If it wasn't for the fact that you're both from the 19th century, I'd be really offended. Just don't look down on people. A tradesman is no lower than a shop keeper, or a policeman, or even a politician or a Lord. You get what I mean, don't you?"

"Yes, in that case," I said, "I shall also invite Mrs Hudson."

Holmes had been silent during this exchange, her point as applicable to him as it was to me, although it is fair to admit, that to Holmes class distinction was never of much concern to him; as his clients ranged from the lowest to the highest and he treated them all the same—or in some instances, he tended to treat the lowly more courteously than the wealthy.

After lunch we escorted Georgina back to Scotland Yard; then at my insistence we set about purchasing some more clothes, shoes, underwear, night wear and various toiletry items. Holmes was pleased with his new pipe and would have lit up and smoked it as we shopped if he hadn't been stopped by numerous shop keepers and one policeman for even considering smoking in a public place. Things have sure changed. He had to wait until we got home.

"I don't know what all the fuss is about," he grumbled.

"I read that smoking causes lung cancer," I said, "and that nonsmokers can get this from just being exposed to a smoker. They can sue a smoker, or company that exposes them to smoke."

"What nonsense!" said Holmes. "Soon they'll have drunks suing bartenders for selling them alcohol if they go outside and get run over!"

"Actually, I think that has already happened," I said.

Holmes just shook his head in disgust.

We caught a taxi home and carried our purchases upstairs. Mrs Hudson came out of her downstairs rooms to watch us with curiosity. After dropping off our stuff, I went downstairs with a small parcel. Georgina's words had made me feel guilty. I felt that I had not given Mrs Hudson her just dues. I knocked on her door.

"John!" she exclaimed in surprise when she saw me. "Do come in," she invited opening her door to a neat parlour.

"Oh, I am not here for a visit. I just wanted to give you this in appreciation for your kindness in taking us in when we were temporarily broke," I said, handing her the gift.

She smiled with delight and unwrapped it. "Chanel Number Five. Ooh, lovely. You are a dear," she said.

"I'm glad you like it," I responded.

"Oh, I do. I say, John. Would you like to go to the pictures tonight?"

"The pictures?"

"There's a new movie playing at the palace theatre tonight."

A movie, yes, well, I knew what that was now. Picture theatres apparently had large screens. It sounded interesting. It occurred to me that this was the experience of a life time being in another century and wondering at all its marvels. "I'd be delighted," I said, and she smiled.

"I'll have dinner ready at six. We can leave at seven-thirty."

"Certainly. I'll look forward to it." I smiled at her. She really was a rather attractive woman. I decided to think of her as Wiona, rather than Mrs Hudson, as the latter name tended to conjure up mental images of a motherly Scottish woman, and this Mrs Hudson was anything but motherly.

I returned upstairs. Holmes had discarded his packages and was now puffing up a blue cloud of smoke from his new pipe. He had an expression of bliss on his face. I hadn't realized his smoke cravings had been so critical.

"I'm going to the picture theatre with Wiona tonight, Holmes. Would you like to come with us?"

"No, Watson. I'd rather stay home and smoke and study those print outs."

I also took the opportunity to fill and light a pipe, and then we both packed away our purchases. I was glad I'd bought some more clothes.

CHAPTER SIX

After dinner, Holmes buried himself with his pipe and print outs whilst I changed for my night out. I called for Wiona right on the dot of seven-thirty, and was greeted with a pleasant surprise. This evening she was dressed sedately in black slacks and a knitted top that showed off her feminine features. She really did have an eye catching figure—without the aid of corseting too! She was wearing the perfume I bought her. Outside we caught a cab and made our way to the theatre. At the theatre however, I was shocked when she attempted to pay for our tickets.

"Good Lord!" I gasped. "What is this? I have never let a lady pay for me in my entire life, and I'm not about to start now no matter what the current trend is!"

She smiled and allowed me the privilege.

We also bought some fairly tasteless stuff called popcorn and some sweet fizzy drinks. It started out to be a rather pleasant evening. Once the lights went out Wiona hooked her arm in mine and cuddled closer. It was not an unpleasant situation, and I must confess that I was pleased that Holmes didn't come with us.

It wasn't until we were into the second half of the movie when all hell broke loose. The audience was silent, watching the screen, when our peace was disrupted by a loud explosion. The screen split into pieces and those seated in the front started screaming as they bore the brunt of the blast. We were seated at the back, but even where we were, we were pelted with flying fragments from the blast.

The lights came on and I gaped in horror. Despite my having participated in the Afghanistan war, the carnage I witnessed this night stayed with me for the rest of my life. Women, children, innocent civilians bled their last. Their mangled bodies draped over seats and flung about like rag dolls. People were screaming and crying; it was chaos.

"Oh my God!" I murmured in awe, disentangling my arm from Wiona's tight grip. "Who would do something like this?"

"The IRA probably," she whispered, just as shocked as I.

"I have to help them," I said. "I'm a doctor." To my gratitude she came with me. Others in the theatre were panicking and hurrying towards the exits. We had to push our way past to get to the wounded at the front.

At close hand the carnage was even more apparent. I set about organizing triage. I ignored the dead, and concentrated on the living. Some were too badly injured; there was little I could do even if I had my medical bag with me. I concentrated on those with lesser injuries, stemming bleeding, securing broken limbs and the like. Wiona had a pair of nail scissors in her bag and used this to cut bandages from the clothing of the dead. I was oblivious to the sirens, smoke and general upheaval as I concentrated on the task at hand.

Other people, more level headed than those in panic also came down to help. Being the only doctor on the scene it fell to me to direct the rescue efforts and coordinate the first aid. Wiona made an able nurse.

I am not sure how long we were at it—it seemed eternal—but I suppose it was only half an hour at most before police and emergency medical staff called paramedics according to Wiona, came swarming in with stretchers and other medical equipment and took over.

There was one other figure too. Sherlock Holmes slipped in with the rescue teams. When he saw me his face lit up with relief.

"I'm glad you're all right, Watson. When I couldn't see you outside…" he left the rest unsaid, his relief evident.

"How did you get here, Holmes?" I asked, as I continued to bandage a young girl's arm.

"I was watching the television when they announced in a news flash about this bombing. I came as quickly as I could."

"It was awful, Holmes. These poor innocents…"

Holmes looked around at the damage. Within moments he was on the platform where the screen had been, examining the actual site of the blast. As yet the police were busy clearing the rest of the theatre's audience out, whilst the medics had begun ferrying the wounded. No one noticed Holmes.

A policeman came over to me. "I am Inspector Harrison, did you witness this?" he asked me.

"Yes." I replied and told him what had happened. He took my name and address and thanked me for my help in tending the wounded. It was then that he noticed Holmes and stormed towards him angrily, calling out. "Here you! What do you think you're doing?"

Holmes straightened up. "Inspector," he greeted, and handed him the butt of a cigar. "The bomber is approximately six feet tall, wearing army greens and boots. He smokes Turkish cigars, I'm not sure of this particular brand. It was a homemade bomb, triggered with a fuse. He used his cigar stub to light the fuse…oh, and he's left handed."

The Inspector eyed him with distrust. "Who the hell do you think you are—Sherlock Holmes?"

"Yes," replied Holmes. "I am quite correct in my findings. I suggest you search for him immediately as he can't have gone far yet."

"Yeah? How come you know so much?" He took the cigar from Holmes. "Maybe you smoked this here cigar."

"Nonsense. I wasn't even in the theatre. I just came to see if Watson was all right," said Holmes.

There was something authoritative about Holmes that compelled action, even from the most unwilling. The Inspector detailed some of his men to search for a man in army greens, and then turned back to Holmes.

"How do you know what he looks like then?" he asked, his tone slightly conciliatory.

"There's a scrap of cloth adhering to a nail, torn from his shirt, this allows me to estimate his height. He had obviously stepped in some animal droppings, leaving a clear imprint of his boots, which show me that they are of military style. The angle of the cut on this cigar shows me he was left handed and the remnants of the bomb tell me the rest. My first thought was that he was an ex-soldier, but I am more inclined to believe it is just someone with military aspirations."

Other police began to scour the scene, while Harrison ordered another policeman to keep us company so that we didn't leave. He was not wholly satisfied with Holmes' explanation. During this time Wiona had looked on silently, watching Holmes as if seeing him for the first time. She had a thoughtful expression on her face.

A short while later, a policeman arrived, looking flushed with excitement and reported that a man in army fatigues was seen leaving the theatre moments before the explosion. A full scale search went out for him, although I think that Harrison suspected Holmes of being the man's accomplice. Wiona was allowed to leave, while we were asked to come to Scotland Yard. Even as we were being taken to the Yard in Harrison's automobile, he received a message saying a man fitting the description Holmes gave had been picked up.

At the Yard, we were put into a waiting room, while the bomber was interrogated. The man, under the influence of drugs, bragged about what he had done. His reason for this senseless violence was simply as a protest against the movie. He was, as Holmes surmised, not in the actual military, it having rejected him on grounds of mental deficiency, but with aspirations of being a soldier. Once the man was locked up, Harrison came back to question us, but was interrupted by Holmes.

"Inspector, you have no right to hold us. Watson here did nothing more than help the wounded. I merely helped the police capture a dangerous lunatic. Since when is that a crime? If you want verification of our identities, I suggest you contact Inspector Georgina Lestrade at Homicide. She can vouch for us."

His eyebrows shot up at that. "You know Lestrade?"

"Yes."

"Wait here," he growled. He left the room, but through the glass partition we could see him talking to someone on a device called a telephone which allowed two people in different places to converse directly. Ten minutes later, an older man arrived.

"Georgina's father," murmured Holmes to me, as the man entered the room. There was a faint resemblance.

"Superintendent Lestrade," greeted Holmes.

"You know me?"

"We know your daughter."

Lestrade motioned for Harrison to leave us. He was silent for a moment as he looked us over. "I'd like to thank you for giving us the information we needed to catch the bomber. Is it correct that you claim to be Sherlock Holmes and Dr. Watson?"

"Quite correct," I said. "I am Dr. John Watson, and this is the Sherlock Holmes—the real and original."

His eyes narrowed. "I can usually only handle one madman a day," he said quietly.

"We're not mad," returned Holmes calmly. "Perhaps a demonstration?"

"What sort of demonstration?"

"I can see you were born in Leeds, you're a mason, your wife is Irish, you have corns on your feet which have been troubling you lately and you have recently given up smoking strong tobacco."

He looked at Holmes open mouthed—which was the usual reaction he got when making deductions. "Explain please."

"Your accent is unmistakable. Georgina doesn't have it, so I assume she was born in London. You wear a mason's tie pin and have clover link cufflinks, a gift from you wife. You walk with a limp but carry no stick, so the cause is not injury related, plus you have tobacco stains on your fingers, but do not smell of tobacco, hence you've given up."

He was silent for a long moment. "Very impressive. Very Sherlockian," he said. "How did you convince Georgina of your identity? She's quite astute."

"She is indeed. You should be proud of her," returned Holmes, smiling faintly. "I identified the tie pin that I had given your great grandfather and recited the inscription on it, also she insisted I show her the scar I received during the Villers case, plus there were one or two other points."

"There is one easy way of proving it for sure," he said.

"And that is?"

"DNA testing. Let us take blood and hair samples from both of you. We can test it with samples from your possessions at the Sherlock Holmes museum. If they match…"

"You don't believe us?" I asked.

"You've got to admit it is not an easy story to swallow. Georgina believes you. Usually I trust her judgment, but if I want to convince my superiors I will need irrefutable proof. If you are agreeable gentlemen, you can leave as soon as we have the samples.

"All right," agreed Holmes, and I nodded.

We stayed with him for almost an hour. I explained to him how we arrived in this century whilst a police doctor took blood and hair samples. I was curious to know what this DNA testing entailed. He then ordered a policeman to drive us home. We left him standing on the steps of the police station looking thoughtful.

CHAPTER SEVEN

We decided to spend the next day at home. Holmes studied his print outs, making notes as he went. I watched television. The midday news mentioned Inspector Harrison capturing the bomber, but fortunately there was no mention made of Holmes and myself.

The previous night on our return, I comforted Wiona as she had been quite shocked by the whole affair. Holmes' behaviour had not been lost on her and I feared that she suspected our real identity. In fact when she brought in our lunch she said as much.

She curtsied to Holmes and said, "You're him aren't you; the real Sherlock Holmes? Don't worry, your secret is safe with me," she promised.

"Er, thank you," said Holmes. He looked accusingly at me when she left.

"I didn't tell her," I protested, "it wasn't hard for her to figure it out though, after all you told that policeman at the theatre who you were, the only difference is she believed you."

Holmes shrugged it off as being of no importance.

That afternoon, Georgina dropped in for a visit and congratulated Holmes on his good work, saying, "Dad was most impressed with you, Sherlock. By the way, you're both invited to dinner on Saturday."

Holmes didn't look too pleased at that, but did not argue, after all the young lady had been most helpful to us, and now that her father was also aware of our identity, it was only to be expected. I also thought that it didn't hurt to have additional contacts. Superintendent Lestrade wielded more power than Georgina should his help ever become necessary.

*****

Next morning, just as we were finishing our breakfast, Georgina arrived in a flurry. "Sherlock," she greeted without preamble, "father sends his regards and asks if you would mind accompanying me to a crime scene. We would really value your advice."

Holmes sighed and put his morning paper down. It was almost as if he had been expecting the summons.

We joined her in her car and she filled us in on the case as she drove. "This is the fifth junkie murder in two months. It's been kept quiet but the MO is the same as the others. Female Caucasian, around twenty years old. Brutally beaten to death with the body dumped in an alley."

"Why do you call it a junkie murder?" asked Holmes.

"The victims are all drug addicts, we call them junkies."

"Is that common?" I asked. "Young women taking drugs?"

"Very common. They get hooked in primary school nowadays and are usually dead before they're twenty-five."

"How?" asked Holmes, then added at her querying look. "How is it possible for school children to get access to drugs?"

"The dealers hang around schools and sell them there, or enlist other kids to act as dealers. It's common enough. Drugs are easy to come by and relatively cheap. That guy the other day, the bomber, he was as high as a kite on ecstasy. He killed seventeen people in that blast just because he didn't like the movie. Drugs are responsible for all the petty thefts and break-ins, the assaults on the elderly, and not to mention crimes of senseless violence."

"So it wasn't anything to do with the IRA as Wiona feared?" I asked.

"No, just drugs."

I was appalled. Holmes' face was expressionless. Perhaps he was thinking of his own drug taking habit and reconsidering its benefits.

We reached the crime scene which was sealed off with yellow tape. Policemen were standing guard. Holmes crossed the line.

"Not even the crime scene squad has been here yet. I didn't' want them to trample on anything that might help you," explained Georgina.

Holmes was about to move forward, but she stopped him for a second and handed him a powerful magnifying glass. Holmes nodded his thanks. There were a lot of people crowding around, some police, some sightseers and some—we later found out—reporters. As Holmes bent down to examine the scene of the crime, there were flashes of light, which came from their cameras. He ignored these peripheral distractions and concentrated on the scene as was his usual wont.

The dead girl had once been pretty, although her body showed signs of self-abuse. Her arms were literally lined with needle pricks. The beating she had received prior to her death was vicious and horrific. Holmes examined the naked body impersonally, paying particular attention to her hands, wrists and ankles and the injuries inflicted, then he perused the ground around her carefully, crawling along this way and that with his magnifying glass, oblivious to his fascinated audience.

Half an hour later he straightened up and indicated that he was finished. The crime scene men moved forward and began collecting evidence and photographing the scene. Holmes stopped one and said to him, "The blood under the fingernails of her right hand bears scrutiny." He then came forward and joined Georgina and me. She looked at him hopefully.

"There wasn't a great deal to be learned," replied Holmes.

"Still?" she prompted.

"Still, there were a few things of interest. The woman was under the influence of drugs at the time of the attack. Despite her appearance, she has not been sexually assaulted, just physically. The attacker is a man of slight build, impotent, red-haired with a sparse red beard. He's right handed, walks with a limp, dragging his left leg slightly. His left shoe should bear marks on the instep of this. Also, the victim managed to scratch her attacker on the left side of the face and down his neck before he could secure her right arm with handcuffs to a brass bed. Hence the ferocity of the attack. He attempted to strangle her, but his strength was insufficient. He picks drug addicts for his victims because he would be no physical match for a normal healthy woman."

Georgina's jaw dropped in amazement. "You could see all that?"

"There were a few other marks but they were indistinguishable," he added casually.

Her eyes were shining now. It was obvious she admired Holmes and relished this opportunity to see him in action. If Holmes noticed her look of hero worship he chose to ignore it.

"I can see why my great grandfather went to you so often," she said, awe in her voice. She then left us to call the Yard and put out a description of the killer. The hunt was on for a red-headed pervert with a limp. Georgina offered to drive us home, but Holmes declined. We left the filthy rundown area, with its dirty big eyed children watching us, and young men and women, looking like living skeletons. These were the modern slums where the junkies, the destitute and the homeless lived. I pitied the children, having to grow up in such a hopeless environment.

Holmes was silent on the journey home. I noticed however, that he threw himself back into his research with renewed vigor. I knew how he felt. It had been a depressing morning. I yearned for the simple innocence of the 19th century. At least children didn't take drugs in those days. Fortunately for our peace of mind, we were unaware that we had been followed home. There was plenty of time to curse fate later.

CHAPTER EIGHT

At two o'clock the telephone contraption on the wall started ringing. Holmes stood up and strode over to the instrument and picked it up, ending its siren like ringing.

"Yes?" he enquired off the instrument. He listened intently for a moment, and then replied, "Thank you." He hung up.

I looked at him enquiringly.

"That was Georgina. They found a red haired man with facial scratches in a bookstore for adults. Apparently he has broken down under questioning and admitted to his culpability. He fits the description I gave."

"So you were right, Holmes."

Holmes shrugged modestly. "It was a fairly simple case. What surprises me is why they hadn't caught him sooner."

"You weren't here," I pointed out.

Holmes smiled faintly. "You flatter me, Watson."

"Perhaps, but nevertheless it's true. Georgina told me that it usually takes a week or more for their forensic experts to study the evidence and come up with a picture of the killer, if there is enough evidence found. By that time the murderer has had a chance to escape or cover his tracks. You were able to do in half an hour what it takes experts to do in weeks. Same with the madman who set off the bomb in the theatre… the police would still be looking for him, but for your quick observations and description. He was still at the scene of the crime when he was caught."

"I suppose so." He was silent for a moment as he contemplated something that troubled him. "I will admit this only to you, Watson. I feel out of my depth here. There is so much I do not know. I can observe, but I cannot always deduce if I do not have the knowledge on which to base those deductions. For example, in our time I can tell a man's occupation at a glance. I look at people in this century and they all look alike. A nurse or doctor looks no different from a bank clerk or shop assistant. Unless they are dressed in a specific uniform, even then I may not know what that uniform represents." He shook his head. "No, I fear that Georgina's father will want to take advantage of my presence here, and I also fear that I will fail."

"What does it matter if you do? They can't expect miracles from you," I countered.

"That's the problem, Watson, they do. Remember, it is your stories that have immortalized me. I am a legend, to use Georgina's words. Legends are not allowed to fail."

"You're overreacting, Holmes."

"You think so?" he replied, his voice laced with doubt.

"I'm sure of it."

He just shrugged and returned to studying his printouts, while I looked at him thoughtfully. I recognized the mood that possessed him and was concerned. With the ready availability of illicit drugs in this century, I knew it wouldn't take much for him to resort to them to counteract the depression that was pressing down on him.

I sat down at the table to read the morning's papers, not having had a chance earlier. That was when I noticed an announcement in the entertainment section.

"Holmes," I said, interrupting him.

He glanced up at me.

"How would you like to go to a concert tonight? There's a fellow named Swasbrick playing at Albert hall tonight. He's supposed to be a violin virtuoso of some renown. He'll also be playing some of Sarasate's pieces," I said.

Holmes' eyes lit up with interest. "Yes, I think I would like that. Thank you, Watson." He smiled and I heaved a sigh of relief. If anything improved his black moods it was music.

*****

We had high tea at five and, dressed in our new black suits, left for the theatre at six. The next two and a half hours were pure delight. Holmes lost himself in the music; a smile of contentment on his face for the violinist was indeed first class.

After the concert we decided to walk part of the way home, for as Holmes pointed out, we never knew when we would encounter another time portal. It was a clear night, not dissimilar to the one that led us into this predicament in the first place.

As we walked through the back streets, we were silent observers of London's night life. All was peaceful until the rumblings of my stomach broke the silence.

"You know what, Holmes, I'm hungry."

"I'm a little peckish myself," admitted Holmes. He pointed to a building across the street with a flashing light. "We could try that place," he suggested.

"Driscoll's Gay bar," I said, reading the sign. "Sounds like a happy place."

"Indeed. Perhaps they serve meals with light entertainment," agreed Holmes as ignorant as I. "I could use a laugh."

We crossed the street and moments later entered the building. It was quite dark inside initially, until our eyes became accustomed to the subdued lighting. Slow music was playing as we made our way to the bar. There was more light here.

We ordered drinks and turned to survey the room and the couple's dancing. That is when I had the biggest shock of my life. "Holmes!" I gasped.

"I see them, Watson," replied Holmes softly.

"Those men are dancing with other men!" I couldn't help stating the obvious in my astonishment. The music came to an end and the couples began to move off the dance floor. What struck me most was the fact that most of these men were big, burly, hairy types, mean looking and rough. Not the sort one would expect to find cuddling up to each other. I had heard of such decadent behaviour, even in our own time, but it was never openly flaunted like this—in fact, it was against the law. What's more the sort of men involved in such practices were usually weak effeminate types, not these big burly aggressively male sorts. I was aghast.

"I think we should leave, Watson," said Holmes softly.

"Definitely," I agreed.

We started to move away from the bar, only to find our way barred by a group of large, hairy men that towered over us, even over Holmes. They circled around us, effectively blocking all movement, backward and forward.

"Well, well, well, what have we here?' said the biggest brute, looking us over with avaricious eyes. If I'd been a woman I would have feared for my virtue. It took me but a moment to realize that given the proclivities of these men, that regardless of my sex, my virtue was in all probability at risk. Holmes' too.

"You are in our way," pointed out Holmes calmly, although I noticed that his fists were clenched and his knuckles showed white. "We are leaving this establishment."

"Not so fast, my pretties," grinned the obscene fellow. "Not until you dance with us."

"I think not," replied Holmes coldly, looking disdainfully at the man.

Suddenly I gasped and leaped forward involuntarily as one vile thug pinched my rear.

"You can dance with me, sweet cheeks," he said, leering at me.

I am afraid my reaction was automatic. I didn't stop to think of the odds, I just swung my fist, clouting the fellow across the jaw. I had the satisfaction of seeing him go down before all hell broke loose. I was struck in the side of the head, and as I staggered I saw Holmes swinging a powerful punch into the biggest thug's midriff.

Within seconds the battle became a free for all, with the ruffians turning on each other as well as on us. The brawl raged undisturbed for almost half an hour.

Holmes and I were very inventive in our defense, using whatever items of furniture came to hand. We made our blows count, although, from the way my head was pounding, we were receiving as good as we gave.

I had just smashed a chair over one brute's head when the door swung open and blue uniformed figures came racing in, police whistles blowing. At that moment, Holmes distracted for an instant, caught a punch and staggered backward, crashing into me and knocking me over. We collapsed onto a table, demolishing it in the process.

Before long we were all rounded up, handcuffed and shoved into a van and taken to the nearest police station. Holmes tried to explain to the officer who was booking us that it was a misunderstanding. That we had wandered into the place by accident and were assaulted when we tried to leave.

"Yeah, right," he returned disbelievingly. "You're allowed one phone call to your lawyer," he advised us.

"Actually, I would prefer you called either Chief Superintendent or Inspector Lestrade, they will vouch for our innocence," said Holmes.

The policeman looked impressed. “All right, I’ll do that, but I’m afraid you’ll have to go into the holding cell in the meantime.” His manner was slightly more polite than before.

The handcuffs were removed and we were led to a separate cell from our adversaries. They were in cells on either side of us and continued to make obscene remarks and suggestions, and when I accidentally made eye contact with one ugly brute, he blew me a kiss! This situation was intolerable.

CHAPTER NINE

We were there for nearly two hours before Georgina arrived and our cell was unlocked.

"Oh, look at you!" she exclaimed on seeing our bloody, battered faces and our torn filthy clothing. "What on earth were you thinking off, going into a gay bar?" she chided, hands on hips looking sternly at us, as if we were misbehaving children.

"We thought it was a comedy club," I explained.

"A comedy club! How the hell did you get an idea like that?"

"Well, by the name. The Gay Bar. I mean the name denotes happiness, laughter, humour, fun…how were we to know it was a venue for deviants," I complained.

Georgina's eyes sparkled as she attempted to suppress the laughter that threatened; her lips twitched for a moment, then her self-control left her and she broke down and started to laugh.

Holmes looked annoyed at her behaviour, while I flushed with embarrassment, especially when the other police officers also joined in. We weren't used to being laughed at.

"I'm sorry," gasped Georgina between paroxysms. She was holding her side and tears streamed from her eyes as she struggled to gain control. It was a good fifteen minutes before she did.

"What planet are these guys from?" asked the grinning police sergeant as he returned our personal effects to us.

"Well they're a little old fashioned," replied Georgina still grinning, "but they're a couple of dears. You can drop the charges. I can pretty much guarantee that it was a genuine mistake."

She escorted us out to her car saying, "You two are a mess."

"What took you so long?" asked Holmes.

"I was at the gym. I didn't get the message until I got home," she said opening her car doors.

I climbed in gratefully.

"Never a dull moment with you is there?" she grinned again.

Before long we were at Baker Street and Wiona Hudson was at the door to greet us. "Jesus Christ!" she exclaimed when she saw us. "John…your poor face!"

As we moved past her she added, "Get them upstairs, Georgina. I'll be up in a minute with the first aid kit."

Upstairs, Georgina made us take our ruined jackets off and sit down.

Wiona joined us a few minutes later carrying a medical box and a couple of bowls, which she handed to Georgina who filled them with hot water from the tap. Then they helped themselves to the antiseptic, adding it to the water and some swabs.

As Georgina began to dab at Holmes' cuts he flinched and said, "This is not necessary."

"It is too," she retorted. "Do you want those cuts to get infected? If you're going to spend the night brawling in bars, then you have to put up with the treatment…now stay still or I'll sit on you."

When she dabbed at a particularly nasty cut above his right eye, he flinched again and swore under his breath. Georgina scowled, hitched up her short skirt and sat on Holmes' lap, straddling him; facing him. She placed one hand under his jaw to hold his head still, while she continued to dab at the cut with the other. He didn't push her away but submitted to her ministrations in this unconventional fashion. I also noticed that Holmes, not knowing what to do with his hands placed them on her exposed thighs. Whether he explored them or not, I could not say for I was distracted from him by Wiona as she leant over me and gently cleansed my cuts and abrasions. She was looking particularly fetching in slacks and low cut top—or so I noted through my good eye, the other having been closed by a fist.

"How did this happen, John?" she asked with concern.

Before I could answer, Georgina did.

Wiona chuckled at her explanation, and then asked with genuine concern, "You're not gay are you John?"

"Gay, hardly, this had been one of the worst nights of my life," I said indignantly.

"Gay means homosexual in this century. It's not used to denote happiness anymore," pointed out Georgina.

"Oh!" I was silent for a moment, and then declared vehemently, "In that case I am most definitely not gay."

She smiled. "Good," then leant down and kissed me gently on the side of my lip—the bit that wasn't cut or puffy.

Georgina, with eyes sparkling mischievously looked at Holmes from where she sat across his lap. "What about you, Sherlock honey, are you gay?"

Holmes did not reply immediately; instead he glanced down at his hands resting on her thighs, felt the smoothness of her skin and looked thoughtfully into her upturned face. "Was I in the mood for intimate company," he said finally, "I would prefer it to be female."

"With long legs?" she teased.

Now he smiled. "Especially with long legs."

She smiled, wriggled forward a little in his lap, placed both hands on his shoulders and whispered something in his ear, her hot breath tickling him. I didn't hear what she said, but it caused Holmes' eyebrows to shoot up, and his hands wandered a little way further up her thighs as he held her.

My heart was thumping wildly in my chest from Wiona's attentions and I could imagine that Holmes' was doing the same. Georgina nibbled Holmes' ear and kissed him on the tip of the nose before sliding off his lap and standing up.

Holmes ran a finger around the inside of his collar. "It's hot in here," he complained.

I agreed; my own face flushed with unaccustomed heat.

The two ladies exchanged knowing glances and smiles.

"Now off to bed the both of you. You're both worn out. When you're ready, we'll come and tuck you in," promised Georgina.

"That will not be necessary," replied Holmes stiffly.

She flashed him another smile. "Okay, promise you will go straight to bed?"

"Yes, thank you for your help," he added, and then said firmly. "Goodnight, Georgina."

"Goodnight, Sherlock," she responded, blowing him a kiss.

Wiona kissed my cheek as she bid me goodnight.

When the ladies left, Holmes said, "We really need to get home, Watson."

"I guess. What did Georgina whisper to you, Holmes?" I asked curiously.

"She said I was welcome to put my shoes under her bed anytime."

No doubt my own eyebrows raised a tad at that. I shook my head. “The women of this century…” I left the sentence unfinished.

“Quite. Goodnight, Watson.”

“Night, Holmes.”

CHAPTER TEN

We slept deeply that night, exhausted by our efforts during the fight. For once I was up before Holmes, clean and spruce, though not quite freshly shaven, due to the care I had to take to avoid the cuts and bruises that sprinkled my face. I was in good spirits for I must admit I had some rather exotic dreams during the night and looked forward to seeing Wiona this morning.

She arrived not long after, bearing our breakfast tray and the morning papers. I smiled a greeting at her but was startled by her expression.

"What is it? What's wrong?" I asked with concern.

She put the tray down and picked up one of the morning papers, holding it up, so that I could see the headline.

SHERLOCK HOLMES LIVES!

The big black letters seemed to scream at me. Before I could make a comment, we were distracted by hearing Holmes cursing. He stormed out of his room.

"Mrs Hudson, call the police," he ordered. "A pervert with a camera has climbed up the drain pipe outside the bathroom and has been spying on me!"

Only then did he notice our expressions. Without a word, I handed him the newspaper. He opened it and looked at the headline.

"This is monstrous," he gasped, as he sat down on the nearest chair to read the story.

"Read it out loud please, Holmes," I requested.

He nodded and began to read. "Sherlock Holmes and Dr. Watson are alive! Carlos White, crime reporter for the Daily News witnessed Sherlock Holmes investigating the latest junkie murder. He was instrumental in the capture of Peter Bradley, who confessed to the crimes after his arrest. We have it on good authority that Holmes and Watson underwent a DNA test at New Scotland Yard to prove their authenticity. These tests were compared with strands of hair from Holmes' brush, currently on display at the Sherlock Holmes museum and samples from Dr. Watson's toe nails. They recorded a perfect match. It is unknown at this point in time exactly how they arrived in our century, but it has been proven without a doubt that they are the genuine article.

"A spokesman for Scotland Yard refused to comment on their enlistment of Sherlock Holmes in solving the junkie murders, but did say that his help was sought in a purely unofficial capacity. This reporter has subsequently learned that Holmes was also responsible for the apprehension of the Palace theatre bomber..."

Holmes stopped for a moment and looked at me. "It goes on to say where we are living. I guess that explains the peeping tom at the bathroom window."

I stood up and went over to the front window. The minute I pulled up the blind, a roar went up from the crowd down below and lights flashed in my eyes from the numerous cameras being directed at me. I hastily backed away. "My God, Holmes. There's a mob out there."

"How did they find out?" queried Holmes throwing a glance at Wiona.

She held up her hands. "Don't look at me. I didn't' tell anyone you were here."

"It must have been at the crime scene, Holmes," I said pointing to one of several pictures which showed Holmes examining the dead woman.

At that moment the telephone rang. I sprang to answer it.

"Can I speak to Sherlock Holmes?" asked an anonymous male voice.

"Who's calling please?" I asked.

"This is Jackson Daniels of the five o'clock news. Is that Dr. Watson I'm addressing? We'd like to interview..."

I hung up on him. The phone rang again. I answered it only to find it was another reporter. I cut him off mid stride. Now the phone began to ring in earnest.

Wiona took it off the hook silencing it.

"What are we going to do, Holmes?" I asked, dismayed by this turn of events.

"I'm not sure. I'll call Georgina," he decided. "The police can move these busybodies away. I have no doubt that the leak of our identities came from them, the least they can do is help us."

He picked up the telephone and dialled Georgina's number. She answered promptly enough. Holmes explained the situation to her and she agreed to do what she could.

Twenty minutes later she arrived with a dozen policemen who set about breaking up the crowd of loiterers. She entered our rooms apologetically.

"I'm so sorry, Sherlock, John. It seems the DNA results were leaked from the lab and that reporter talked to Inspector Harrison, who always was an idiot. Dad is as upset about this as I am. The DNA test was supposed to be only for the police commissioner's benefit and to clear you of suspicion with regard to the bomber case.

"What are we to do now? That situation out there is insufferable," I said.

Georgina bit her lip and said nothing. She knew better than we did at this time just what was in store for us. "I'm sorry," she repeated ineffectually.

Wiona tried to entice us to the breakfast table which she had just finished setting up. I went over and made a half-hearted attempt at eating, but Holmes had lost his appetite, and lit his pipe instead.

"Have you made any progress with your research?" asked Georgina at last.

"No," replied Holmes shortly, puffing furiously, creating thick blue clouds.

She was uneasily silent until he relented and elaborated.

"I have studied it. There are certain times of the year when the phenomenon is more prevalent, but they never appear in the same place twice. I have come to the conclusion that it is impossible. Watson and I cannot sit for twenty-four hours a day in one place in the hope that a time portal will open up. It could take years. It's hopeless."

"Maybe the commissioner can help you," suggested Georgina. "He'd like to see you both today, if you're willing. I mean, he's got more clout than either Dad or me." She looked at Holmes pleadingly. "Will you come with me?"

Despite her couching it as a request, we knew that she had been ordered to bring us.

“I don’t see that we have any other choice,” replied Holmes. He looked at Georgina for a long moment, his eyes searching for something. Whatever he did see seemed to satisfy him.

I was at a loss myself, wondering what was going through his mind. A new thought seemed to have occurred to him. I finished my breakfast and then we left with her.

Despite the police outside keeping the crowd back, a few managed to break through. One woman shoved a fur padded stick in front of Holmes’ face.

“Mr Holmes, how did you come to be in this century?” asked the woman aggressively.

Holmes pushed the stick (a microphone I later found out it was called) away without deigning to reply. It was an effort to reach Georgina’s car. It was also something of a relief to be driving away from the maddening throng.

Holmes was silent, lost in cogitation. I thought that the worst was behind us, but I was wrong. Georgina had no sooner pulled up at Scotland Yard than we were besieged again. Not by reporters this time, but by, unless I was greatly mistaken, Japanese tourists. A bus had pulled up in front of us and as we stepped out of the car, a horde of Asians surrounded us, all manner of camera’s snapping wildly, blinding us with their flashes.

It took one who knew Holmes as well as I did, to see the anger mounting by the minute and that he was making an effort to contain it. Holmes had always been an intensely private man, who guarded his privacy jealously. This blatant intrusion into our lives was sheer torture for him.

Once inside the building, Georgina turned a distressed face to Holmes. “I’m so sorry, Sherlock!”

To my surprise, Holmes squeezed her arm reassuringly and said, “I don’t blame you, Lestrade. You’re just a pawn.”

She frowned at his cryptic comment. It puzzled me also, but now was not the time to ask for an explanation.

Georgina stopped at the front desk and rang the commissioner. When she hung up, she led us upstairs to his office, saying, “We’re to go straight in.”

CHAPTER ELEVEN

The commissioner of police was a hearty looking fellow in an elegant suit. He looked more like a businessman than a policeman.

"Mr Holmes, Dr. Watson," he greeted, holding out his hand to shake. "A pleasure, a real pleasure."

"Too bad we can't say the same," replied Holmes rudely, putting his hands in his pocket and not shaking the outstretched hand.

The commissioner frowned at Holmes for a moment, then dismissed Georgina with a curt, "That will be all, Inspector." He motioned us to seats, but Holmes remained standing. "Why have you brought us here?" he demanded.

"Why? Er...because I wanted to meet you," replied the commissioner somewhat hesitantly.

"Don't be coy. You know what I am referring to," said Holmes, staring at the man coldly, his grey eyes piercing the other.

"Actually he doesn't know," said a voice from behind us—a familiar voice.

We turned.

Standing in the doorway was none other than Mycroft Holmes!

"Mycroft!" Holmes was stunned for once. Whatever he suspected was happening he certainly did not anticipate seeing Mycroft. I was just as thunderstruck, for he was the last person I ever expected to see in this century.

He came into the room. "Sherlock, my dear brother, and you are my brother despite the fact that we have never met," he said enigmatically.

"You're not my brother, you're an imposter," declared Holmes, recovering some of his poise.

"Au contraire. Genetically I am of the same flesh and blood, the same substance. You see Mycroft was so indispensable to the British government that we couldn't just let him die. Scientists have been experimenting with cloning since World War I. Mycroft voluntarily provided the cells that enabled scientists to clone him, making an exact copy. In a way..." here a smile broke across his fat face. "I could be considered Mycroft's son. My name, by the way, is Morelock." He offered his fat flipper like hand to Holmes, who scrutinized him closely.

"You work for British intelligence?" asked Holmes.

"I am British intelligence, just as your brother was."

"What do you want from us?" I asked, still a little confused by this remarkable turn of events.

"Good question. In fact, Sherlock, why don't you tell me what you already know, or suspect?"

"I suspect that the time portal we came through was artificial, engineered by you for the express purpose of bringing us into the 21st century. Something went wrong though, and we did not materialize where you expected us to. It was purely coincidence that we were traced through the sale of our money…"

"No, not a coincidence. We let it be known that a private collection of old pound notes had been stolen and that any sale of such was to be reported. I know how you think, Sherlock. I knew it wouldn't take you long to realize the value of your money in this century and cash in on it."

"I see. Very well, you allowed Inspector Lestrade to contact us, counting on her name being sufficient to win us over. You also wanted to test us, so enlisted our aid in the junkie murder."

"Well I had to be sure you made the transition through time with all your faculties intact. Catching the bomber was an unexpected bonus," added Morelock with a smile.

"What it gets down to," said Holmes, "is that you have a case for us. You have manipulated us and others all for your own end." Holmes was coldly disapproving now.

"I did no more than your brother would have done for his Queen and country," countered Morelock, a trifle defensively.

"That means that you can send us home," I said. "If you brought us here, you can send us home!" This knowledge was like a huge weight being lifted off my shoulders.

"Possibly," he replied. "After you handle a small task for me."

"And if we refuse?" asked Holmes.

He shrugged. "I hope you like the 21st Century; you're going to be here for a long time."

"Is that a threat?" I asked, a knot forming in my stomach.

He shrugged again. "The government is unlikely to waste money, time and resources on sending people back to the past if they have done nothing to earn it."

"Blackmail!" I was as angry as Holmes over having been exploited by this fake Mycroft. "First you kidnap us, then you try blackmail. Have you no shame, no honour?"

"Sorry, Doctor, but it is a matter of national security."

"If you have Mycroft's brains and abilities, why can't you attend to it yourself?" asked Holmes almost scornfully.

"It is because I have all his abilities that I cannot. If this was in your century, he would turn to you to help him. I have had to bring you to my time for the same purpose. Help us and I will return you to the past." He looked at Holmes' stubborn face and cold grey eyes.

Would Holmes jeopardize our only chance of getting home by refusing to help, or would he concede defeat to Mycroft's clone? These thoughts crossed my mind as I also looked at Holmes' unrelenting face. Morelock also sensed Holmes' irritation and the stubbornness it engendered. Holmes did not take kindly to being manoeuvred like a pawn on a chess board. He was a man very much in control of his own destiny, and to have it taken away galled palpably within him.

"I'll tell you what," said Morelock over the ensuing silence. "We still have some time on our hands. Why don't you go home and think about it. I'm sure you will see reason within a day or two." He held out his card to Holmes.

Holmes glanced at it, but refused to touch it, as if it was contaminated with a deadly disease.

I stepped forward and took it.

"When you change your mind, call me," he said.

We left the office without a further word. There was a police driver waiting to take us back to Baker Street.

Holmes said nothing during the drive but it bothered me not, for I was lost in my own ruminations.

The car pulled up in front of 317, which was once again besieged with hordes of people. We stepped out of the car and attempted to make our way to the front door. These people were not reporters, they were a hysterical mob!

They tore at our clothing as we tried to fight our way through. We were trapped in the centre when Wiona Hudson emerged from the front door, spraying the crowd with a fire extinguisher. They parted and we staggered past. Once through the door, Wiona slammed and locked it. Holmes was pale and I was also feeling rather shaken.

"Were they trying to kill us?" I asked.

"No, John. They're just fans. They were mobbing you to get a souvenir," she replied.

As our clothes were in tatters, it was fortunate Wiona appeared when she did, for any longer and we would have been stripped naked.

"I need a smoke," growled Holmes, taking to the stairs two at a time. I knew how he felt. Also, I didn't need Holmes to explain to me that it was Morelock who was responsible for our public exposure. More fuel for his blackmail, more incentive to make us want to leave. The man was diabolical.

CHAPTER TWELVE

Holmes took his pipe and a box of tobacco and curled up in the armchair by the cold fireplace. He had withdrawn into himself and not a word came from him. He didn't even bother to change out of his tattered clothing. I did, and when I emerged from my bedroom Wiona arrived with a tea tray. I offered Holmes a drink but he ignored me, his brows drawn, his eyes hooded, his lips a straight thin line.

He remained that way, unmoving. He could have been dead but for the spiraling smoke from his pipe. He said nothing, and as the day wore on I became worried. Only once or twice have I seen him in such a black depression. Sometimes, in the past, he resorted to cocaine, which did nothing to lift his mood, and only made it worse. It was at such times that I actually feared for his life, for he was not above self-harm on such occasions.

It went against his grain to acknowledge defeat, yet Morelock held our only means of returning home. We were powerless without his help. I didn't know what to say or do. As far as Holmes was concerned, at this moment I did not even exist; he was alone in his misery.

When he ate neither lunch nor dinner, and had not budged an inch, I decided to act. The worst he could do was yell at me.

I went downstairs to Wiona's apartment and used her telephone to call Georgina. Her presence seemed to strike a chord in him. I knew he liked and admired her, so I hoped that she would be able to rouse him from his black mood. She told me that after she had been dismissed by the Commissioner, she had been kept busy all day on nonsensical tasks, but that she was due to knock off soon and would be at Baker Street within the hour.

She was true to her word. When she arrived, both she and Wiona came into our rooms. Wiona slipped an arm around my waist in moral support, whilst Georgina approached Holmes cautiously.

She stood in front of him. "Sherlock?" she queried, looking at him.

He continued to stare moodily at the fireplace, unseeing.

"Sherlock!" she said louder, more forcefully.

Still he ignored her.

She looked at me helplessly.

I shrugged. I had hoped that her presence would at least bring him out of his withdrawal from the world around him.

She stood looking at him for a moment, then moved around behind him and began to gently massage the back of his neck, then his shoulders. For a long five minutes nothing happened, then his eyes closed and he leaned back into her hands. She continued to massage him. When his eyes opened, gone were the introspective look and the haze that had seemed to cloud his spirit.

"Georgina," he said with surprise, as if seeing her for the first time.

"Sherlock, I can't tell you how sorry I am at what has happened," she moved around in front of him again.

He looked at her, his eyes filled with a pain I couldn't quite understand. It occurred to me that there was much I did not know about Holmes, despite our long acquaintance. Perhaps this situation reminded him of something similar that had happened to him in the past, before I met him. I could only conjecture at the cause of his hidden pain, at the reason for his melancholy.

"My dear girl, it is not your fault, or your father's. You are merely being used by forces beyond your control. We all are," he said, and then fell silent again, but to my relief did not begin brooding.

"If only I knew where he kept it, we could steal it and return ourselves home," he said.

Georgina looked at him blankly, not knowing what he was talking about.

I did. Quickly I explained what happened in the commissioner's office.

She was aghast at the enormity of it. "I had no idea!"

"Of course you didn't," I replied, and then to Holmes I said, "Even if you could steal the time machine, Holmes, there is no guarantee that you would know how to use it. Even in experienced hands something went wrong—we were supposed to end up with Morelock, not left to fend for ourselves," I pointed out.

He sighed unhappily. “I know you think I should just take the case, whatever it is, but it is not that simple, Watson. We have no guarantee that he will return us to our time. He is not to be trusted. He may look like Mycroft, but he is not my brother; he is not half the man my brother is. He could force us into one case after another. I prefer to pick and choose what I do and for whom I do it. To have no say, to be powerless…”

To my surprise he suddenly changed tack, and looking at Georgina he said, “That was nice, what you were doing before.”

She smiled. “The massage?”

“Mmm.”

She looked at him, her eyes luminous. Suddenly she leant down and took both his hands in hers, pulling him up from the chair. “Come on,” she said, “I’ll give you a proper one.”

She pulled him unresistingly towards his bedroom. If we were in our old rooms in 221B, I would have been shocked at such wanton behaviour, but here, now, in this time and place, it seemed the most natural thing. I looked at Wiona; she smiled knowingly and, with her hand in mine quietly led me downstairs to her apartment.

CHAPTER THIRTEEN

The next morning I helped Wiona bring the breakfast tray upstairs and entreated her to join us. I had just poured the tea, when Holmes emerged from his room followed by a tousled haired Georgina, still tucking her blouse into her skirt. Holmes looked well this morning, his eyes were bright and his cheeks bore a healthy flush.

"Good morning, Watson, Wiona," he greeted us cheerfully. "What's for breakfast? I'm ravenous."

At the table, he pulled out a chair for Georgina, then seated himself and began helping himself to the most enormous breakfast I have ever seen him eat. Of course he did miss his meals the previous day—but still!

Naturally it was relief to see him like this after the gloom of the previous day. I smiled at Georgina in silent thanks and she nodded in return, understanding me completely.

It wasn't until Holmes was half way through his second helping that he said, "Georgina has a splendid idea for getting rid of those busybodies outside."

"She has?" I was eager.

"We'll put it into effect after breakfast," he promised, but did not elaborate.

After breakfast, we tidied ourselves up (I hadn't shaved yet); then when we were all immaculate and groomed, Holmes said, "All right, let us beard the lion."

We marched out and stood on the front step, Holmes, Georgina and me. The crowd let out a sound resembling a roar and surged forward. Holmes held up his hand for silence. Cameras began flashing nonstop.

"Ladies and gentlemen, a moment of your time," began Holmes. The crowd became quiet.

"My name is Irving Brown and this is Phillip Barton, we are the actors who portray Holmes and Watson in the new movie currently in production called Sherlock Holmes in the 21st Century. This, my friends, is nothing more than a publicity stunt; a very successful one, I might add. The producers wanted to know if the plot line was believable and apparently it is. The good news is that you the public have been filmed as part of the crowd scene and will also appear in the movie…"

There was uproar from the crowd. A journalist thrust himself forward and shoved the microphone at Holmes. "What about the DNA tests… and you being at the scene of the junkie murder?"

Holmes smiled. "The DNA information was a hoax; that is why it was deliberately leaked. You should never believe everything you read. As to the 'murder', the victim was an actress cleverly made up. Inspector Lestrade here from Scotland Yard consented to appear, as did Inspector Harrison, for the sake of a large donation to the police widows and orphans fund. Their presence gave it authenticity," explained Holmes convincingly.

Most of the faces in the crowd showed their disappointment. Then suddenly, we heard a squeaky old voice. "Let me through, let me through." And old lady of perhaps ninety years struggled through the crowd. She was tiny with thick trifocal glasses on her long nose as she peered owlishly at Holmes. She poked at him with her battered old parasol.

"I could have told you this young man was an imposter," she cried. "I knew the real Sherlock Holmes!"

The reporters turned their attention to the old biddy, while Holmes smiled with amusement. She came no higher than his waist, but had a fearsome temperament.

"Sherlock Holmes and I were lovers. I bore his illegitimate child!" she declared. This naturally caught the crowd's attention, as all eyes focused on her. We discreetly moved back inside and allowed her the limelight. Once inside, Holmes began to laugh in that peculiar silent fashion he had.

"Who was that woman, Sherlock?" asked Georgina curiously.

"No idea. I have never met her," he said, laughing harder still as we listened to the old girl's story. According to her she had been his mistress during the great hiatus, whatever that was, and that she had born him two children who had since died. She claimed to be a French courtesan despite speaking with a very strong lower class British accent. If she was French then I was Queen Victoria. The woman was lapping up the attention of the gathered media.

"What absurd claims, Holmes," I said.

"Let her have her moment of glory, Watson. We know it's nonsense. I cannot see myself taking up with a semi-literate French courtesan in the near future, although…" here he glanced at Georgina, "it is possible I may have developed a taste for something I have hitherto not experienced."

I said nothing to that; there was little I could say, although personally I thought it was a good thing. Maybe Holmes would even consider marriage in the future now that had experienced one of its benefits.

A short while later when I looked out the window, I noticed that the crowd had dispersed, taking the old lady with them.

"Well your subterfuge worked," I said.

Georgina grinned. "I knew it would." She moved over and kissed Holmes' cheek and then bid us a cheery goodbye. "I'll catch you all later," she said as she left.

It proved to be a very pleasant day. We went to the bank and withdrew some money. Holmes bought a computer and spent most of the day, with Wiona's help, setting it up. While they were thus occupied, I visited the local news agent to buy the papers.

There was a copy of the book entitled His Last Bow, written by me. Holmes had specifically ordered me not to read any books about him that I had written, insisting that it never paid to know too much of one's future. It was tempting though, I must admit. I couldn't resist flipping through the pages and glancing through the stories. It gave my own ego a bit of a boost to know that my stories would survive me, that they were still being read a hundred years after my demise. It gave me a certain pride of accomplishment, for how many writers are remembered eternally. Most eventually fade away to some musty old library shelf. The temptation was too strong for me to resist. I bought the book and stashed it in the inside pocket of my coat.

Back in our rooms I put the papers down on the table and went to my room intending to conceal the incriminating book. When I took it out of my pocket, I had the shock of my life. Even as I looked at it, the writing began to fade.

"Holmes!" I cried, racing out of my room and into the sitting room, waving the book at him. When I reached him, I stopped and shoved it in front of him. "Look! It's disappearing! What can it mean?"

Even as we watched all the print disappeared, leaving a blank book in my hands. Holmes looked grave.

"It means that the past has changed. History has changed. When we first arrived here the probability was strong that we would return home. Something has happened since then to change that. That the book has faded proves that it was never written."

"Is it Wiona and Georgina?" I asked.

Holmes thought for a moment, seriously considering the possibility. "No, I think not."

"Is it because you have decided to refuse Morelock?"

"How did you know I have decided to refuse him?" asked Holmes.

I tapped the book. "What other reason could there be. He is the only one with the ability to get us home. If we don't deal with him, we are stuck here." I am afraid my face revealed my distress at the thought.

Holmes looked suddenly contrite. "I am sorry, Watson. I have been incredibly selfish. I have not spared you or your feelings a thought. It is just that the man rubs me the wrong way. He looks like Mycroft but he is not. My brother has more honour than that. I do not like to be manipulated or dictated to. I had enough of that growing up. Did you know, Watson, that I was disinherited because I chose to follow my own career path, rather than the one my father had decided for me?"

"Yes, I believe you have mentioned that before, Holmes, during the Kathryn Wilson case."

"He was the sort of man that was very strict, and believed his sons should do as they were told and he had an antipathy for creativity and imagination. As you can imagine, we did not see eye to eye. Even Mycroft, the real one, rebelled against his influence. Ever since I have had an intense dislike of doing what is expected of me. I suppose that is why I invented my own occupation. At times I have been judge and jury. I have been the deciding force, the one in power. It is not easy for a man like me to become submissive to another's will."

It surprised me that Holmes was so forthcoming with hitherto unmentioned personal information but I appreciated it, for it helped me understand his mood of the previous day.

"Still, my own feelings aside, I should have asked you what you wanted to do, Watson. It was remiss of me and incredibly selfish."

"Well, I would like to go home," I said simply. "I admit that I am attracted to Wiona, but like you, I feel useless here. I am an anachronism. That incident at the gay bar; we were both so ignorant that we wandered blindly into such a place. There are so many things around here that I don't understand; that a child of this century could explain in detail. I know sometimes in the past you have accused me of being dull, and perhaps I am at times, especially when compared to you, but I feel worse than dull here."

Holmes looked at me for a long moment. "I have been self-centered."

"It's not just that, Holmes. I...I glanced at one of the stories in the book. I know you said I shouldn't, but I couldn't help it. You have to go back; you owe it to this country. You play a major part in the First World War. If we don't go back you will not be there, you will not play your part, and it could even mean a change in Britain's fortunes in the war. It is not just you and I as individuals whose lives are at stake, but a great many other people. We cannot, we must not change history!" I became vehement.

Holmes looked thoughtful. "There is a great deal of truth in what you say. I must admit I haven't considered the ramifications of what my absence in the past would mean. There would be many a case left unsolved, many a criminal free...and that which you are referring to, my contribution during war time...I suppose it is a small sacrifice on our part to give up our present pleasures for the sake of preserving history."

"Everyone has to make sacrifices," I pointed out.

"Mmm." Holmes looked none too happy, and I felt a trifle guilty. He was my best friend. He had finally found happiness with a woman, something I had always wished for him, and now I was asking him to give it up.

"Well, Watson, when you're right, you're right. It would seem we really have no choice in the matter. Do you have Morelock's number?"

"Yes."

"Very well, ring him and make an appointment for tomorrow."

"All right...Holmes!" I held up the book again. The writing that had disappeared was now gradually reappearing.

"It would seem we have just made the right decision," Holmes mused.

"It also means one other thing."

"What?"

"That despite your misgivings about Morelock's trustworthiness, he does send us home."

"And you said you were dull!" Holmes smiled at me.

I telephoned Morelock and he agreed to a meeting the following day. His voice sounded smug, as if he knew he would win in the end.

That evening we made the most of our new found freedom from the crowds that had stalked us and took the ladies out to dinner at the finest restaurant in London. After dinner we returned to Baker Street. At 317, Georgina took a bag from the boot of her car, and at my enquiring glance said, "Just a few necessaries."

It seemed she planned on staying the night again. I also noticed that Holmes offered no objections. I have to admit I was having a few qualms about our developing intimate relationships with the ladies, especially now that we had decided to return to our own time. It wasn't fair to lead them on. I was wondering what Holmes felt on the subject, but not for long, for as we lounged around in the sitting room, enjoying our night cap of fifty year old French cognac, with Wiona sitting beside me on the couch, and Georgina and Holmes curled up together in the big arm chair, Holmes brought up our leaving.

"There is something you should know," said Holmes evenly. "About our future plans," he continued, preparing himself for tears or a scene of female outrage.

"You're going to take Morelock up on his case and return home," deduced Georgina calmly.

"Yes." Holmes gave her a squeeze around the waist. "How did you know that?"

"It is pretty simple. You have to go back. Morelock is the only one who can get you back. If you don't go back you change history. In fact if you don't go back you are effectively killing me."

"What!"

"Yes, Sherlock dear. You see, in 1892 you save Arnold Lestrade, my grandfather's life. If you aren't there to do it, he will die without ever having fathered a son—my father, which means I will never be born."

"Arnold Lestrade?" Holmes frowned in confusion, the name not being familiar to him.

"Inspector George Lestrade's son. He becomes a policeman too, just like his father. He is still a junior constable when you save his life. It's kind of funny just how big a part you play in the history of the Lestrade family. It must be fate." Here she grinned impudently at him. "You are linked to us for eternity it would seem."

"I can think of worse things," he answered, smiling tolerantly at her.

"But does it not bother you, either of you?" I asked. "I mean, in our time we would never consider intimacy without marriage…"

"Dear old Dr. Watson," smiled Georgina.

"John dear, the time I spend with you will be a cherished memory. After having put up with Mr Hudson for seven years, I can tell you I have no interest in marriage, but I am a woman in the prime of life. I have needs. I think that old fashioned Victorian attitude of yours is cute, but unnecessary. Don't ever think that you are taking advantage of me; consider it more a mutual fulfillment."

What could I say to such a statement—nothing. So I did the next best thing, I kissed her with all my heart.

"That goes for me too," said Georgina, "besides," she added with a wide grin. "I'm thinking of renting these rooms when you leave. The place I live in at the moment is a real dump."

"Trying to get rid of us already?" asked Holmes.

"Well, it never hurts to make plans," she replied, still smiling.

CHAPTER FOURTEEN

Breakfast the next day was a merry affair, as both ladies joined us. We were all up reasonably early as Holmes and I had our appointment with Morelock to keep and Georgina didn't want to be late for work again. I couldn't get over how well Holmes looked. Georgina was certainly beneficial for him. Her company did wonders for his appetite as well.

After breakfast, Georgina left for work and we caught a taxi to the address Morelock had given me the previous day.

It was a dingy non-descript place on the outside, but inside was another matter. A man was seated at the front desk and directed us to an elevator. There were no controls on the inside which meant that it was controlled from the outside.

My stomach rose to my throat as we shot downwards at a tremendous rate, then suddenly, the cubicle we were in went sideways for a short distance before coming to an abrupt halt. The door whooshed open and we were greeted with bright lights and bustling activity. Morelock also stood there, smiling a welcome. We stepped out into another futuristic world.

"Welcome to the nerve centre of the British Empire," he greeted proudly, as we looked around in awe. It was a vast underground room. Huge screens covered the walls with banks upon banks of computer consoles and other paraphernalia. People wandered around in white smocks or overalls.

"Those are the spy satellites," he said pointing to one screen. "At a touch of a button we can see what is happening anywhere in the world." As we walked he pointed out various other things, much of his explanations going over my head.

Finally we came to a locked door. He leaned forward and a blue light shone into his eye before the door opened and admitted us.

"This is what you want to see, isn't it?" he said, pointing to a platform with two circular pads on it.

"The time machine?" Holmes moved forward with interest.

I knew one thing, there was no way we could steal it, for it practically occupied the whole room.

"What went wrong?" asked Holmes.

"The electromagnetic pulses emitted by the machine caused a natural time portal to open up. It was the natural one you stepped through. If you had waited but a few moments before stepping into it, you would have been encompassed by ours."

"Just as well we didn't wait then," replied Holmes with a smile. "What is this case that you had to drag us here for?"

Morelock led us to his office located in a glass enclosure that overlooked the main room, but was sound proofed against the noise. "There have been death threats made against the royal family," he began.

"That's nothing new. They are always receiving death threats," interrupted Holmes.

"True enough, but these are different, they're real. It started three years ago and has been ongoing. The assassins have already succeeded in killing Princess Diana. And it is not just the usual hatred against royalty involved. Large ransoms are being demanded for the lives of various royals. Her majesty Queen Elizabeth II has paid out a fortune in ransom to the assassins to spare her grandsons, Harry and William, but even she, despite being the richest woman in the world, cannot afford to buy the life of everyone."

"So the death threats are merely incidental? It is more like a protection racket?" I asked.

"Yes. Before Princess Diana's death in 1997, the Queen received a ransom demand requesting twenty million pounds for Diana's life. She ignored it. That same week, Diana was dead and the country was in shock. Naturally we covered it up. The public believe she was killed in a motor car accident caused by the paparazzi. Six months after her death, the Queen received a further demand for forty million for Diana's sons, with the threat that they would be next. There was little she could do, she paid.

"The boys were safe and there were no further demands for a year and a half until another demand came. This was for fifty million for Prince Charles. She paid twenty-five because that was all she could spare and had Charles guarded around the clock by the best security men in the business. Two months later he was found in his bed chamber still alive, but with his ears cut off…"

"That can only be an improvement," sneered Holmes. "I've seen pictures of him."

I glanced at Holmes, rather surprised by his attitude, for he had always supported the royal family. However I recalled that he had been reading some of Wiona's women's magazines. It seems the Crown Prince has a mistress—a married woman with whom he continued to have an affair whilst married to Princess Diana. Obviously the scandalous public behaviour of royalty in this century did little to win Holmes' approval.

Morelock frowned. "Granted, Charles is not all that popular, but Queen Elizabeth is, and so is her mother—who you will come to know in your own lifetime. Her Majesty received Charles's ears as proof that despite our precautions they are not safe anywhere. Now they are asking for two hundred million for the life of the Queen Mother, and five hundred million for Her Majesty herself."

I gasped in surprise. Holmes remained inscrutable.

"We have taken care to keep it out of the press, no one knows," added Morelock.

"I still do not see the reason for my presence," pointed out Holmes.

"You will, when I tell you that recently we managed to catch one of the men who made the attack on Diana. With a little persuasion and lots of drugs we managed to get the name of his employer…it is Professor James Moriarty," announced Morelock looking at us expectantly.

A hushed silence followed his words.

"How is that possible? Moriarty would be at least 150 years old!" protested Holmes.

"Mycroft is dead, yet I live," pointed out Morelock.

"You are saying that this is Moriarty's clone?"

"Yes. You see he was created the same time as me."

"Why?" I felt dumbfounded. "Why on earth would they clone a criminal?"

"It wasn't official. One of the scientists involved on the project that begot me was a descendant of the Professor. His name was Paul Bishop and he inherited a locket which contained some of Moriarty's hair. Unbeknownst to the other scientists, he used the facilities of the laboratory to reproduce Moriarty."

"I still have to ask why?" I said.

"It seems he considered it unfair that they would resurrect a Holmes and not even consider his ancestor. Needless to say, that once Moriarty had fully matured, he no longer needed his misguided kinsman, who despite being stupid, was honest. He killed him and fled to Ireland, where he set up an organization ostensibly to assist the continued development of the IRA, but was actually just a front for other crimes. For example, when members of the IRA set bombs in the financial district, Moriarty's men were emptying bank vaults under cover of all the confusion that ensued."

"Why me?" asked Holmes. "If you know who is behind it why can't you deal with him, with all your modern ways?"

"Because this is Moriarty. You are an expert on him. You know how he thinks and how he works. We have tried, but we cannot get close. Two months ago, we raided his headquarters in Ireland. We caught a lot of revolutionaries and small fry thieves, but Moriarty disappeared without a trace. You are the only man who has ever defeated him."

Holmes looked thoughtful. "This isn't the Moriarty I know. If he is just a clone, he may think similarly, but he is not the same," Holmes pointed out.

"Technically he is the same; the only difference is that he doesn't have Moriarty's memories. Just as I do not have Mycroft's memories, yet in every other way I am the same. He has Moriarty's abilities. Furthermore, you know what he looks like. In fact you are the only person to have met him and lived. We can catch his underlings, but they refuse to talk. As a matter of fact, many have taken their own lives in preference to talking."

"That sounds like Moriarty," agreed Holmes, nodding.

"That is why we have brought you here. He was a criminal genius in your century; imagine what he could do in this one with all the advances in technology. You are the only man who can find him and stop him," declared Morelock.

CHAPTER FIFTEEN

Morelock had Holmes' interest now. Gone was his studied indifference. "You said I defeated the original Moriarty?"

"What you've done once, you can do again," stated Morelock.

"I assume that this 'defeat' is still in my future, as it hasn't happened yet. I know of him of course and our paths have crossed numerous times, but always at the fringes. I have yet to deal direct with him, so I do not actually have anything to go on," Holmes pointed out.

"Perhaps not, but you are familiar with his ways, even in 1890. Unless I am mistaken, you have already commenced to amass the information you need to use against him and his hirelings."

Holmes nodded. "True enough. Like you, I can get information on his peripheral activities, but cannot get close to Moriarty himself. He covers his tracks too well. Am I right in assuming that Moriarty has shifted his base of operations in Ireland to England?"

Morelock smiled. "Yes. No fooling you is there. When my agents broke up his organization in Ireland, as I said before, Moriarty escaped. We know he came to England, but he's gone to ground and we have no idea where to begin looking for him."

Holmes nodded grimly. "That sounds like Moriarty all right." He took his pipe out of his pocket, ignored Morelock's look of dismay and proceeded to fill and light it with the strong offensive smelling tobacco.

"I have a question," I began, somewhat hesitantly.

Morelock looked at me, his expression one of polite disinterest. I knew that they hadn't intended for me to come, just Holmes. He considered my presence as unnecessary.

"You're a clone, Moriarty's a clone. Rather than bring Holmes from the past, why didn't you just clone him? After all you had hair samples from him, if it's true about the DNA test being compared to hair samples from his brush."

"Good question, Watson," approved Holmes. "I wondered that myself."

Morelock looked uncomfortable for a moment. "They did consider making you as well, but you would have been manufactured for government service. They wanted someone with the Holmes brains and abilities, but who was as willing to accept orders as give them. They wanted someone unambitious. You were considered too unstable…"

"Unstable!" growled Holmes.

"Your moods are too volatile. You do not take well to authority, you have a history of being a law unto yourself, and you take drugs," pointed out Morelock. "Whereas Mycroft was happy to do his bit and go with the flow. They felt that if they created you, they wouldn't be able to control you, just as Moriarty's creator was unable to control him."

Holmes was somewhat mollified by this explanation, and I have to admit I agreed with Morelock's assessment. Holmes, even a cloned Holmes with his inexhaustible energy would never have been happy with the mundane paper pushing of intelligence work. He was a man of action.

Holmes puffed contentedly on his pipe. "Well, if you want me to take on Moriarty I am going to need a few things."

"Whatever you want, we can get it," Morelock promised.

They fell to discussing the situation and Holmes' needs. I'm afraid that I tuned out, as this was the sort of thing that Holmes relished, and where, judging from some of his requests, his unique talents would be at their best. There was little for me to do until all the ground work had been done. Holmes always worked alone during such times. He usually only enlisted my aid when it came to the final moments of any case.

When everything was arranged to Holmes' satisfaction, I interrupted their conversation again to put forward a thought that had just occurred to me. "I have another question," I said, noticing that this time Morelock looked at me with a little more respect. "If this has been going on for three years why have you waited until now to approach Holmes?"

Holmes smiled. I was certainly putting Morelock in the hot seat.

Morelock looked shamefaced as he confessed. "It is only recently that we found out about Moriarty's existence, let alone his involvement. Once we did, we applied all our resources, but have had little success. He seems to be able to strike wherever he likes with impunity; the way he is striking at the royal family is like he is laughing at us."

"These ransom demands on the royals," began Holmes, "They've been getting bigger with each claim?"

"Yes. They're impossible demands. Her majesty cannot pay."

Holmes puffed for a few moments in silent contemplation, and then said finally, "It seems to me that he is trying to build up his finances rapidly for some purpose. Previously he demanded manageable sums and did not rush to make the next demand. But two demands simultaneously for seven hundred million pounds prove he is desperate for a large amount of money quickly. General crime takes a while to amass large sums. He needs a great deal of money in the near future; by threatening the royal family, he knows that if they don't pay, the government probably will. The question of course is why. What is he planning? What sort of things can a person buy in this century that costs a fortune, but can be turned to the purchaser's advantage to generate an even larger fortune—or power?"

Morelock frowned. "A weapon. A weapon of mass destruction could be used to blackmail countries."

"You have weapons like that?" I asked, amazed at the foolishness of mankind.

"Yes." Morelock turned to his computer on his desk and punched in some codes. He was silent as he scanned the information that came up. Even as we waited, we noticed that his fat face paled and sweat beaded his brow. "Oh, God!" he gasped, his shock and horror evident.

"Something?" asked Holmes.

Morelock turned a stricken face to us. "Last night a top secret military installation situation in the Arizona desert in North America was broken into and a prototype weapon was stolen. There are only four people in the world capable of using it as it functions on complex mathematical algorithms. Those four people are above reproach.

"If it operates on mathematics, then you can make it five people, for this Moriarty has no doubt inherited the original ones mathematical abilities," pointed out Holmes.

"What does this weapon do?" I asked.

"Anything, anything at all. It is equipped with laser technology. It can destroy whole cities, a single building, even an individual item if need be. It is wirelessly connected to a satellite which can be directed to any part of the world. It can control the weather, or worse, it can be focused on a fault line and cause earthquakes, even volcanoes to erupt."

I was open mouthed and dumfounded. "Why would anyone create such a dastardly weapon?"

"The ruling nation is the one with the best weapon. Governments are shying away from nuclear weapons because of the long term complications from the fall out. Instead they have focused on designing 'clean' weapons. There has long been a market for stolen weapons, in fact, the modus operandi in this latest theft tallies with that of an international gang which specializes in weapon sales. If Moriarty plans on bidding for it…" he left the sentence unfinished.

Holmes nodded. "With a weapon like that he could hold the world to ransom."

"Exactly. He has to be found, Sherlock."

"How long do I have?"

"The deadline for the Queen Mother falls next Saturday. If we don't pay, they will kill her. I truly believe this. If they could get to Charles, despite the security, the Queen Mother doesn't have a chance."

"And Her Majesty?"

"Four weeks. She has four weeks to pay, or they target her."

"You have been looking for Moriarty for three years and you expect Holmes to find him in a week!" I exclaimed incredulously.

Morelock had the grace to look ashamed. "Well, he is the master detective of all time."

Holmes smiled weakly. "What did I tell you about miracles, Watson?" He stood up and added, "I suggest you pay the two hundred million for the Queen Mother. It will buy us some time. If there is a four week deadline, it means that the weapon will not come up for sale before that time, and as he is the only one capable of using it, you should be safe from other threats until he gets his hands on it."

Morelock nodded in agreement.

"Now, as I haven't much time, I want everything I asked for at Baker Street by this afternoon. I'll take the maps with me now, though," said Holmes.

"Yes, sir," replied Morelock.

I couldn't help noticing the change in him. He was deferential in his attitude to Holmes now. The tables had turned.

Before we left, Morelock gave Holmes a large case containing in-depth maps of London and surrounds. Holmes needed to familiarize himself with this new London. It had grown considerably since our time.

CHAPTER SIXTEEN

Back at Baker Street, Holmes immersed himself in the maps, while I amused myself browsing through the internet. I was getting quite good at it, even if do say so myself, and I have to admit I was getting rather hooked on watching those hilarious cat videos on a site called You Tube. It was rather amazing really. Who would have thought a cat could play a piano, and use the lavatory. Occasionally I heard Holmes mutter, or make an exclamation as he studied and jotted notes on a pad beside him.

Three hours later a young man and woman arrived, followed by a procession of delivery men brining up several large trunks and boxes and even furniture. Holmes directed them to his bedroom with a mirrored dressing table that had lights around the edge, while the trunks were dumped in our sitting room. It had been spacious before, but now, with his maps spread every which way one looked and heavy trunks and boxes scattered about, it was starting to look like our rooms of old.

The delivery men left, but the young couple stayed. They introduced themselves simply as Melvin and Delilah and claimed they were makeup and wardrobe artists. Holmes disappeared with them into his bedroom. Delilah came out several times to select items from the trunks, before returning to Holmes' room.

I did glance in once, out of curiosity. Holmes turned and grinned at me, showing rotted crooked teeth and a battered misshapen countenance. His nose was bent and he had the traditional cauliflower ear of a boxer, not to mention his eyes were blue.

"Holmes, your eyes!" I exclaimed, startled.

"Contact lenses," he replied. "Aren't they great?"

I just shook my head. Obviously modern disguises were far superior to what Holmes was used to. He was enjoying himself immensely. Although I didn't say it, I wondered why he even needed to bother with a disguise. It's not like anyone knew him by sight in this century. Still, he deserved to have some fun after all there was enough pressure on him with having to contend with a four week deadline.

This deadline did not seem to worry Holmes, for as he pointed out during our journey home, if he had to act quickly, so did Moriarty, as his time was also limited. It did not make me feel any easier in my mind.

At six o'clock the couple left, congratulating Holmes on his natural acting ability and skill with makeup. He was delighted.

"Remarkable couple, that," he said to me after they had left. "They work for a movie studio."

Georgina arrived at seven, but not to stay the night. Apparently she had been detailed, at Holmes' request, to act as the liaison between him and the official police, plus to act as his aide and general dog's body, and to keep him up to date with current information where necessary.

She gave Holmes a portable telephone and showed him how to use it—a mobile she called it.

"In case you need to call me or John," she said. "After all, some of the places that you're going to visit aren't likely to have easy access to phones."

Holmes thanked her. She asked for more details about his case, but Holmes shook his head. "Sorry, Georgina, as much as I would like to take you into my confidence, I cannot reveal the entire case. Suffice to say that we are dealing with a clone of Moriarty which is why I have been brought here. I am supposedly, the authority on Moriarty." He then proceeded to give her a list of instructions which she jotted down. From the look on her face, it was obvious these tasks were going to keep her busy.

Just before she left, she kissed him and said, "Be careful won't you, Sherlock. There aren't any gentlemen crooks anymore; and they'd sooner kill you than look at you. I know from Watson's stories that you never pay much attention to your own personal safety, but please do so this time, if not for yourself then for me. After all, without you, I won't be born. Plus…" here she held his hand wistfully. "I care about you."

Holmes gave her a hug and replied, "Don't worry, I'll be fine. I assure you, I have been in much worse situations than this. Get Watson to tell you about the giant rat of Sumatra one of these days."

It was nearly midnight when I decided to retire. Holmes was still up studying his maps and various dossiers that Morelock had sent of known associates of Moriarty.

"Is there anything I can do for you, Holmes?" I asked him.

"Not at the moment, Watson. Although please do continue to improve your proficiency with the computer. I am probably going to need some research once I get a lead. That will be your department. Also my computer is connected to Georgina's, so I would appreciate a printout each day of any information that she sends to me. Please leave the printouts on the table, as my hours over the next few weeks are bound to be irregular."

"Yes, I can do that for you, Holmes," I said, pleased to be of some use. "If you need me for anything else…"

"I know where to find you, old chap, don't worry. You will be the first to know."

"Goodnight, Holmes."

CHAPTER SEVENTEEN

Next morning as I came out to breakfast, I stopped in shock. There, sitting at our table reading confidential papers was one of the punks that we had encountered on our first day here. Surreptitiously, I picked up a chair and was about to advance on the hooligan.

"I hope you are not planning on hitting me with that chair, Watson," said the punk in Holmes' voice.

The punk turned and grinned at me with uneven teeth. "Morning, Watson."

"My God! Look at you. How could you do that to yourself!" I exclaimed, referring to the rings piercing his eyebrows, nose and lip.

"They're fake, Watson. It only looks like I'm pierced."

"And your hair?" It looked as if he had shorn his head, leaving only a strip down the centre.

Holmes patted his head. "Nifty isn't it," he said, grinning at me. "I'm going to visit our friends down in the East End. I want to see what the word is on the street."

"No offense, Holmes, but are you sure that you will blend in. These are different people from the ones you are used to. In our time you know every nuance of every class and occupation, but here?"

"Fear not, I only have to sit quiet and observe their behaviour for a while. It is not difficult to imitate a thug. Their appearance may change over the years, but their behaviour rarely does."

Holmes ate a hearty breakfast and then left. Such was to be the pattern of our existence for the next two weeks. I saw little of him, and usually only in passing as he came home to change costume. He would leave early and return late, and sometimes not at all. When I didn't see him, he checked in by telephone with instructions for either me or Georgina. In turn, I looked up the things on the internet for him that he requested, printing out the pages.

They were odd things: chat channels, advertisements, home pages etcetera; they didn't seem in the least bit related, but Holmes seemed pleased with the results of my searches.

I spent a lot of time with Wiona, too, although Holmes saw little of Georgina. I wondered how Georgina felt about that, but to my surprise she seemed not the least bit put out.

"It's the work, Doctor. It gets in your blood. I am a career woman myself, I know all about sacrificing personal life for career. Whether it is this century or the last, Sherlock will always put work first. He just wouldn't be Sherlock if he didn't."

On Tuesday of the third week, Georgina turned up at Baker Street at three o'clock. "Holmes not here yet?" she asked.

"Not yet, why?"

"He called and said to meet him here."

"Oh." I had not seen Holmes for two days.

Half an hour later, Holmes arrived. Today he was dressed in jeans and T-shirt, long hair and beard, with fearsome tattoos down his arms.

"Hey, dudes," he greeted. "Gladya could make it, Sweetheart," he leered at Georgina, and I noticed he had two teeth missing.

Georgina smiled at him and said, "You look disgusting. What do you have for me, Sherlock?"

"Give me a minute to change," he returned in his normal voice, leaving us for a moment. When he returned, he still wore the jeans and T-shirt, but the hair and beard were gone, and all his teeth were intact.

"You know, you look kind of spunky in a T-shirt," Georgina said with a grin.

"You can tell me how much later," he invited. "But for now, I would like you to listen."

From his back pocket he pulled out a notebook. "Moriarty is going to make a big strike on Friday afternoon," he said, thereby ensuring our undivided attention. "Every major criminal, petty thief, low life, drug dealer and thug has been recruited for an all-out assault on every bank in London."

"What!" gasped Georgina, stunned. "How do you know this?"

"Because I've been recruited, too. We're going to need every police officer available, possibly the military as well, to be able to cover every bank. I'm afraid I cannot give you a list.
There may be a few of the smaller branches which are ignored, however to be safe we need to have men planted everywhere.

Moriarty is desperate for cash, which means that either the weapon thieves have upped their price, or he has doubts that the Queen will pay. I am inclined to believe the former."

"Weapon thieves?" asked Georgina. "The Queen?"

Holmes grimaced, and I realized just what a strain he must have been under during the last few weeks to make slip like that. He hadn't told Georgina about these aspects of the case.

"Sorry, Georgina. I will fill you in on the other details at some later date. I cannot do so now. All you need to know is that there is a great deal at stake, more so than mere thievery."

"You've seen Moriarty, Holmes?" I asked eagerly.

"No, Watson. He doesn't mix with the lowly, except when they fail, and they never survive the meeting. I've just seen his chief henchmen. If we swoop on Friday, we will deprive him of his army, and the money of course. This will make him desperate, may even bring him out in the open. It will certainly make him act rashly."

"I can't believe that you've gathered so much information in just a few short weeks," said Georgina, admiration shining from her eyes.

"Well, actually Watson is the one who gathered most of it. These home pages that you have been keeping track off for me, Watson that is how Moriarty contacts his group leaders. Once I cracked the code they were using the rest was easy. I suppose the internet is the modern equivalent of the agony columns, and no less informative."

I was delighted that I had played such an important role, even if I wasn't aware of it at the time.

"The important thing, Georgina, is that we cannot let anyone get away. I don't care if your prisons are overflowing. They must stay in jail until the deadline for the sale has passed. After that I will concentrate on retrieving the weapon. However, first we must smash Moriarty's forces, hit him hard and ruin him. Without the weapon he is nothing, and without him the thieves who stole it have no customer."

I nodded in agreement, while Georgina strove to contain her curiosity. Instead, she questioned Holmes as to further details for Friday's raids.

"I don't know how I'll get the commissioner to approve such a wide scale plan," she said worriedly.

"Don't worry. He is under orders from a higher authority. He will give you every cooperation," reassured Holmes. "I will see Morelock tomorrow and fill him in. it is possible he will be able to organize most of it for you."

Dinner that evening was a celebratory meal and Georgina stayed the night with Holmes, but left early the next morning, as she had a great deal of work to do to organize a counter attack on the raid.

Holmes, after visiting Morelock, decided to take it easy, searching the web for possible clues as to the weapon's thieves.

"It would seem, Holmes, that you have managed to pull off a miracle after all," I said.

"Not yet. The capture of Moriarty, the return of the extorted money and recovery of the weapon would be a miracle."

"Perhaps, but you have achieved quite a bit in just two weeks. Far more than Morelock's crowd have in three years."

"That's where it pays to have energy and an independent turn of mind. Additionally there is the fact that I was in the right place at the right time. Crime hasn't really changed, Watson. There are still the same old motives. Of course drugs cause some people to go berserk and attack innocents for no reason, but on the whole it is pretty much as it was in our day. The underworld still exists, and in much the same places."

"You know, I have often wondered what it would be like in the 21st century," I said. "I imagined that people would travel to the moon, and there would be peace and harmony throughout the world. No war, no racism, no crime. I guess I was wrong. It is rather depressing to think that things will never change."

"Well, they do travel to the moon, though why on earth they should want to, is beyond me, but I am afraid it will take another millennium before there is world peace. Especially if man continues to invent weapons as deadly as the one we are after. For all we know, there may not be any humans left by that time. They may have destroyed themselves."

I nodded in agreement. "I wish I could have more faith in my fellow man, but I only have to watch the nightly news and see daily reports of children in America killing their classmates, war, violence and brutality, children being molested, natural disasters and famine rampant around the globe, to fear for our future as a species. Surely it was never so violent in our time?"

"I don't know, Watson. There are certainly less instances of children killing children, although it is not unheard of. But news did not travel so quickly; here, outrages are reported almost as soon as it happens. In our time, it may take months, or even years for such things to come to light. Brutality exists in all centuries, but in the 19th, it tends to be covered up to hide scandal. Here, everything is exposed and open—perhaps that is why it seems there is more crime and violence now. Personally, I don't think there is much difference. It is only that it is publicized now, where in our day it used to be kept secret. Whether that is good or bad, I cannot say."

"Bad, I would say," I rejoined. "Too much public exposure to violence where even children have access to this knowledge, destroys their innocence and may even beget violence."

"You could be right. Let us hope that one day they will find a solution and eradicate violence altogether."

I nodded fervently. I had always been an optimist, but my optimism had taken a severe thrashing in this century.

CHAPTER EIGHTEEN

The week progressed slowly. Holmes made several forays into the underworld for last minute orders. The police were gathering their forces together, ably led by Georgina, who was probably going to get a promotion out of this business. Morelock stopped by for a visit and congratulated Holmes on having infiltrated the gang so easily.

Friday dawned clear and sunny. I decided to go to the bank that Holmes was going to raid with his motley group of punks. Three thirty rolled around; suddenly the power in the city went off, leaving all banks without electricity or the ability to lower their security shields. The thieves stormed in with masks over their faces, guns drawn. Imagine their shock when the 'customers' turned out to be police in disguise, who quickly turned the table on them. One overzealous fellow tried to arrest Holmes, but I stopped him. This same scene was repeated all over London. By the end of the day there were only six banks that hadn't been targeted. Then again, perhaps they had been but the thieves were apprehended elsewhere and couldn't make it. All in all, it was a well laid trap with the forces of law triumphant. Georgina got the credit. It was all over the nightly news.

Holmes was home by this time and was gleefully monitoring the Moriarty home pages. Poor Moriarty was sending desperate messages, but receiving no replies. I almost felt sorry for him.

Homes grinned as he read one frantic message asking for one of his henchmen to check in and report. "I think I will send him a little message, just to put him out of his misery," he said.

I walked over and stood behind him so I could see what he typed.

"Greetings, Moriarty. How does it feel to be beaten so easily?" He pressed send, then sat back to await a response. It wasn't long in coming.

"Who are you?" came the reply.

"Sherlock Holmes," typed Holmes with relish.

"Clone?"

"No. The one and only."

"You may have got my men but you will never get me!" wrote Moriarty.

"I don't know about that, after all I got the original," Holmes bragged.

"Enjoy yourself, for tomorrow you die!" The screen went blank.

"Guess he doesn't like losing," said Holmes mirthlessly.

"He's a nasty piece of work all right," I agreed. "Still, you had better be careful, Holmes. I am quite sure that was no idle threat."

"Don't worry, Watson. I do not take it lightly. We must be on our guard from now on."

*****

Saturday morning dawned bright and sunny. Wiona delivered our breakfast, the papers and a gift box.

"Where did this come from?" asked Holmes suspiciously.

"With the papers," said Wiona, looking surprised at his behaviour.

"Is it a bomb, Holmes?" I asked.

"A bomb!" gasped Wiona.

Holmes looked at the box carefully, felt its weight, then, to my surprise he dropped the newspapers onto Wiona's tray and poured our pot of coffee over them.

"What the devil, Holmes. Have you gone mad?" I asked staring at him.

"Moriarty has threatened me. He knows my capabilities; would he send so obvious a trap as a bomb in a box? No. His attempt is likely to be more subtle than that." Holmes used his fork to open the sodden newspaper. Concealed within the centre was a flat mechanism attached to an explosive substance. The water had rendered it harmless.

"You see, he anticipated I would concentrate on the box, and then when I destroyed it and felt safe, I would unsuspectingly open the paper."

"Brilliant, Holmes!"

"Elementary. Trust nothing and no one," cautioned Holmes.

We decided to stay in for the day. The man from the tobacco shop stopped by with Holmes' weekly delivery. I brought it upstairs. Holmes noticed my frown as I put the packet on the table.

"What's the problem, Watson?"

"Did you order more tobacco? I thought your regular delivery came on Thursdays."

"It does and did."

"Well, this just came," I said indicating the package.

Holmes opened it cautiously. It contained nothing but tobacco. Holmes hunted through one of the boxes that Morelock sent him and began removing some laboratory apparatus. I sniffed the tobacco but could not detect any other odour than that of tobacco. It only took Holmes a short while to set up an impromptu lab. He began to test the tobacco for various poisons and substances but to no avail.

"Perhaps it is only noxious when inhaled," I suggested.

Holmes took a table spoon, placed some tobacco in it and began to heat it until it smoked.

My eyes began to water and my throat seemed to clog.

"Stop it, Holmes!" I gasped, staggering towards the window to open it.

He did, dropping the smoking tobacco into a jar with a lid. I forced the window open and inhaled the fresh air. Holmes looked a little green also. He joined me by the window, drawing in a lung full of air.

"Similar effect to the incident with the devil's foot," he said, when he could breathe normally. "Quite ingenious."

There were no more attempts on our lives on Saturday. On Sunday we decided to take a stroll down Baker Street. There were some children playing nearby and one cute little girl with a posy came up to me and offered me her flowers.

I took them, bowing my thanks to the child who skipped away merrily. "Isn't she cute, Holmes?" I said.

To my astonishment, Holmes knocked the flowers from my hands and sent them flying onto the roadway. A car driving by drove over them and they exploded. The car swerved and crashed into a lamp post. We hurried over and helped the stunned driver out. The whole front left corner of his car had been demolished. We reassured the poor fellow and Holmes promised to pay for his damages. We stayed with the chap until a tow truck came and hauled his car away.

"Holmes, surely that child wasn't in league with Moriarty?" I asked when they disappeared from view.

"No. but easily persuaded to give a stranger flowers for a few coins and some sweets."

"Unbelievable!"

"Trust no one, Watson," Holmes reminded me.

"Well, I trust Wiona," I replied emphatically.

"Wiona and Georgina," Holmes agreed.

Due to the danger surrounding us, Holmes rang Georgina and told her to stay away from Baker Street. He was surprised that she agreed so meekly. After he rang off, he turned to me and said, "It wouldn't be beyond Moriarty to use Georgina to get at me."

That evening when Wiona brought up our evening meal, I smiled a welcome at her and I must admit, due to our intimacy, I was a little familiar with her, patting her bottom as she laid the table.

Holmes was at the computer.

Uncharacteristically she stiffened when I touched her and she turned around and glared at me.

"What's wrong, Wiona?" I asked with concern.

Her eyes flushed, but her face remained strangely immobile.

"That's not Wiona!" cried Holmes, leaping up. "Grab her, Watson."

I attempted to do so, but she sliced her hand down at me, striking me at the base of the neck and shoulder, numbing me painfully. I collapsed back into my seat. She swung on Holmes and as she approached lashed a kick out at him that caught him on the hip and sent him staggering away.

At that moment, Georgina burst into the room. The woman, I knew it wasn't Wiona now, turned on her with a snarl. Georgina brought her hands up in a strange manner and the two women circled each other. She launched a kick at Georgina that missed and hit the doorknob, leaving a deep dent in it. Georgina retaliated with a graceful side kick, which did land.

It was incredible watching them fight as they used some strange oriental technique. Holmes called it Jujitsu. By this time, Holmes had regained his balance and stood rubbing his hip;

while the sensation was only just beginning to return to my arm and shoulder.

The end was never in doubt. Georgina made every kick count. She landed a straight kick into the impostor's abdomen, and then while the other was gasping for breath, leaped forward and handcuffed her. With her prisoner secured, she reached down and pulled a rubber mask from her head, revealing an altogether different countenance from Wiona's.

"Where's Wiona?" I asked. "By Jove, if she's hurt her…"

"In the kitchen, she's tied up. I'm afraid I never stopped to free her," replied Georgina.

Holmes looked at this particular Inspector Lestrade with respect. "I thought I asked you not to come," he said mildly.

"Aren't you glad I did?" she said with a grin. "As you can see, I am quite capable of looking after myself. I don't swoon from a little thing like danger."

Holmes smiled at her, no doubt thinking how different she was from her great grandfather.

She moved over to the telephone as I left to go downstairs to Wiona. I heard her calling Scotland Yard. It didn't take me long to free the bound and gagged Wiona in the kitchen and lead her upstairs.

Holmes meantime had bagged the food. There was a high probability that it was poisoned.

It was a scheme that probably would have succeeded, except that they never took into consideration, or more likely, never knew about my relationship with our landlady.

"Clone Moriarty is rattled," said Holmes later, after the police had come and taken the prisoner away and we were all enjoying a Chinese takeaway that Georgina had fetched.

"What makes you say that?" I asked.

"The Moriarty I know would have checked all his facts before attempting something like this. Certainly he would of if he had the time and man power. It is safe to surmise that Moriarty does not. That mask was quite clever, but not an exact replica of Mrs Hudson, that's why she kept her face averted until you startled her with your lewd behaviour," said Holmes.

Lewd behaviour indeed! Really! This from a man who never missed the opportunity to caress Georgina's legs!

Wiona noticed my irritation at his comment, patted my hand and said, "I like your lewd behaviour."

"You know, Sherlock. I'm thinking that we ought to move your base of operations for a while. You've only got a week until your deadline. You can't work properly if you're worried about being attacked every minute of the day. We have a few safe houses scattered around London. I'm sure I'll have no trouble getting permission to use one."

Holmes stood up and went towards the computer table to collect his pipe from where he last left it; as he bent, the window suddenly shattered. Holmes threw himself to the floor, just as I pushed Wiona off her seat and threw myself on top of her to protect her from the flying glass. Georgina was also down and crawling towards Holmes.

The bullets came in a rapid staccato, an unusual sound, so much so that I couldn't help remarking on it to Wiona as we lay on the floor.

"Machine gun," she replied a little breathlessly for I had landed rather heavily in my haste.

The room smelled strongly of cordite fumes, and it was a long moment after the deafening noise had ceased before we dared to stand up again. Holmes had a cut on his face from flying glass, but was otherwise unhurt. I couldn't say the same for the wall opposite the window. It was riddled with bullet holes.

"That settles it," said Georgina surveying the damage. "We're moving to a safe house tonight."

She contacted he father who was on duty at the Yard and explained the situation. She also organized for police to come and board up the broken windows and guard the house in our absence. She then directed us—Holmes, Wiona and myself to pack some bags.

Within the hour we were on our way to the safe house. Chief Superintendent Lestrade met us at the door with a bag for Georgina and the house keys.

"You should be safe here. If you want anything from Baker Street I'll send a police officer for it, who in turn will bring it to me at the Yard. Only the five of us know your location. I'm not even going to tell Morelock. It's safer that way."

He shook our hands and kissed Georgina before leaving.

CHAPTER NINETEEN

Over the next few days we lived an idyllic life. We pretended to be two married couples sharing a quaint old style house. Mr and Mrs Page (which is the name Holmes and Georgina went by), and Wiona and I were Mr and Mrs Harris. The house was fully equipped and well stocked with provisions.

For Holmes it was an opportunity to experience the domesticity of marital bliss without having to take that final step. I must admit that it agreed with him. He actually put on weight. For the first time for as long as I've known him, he had a bit of meat on his bones, as opposed to the emaciated underweight figure he usually sported. Not that he was fat by any means, but his face seemed a little fuller, less sunken and not so sharp and angular. He'd also lost his natural pallor and looked the very positive picture of health. I dare say I put on a few pounds too. One thing Wiona Hudson had in common with Martha Hudson was her cooking.

Holmes and Georgina spent most of their time on a couple of computers searching for I know not what. I did know that Holmes had taken Georgina into his full confidence regarding the stolen weapon and the threats to the Royal family. Wiona, I am afraid to say, we kept in the dark as Morelock had stressed the information was privileged and should only be divulged on a need to know basis.

Whatever Holmes was searching for, he found it at eleven pm on Thursday. I heard his shout of triumph, and then heard him enter his room to wake Georgina. I decided to get up as well and find out what was going on.

"What is it, Holmes?" I asked, knotting the tie on my dressing gown as I stopped by the door of his bedroom. Delicacy prevented me entering as Georgina was in bed.

"Get dressed, Watson, Georgina, we've got some arms dealers to catch!" Holmes was already at the wardrobe pulling out clothing. I left to dress hurriedly, waking Wiona in the process. Holmes was ready first, and when I entered the sitting room, he was on the phone to Morelock. Georgina, dressed in jeans and jumper, as the night was cool, unlocked a cupboard and distributed weapons to us, showing us how to load and empty the unfamiliar guns, the safety catch and the like. The gun was a far cry from my heavy old service revolver.

Holmes pocketed his, and in less time than it takes to tell we were in Georgina's car and headed for a village just outside London. As she drove, Holmes explained:

"There is to be an illicit arms auction tonight. Like any other business, they have to advertise so that their customers know where to find them. If you know what to look for, it is not difficult to locate them."

Not difficult? It had taken him three days of constant searching.

"Of course," he admitted. "I cannot be certain they are the ones we are after, but…"

"You mean they may not be?" I asked.

"It is always a possibility, Watson. But there cannot be too many groups about with the skills necessary to raid a military installation. The wording in the advertisement was distinctly American. It stands to reason that they have come to England for the upcoming sale next week, especially as their main customer is here. You know, the more I think about it, the more I believe that Moriarty is the only buyer for the weapon we are after. It is my contention that he actually requested this particular weapon and the group merely fulfilled his order. Like any business though, they are not about to hand it over until they have been paid. The weapon is useless to anyone else if they do not have the mathematical ability to use it."

"I suppose that is possible," agreed Georgina. "In fact it makes sense, and it's been known to happen before. Some rich dude, hints to thieves that he's after such and such an object. The thieves steal it, as they know they have a ready customer for the item. Happens all the time."

"Well I hope that these are the ones we are after then," I said.

"So do I," Holmes returned. He pulled his pipe out of his pocket and made to fill it, but put it away quickly at Georgina's reprimand.

I smiled faintly. His main complaint about sharing a domicile with Georgina was that she didn't allow him to smoke in the bedroom, dining room or kitchen, and barely tolerated it when they were working together on the computers. He had to go outside if he wanted a decent smoke. In fact, I had just about cut out smoking altogether because of these restrictions. Holmes never could, or it would be more to the point to say, he never would, just out of plain old fashioned stubbornness.

As we approached the village, we stopped at an all-night petrol station and asked for directions to a local farm. The farm-house itself was quiet and appeared to be deserted, but the barn was a hive of activity. We were about to approach, when More-lock materialized from the darkness.

"My men are in position," he said by way of greeting. "They've neutralized the perimeter guards." He was rubbing his fat hands together nervously. "I hope you are right."

We advanced to the barn and stopped just inside the door. The customers—there were ten in all, were bidding for a wicked looking missile balanced on a stand on a makeshift platform. The prices being bandied about were in the hundreds of thousands. Morelock's men closed in, and soon joined us, some taking up positions at the barns windows, ready to enter on Morelock's command. In the barn itself were five heavily armed men. The auctioneer was an American, judging by his accent. We drew our guns and entered with four of Morelock's men following behind, then fanning out to cover the room with their guns. The others burst through the windows.

It only took a few moments to take control of the room and secure the gun runners. The customers were also rounded up and taken in for questioning. To my regret Moriarty was not pre-sent, but Holmes was not disappointed, for he pointed out that he hadn't expected him to be here, as his was likely to be a private sale.

Several hours later, all the weapons dealers had been photographed and fingerprinted. This information was then sent to the CIA of America, who returned a positive identification within half an hour. The fingerprints of one man matched those found at the scene of the robbery at the military installation in Arizona. We had the right men.

The prisoners retained a tight lipped silence as to the whereabouts of the other weapons. During the interrogation, the big American who was the auctioneer and also the leader of the gang stared insolently at us, and refused to cooperate.

Holmes cold eyed him, his eyes missing nothing about the man. "It doesn't matter, Morelock," he said. "I know where the weapons are hidden."

The American sneered at him, but that sneer soon changed to shock as Holmes continued.

"There is a secret storehouse beneath the pig sty at the farmhouse."

"How do you know that, Holmes?" I asked.

Morelock, also looking the man over nodded with understanding, obviously following Holmes' reasoning (but then he did have Mycroft's abilities).

"The mud on his shoes," Holmes said. "At my blank look, he elaborated. "Why would a weapons dealer walk through a pig pen. He'd hardly bother feeding them; that is a task best left to menials. The mud on his boots testify that he has spent quite a bit of time in the pen, also, you will note where it has dried, only to be layered over with fresh mud. Why would such a man keep revisiting a pig pen? I doubt he has a love of pigs, hence the simple deduction that he has something of value hidden there. The weapons are rather large therefore there must be an underground cellar of sorts with its entrance via the pig sty. The last place anyone would think to look."

Morelock was quick to get to a telephone and bark out orders. Within the hour he received a call and turned to us, his fat face beaming with delight.

"You were right, Sherlock. We have the weapon, not to mention a few other missiles and assorted deadly arms. The customers have a lot of explaining to do. Thanks to you we have prevented quite a few nefarious enterprises from going ahead. I can't thank you enough. You have achieved everything I hoped you would." He was smiling broadly.

"Not quite," said Holmes. "Moriarty is still free."

"Never mind, his back is broken. We have his minions in custody. Even if he did have the money, the weapon is no longer available," rejoiced Morelock.

"Never the less, I prefer to remain here a little longer," said Holmes. "Just in case. I don't like the thought of Moriarty on the loose. All he needs is half a chance and he will regroup and start again."

"Stay as long as you like," grinned Morelock.

"Will it be safe to return to Baker Street now?" I asked.

Holmes nodded. "I think so. Moriarty has nothing more to gain from killing me, other than personal satisfaction. He certainly will not waste his few remaining resources on the task."

Dawn was breaking before we returned to the safe house and climbed wearily into our beds.

CHAPTER TWENTY

We did not rise until nearly midday, so had lunch instead of breakfast. After that we made preparations for our return to Baker Street. Georgina teased Holmes that he wanted to get rid of her.

"Of course," he agreed imperturbably. "If I don't, I will be as fat as Mycroft," he said, patting his flat stomach.

She poked her tongue out at him and said, "Never mind, you'll be going home soon, time enough then to revert to your unhealthy ways again."

By afternoon, we were back at 317. The windows had been repaired and the bullet pocked wall replastered and painted. Morelock's doing. Wiona was delighted by this.

Once we were settled in and puffing contentedly on our pipes, Holmes said, "Watson, it is only a matter of time now before we leave. The money we have in the bank is useless to us in our own century. Do you have any objections to my leaving it to Georgina?"

"Yes, Holmes, just one."

"Oh?"

"I'd rather you left it to Georgina and Wiona equally," I said.

Holmes smiled. "Stout fellow! My apologies. Yes, that seems equitable. I will arrange it with Morelock to have our assets distributed to the ladies on our departure."

I smiled as well. "Good. I'm glad, Holmes. I'd like to do something for them. These circumstances do not permit us to marry them, more's the pity."

Holmes did not reply, but fell into a contemplative silence instead.

On Saturday morning, we received an invitation from Morelock to attend a grand ball at Buckingham Palace, on the express orders of the Queen Mother who wanted to meet Holmes again. When Holmes pointed out that they hadn't met yet, Morelock just laughed and said,

"You will."

Considering that the Queen Mother was ninety-nine years old, I suppose this was true.

Morelock was a different man ever since the business with Moriarty had been resolved. He was more affable and likeable, in fact he was a great deal more like Mycroft now than he had been when we first met. Of course, he had been under considerable pressure to solve their problems. Now that Holmes had succeeded where he had failed, he was a new man.

I asked if it was possible to bring the ladies and Morelock heartily agreed. I think that at this point in time, he would have agreed to anything. I raced downstairs to tell Wiona and gave her money for a new dress. The ball was on Sunday night. Holmes telephoned Georgina.

They were both delighted, Wiona especially, as she had never expected to be meeting royalty through her association with me. Of course, I was rather blasé about the whole thing; after all, I was used to dealing with august personages through my affiliation with Holmes on his cases. Wiona was as excited as a school girl.

*****

As Saturday evening dawned, both Holmes and I were dressed elegantly in tuxedos, which I thought made us look rather dashing. Morelock had promised to send a limousine for us.

It was while we were waiting for the car and Wiona to present themselves that Holmes said, "Watson, do you still have the revolver Georgina gave you?"

"Yes, Holmes."

"Then I suggest you put it in your pocket."

"Surely there is no danger now," I protested.

"There is. I believe Moriarty will put in an appearance tonight."

"But why…why should he?"

"Everyone seems to have forgotten that the deadline for her Majesty expires today. She will not pay the ransom for her life, which means she has to die. If she does not, Moriarty loses credibility, and will never be able to hold his head up in criminal circles again."

"But would Moriarty show up in person?"

"Most likely. I doubt if he has anyone left who will follow him, after the failure of his grand schemes."

"We have to tell Morelock..."

"No," snapped Holmes. "This is the only way we will stop Moriarty once and for all. If he sees an increase in Morelock's men, he may pull out. I want him to think we are off our guard."

I noticed that Holmes put his own pistol in his pocket. We went downstairs and I knocked on Wiona's door. When she opened it, my breath caught in my throat. She was absolutely beautiful in a figure hugging, low cut white ball gown that flared out from the tight bodice at the hips to a wide long skirt.

She smiled at my reaction, greatly pleased. Even Holmes was moved to compliment her. She hooked her arm through mine as I escorted her out. In the street, a long car—a limousine—awaited us. Our next port of call was Georgina's flat, where Holmes went in to collect her. She was radiant in a white, sleek fitting gown that emphasized her curves. When she walked, a slit down the side of the skirt revealed one shapely leg. No doubt she wore this dress especially for Holmes.

Before long, we were at Buckingham palace, where Holmes and I were spirited away to the private chambers for a meeting with Queen Elizabeth and her mother.

The old lady was charming. She mentioned how she had the pleasure of meeting Holmes in 1920. She smiled and said, "Of course I was younger than you at that meeting, now our roles are reversed."

Holmes bowed low to her and said courtly. "I will look forward to meeting your Highness again, though I doubt you have ever looked more beautiful than now."

The old lady laughed delightedly and patted his cheek with the familiarity of a grandmother. She was just as warm and pleasant with me, praising me for my stories about Holmes and mentioning how much she enjoyed them as a girl. Next, Queen Elizabeth graciously thanked us for our help in eliminating the threat from Moriarty.

"I wish that were true, Your Majesty, but I fear there may be more developments on that front."

"Oh," she looked down her nose at him. "Nothing you cannot handle, I trust?"

"I have every confidence," responded Holmes, bowing slightly.

As we left the private chambers, I whispered to Holmes. "The mother is a charming old dear, but I'm not so sure about the Queen."

Holmes smiled faintly. I knew he shared my feelings. We rejoined the ladies and I noticed that Holmes seemed to be scanning the crowd. I did also, but as I have never seen Moriarty, I wasn't quite sure for who I was looking. I guess I was hoping to spot someone acting suspicious.

The guests had all gathered before the royal party put in an appearance. Holmes tensed, but nothing untoward happened. When the music began, Georgina enticed Holmes onto the dance floor. Imagine my surprise when he proved to be a consummate dancer. I was waltzing with Wiona when I noticed Holmes whirl past with Georgina.

"To think I have lived with Holmes for all these years and I never knew he could dance," I said to her.

She smiled winsomely. "What's unusual about that? It's not like you ever had call to dance with him."

I chuckled and made a few fancy moves of my own, much to her delight.

It was a delightful evening and it seemed that despite Holmes' fears, nothing would happen. During the interval between dances, Wiona and I went over to join Holmes. Morelock had just presented Georgina to the Queen who was chatting with her in a friendly manner.

Georgina curtsied and turned to leave the Queen's side to rejoin us, when a waiter passed us bearing a silver tray loaded with refreshments. He approached the Queen with his tray held at chest level.

Holmes suddenly leapt forward and cried out, "Stop there, Moriarty!"

The waiter whirled and dropped the tray with a clatter, causing a hushed silence to descend upon the room. He had a gun in his hand. Georgina, almost level with him was taken unawares as he grabbed her around the waist to use her as a shield. Holmes had his own gun out now.

Georgina was in an awkward position, for despite her incredible talent in self-defense, she was hardly dressed for such action. The dress constricted her legs, to make kicking impossible, and Moriarty held her in such a way that she could not use her hands effectively either. Plus the fact that the gun was held cocked at her temple.

"Drop your gun or I'll kill her," snarled Moriarty. He was tall and lean, and his head with its high forehead had a strange reptilian oscillating movement.

"Don't drop your gun, Sherlock," retorted Georgina emphatically.

Holmes looked stricken and at a loss at what to do. In the meantime, I was surreptitiously edging around to the side. If I could get a clear shot at Moriarty whilst Holmes held his attention…

"Shoot me, Sherlock," instructed Georgina calmly. "That way you'll have a clear shot at him."

Moriarty's eyes were wild, sweat beaded his massive brow and his face was incredibly pale, almost translucent, like a death's head.

Georgina mouthed a silent 'I love you' to Holmes and closed her eyes.

I couldn't believe it. Holmes shot her and as she dropped, Moriarty released her. He fired wildly at Holmes, missed and hit Morelock instead, who gasped and staggered back.

By this time I was at his side. I thrust my pistol into his ear and snarled with uncharacteristic savagery, "Drop your weapon or I will blow your head off!"

Holmes brought his own gun up and aimed it at him.

"Never! You will never take me!" Moriarty cried, pointing his weapon at Queen Elizabeth. He never had a chance to pull the trigger for both Holmes and I fired simultaneously. My bullet exploded in his head, Holmes' went through his heart; either would have killed him.

I moved over to help Georgina who was struggling to rise. To my relief I saw that she had not been shot, but it was a near thing for I could see the bullet burn on the material of her dress. She had been pretending.

Holmes moved over to where Morelock lay. At a glance I could see he was fatally wounded and there was little I could do for him.

He looked up at Holmes, his grey eyes clouding. "Tell Mycroft I did my best to carry on his work and that I tried to live up to his standards…"

With more compassion than I would ever have given him credit for, Holmes took Morelock's hand in his and said softly, gently, "I'll tell him you did," he promised.

Morelock smiled and blood trickled from his lips. His eyes closed and his hands fell limply to his side.

CHAPTER TWENTY-ONE

The shooting put an end to the festivities and it wasn't long before we were back at Baker Street.

"Did you know Moriarty would lose control like that, Holmes?" I asked.

"I suspected he would. Although the clones look and act like the real thing, I couldn't help observing with Morelock that they cannot handle stress as easily as the original. I theorized that Moriarty would have the same flaw and would slip up when challenged." He was silent for a moment. "I am sorry I wasn't quick enough to prevent Morelock's death though. He wasn't such a bad fellow."

"Well you've done everything you were brought here to do, Sherlock, so what now?" asked Georgina looking him in the eyes.

His eyes held hers and he didn't answer.

"You'll be leaving now, won't you?"

Holmes nodded. "You know I have to," he reminded her gently.

"I know." She sighed. "A girl can dream though, can't she? When?"

"Tomorrow."

"In that case, my dearest Sherlock, what are we sitting around here for? Let's make tonight count for something," she said, pulling on his hand to make him stand up.

Holmes smiled and went willingly with her.

I held Wiona to me. "You could come back with me," I suggested. "We could get married..."

"Oh, John, I'd like to, really I would, but I'd be a fish out of water in that time. I'd be lost without my household appliances, and unlike you, there would be no way for me to return if I didn't like it."

"I'm sorry," I began, but she put a hand to my lips.

"Don't be. I have had the best time of my life with you. Hell, I even met the Queen." She smiled roguishly at me. "Now, I think Georgina had the right idea, let's make this a night to remember, shall we?"

*****

The next day was Monday. We had a sad last breakfast, sad for Holmes and I, and possibly the ladies too, but they chose to conceal their feelings with bright smiles and forced cheerfulness. They insisted however, that they were coming with us to see us off. We didn't argue.

It was ten o'clock when we arrived at the nondescript building and went inside. The guard at the front desk gave us some argument about allowing the ladies to proceed further, however at Holmes' insistence he made a phone call to someone who gave their permission. We crowded into the lift and shot downwards. Wiona held my hand, feeling rather nervous.

The lift reached its destination and the doors whooshed open. We stepped out and stopped in surprise, for there, waiting to greet us was Morelock.

"Morelock!" exclaimed Holmes. "But you died!"

"Morelock died," said the Mycroft lookalike. "I'm Myron."

"Myron?" I eyed him in askance.

"I am clone number two. I have been activated from stasis to replace Morelock."

"Just how many of you are there?" asked Holmes.

"Six."

Holmes shook his head and said with a faint smile. "For a bachelor, Mycroft certainly has a lot of offspring."

Myron led us to the time travel chamber. Once inside, I turned to Wiona to say my goodbyes, not that there was much to say as we had said it all the night before. Instead, we merely embraced and kissed.

Holmes turned to Georgina. "You know, you can put your shoes under my bed any day," he said to her with a faint smile.

"Is that a proposition, Sherlock?" she asked with a grin.

"Proposal," he corrected seriously.

She sighed. "Oh, Sherlock! I do love you, but it would never work. I couldn't live in your time. The constraints and restrictions on women in the 19th century would kill me. I couldn't bear to lose my independence, or my job. I'm pretty sure there are no female Inspectors in your Scotland Yard."

Holmes nodded. "More's the pity, but I do understand. I won't forget you."

"Nor I you," she replied, making a supreme effort to hold back the tears that threatened to spill from her eyes.

Holmes noticed their brightness, but said nothing. Rather, he took her in his arms and kissed her passionately for the last time.

After a long moment, Holmes released Georgina and stepped onto the platform where I awaited him. The ladies stepped back to stand behind the protective screen with Myron. For a moment nothing happened, then lights shimmered before our eyes. A wave of disorientation beset me. When my head finally cleared I found that I was in the same alley that we had wandered into at the start of the month before our incredible adventure began.

I looked towards Holmes, who also seemed a little disoriented for a moment. He straightened himself up and looked about. "We're home, Watson," he said, and I detected a note of sadness in his voice.

Once out of the alley we were greeted with the sights and smells of the 19th century once more. The horse drawn vehicles were moving slowly along the street; people were once again dressed fashionably and decorously. Our own dress received frowns of disapproval as we were dressed in 21st century clothes, jeans, shirts and jackets.

We hurried on to 221b and as Holmes was about to open the door, the knob turned from the inside and Mycroft emerged.

"Brother Mycroft?" asked Holmes, as if he had some doubts.

"Sherlock, where have you been? Half of Scotland Yard has been out looking for you and the doctor." Mycroft looked us over, taking note of our strange garb.

Holmes smiled and slapped his brother on the back. "I'll tell you all about it."

We entered and were greeted by a jubilant Mrs Hudson, who shook Holmes' hand and hugged me. Apparently time ran parallel. We had been missing for a month and the police and Mycroft feared foul play. It did not take Holmes long to fill his brother in on our adventures. He was a very thoughtful man when he left.

Later as Holmes was puffing happily on his cherry wood pipe with his most obnoxious concoction of tobacco, I said, "It's too bad we couldn't bring them back with us. You really fancied Inspector Lestrade, didn't you, Holmes?"

"I would appreciate it, Watson, if you did not use the words fancied and Inspector Lestrade in the same sentence."

"Oh, sorry. I meant Georgina of course. Didn't mean anything else by it."

"Of course you did, you've been dying to use a line like that ever since we met her," replied Holmes, right like always.

I smiled.

"By the same token, I could accuse you of having carnal knowledge of Mrs Hudson," he suggested.

I pictured Mrs Hudson in my mind—kind, motherly, rotund Mrs Hudson and shuddered at the context of Holmes' words.

At that moment the door opened and Mrs Hudson entered, carrying a tray of tea and cakes. I glanced at her, then at Holmes as he also looked at her.

Carnal thoughts indeed!

My eyes met Holmes' amused grey ones and I couldn't help it, I burst into a hearty, uncontrolled laugh being joined by Holmes within seconds. Mrs Hudson, that poor long suffering soul looked at us laughing like a pair of lunatics and shook her head in disgust. No doubt she thought we had gone stark raving mad. She put the tray down and left us to our laughter.

"Carnal knowledge!" I panted, holding my sides as they ached from laughing.

"Mrs Hudson!" added Holmes laughing so hard tears ran from his eyes.

"And Inspector Lestrade!" I added gasping, my words triggering a new paroxysm of laughter from the both of us.

It was good to be home.

EPILOGUE: JANUARY 6TH, 2001

(Author's note)

Georgina woke up feeling a heavy pressure in her abdomen. She dragged herself out of bed and raced into the bathroom. Ten minutes later, she dressed herself hurriedly and staggered downstairs, banging on Wiona's door.

"Georgina, what is it?" asked Wiona, helping her into the sitting room.

"My water's broke!" cried Georgina in panic. "Call an ambulance."

Wiona did, and then hurried back to her, to comfort and reassure her. "It's a month early," she added, patting Georgina's hand. The two had become close friends since Holmes and Watson left and Georgina had moved into the upstairs apartment.

"I know, but he can't wait." Georgina winced as she felt a contraction.

"What are you going to call him?" asked Wiona.

"Sherlock Holmes Lestrade of course, what else could I?" she answered with a faint smile of pride.

Wiona smiled and patted her own maternal abdomen. "I'm going to call my daughter Joan Watson Hudson," she said.

Georgina tried to smile at that, but little Sherlock made his presence felt with an extra severe contraction. Georgina gasped and grimaced and started panting.

He was impatient to come out into the world and face the challenges of life.

BOOK TWO

THE MORIARTY GENE

by Magda M. Jozsa

CHAPTER ONE

February 3rd, 2022

Chief Superintendent Georgina Lestrade paced about in front of the restaurant. She was an attractive brunette, intelligent and competent and the youngest Chief Superintendent at New Scotland Yard. Her son had rang earlier in the day saying he wanted to discuss something important with her and invited her out to dinner. She had no idea what it was about and had been worrying that it might be bad news. Perhaps he'd gotten into trouble at Oxford University, or worse perhaps he wanted to quit school. After five minutes of pacing she stopped when she recognized her old friend Wiona Hudson crossing the street. That meant that whatever he wanted to talk about also concerned Wiona's daughter Joan, as the two of them were inseparable and had been pretty much since birth.

She gave Wiona a wave to attract her attention.

Wiona joined her a moment later. "Hi, Georgina. I didn't realize you would be here as well."

"Joan rang you?" asked Georgina.

Wiona nodded her head, her shoulder length blonde hair framing her face attractively. Despite being in her early fifties she had maintained her hour glass figure and knew how to dress to offset her best assets. "Yes, she said she had something important to discuss with me and invited me out to dinner. Sherlock rang you?"

"Yep. He was very mysterious. I've been worrying that he wants to drop out of school, but if Joan is involved as well then it can't be that."

"Do you think they're engaged?"

"What?" Georgina stared at her. The thought hadn't even crossed her mind. "You know, Wiona, I hadn't thought of that. Still, it would be only natural given how close they are."

"That's what I was thinking. Neither of them have bothered dating other people. It's always just been the two of them. I'm sure they love each other."

"Up until now I've assumed that to be a platonic love," said Georgina.

"True enough, but Sherlock is twenty-one and Joan will be turning twenty-one this month. They've grown up. Feelings change as you mature. Maybe they've moved onto the next level."

Georgina smiled. "Well, I wouldn't complain about that. They're perfect for each other. It wouldn't seem natural if they married someone else."

"I agree. It's well past time the Hudson's and Lestrade's joined forces."

"That would make you related to the Holmes' and the Lestrade's."

Wiona smiled at that. "And you to the Watson's and Hudson's."

Georgina chuckled at that. "What a mix, huh?"

"I think it's a pretty good mix."

"Well, we are going to find out shortly because here they come. Let's pretend we haven't figured out what it's about. I don't want to ruin their surprise."

"Agreed." Wiona turned around to see the young couple in question walking up the street towards them.

Sherlock Holmes Lestrade was tall, just over six foot, and lean. His features were slightly angular, and his hair was thick, dark brown and tended to flop over his eyes so that he was forever pushing it back. He wasn't a particularly handsome young man, but he wasn't ugly either. There was something about him, the way he carried himself, that set him apart and made him stand out. Top that off with a set of piercing grey eyes that seemed to see through you and miss nothing and he was a chap to be reckoned with. He also excelled in biology, genetics and chemistry.

She straightened a little with pride as she looked over her daughter. She'd named her Joan Watson Hudson. Joan had inherited her blonde hair and figure, but the hazel eyes of her father. She was also something of a computer whiz. Wiona didn't understand half of what she was talking about when she spoke of computers, but she did know that big software companies were already head hunting her to come work for them when she graduated; she was at the top of her class, and in fact was even more proficient than her teachers.

The young couple waved to them when they spotted their mothers. They had a lot in common. Both had grown up in a single parent household. Neither knew their fathers. They'd been told that their fathers were actors named Irving Brown and Phillip Barton and they had been killed in a car crash, and that Wiona and Georgina had met them when they rented the upstairs flat while they were here filming. As for their names, their mothers claimed they were huge Holmes and Watson fans and couldn't resist naming their babies after them, much to Sherlock's disgust. He tended to be teased quite a bit because of his name and so preferred to be called Lockie. Not surprisingly he developed his observation and deductive skills; after all with a name like Sherlock Holmes it was expected. As for Joan, whenever she signed her name, it was merely as JW Hudson. It was a little hard to explain Watson as a middle name.

Georgina rented the upstairs flat at Wiona's until she could afford to buy her own house, so the two grew up together. One upstairs, one down. Wiona usually babysat for her when she was at work. The kids called each other's mother auntie. Georgina moved out when Sherlock was twelve, but that didn't stop the pair from seeing each other. They went to the same school and were in the same grades, and now they were both at Oxford together.

"Hi, Mum," greeted Lockie kissing his mother on the cheek, while Joan greeted Wiona.

"Sorry to keep you waiting," she said. "We couldn't find a park. Shall we go in?" She hooked arms with her mother and the four entered the restaurant.

Georgina and Wiona exchanged several glances as both Joan and Sherlock seemed intent upon the menu. It was hard trying to pretend to be clueless.

Once the meal was ordered, Georgina could hold off no longer. "All right you two, what is so important that you had to drive all the way up from Oxford to discuss with us?"

"We'd like to know who our fathers are?" said Lockie.

"What?" gasped Wiona and Georgina simultaneously. This wasn't what they were expecting.

"What do you mean," continued Georgina. "You know who your fathers are."

"Then why aren't I called Sherlock Brown and Joan, Joan Barton?"

"We weren't married. You know that."

"Uh huh. They're not listed on our birth certificates either. In fact, under father's name for both of us, it says unknown."

"That's because they died before you were born so it didn't seem right to put their names on it. We didn't want their parents trying to come claim you," explained Wiona.

"You said that they were here making a movie called Sherlock Holmes in the 21st Century," continued Joan.

Wiona nodded. "That's right."

"There is no such movie. It was never made. It doesn't exist."

"They died before the movie was finished."

"In that case, wouldn't they have just got a couple of new actors?" asked Joan.

"The studio was broke and couldn't afford it," replied Georgina.

"Well, here's something else that is interesting," added Lockie. "Irving Brown and Phillip Barton not only do not have death certificates, they don't have birth certificates either. How do you explain that?"

Georgina and Wiona exchanged glances. They should have known that once their kids came of age they would go looking for answers.

"Tell me, Mother, is my father Sherlock Holmes, the Sherlock Holmes?"

"And is my father Dr. John Watson, the Dr. Watson of literary fame?" added Joan.

Both young people looked expectantly at their mothers. Again the two women exchanged glances.

Georgina sighed. "You wouldn't be asking that unless you already knew the answer. How did you figure it out?"

Lockie smiled. "One, you and Aunt Wiona claim to be huge Holmes and Watson fans, so huge in fact that you named us after them. If that's the case how come Aunt Wiona only has one Sherlock Holmes book in her house? You've got the whole set of original stories, but real fans can't get enough of them and buy all the Holmes stories they can get their hands on, including the pastiches by other authors. And two, I analyzed mine and Joan's DNA. She hacked into the government's DNA database to see if she could find and a match. Can—"

"Hacked in? Joan, that's illegal!" gasped Georgina, shocked. "You can't go breaking into government databases."

"It was easy. If the information in it was that secret you'd think they'd make it harder. Anyway, I covered my tracks. They won't be able to trace it back to me or the university," replied Joan.

"That's beside the point. You can't go confessing to crimes, I am a Chief Superintendent after all."

"You're not going to arrest me, are you Aunt Georgina?"

Georgina sighed. "No, but don't go making a habit of it. I don't want to have to arrest you."

"Anyway," continued Lockie, "Getting back to the point, can you imagine our surprise when it came back with a match. I'm not sure how the government had a copy of Holmes and Watson's DNA in their data base. I didn't think they could do that sort of stuff back in the early 20th century, and if they could it would have been fairly primitive. They would have had to do it then, maybe during WW1. My question is how did you get hold of their viable DNA? Were we test tube babies?"

Georgina once again exchanged looks with Wiona. "I suppose," she said, "That they deserve to know the truth."

Wiona nodded.

"What I am about to tell you is top secret. You cannot discuss it with anyone else. It is to stay between the four of us, is that understood?"

Lockie's grey eyes sparkled as he nodded.

"You can trust us," said Joan. "We just want to know the truth. How can Sherlock Holmes and Dr. Watson be our fathers?"

Before Georgina could reply, the waiter arrived with their meals.

"Let's eat first," suggested Wiona.

"Oh, Mum!" groaned Joan.

"Well, I don't want our food to get cold. I promise we'll tell you everything after, but perhaps it would be better to do that at home rather than in a public place."

"Good idea, Wiona," agreed Georgina. "It would be safer that way."

"You just want us to suffer," complained Lockie.

Georgina smiled faintly. "You've lasted twenty-one years. Another hour isn't going to make much difference."

*****

After dinner, they skipped dessert and drove to Wiona's house as it was closer. Both young people were champing at the bit with impatience, but their mothers refused to say anything until they were behind closed doors.

"Okay, we're home," said Joan. "Now don't keep us in suspense any longer."

They all trooped into the sitting room, with Joan and Lockie perching expectantly on the couch.

Wiona sat down, while Georgina paced.

"It's hard to know where to start," she said.

"At the beginning," suggested Lockie.

"Our beginning or theirs?"

"Whichever makes more sense."

Georgina took a deep breath in. "All right. You are not far wrong, Sherlock in surmising that the government was dabbling in genetics way back as far as WWI. Only they didn't take Holmes and Watson's DNA. They took Mycroft Holmes' DNA, and what's more they cloned him."

"Holy shit!" gasped Joan. "They cloned Mycroft?"

"He was so indispensable to the government during the war that they wanted a Mycroft in the background secretly controlling and running the government. Unfortunately a rogue scientist—a direct descendant of Professor James Moriarty—decided to make a clone of Moriarty as well. This clone was extorting the royal family and indeed was responsible for the death of Princess Diana, not to mention he cut off Prince Charles's ears."

"He's still got his ears," pointed out Lockie. "And they're as big as ever."

"Prosthetics."

"Oh."

"Anyway, Morelock, who was the first Mycroft clone decided the only way they were going to catch Moriarty was to bring an expert onto it. They used a time machine to bring Holmes and Watson from 1890 to the year 2000."

Lockie almost fell off the couch. "They've got a time machine? Wow! Are you for real?"

Georgina smiled. "I am. This is the truth, Lockie, the whole truth, incredible as it may seem. We didn't use their DNA to have you, we begot you the old fashion way."

Joan's eyes gleamed. "Dr. Watson is really my biological father?"

Wiona nodded. "I have the stretch marks to prove it."

"Holmes and Watson stayed here. They rented the upstairs flat. When reporters spotted Holmes at a crime scene word went out that the real Holmes and Watson were here. As you can imagine it was chaos. So Sherlock made up the story that he and John were actors portraying Holmes and Watson in a movie and that the crime scene that the reporter saw them at was staged as a publicity stunt. It worked. It also gave them the freedom to continue to pursue Moriarty without being followed everywhere they went," explained Georgina. "Anyway, they found Moriarty and stopped him and then they returned to the past."

"What! They came, they had their way with you, got you pregnant and then cleared off? What mongrels!" growled Joan indignantly.

"No, Joan. It wasn't like that at all," countered Georgina. "For one, they were perfect gentlemen. It was Wiona and me that came onto them. They were pretty irresistible you know."

"And John was a real cutie," sighed Wiona.

"They wanted to stay but couldn't. If they had, I would have ceased to have exist which means you wouldn't have existed either," said Georgina. "In 1892 Sherlock Holmes saves my great grandfather's life. If Holmes wasn't there to save him our family would have ended with him and your grandfather and I would never have existed. Not to mention Holmes was important during the war as well. He had to go back; too many lives depended on him. They wanted to marry us. They wanted us to come back with them, but we couldn't go. I couldn't live in a world where women were thought of as dainty brainless things.

I loved my job too much. I couldn't see Scotland Yard in 1890 wanting to hire a woman detective."

"I didn't think I could live without my creature comforts and all my electric gadgets," added Wiona. "They had to do everything by hand back then. We couldn't go back. If we went back and hated it there, there was no way of returning. And anyway, we didn't even know we were pregnant then. Didn't find that out until a month or so later."

"Oh." Joan felt somewhat mollified by their explanation. She would have hated to know her father was a cad.

"So they don't know about us?" asked Lockie.

Georgina shook her head. "No."

He exchanged a quick glance with Joan, and then turned his attention back to his mother. "So does this mean I have an uncle named Morelock Holmes who looks like Mycroft Holmes?"

"No. Morelock was killed by Moriarty. He was replaced by another clone called Myron."

"Another Mycroft?"

"Yes."

"Cool!" Lockie grinned. "Can we meet him?"

"What! No, I don't think so. He works for the secret service."

"Does he know about us?"

"I would imagine so, yes, although he has never met you. There is not a lot he doesn't know."

"I want to meet him. We're family after all. He's my uncle."

"It's not as simple as that, Lockie."

"Please, Mum? I'm sure he's curious to know how I turned out, and I'm dying to meet a clone of the one and only Mycroft Holmes. He could show us the time machine."

"I seriously doubt he'll do that. It's top secret and you don't have clearance."

"Please, Mum. You could ask him couldn't you? Tell him we know all about him and want to meet him. Joan too. He can trust us not to blab. Tell him we're thinking of applying for jobs with him when we graduate. They could use someone with Joan's skills, and maybe mine too."

"Well…" Georgina hesitated.

"Please," wheedled Lockie, trying to give her a puppy dog look.

"Don't give me that look, and stop wheedling. I will call him, but I can't promise anything. It will be up to him."

Lockie smiled, and reached out and squeezed Joan's hand.

They talked for a while longer, Wiona and Georgina sharing memories of their fathers, then Georgina said, "Well, we'd better head home, Lockie. I have to work in the morning."

"Actually, is it all right if I bunk here, Aunt Wiona? That way Joan and I can get an early start back to Oxford in the morning. Save her having to come pick me up," asked Lockie.

"Not a problem," smiled Wiona. "You can sleep on the couch."

"Is that okay with you, Mum?" asked Lockie.

Georgina nodded. "It makes sense. In that case I'll call it a night. I will ring you if I hear anything from Myron, all right."

Lockie nodded. He stood up and kissed his mother goodnight.

She stopped and stared up at him wistfully, "You look so much like your father. Of course he was older than you when I met him, but I imagine he looked exactly like you at this age."

"I wish I could meet him."

"It's a little hard. We're separated by one hundred and thirty-two years."

He grinned, "That didn't stop you."

"Well, our meeting was accidental. I don't think Myron is going to let you and Joan go joyriding to the 19th century using top secret government equipment."

"Too bad."

*****

After Wiona went to bed, Lockie waited ten minutes then made his way to Joan's room. He knocked softly and opened the door. "Are you awake?"

"Yes, come in." She turned on the bedside lamp and sat up.

He came over and jumped into her bed with her, pulling the blankets up. “It’s freezing in here.” Now he looked at her and grinned. “So, how about those revelations tonight?”

“We have to go back,” she stated. “I want to meet them.”

His grin widened. That’s how he felt too. “Thing is we don’t want to go back and be stuck there. Not much use for a computer expert in the 19th century is there?”

“Uh huh. We can only go back if there’s a way of coming back.”

“The only way we’re going to find that out is if we meet Myron and get him to show us the time machine. I’m sure you can weasel how it works out of him. You just have to turn on your charm. Then we’ll have to figure out a way of breaking into a top secret government facility and using it.”

“Piece of cake,” replied Joan, smiling at him.

“And we’ll have to rig something so they can’t zap us back immediately. We want to spend some time with our dads.”

“Too true. If it operates on a computer system, I could probably input some codes to stop them zapping us back, maybe I can even add in an automated safeguard to return us at a set time, so we don’t get stuck in the past.”

“If anyone can do that, you can.”

“Of course we’ll be in a shit load of trouble when we do get back,” Joan reminded him.

“What’s he going to do, arrest us? He’s my uncle. They can’t try us in public as word would get out about the time machine.”

“No, they can just charge us with treason and lock us in a dungeon and throw away the key.”

He shook his head. “They won’t do that. We’ll just show them that their security is a joke and that they would be better served having us help them fix the flaws in their systems rather than lock us up. I’m sure I’ll be able to convince Uncle Myron to go easy on us.”

“I hope so. Anyway, it’s worth the risk.” Now she smiled. “To think our fathers are really John Watson and Sherlock Holmes. How incredible is that? I don’t mind my name as much now.”

"I still don't like mine, but I guess I'll get over it in time. To be named after someone so famous is just begging for trouble."

"Still...can you imagine? I wonder what they're really like. It's hard to imagine Sherlock Holmes and your mother. I mean, everything you read about him says he's not particularly interested in women, but I guess that's not true, is it?"

He grinned. "I'm here, aren't I? Can't believe everything you read I suppose. At least he's not gay. I'm pleased about that. Sometimes when I've read those stories I kind of wondered."

"Wonder no more. There were never any such doubts about my dad," she added smugly.

"Well my dad's Sherlock Holmes, the one and only," countered Lockie.

"Uh huh, and the only reason anyone has heard of him is because of my dad."

"Ouch. Okay, you win. Let's say they're both pretty impressive."

"Now, Lockie, it's late and I want to get some sleep, so go back to the couch, will you?"

"But I'm nice and snug here."

"Go!"

He grinned, kissed her cheek and slipped out of her bed. "We'll plan more on the drive back to school tomorrow."

"Okay."

CHAPTER TWO

Joan was keeping Lockie company in his dorm room two days later when his mother called.

"Hi, Mum," greeted Lockie. "What's the news?"

"You're in luck. It seems Myron has been keeping tabs on the two of you. He's impressed with your academic credentials, Joan's too, and has agreed to a meeting."

"Really? That's great." Lockie gave Joan a thumbs up and she smiled. "Where and when?"

Georgina gave him the address and then added, "He'll expect you both at ten o'clock Sunday morning. Don't be late."

"We won't. Thanks awfully, Mum. I really appreciate this."

"Just don't do anything to make me regret it, and tell Joan no more hacking into government departments."

"No worries." Lockie hung up and looked across at Joan. "Myron has agreed to meet us. Sunday morning."

"Whereabouts?"

"Some place in the city."

"I wonder if it's their headquarters. We're going to have to convince Myron to show us the time machine. How are we going to use it if we don't get a look at it? I'll need to be able to understand how it works, and if it's computerized come up with an alternative program. Also, you're going to have to figure out a way of getting us in after hours so we can access it."

Lockie nodded. "I'm thinking this is their headquarters and he wants to meet us on Sunday because there will be less people there. He might be planning on showing us around. I mean it's the least he can do, isn't it, seeing as how we've been deceived our whole lives as to our heritage. If it isn't his headquarters, then we'll have to work on him until he does show it to us. Can't break in unless we know where it is."

"Exactly! And I can't write a computer program until I know what I'm working with."

He smiled. "I can hardly wait. I wonder what Myron is like. He's Mycroft's clone, so meeting him will be like meeting the genuine article."

"Cool. I've always liked Mycroft in the Holmes stories. Watson never really went into much detail about him, but he always struck me as a rather enigmatic man; a lot like Sherlock but less physically industrious. It's his great brain that does all the work. I'm a little in awe of him actually."

"Don't be, and don't forget to turn on the charm. If he is like my dad, then he should be susceptible to flattery. I recall Dr. Watson writing that Holmes was, so hopefully his brother is as well."

Joan grimaced. "I'm not sure I know how to turn on the charm."

"You're a girl aren't you? All women know how to charm men."

"That's a sexist generalization. I'm sure I don't know."

Lockie looked her over. She was dressed in her customary jeans and sweatshirt, her hair gathered back in a short pony tail. She never wore makeup and rarely a dress. He'd never given much thought to her appearance before, just accepting her as she was. She was his best friend and that was all that mattered. Sometimes he didn't even think of her as female.

"Maybe you ought to wear a dress."

"I don't have a dress."

"We can buy one. We want to impress him."

Joan rolled her eyes. "I don't want to date him."

He grinned. "I'm not asking you to date him. But still, you want to look female and helpless."

"I'm not helpless."

"I know that, but he won't. We want him to take pity on you and explain everything so your feeble female brain will understand—"

"Ooh!" Joan threw herself at him. "Feeble female brain!" She grabbed his arm, twisted it behind his back, kicked him in the back of the knee so he lost his balance and fell to the floor with her on top, pulling back on his arm.

"Ow! You're breaking my arm!"

"Apologize."

"All right, all right. You're not female!"

She pushed on his arm again.

"Ow! All right, you don't have feeble brains."

She released his arm, but continued to sit on him. This time she grabbed a handful of his hair and pulled his head up off the floor, then leant down to look him in the eye.

He winced from her grip.

"Say it like you mean it."

"Sorry. You don't have feeble brains. You're an incredible genius equal to none. I am your slave, unworthy in your presence."

She chuckled, released his hair and got off him. "That's more like it."

He sat up and rubbed at his head. "Wait until I tell your father how mean you are."

She smiled serenely. "He will no doubt understand. After all I have to deal with another Sherlock Holmes. I am sure there is many a time he would have liked to have clobbered Holmes himself."

"What I was trying to say before I was so viciously attacked is that you need to show interest, and flatter Myron and act a bit dumber so he tells you everything you need to know while trying to impress you. Hopefully while you're keeping him distracted I'll be able to case the joint."

"Now if you'd said it like that, I wouldn't have had to viciously attack you."

He rubbed at his head again. "You need to buy a dress and do something with your hair. Try and look more like a girl."

Joan stuck her tongue out at him.

"I'm serious. We'll only have one chance at this, so we need to make a good impression. I'll be on my best behaviour and you need to exercise your womanly wiles."

"Sometimes I think you live on a different planet to me. Have you ever seen me exude womanly wiles? I'm not even sure I know what they are."

"Yes you do, act like Patricia. She's always flirting with me, inviting me out."

Joan screwed up her nose. Patricia Woodhart was a biology student that fancied Lockie. "Yeah, she's always sniffing around you like a dog on heat."

"You could try being a bit like her."

"You find that kind of behaviour attractive?"

"Well, I don't. I find her annoying, but I have observed that a lot of men do. One thing I will say for her is that she's feminine."

"And I'm not?"

He nodded.

Joan wasn't sure if she should be angry or upset at his response. She tended to be something of a tomboy and a computer nerd. She also wasn't particularly interested in chasing after men. It wasn't her scene, and she rarely, if ever, dressed to impress. Finally, she said, "Should I be offended by that?"

He smiled affectionately at her. "No. I like you the way you are. After all, you're my best bud."

"The question is would you want to date me?"

"Um…" he hesitated. "Dating is a whole different thing. I mean, if uh, I was going out on a date with you, I'd prefer it if you looked like a girl. Wouldn't want folks to get the wrong idea."

"Gee thanks."

"Now you're upset."

She sighed. "No, I'm not. It's true what you say anyway. I guess I should dress more like a female. I just can't be bothered. And I'm not interested in trying to attract a man. Women only dress to impress when they want to get a man's attention."

"Is that so? So does that mean if you should suddenly turn up in a dress I should be wary?"

"Huh! What makes you think I'd be dressing to impress you?"

"Well, who else would you want to impress?"

"Ooh, talk about conceited."

He chuckled. "Seriously though, we're all right aren't we? You don't really want to date me do you? We're friends, and you'll always be that. Dating can make things complicated."

"True enough, and you're right, I don't want to date you. Now that I know how demanding you are, I couldn't be bothered dressing like a woman just so I can be seen out in public with you."

"It's all right, Joan. I don't mind being seen out in public with you just as you are."

"You're too kind."

CHAPTER THREE

"Come on, Joan. Aren't you ready yet? We don't want to be late. We still have to drive up to London." Lockie paced impatiently outside her door.

"Don't get your knickers in a knot, I'm ready." Joan pulled open her door and stepped into the corridor.

He stopped pacing and stared at her. "Wow! You know what, you scrub up all right. Maybe I should date you."

"In your dreams, Lockie. In your dreams." Despite her comment she felt pleased at his compliment, given that she'd been up since six trying to make herself presentable. Her shoulder length blonde hair shone from brushing and gently framed her face, the mascara that took her so long to apply made her hazel eyes look larger and her lips were perfectly formed. The dress she bought the previous day also suited her and flattered her figure.

She looked up at him. "I thought you were in a hurry to go?'

"I am." He grinned at her. "You know, you're not half bad."

"Well, it better be worth it, dressing up like this. It took me hours."

He grinned again. "Dressing to impress me?"

She hooked her arm through his and started to pull him along the corridor. "You really are a conceited prick. I'm dressing up to impress Myron, remember. It's got nothing to do with you."

"Too bad."

She glanced at him and frowned. "Don't you start going all mushy on me now, will you?"

"I won't. Promise."

*****

Two hours later, Lockie pulled up in front of the building. They looked it over curiously. It was old, fairly dilapidated looking and badly in need of a coat of paint.

"It doesn't look much does it?" said Joan.

"Maybe not, but it could be the perfect headquarters for a secret government agency that wants to look inconspicuous, plus this building looks old enough to have been around in the real Mycroft's time."

Joan looked up at the stone work at the top. "Built in 1852. You could be right about that."

They got out. Joan slammed her door shut, took two steps and came to a sudden halt.

Lockie made it all the way to the door before he noticed her absence. He turned around and grinned. She'd got the skirt of her dress caught in the door. He used the remote to unlock the door so she could free herself.

"Now I know why I don't wear stupid dresses," grumbled Joan as she joined him.

"I guess it takes practice. Ready?"

She nodded.

Lockie opened the door and stepped in. The lobby was not much more impressive than the outside. It was just an empty hall with a few bench seats scattered around the walls, old parquetry flooring that was in dire need of polishing and a desk at the other end with two computer monitors on it and a security guard behind it.

They walked over to him, their footsteps echoing every step of the way.

"Hello," greeted Lockie. "We're here to see Mr Myron Holmes. He's expecting us."

"ID please," he replied.

They both fished out their licenses and handed them to the man. He studied them, his eyebrows rising a notch on noting their names.

"Business?"

"Personal," said Lockie. "He's my uncle."

The guard reached into a draw and took out two name tags with visitor written on them. He slipped their licenses into each holder and handed it to them, and then nodded towards the lift at his right. "Take the lift."

"Thank you."

They pinned their name tags on and went over to the lift.

"We should have asked him what floor we have to get off," said Joan as they stepped into it.

"I don't think it matters." Lockie pointed to where a lift's control panel was usually located. In this case there was none. "The security guard must operate it."

"That's going to make it awkward," replied Joan. "If someone has to be out there to operate it, we both can't go down at the same time."

"There'd have to be a corresponding control downstairs. Might have to take turns to come down."

The lift whooshed down at tremendous speed, then just as their stomachs hit their throats, it suddenly went sideways.

It stopped as abruptly as it started and the door slid open silently.

They blinked against the bright lights that hit their eyes as they stepped out into a totally white room. In front of them stood a large man, taller than Lockie's six foot one, and three times as wide. His face was round and double chinned, but his eyes were grey and piercing.

"Uncle Myron, I presume," said Lockie, stepping forward and holding out a hand. "It's a real pleasure to meet you finally."

"Mr Lestrade." He shook his hand, then turned to Joan. "Miss Hudson."

She felt suddenly nervous. "Mr Holmes. This is a real honour, sir."

Myron smiled. "Chief Superintendent Lestrade has told me how the pair of you figured out your true heritage. I must say that was a rather impressive piece of detective work, Sherlock. As for you Miss Hudson, I would be most interested to learn how you managed to hack into the government DNA database. We have numerous security codes and firewalls in place to prevent such a thing."

"It wasn't that hard. I can give you some recommendations on how to prevent back door entries if you like. That's how I got in. Going in via a roundabout route one can bypass a lot of your security."

"That's why I invited you here today. I have followed your progress over the years. Your professors are extremely impressed with you both, you Sherlock in the strides you've made in chemical analysis and also in genome isolation, and you, Joan, if I may call you that, your acuity with a computer. There may very well be a place for you here when you graduate. Please take it into consideration. It occurred to me, that if I showed you a little of what we do here, it may pique your interest."

"There's so many questions we want to ask you," said Joan. "Did you meet our fathers?"

"Yes, I had that pleasure, briefly. It was mostly Morelock that dealt with them."

"What were they like?"

"Impressive."

Joan smiled.

"I don't mean to be offensive, Uncle Myron, but you're really a clone of Mycroft?" asked Lockie.

"Indeed I am."

"That's so amazing. All we ever hear about is them cloning sheep and the like, but a human that's as perfect and capable as the original, well…" Lockie looked admiringly at Myron, whose chest puffed out a little.

Joan smiled faintly. Lockie told her to turn on the charm, but he seemed to be doing a good job of it himself.

"The government has been experimenting with cloning since the 1920's. Not always successfully, but as our technology improved so did the quality of the clone. The first Mycroft clone was a bit of a disaster. He looked like Mycroft sure enough, but did not develop the same mental capacity. Mycroft's DNA was stored and the project put on hold for some seventy years, when they tried again in the 1990's. This time successfully."

"I'd love to read the documentation on that project," replied Lockie truly interested as this was one of his fields of expertise.

"Unfortunately that's classified. The only way you would get to read such material was if you were actually working for us."

"Recruiting, Uncle Myron?"

"The best of the best work here. As I said I've been keeping tabs on you both. You would fit in well here."

"I'll tell you what I'm interested in, Mr Holmes," said Joan.

"The time machine," he replied.

She smiled at him. "Can you blame me? I thought that was the stuff of science fiction, and to think our government actually has one. Wow! It just blows my mind."

Myron paused for a moment. "You understand that everything you see and hear here is strictly classified. It cannot be discussed with anyone else, except your mothers. They've both been here before. It is top secret and must remain that way. Good lord, can you imagine what would happen if the media got wind of the Mycroft project or the time machine? Do I have your solemn oath to not divulge anything you learn here?"

"Yes, Mr Holmes, you have my word," replied Joan solemnly.

"You can count on me, Uncle Myron," replied Lockie just as seriously.

"Very good, I'll hold you to that." Now he indicated the room they were in, and it was only now that the visitors took in their surroundings in more detail.

"There is always someone on duty here, but being a Sunday it is only minimal staff. It is a lot busier during the week and during times of crisis. Those monitors cover all the hot spots around the globe via our satellites."

They walked through the huge room. There were only half a dozen techs in white coats at the consoles who glanced their way as they passed.

Lockie nodded and smiled at them, his mind already making plans.

From the main operations room, Myron led them down a long corridor covered by half a dozen security cameras.

"You must have a lot of security in here," said Lockie. "You'd have to I guess."

"Not as much as you'd think," replied Myron unsuspectingly. "No one suspects all this is under the building upstairs. We're one hundred feet underground. We have some fake offices on the first floor, which is where we direct people if they need to come here. Our exterior is so nondescript that no one even notices us. Mycroft Holmes is the brains behind this installation. He said it was easier to be invisible in plain sight, and he was right. This underground installation actually connects to what used to be the Diogenes club in his day. In fact that was the entrance back then. It was destroyed during the war. So we relocated to this entrance, which originally was considered the back door."

Lockie smiled. "Pure genius."

Myron stopped at a door at the end. He leaned into the scanner and it scanned his eyes. The door opened.

Joan and Lockie exchanged looks at that. The thought occurred to both of them that this entry might be a little harder to crack. They entered the room and stopped, their mouths falling open as they stared at the time machine. It consisted of a platform with two circular rings on it, above and around it was the actual electronics of the machine with a multitude of cables connecting up various parts of it.

"Wow!" gasped Locky.

They both walked forward.

"It's amazing," said Joan.

They stepped onto the platform and looked back at Myron, their eyes gleaming brightly with excitement.

"Uncle Myron," said Lockie. "How do you bring the people back? This machine is here and sends them to the past or future or whatever, but how do you bring them back? Do they have a portable machine?"

"Good question, Sherlock. No, we use transponders. They're implanted in the operative's arms as a safeguard against them being lost or damaged. When we want to bring them back we lock onto the transponder."

"That makes sense. Can I see one?"

"Of course."

Myron went over to a shelf at the side of the machine.

They followed him.

He opened a small black case. It contained a dozen microchips."

"They're tiny," said Joan.

"They need to be, however they do the job." Myron replaced the case on the shelf.

"Myron, oh, sorry, I mean Mr Holmes..."

"It's all right, my dear. You can call me Myron."

Joan gave him her best smile at that. "Thank you. Myron, as impressive as the machine itself is what really fascinates me is the programing that went into making something like this possible. You couldn't show me the program could you? You don't have to start the machine or anything like that, but just the thought of the coding required is pure genius. Who came up with it all?"

"There were several experts involved including Morelock. He had a great deal to do with developing the software to operate the time machine, and of course his knowledge was passed onto me before I was activated to take his place."

"So you and Morelock being clones, makes you one and the same almost, which technically means you invented it."

Myron harrumphed and cleared his throat. "Well, I don't know that I could say that but I certainly know the ins and outs of it."

"Will you show me, explain it to me," Joan looked up at him hopefully.

"Of course, my dear. Of course. You are probably the one person outside this facility that can actually understand the intricacies of the programming."

The main consoles controlling the time machine were behind a protective screen. Joan sat down at the computer while Myron stood beside her, his back to Lockie.

Lockie, still standing by the shelf helped himself to the black case and took out two transponders, slipping them into his pocket, before wandering over to the time machine itself. As he did so he studied the room. There were no cameras in here, he noted. Getting into the room would be the hard part. Meantime, Joan was doing a good job in getting Myron to teach her about the software associated with the machine.

After a while he wandered over and joined them. His knowledge of computers was fairly average when it came to everyday stuff. When it came to manipulating gene strands via a computer that was something different. He certainly wasn't in Joan's class though when it came to reading and writing computer codes.

He waited patiently until she leaned back, indicating she'd covered everything she was interested in. "How do you actually turn the machine on?" he asked.

"That would require the activation code, which I'm not going to tell you," replied Myron with a faint smile. "I am sure you would love to go back in time and meet your fathers, but this is an extremely expensive piece of machinery and software. We can't let just anyone use it. It's for trained operatives only."

Lockie smiled. "Too bad. It would be pretty cool to go back in time. What year did you send our dad's back to?"

"1890. That was the year they came from. Back then past time ran concurrently with present time, so they were here a month, when they returned, they returned a month later. We've since fixed that flaw in the programming and can now return people pretty much to the same time as they left give or take five or ten minutes."

"Have they ever been back?" asked Joan curiously.

"No. We haven't needed their help again. The reason Sherlock Holmes was brought here in the first place was to tackle Moriarty. We felt he was an expert on that subject."

"And my dad?"

Myron shrugged. "His arrival was accidental. We only wanted Sherlock, but Watson was with him and came along for the ride."

"Oh." Joan looked disappointed.

Myron patted her shoulder with his fat flipper of a hand. "Your father proved quite useful to Holmes. I am sure he wouldn't have been able to locate Moriarty as easily if it weren't for his help. We underestimated Watson's value."

Joan smiled. "Thank you, Myron. I appreciate you saying that."

He returned her smile. "So, that's about it. Anymore questions?"

"Yes, can I have some of your DNA?" asked Lockie.

"What?"

"I'd love to study it and see if there are any differences in cloned DNA compared to the original."

"You'd have to have Mycroft's DNA for that."

"I have the pictures of them."

"Ah yes of course, I forgot you'd already accessed that information."

"So can I?"

"I don't think so. You might get tempted to write a paper on it. But, perhaps if you were working here…"

Joan grinned. "He's dangling the bait again. For my part I have to say I'm interested. If I could work with computers this advanced that would be real interesting. Far more interesting than working for software companies developing games or word processing programs and the like. I could do them in my sleep."

"What's the pay like?" asked Lockie.

"Reasonable," replied Myron. "Perhaps I will attend your graduation."

Lockie smiled. "I'd like that."

Myron glanced at his watch. "Well, that is all I have time for now. Again, you are sworn to secrecy about everything you saw here. You know where to find me now and here's my card in case you have to call me. But bear in mind I am a busy man so I don't want to be bothered with nuisance calls. Understood." He tried to look sternly at them but failed.

"We won't bother you," promised Lockie. "But I am pleased to finally have a relative on my father's side of the family."

Myron escorted them both back to the lift.

They said their goodbyes and went back up to the lobby. The same security guard was on duty. They went up to the desk and detached their passes, removing their driver's licenses from the holders. Lockie managed to stand to the side so he could glance at the computer screens on the guard's desk. It showed the main room, the corridor they went down towards the time machine room, and various other laboratories, most of which were empty.

They smiled at the guard and left. As soon as they got in the car, Joan pulled her notepad out of her handbag and started scribbling down lines of numbers and symbols. Lockie stayed silent, not wanting to interrupt her train of thought. It took her nearly fifteen minutes to write it all down.

"Finished?" asked Lockie finally.

Joan nodded. "Yep. I just wanted to get it all down while it was fresh in my mind. That's the code that controls where a person is transported to; this is the one I'm going to have to put a block on so they can't bring us back prematurely. I take it you managed to nick a couple of transponders?"

"Of course."

"Getting down in the lift won't be so hard. One of us just has to stand in the doorway holding it open while the other sets the controls. Of course we'll need to get past the guard."

"I might be able to come up with something for that."

"What about downstairs?"

"We'll have to come on a Sunday, obviously there're less people around then. Those workers downstairs only glanced at us. They saw us with Myron. They may think we're potential new employees. After all, how many people would be shown the time machine? After we take out the guard, we can just make up a couple of name tags and pretend we belong here. With the guard out, he won't notice us going along the corridor to the time machine. As Myron said, there's not a lot of security here. They don't need it because no one, other than those that work here, know of its existence. The trickiest bit will be getting into the time machine room itself."

"You've got grey eyes—Holmes eyes."

"But not Mycroft Holmes eyes. Our eyes are as individual as our fingerprints. That one I'm going to have to think about for a bit."

"It's too bad you couldn't get Myron's DNA, you might have been able to grow a pair of eyes."

Lockie chuckled. "Hey I'm good, but not that good. Besides it would take weeks. I'd like to go sooner rather than later. What about you?"

"Likewise."

"Will you be able to operate the time machine without the operating code?"

"Please. I already know what the code is."

"What! How? What is it?"

Joan grinned. "HG Wells."

"Would they be that obvious?"

Joan nodded. "Yep. I couldn't help noticing some of the other passwords that Myron put in, most of them were references to Sherlock Holmes stories. If you were referring to a time machine, wouldn't you reference the author of the book of the same name?"

"It's really that simple?"

"Yep, because they don't expect anyone to be able to break in."

"So really, it's just that door that will pose a problem."

"Maybe you should go to the electronic engineering lab and see if they can help you with that."

Lockie smiled. "Good idea. I'll do that while you work on your lockout program."

CHAPTER FOUR

The week passed fairly quickly for the two conspirators. Their mothers rang them to find out how their meeting with Myron went, little suspecting their children's plans.

On Friday afternoon, Joan and Lockie gathered in her dorm room.

"Have you completed the program blocker?" asked Lockie.

Joan smiled. "Have I ever! I'm using a question and answer blocker program, so unless they know the questions and the answers they won't get anywhere with it."

"They're not obvious like Myron's passwords?"

Joan gave him a filthy look. "Of course not! They'll never get these. I'm using obscure references in Latin. I guarantee they won't figure them out. I've set the program to lock them out for one week, at which time it will activate the transponders and bring us back. A week should be enough, shouldn't it?"

Lockie nodded. "It would be nice to stay longer, but they may not be that happy to see us, and if that's the case we don't want to over stay our welcome."

"Considering they don't even know we exist, I reckon they're going to be in for a big surprise."

"What year are we going back to?"

"I figured 1892. Their visit was in 1890. It was fairly eventful. I figured it might be too much of shock if we turned up just after they returned. This way they've had time to settle into their lives again and hopefully be more receptive to us. Plus, it's before Dr. Watson gets married and before Holmes is supposedly killed in his battle with Moriarty."

"Sounds good."

"What about you? Have you figured out how to take out the guard? We don't want to hurt him."

"The guard is easy. I've mixed up nice little concoction that will knock him out in seconds. All I have to do is spray it in his face. Should last a couple of hours."

Joan smiled. "That sounds good. What about the eye scanner?"

"Yep, I know how to disable that as well. Now all we need are lab coats to make it look like we work there and some suitable clothes to wear in their time period."

"I thought we could go to the costume shop and hire some outfits. Obviously we won't be able to take a suitcase with us. People would stare, but if we bundle it up in a package and carry it, it won't look quite so conspicuous."

"Travel bags would look a little obvious. Now I suppose we had better implant the transponders."

"I'm not looking forward to that," replied Joan.

Lockie had brought a small box with him. Now he opened it. It contained a scalpel blade, forceps, alcohol swabs, the stolen transponders, some gauze, steri-strips and some band aids. "Would you like to go first?"

"No, but I will. Where are you going to stick it?"

"Upper arm would be best. Not likely to accidentally hit an artery there."

"Given you're majoring in biology I should hope not."

He smiled. "I was thinking more for myself. I don't want you hitting my arteries when implanting it in me."

She rolled up her sleeve. "Okay, go for it."

Lockie wiped her arm with an alcohol swab, then picked up the blade and made a small one centimeter incision.

Joan winced.

He used the forceps to pick up one of the transponders and inserted it under the skin in her arm. He wiped the blood away with the gauze and then stuck on a couple of steri-strips (thin medical tape for exterior wound closure) to draw the wound shut, then stuck a band aid over the top. "There. Perfect, even if I do say so. Perhaps I should be a doctor."

"Don't get too carried away. Okay, your turn."

Joan repeated his movies and soon had the second transponder in his arm.

"What did you tell your professors about being away for a week?" asked Lockie when she'd finished.

"I said I had a family emergency. That my grandfather was seriously ill."

"Oh, that's what I said."

Joan grinned at him. "Great minds think alike."

He nodded. "Looks like we're all set then. We might as well go to the costume shop now."

*****

Both were awake early on Sunday morning, being too excited to sleep. They knew the risk they were taking, and also the laws they were breaking, but it was a once in a lifetime chance to meet their fathers so it was worth the risk.

Not knowing what time headquarters opened, they decided to time their arrival for nine o'clock. Both had their costumes wrapped up in brown paper and just wore jeans and sweatshirts. They also had white lab coats with them. Joan had also added a photo album in her package as a gift for their fathers. She'd spent Saturday doing it up.

They came up to London by train this time as there was only short term parking near the dilapidated building. They didn't want to come back and find their car had been towed.

Outside the door, they paused.

"It's now or never," said Lockie.

Joan nodded. "Let's do it."

He pushed open the door and they walked in boldly, their steps echoing up to the guard. It was the same man that had been on duty the previous weekend.

"Good morning," greeted Lockie cheerfully. "We're here to see my Uncle."

The guard looked down at his appointment book, then looked up at them. "I don't see you listed h—"

He never finished his sentence as Lockie sprayed him in the face with his sleeping draught.

They quickly put on the white lab coats that they'd had bundled up under their sweatshirts, then Joan hurried around behind the desk.

"Go to the lift, Lockie."

He did and when the door opened, stepped halfway in so the door couldn't close. Joan quickly punched up some keys on the control panel in front of the sleeping guard, then raced across and joined Lockie. He stepped fully inside. The door closed and the lift began to move.

When the lift opened they stepped out confidently as though they belonged there.

A couple of heads turned at their entrance, noted their lab coats and turned back to their consoles. Lockie noticed that two of those that glanced their way had worked the previous weekend. No doubt they assumed Myron had hired them and was giving them the tour last week.

"So far so good," muttered Joan. Her pulse was racing, but she held her head up and tried to look like she belonged there.

As they walked through the central operations room, Lockie smiled and nodded to anyone who chanced to meet his eyes. Once again there were only half a dozen or so people there. They passed the main section and into the corridor that led to the time machine.

"So how are we going to get past the eye scanner?" asked Joan.

Lockie grinned at her. "Piece of cake." He pulled a multi toolkit from his pocket. It looked like a pocket knife except it contained pliers, scissors, a chisel and two screwdrivers. He used the Phillips head screwdriver to remove the outer cover on the panel, then using the chisel he prized up the inner cover and exposed its inner workings. Now he fetched out a small plastic packet that contained some clear thick substance.

"What's that?"

"Vaseline," he replied. He stuck his finger in the packet, scooped up the goop and smeared it over the scanners inner lens.

Joan frowned. "Do you know what you're doing?"

"Yes. I asked the tech boys at school how one could interfere with a scanner to have it still be able to read but not be able to differentiate between family members if those family members had similar eye colour. This is the way. The Vaseline will distort the image. I'm related to Myron. His eyes are the same as mine. Grey is not that common a colour. The scanner will see its grey but won't be able to narrow it down, so it will go into its memory bank and look for a match. It will base its match on colour, not on iris striations." He put the covers back on the scanner and screwed them in. "Okay, here we go."

"If it doesn't work, it will probably set off an alarm of some kind."

“Oh you pessimist!” Lockie leaned forward and put his eye to the scanner.

Joan held her breath. While it only took less than two seconds, it felt longer.

The door clicked upon.

“Open sesame!” Lockie stepped forward, grinning.

They entered and Joan closed the door behind them. “You know, it’s not a very good security system if it can be bypassed so easily.”

“It’s not a known fact. Actually the techs are working to eliminate this particular flaw. So, six months from now this may not have been possible.”

“It’s all in the timing.”

“Isn’t it always? That’s how we came to be.”

Joan chuckled. “Fool.” She hurried over to the computer and sat down. She pulled a USB stick out of her pocket and connected it, quickly downloading her program. While it was downloading she brought up the screen that allowed one to operate the machine. When the password box came up, she confidently typed in HG WELLS. “Predictable,” she muttered.

Lockie stood behind her. It never ceased to amaze him how adept she was with a keyboard. “You were right.”

“Yep,” she replied, but she wasn’t really paying much attention to him, her focus was on the monitor as screen after screen of numbers came up.

“What are you looking for?” asked Lockie, noticing her input several figures.

“I’m trying to find the exact location they sent our fathers to when they sent them home. Obviously it was in a discreet spot. We don’t want to materialize on a main thoroughfare in front of hordes of witnesses, or worse get run over by a carriage or something.”

“Good thinking.”

“Here is it,” she said a couple of minutes later. She brought information up and input it into the time machine’s time and destination file. “Now all I have to do is integrate my lock out codes.”

Lockie nodded. “How long will that take?” he added, glancing at his watch. “I’d like to be away before the guard wakes and alerts everyone.”

"I'm working as fast as I can. I just want to make sure I haven't made any mistakes. I can't afford to screw this up or else we'll be stuck there for the rest of our lives."

"In that case, take all the time you need."

Joan turned her attention back to the computer. She inputted her codes, and then double checked making a few minor alterations so the data corresponded with that on time machine. She'd been working from memory before.

The minutes ticked by.

Lockie was starting to feel nervous. He wasn't sure how often this room was used. What if someone came in? He walked over to the door and peeked out into the corridor, then hurriedly shut it. "Joan, Myron's coming. Are you finished?"

"One second. Take your position on the platform." Lockie picked up Joan's clothing bundle and hurried over to the platform, stepping into one of the rings on it.

The door opened and Myron stepped into the room.

"Now, Joan!" called Lockie urgently.

Joan activated the five second delay and ran across to join him on the platform.

"What the hell—!" gasped Myron only just realizing there were intruders in the room and who those intruders were. "Stop this instant," he yelled, but too late. The platform shimmered and the young people disappeared. "Damn it!" he swore and hurried over to the controls. When he tried to activate the machine to bring them back a cartoon of a Roman centurion came on the screen. He went from a standing position to gripping his spear and pointing it at Myron.

"No entry," it said, and continued to stand in its on guard position.

"What the…" Myron sat down and tried to several ways to access the transportation program. Each time another picture came up of some creature from Greek or Roman mythology barring his way. He grabbed the telephone and called the guard on duty in the lobby. There was no response. The first thing the intelligence council would ask is how these two knew about the time machine and where it was located, and worse how they knew how to operate it. He had happily explained it all to Joan.

They'd tricked him and took advantage of him. When they came back they were going to be in serious trouble. He was going to be in almost as much trouble as well. Perhaps he could hold off reporting it. Joan was truly a genius when it came to computer codes. No doubt she had created a fairly involved lock out, but it was for sure they weren't intending to stay in the 19th century. With that thought, he got up and hurried over to the box containing the transponders. Sure enough, two were missing. Obviously the lockout was operating on a timer and would bring them back in a week or so. He doubted they would only go for one day, but they were dedicated students and were unlikely to want to miss too many classes so it stood to reason it would be no more than a week, maximum two weeks. That would be more than enough time to meet and get to know their fathers. All he had to do was wait for them to return on their own accord and then hush up the whole thing. As long as no one wanted to use the time machine in the meantime, he just had to stay patient and wait it out.

He pulled his handkerchief out and mopped his sweating brow. He should have known they were plotting this. That's why they wanted to meet him. That's why they wanted to come here. Mycroft wouldn't have fallen for their sweet innocent act. They had been rather flattering to him, and it was rather nice to actually have a real relative as in young Sherlock. They were blood kin, genetically related. For a little while there last Sunday he didn't feel like a clone, something he was constantly reminded off. For a while he felt like a real person and had let his guard down, and this is how they repaid him for his trust. He scowled. Perhaps he'd better put a memo out informing all and sundry that the time machine was undergoing routine maintenance and would be unavailable for use for the next ten days.

*****

The journey through space and time occurred in milliseconds. They were barely conscious of the experience except for the strange tingling throughout their bodies. One minute they were on the platform looking at Myron's shocked face. The next they were standing in a dingy alley. For a moment once the shimmering dissipated, they were a little disoriented and dizzy, then their heads cleared and they looked about them in curiosity.

"Are we there?" asked Joan.

"Hold on." Lockie jogged to the end of the alley and peered around. His eyes widened as he took in the horse and carriage traffic on the main road. He grinned and ran back to her. "We're there all right. Let's get changed. We can't go out on the street looking like this."

She nodded.

They unwrapped their packages and put on their costumes, shivering a little as they did so. They should have set their visit for summer instead of winter.

Joan only removed her sweatshirt and pulled the dress on over her jeans and blouse. It wasn't the most elegant of dresses or the best fitting but it was the best she could find in the costume shop.

Lockie's was a little better. His were dark grey pinstriped trousers and frock coat, a light grey vest and blue cravat. The only thing that jarred with his costume was the fact that he forgot to get suitable shoes and was wearing his sneakers, and he didn't have a hat. Joan didn't either. The hats that went with the costumes had been too bulky.

Joan frowned as she looked at him. "Didn't you try the pants on in the shop?"

"Uh, no." He looked down They were about two inches too short. He sighed. "Oh well, you're not exactly a poster girl for elegance either, so I guess we match. Folks will just think we're a couple that's down on their luck."

"That's exactly what we're going to be if our dad's want nothing to do with us. I don't know about you, but it never occurred to me to bring money, or something I could sell to get money."

He grimaced. It hadn't occurred to him as well. "I'm sure they won't turn us away."

Joan crossed her fingers. "Let's find out, shall we?"

"Okay."

They wrapped the clothes they'd taken off up then moved along the alley and stepped out onto the Baker Street made famous by Dr. Watson.

Several people glanced at them, and looked down on them. Comparing their clothes to their own it occurred to them that the salesperson at the costume shop lied to them when she said the costumes were authentic.

"Ignore the looks," said Lockie.

She nodded and together they walked along the street looking at the numbers as they went. They stopped outside number 221B.

Joan reached out and squeezed Lockie's hand. He smiled at her and reached for the brass knocker.

CHAPTER FIVE

Narrative by Dr. John H. Watson

"There is no interesting crime anymore, Watson," complained Sherlock Holmes, and not for the first time. He'd been moaning all week.

"How do you know there is nothing interesting to occupy your mind? You haven't even bothered to check your mail. It's piling up on the mantel. If you don't start sorting through it soon it will be accidental fuel for the fire. For all you know there could be something of great significance amidst your correspondence."

"Hmm," grunted Holmes. He walked over to the fireplace and grabbed up a handful of letters, then walked over to the window. He opened one, glanced at it and threw it to the floor. About to open another, he stopped. "Hello, what's this? Unless I'm mistaken, we're about to have visitors." He frowned. "They're rather poorly dressed, no hats, gloves or overcoats."

I raised my eyes to the ceiling and said a silent prayer that these visitors would have an interesting case. Holmes was a nightmare when he was bored, and worse; I had to listen to him complain about it incessantly. Add to that the fact that it was so cold and miserable that one did not feel like venturing out, it made my existence almost as miserable as his.

Mrs Hudson opened our door and stuck her head in. "There's a young couple out here to see you. They're frozen clean through, poor dears. I'll bring up a pot of tea."

"Thank you, Mrs Hudson," said Holmes. "Send them in."

"In you go, dears," came Mrs Hudson voice as she addressed our visitors out on the landing. Clearly the newcomers had brought out her motherly instincts.

I put down the book I was reading and looked up with interest. A young woman entered the room, blonde, pretty, not yet of age I surmised and wearing the most appalling frock. She was followed by a young man who seemed strangely familiar.

Tall lean, angular features and wearing trousers he'd long since grown out. As Holmes had said, neither were dressed for the outdoors. I looked at the young man's shoes and a memory came back to me.

Holmes stared at them, not speaking for a moment. He seemed frozen; in shock almost. Finally, he shook himself figuratively and said, "Why don't you come seat yourselves by the fire. You must be cold after your long journey."

The young man met his eyes. "Long journey?"

"I would consider traveling a hundred plus years a long journey. You're from the future, aren't you?"

The young lady smiled and moved forward to warm herself in front of the fire. "You don't disappoint, Mr Holmes." Now she looked across at me. "And you're the one and only Dr. John Watson."

I nodded and smiled back at her. She also looked familiar—now who did she remind me off?

"How did you know we were from the future?" asked the young man.

"Young man, no one wears shoes like that in this century; as for your clothing, even the destitute would not be seen dead in it."

The young man smiled.

"Perhaps you would care to introduce yourselves," continued Holmes.

"You wouldn't like to guess?" he asked.

"I'm good, but not that good," was his dry rejoinder.

"In that case may I present my friend, Joan Watson Hudson, and…"

"Hudson!" I gasped. "Joan Watson...!"

"And my name," continued the young man as though I hadn't interrupted, "Regrettably is Sherlock Holmes Lestrade, but I prefer to be called Lockie."

Two sets of grey eyes met, each measuring up the other, while I stared at the young woman. I was speechless for a moment. In fact, I hardly knew what to say despite the first thought that flit through my mind on hearing her name.

"Your mother is Georgina Lestrade?" asked Holmes.

Lockie nodded.

"And she named you after me because…" Holmes paused also not quite wanting to voice the thought that must have entered his head on hearing the young man's name.

"Because you are my father," replied Lockie.

I finally found my voice, "And you, Joan, you're my…daughter?"

She smiled at me with warm hazel eyes and nodded. Her eyes were shining brightly as though she was near to tears.

"I…uh…I had no idea," I said. I stood up and moved closer to her, studying her. There was a resemblance to Wiona in her looks. I could see it now, even more, there was a slight resemblance to me as well.

"Our mothers didn't know either, not until you were long gone."

"I'm sorry."

She smiled at me again and shook her head. "Don't be. You weren't to know, and there was nothing you could have done to change anything anyway."

There was a lump in my throat which I swallowed down. "I have a daughter, and a lovely one at that." I held out my arms to her and she moved into them, hugging me tightly.

"I knew you'd be nice," she said. "I just knew it."

Holmes looked his son over. "As incredible as it may seem I have to believe you as there is an obvious familial resemblance. How old are you? Are you of age?"

Lockie nodded. "I'm twenty-one, or one and twenty as you'd say in this century. Joan's twenty. It's her birthday at the end of the week. Mine was the 6th of January."

"Interesting," mused Holmes. "Mine is the 8th of January."

"Your birthday is not in February, is it, Dad?" asked Joan.

I shook my head, smiling a little at being called dad. I was a father. To think I'd been a father for twenty years and had no knowledge of it. "No, it's in June."

Suddenly Holmes frowned. "You said your name, regrettably was Sherlock Holmes Lestrade. Why regrettably?"

"Well how would you like to go through life with a name like that?" countered Lockie.

"I do."

Joan chuckled at that and at her friend's discomfort. I couldn't help smiling also.

"I mean," said Lockie hurriedly, "that it's all right for you as you're the original, but you've been to our time. You know how famous you still are. I've had to cop a lot of flak over it. All the jokes and teasing and expectations to be just like you. It gets tiresome."

"And you haven't been able to handle it?"

"Well, no, I can handle it. I just don't like it."

Holmes smiled, his grey eyes twinkling a little with humour. "Sorry, but I didn't name you. For that matter, I didn't name myself either."

"Out of curiosity, if you had the opportunity, what would you have named me?"

"I'm not sure. It's not something I've ever given much consideration. I certainly wouldn't have named you Mycroft. There are enough of him running around in your century, which brings me to an interesting point. I find it difficult to believe that Myron Holmes would allow you to use the time machine for this jaunt to the past. You would still be at university, would you not?" said Holmes.

Joan and Lockie exchanged guilty looks.

Even I could tell that Holmes' surmise was correct. "What did you do?" I asked.

Before they could answer, Mrs Hudson came in carrying a laden tray. "Here we are, a nice hot cup of tea will soon warm you up, and I've added some pastries too." She placed her tray on the table.

I smiled at her. "Thank you, Mrs Hudson. By the way, those two spare rooms you have, would you be able to make them up? This young couple will be staying with us for a few days. We'd like to rent the extra rooms from you."

"Aye." Mrs Hudson nodded, and looked at the young pair curiously.

"It turns out they are relatives of ours," explained Holmes. "From the country."

"Oh, that's it then," she said looking relieved. "I was wondering why they looked so familiar."

When she left I repeated my question. "What did you do? How on earth did you gain access to the time machine—it was in a government facility? I can't imagine they would let anyone wander in."

"Those cakes look nice," said Lockie. "I'm starving. We left Oxford pretty early this morning."

"You can eat, and you can drink, but don't try changing the subject," said Holmes.

"Those cakes do look nice," added Joan. "We really are rather hungry."

"Eat," I said, "and then you can talk. I am sure you have an interesting story to tell."

The young pair—our children (it feels strange saying that), moved across to the table and tucked into the pastries with the ravenous appetite of the young.

"How is Georgina?" asked Holmes.

"Sheeza chif soopa intender," replied Lockie, his mouth full.

"What?"

Lockie chewed hurriedly and swallowed. "She's a Chief Superintendent now."

"Ah, I'm not surprised. She was very competent."

"And Wiona; how is she?" I asked.

"Mum's great. Still renting the flat upstairs. Plus she's got a couple other rental properties as well. She's doing all right," replied Joan.

"I'm glad to hear that. It must have been difficult for her to be on her own with a child."

"She wasn't on her own. Aunt Georgina rented the flat upstairs. Mum looked after us when Georgina had to work, and Georgina looked after us when Mum had to go somewhere. They supported each other. They had things in common."

"Like knowing us," I said.

She nodded. "They've become close friends. Mum told me that you and Mr Holmes left them a lot of money when you returned home. That was more than enough to help them through their pregnancies and our early years, and in fact has even paid for our education. It was kind of you to do that for them—and us."

"The money was no use to us."

She nodded again. "Lockie and I grew up together. Pretty much do everything together."

"I've seen her in the bath," added Lockie, winning a withering glare from my daughter.

"He is often inappropriate like that. To set the record straight, I should say I've seen him in the bath also, and he's got nothing to brag about."

I chuckled. I couldn't help myself.

Joan smiled at me and added, "For clarification we were toddlers at the time."

"I assumed as much."

"If you've finished eating," hinted Holmes.

Joan poured out a cup of tea for each of them and they returned to the seats near the fireplace.

They couldn't put it off any longer. I had a feeling it must have taken considerably ingenuity to be able to access the time machine. Somehow they'd managed it.

"Shall you tell it, or shall I?" Lockie asked Joan.

"You tell it, I'll just butt in if you miss anything."

Holmes and I seated ourselves and looked at them expectantly.

"Well," began Lockie, "Our mothers always told us our fathers were a couple of actors who were playing the role of Sherlock Holmes and Dr. Watson. And that they rented the upstairs flat. They also claimed they were killed before we were born, and we accepted that when we were little. Once I turned twenty-one I was able to access the public records and found there was no record of the births or deaths of Irving Brown and Phillip Barton. That meant our mothers had lied to us. I'm studying chemistry, science, biology and genetics at University. I mapped Joan's and my DNA, and Joan, she's studying computer sciences at Uni and she's pretty smart at it too, so she hacked into the government's DNA data base. Can you imagine our surprise when we found your DNA in the system and they matched ours? We thought we might have been test tube babies..."

I'm sure I looked confused for a moment. This was a term I'd never heard. "Test tube babies?"

"Scientists can combine a viable egg with sperm in a petri dish and implant it in a woman's womb and create a baby that way—it's the treatment used for infertile couples."

"Oh. Thank you. I hadn't come across that term when we were in the future."

“Anyway, that’s when we confronted our mums and they finally told us the truth. They didn’t have much choice, they had to. We asked my mum to get in contact with Myron. We wanted to meet him, and we wanted to get a look at the time machine. Myron was happy to meet with us. He showed us the secret underground headquarters and he showed us the time machine.”

“And,” added Joan, “he was more than happy to tell us how it worked and show me the operating codes and programs.”

Lockie nodded. “To cut a long story short, we stole a couple transponders which we implanted in our arms and…”

“Sorry,” said Holmes. “Transponders?”

“They’re little microchips that allow the time machine to locate us and return us to our own time.”

“Ah, that’s new. They didn’t have that when we were there. Thank you. Continue.”

“That’s pretty much it.”

“I’m sure it’s not,” murmured Holmes.

“Well, we waited a week. I figured out how to disable the security scanner to get into the time machine and devised an aerosol form of sleeping draught to knock out the guard. Because the workers had seen us with Myron the previous week, they figured we were new employees and didn’t give us a second glance when we returned.”

“I wrote a program that has temporarily blocked their access to the time machine so that they couldn’t bring us back prematurely. It is counting down. I have it set for a week. We were hoping you would let us stay with you. We wanted to have a chance to get to know you. In a week’s time, the machine will activate and return us to our time,” added Joan.

“That’s rather clever,” I said.

“Clever,” agreed Holmes, “And also illegal. You broke into a secret government facility. Disabled the guard, entered a secure area, tampered with, I imagine, extremely expensive top secret equipment and came here without a thought for the future consequences of your actions. No doubt when you return, Myron will have you arrested.”

“No he won’t,” countered Lockie. “If he has us arrested he will have to admit that he shared top secret information with two university students who had no security clearance whatsoever. He's in as much trouble as us. I think he will simply wait until we return, tell us off and cover it up. He will want to save his skin just as much as we want to save ours."

Holmes smiled faintly. No doubt he agreed with his son's assessment of the situation. "Let's just hope nothing goes wrong and they don't need to use the machine for an emergency. In that instance your tampering would become known."

"The world's pretty peaceful at the moment," said Joan. "No great and looming crises. I'm sure they'll survive for a week without it."

"I have to admit, I'm impressed," said Holmes. "You are both very resourceful young people."

Joan flashed me a smile. "We must get it from our dads."

I beamed proudly at her. My daughter was certainly something. Intelligent and courageous, and to think she would willingly take such a risk just to meet me. It warmed my heart.

"So you are here for the week then," said Holmes.

"Yes…do you mind?" asked Lockie, a little anxiously.

Holmes shook his head. "Not at all, Junior."

Lockie frowned. "I'm not called junior."

"But you are my son, you are named after me, therefore you are Sherlock Holmes Junior."

"I prefer Lockie."

"So here is your first lesson in life; you can't always get what you want, Junior."

Lockie and Holmes locked eyes in a silent battle of wills. I knew Holmes was testing him. I was wondering which would give in first.

"You could always call him Shirley," suggested Joan.

Holmes frowned and looked across at her. "Pardon?"

"When we started school he used to get called Sherl, or Shirley, short for Sherlock. If you don't like Lockie, you can call him Shirley."

"No he can't," growled Lockie.

A wide smile split Holmes' face. He was obviously amused. "There you go, son. Sherl or Junior. Your choice."

"How about son or neither?"

Holmes chuckled.

I'm not quite sure what was going on with him, or why he wouldn't call his son Lockie. All I could assume was that he was either testing him or trying to assume the role of a paternal disciplinarian. Or then again, Holmes could be rather contrary, so perhaps he was just teasing his son to see how he would react. The easiest was to test a person's mettle was to stress them and see if they lost their temper or coped, or if they came up with an alternative solution or countered it with humour.

"I would assume, Joan, that it must be a bit awkward for you also with having Watson as a middle name. What on earth was your mother thinking?" I said.

"I guess she was thinking of you—probably cursing you if childbirth is as painful as they say."

I smiled at that.

"Anyway," she continued, "When I sign my name I just sign it JW Hudson. Now that I've met you, if anyone asks I'll be proud to say it's my father's name."

"Thank you, my dear. That means a lot to me."

"Which reminds me," Joan stood up and went over to the scruffy looking package she had put down when eating. She unwrapped it. "I compiled this photo album for you and Mr Holmes. I thought you might like to see photographs of us growing up."

"Why, thank you. How thoughtful. I wish I could have been there for your milestones, but this is the next best thing."

She brought the album over to me. Holmes got up and came across to stand behind me so he could also look at the pictures.

I opened the book. The first pictures were one of Wiona holding newborn Joan and Georgina holding Lockie. Both women looked exactly as they had the last time we saw them two years ago. That dreaded lump came back into my throat on seeing Wiona looking so happy.

Lockie came across to check out the pictures as well.

"That's me and Lockie on the proverbial sheepskin rug," said Joan. "I hope you can tell us apart."

"She's the one with the bigger bum," offered Lockie.

I smiled, both infants were cute. It was obvious to me from the banter between the two, the constant trading of insults and the like that they were very close.

The next showed the two of them as two year olds in the bath. Joan was chewing a rubber duck, while Lockie was covered in foam with only his eyes showing.

The rest of the photos showed them growing up. School photos, birthday photos. Graduation photos. There was one of Joan dressed up in costume performing on stage, and one of Lockie playing the violin.

"You play the violin, son?" asked Holmes on seeing that.

"Yes, and piano, viola and cello."

"I would like to hear you play."

"I only play under the professional name of Lockie Lestrade," he replied quickly.

Holmes smiled. "Touché."

"Do you play an instrument, Joan?" I asked.

She shook her head. "Not really, although I can make computer music. Lockie is the talented one."

"Joan has a beautiful singing voice," added Lockie.

After we finished going through the photo album, Holmes went over to his violin case and opened it.

Young Sherlock looked instantly eager. "Rumour has it that you own a Stradivarius."

Holmes nodded. "It was a gift. Will you play something...Lockie?"

Lockie grinned and came across, accepting the violin from him, awe on his face. He fondled the instrument. "It really is a Stradivarius." He tentatively plucked at a couple of strings then accepted the bow from Holmes and tried a chord. "Wow! Listen to the tone on that."

"I'll leave it to you in my will," said Holmes.

Lockie's eyes widened. "Really?"

Holmes nodded.

"That means when we go home, history will have changed and you will already own it," said Joan. "Don't you just love time travel paradoxes?"

Lockie wasn't listening to her; he was too distracted by the violin. He sat down on the arm rest of the couch, closed his eyes and began to play. The music was hauntingly beautiful.

I looked at him and it was like looking at Holmes when he played: he had that dreamy expression on his face as he lost himself to the music.

Holmes' eyes lit up with pleasure. He moved over to his customary armchair and sat back to listen with rapture.

Holmes usually played the violin well. Sometimes he played it terribly, making it sound like a chicken scratching at the strings; other times the pieces were complex and tuneful, but I have to say on listening to Lockie play, his son was an even better musician. I glanced at my daughter. She was staring at Lockie as if seeing him for the first time.

"Surely you've heard him play before," I said softly to her.

"Not like this."

"It must be the quality of the instrument." I replied.

She nodded.

Lockie gave us an impromptu concert of half a dozen tunes. We applauded enthusiastically and he blushed with pleasure. Obviously he was as susceptible to praise and approbation as Holmes.

Reluctantly Lockie held the instrument out to Holmes. "Would you play something, Dad?"

Holmes took the instrument. "I fear I won't be able to match you. I am just a rank beginner by comparison. You have real talent."

Lockie grinned. "I wonder where I get that from?"

Holmes returned his smile, then put the violin to his shoulder and broke out into a merry tune.

Lockie jumped up and grabbed Joan's arm and began whirling her around in a wild dance, until eventually the pair collapsed on the couch panting from their efforts.

It turned into a rather pleasant day. Holmes sent off a telegram inviting his brother to dinner that evening but did not tell our young guests. No doubt he was hoping to surprise them.

*****

It was almost six o'clock in the evening. Our conversation had covered considerable ground and I already felt like I was starting to get to know my daughter.

Caught up in conversation we never heard the heavy footfalls upon the stairs, so the loud knock caught us off guard.

Joan jumped and looked up in surprise, while Lockie, who had been flipping through Holmes' monographs, also glanced across at the door.

Holmes merely smiled. "Come in," he called.

The door opened and Mycroft entered.

"Myron!" gasped Joan. "How did you get through my lockout?"

"You're not here to take us back are you, Uncle Myron?" asked Lockie looking disappointed.

Mycroft stopped by the door, his keen grey eyes studying first Lockie intently then Joan, and then his eyes went briefly back to Lockie, before he shucked out of his overcoat and hung it on the coat stand by the door. "I am not your Uncle Myron; I am your Uncle Mycroft."

"Mycroft!" Joan looked delighted. "The original."

Lockie put down the monograph he was holding and strode forward. "This is a real honour, sir," he said, holding out his hand. "How did you know we were related?"

Mycroft looked at him again, raised an eyebrow and asked, "Do I really need to answer that?"

Lockie smiled. "No, of course not. Silly question. I resemble my father. Put it down to the shock of meeting the one and only original Mycroft."

Mycroft glanced across at his brother. "From the future?"

Holmes nodded.

"Hmm. Perhaps introductions are in order?"

"I'm Sherlock Holmes Lestrade," offered Lockie, "and sitting next to the Doctor is Joan Watson Hudson."

Mycroft shook Lockie's hand, then nodded to Joan, "Miss Hudson." He entered the room fully and sat down on the settee. "They often say the sins of one's past will come back and haunt them, but I don't think anyone ever thinks that the sins of their future will."

I chuckled. "I suppose that makes us unique."

"Indeed," agreed Mycroft. "I assume that's why you invited me to dinner, Sherlock."

"I didn't…" began Lockie before he realized his uncle was talking to his brother. "Oops, sorry. It might be confusing having two Sherlocks."

"And that is why I call you Junior," added Holmes, somewhat triumphantly I thought.

Lockie ignored that. "Just call me Lockie, Uncle Mycroft."

Mycroft nodded. "From what my brother has told me about the future, you two appear too young to be working for British Intelligence. Am I to assume you are here illegally?"

Joan and Lockie exchanged guilty looks.

"They rather ingeniously tricked Myron, the current clone in charge in their time. Learned about the time machine and how it functioned, broke into the top secret facility, integrated a new program into the time machine so that it would activate in a week's time and bring them home. It is nice to know that the future generations of Holmes and Watsons are so resourceful and imaginative," explained Holmes proudly.

"And criminal," added Mycroft. "Clearly, the clone is a poor copy of the original if he can be so easily tricked. I am sure your connivance would not have deceived me."

Joan smiled at him. "I am sure it wouldn't. Nothing beats the original. No one could. No matter how good the copy, it is after all still just a copy."

Mycroft returned her smile, flattered at her obvious hero worship.

Immediately I knew just how Joan had charmed Myron into giving her top secret information about the time machine. Perhaps Mycroft would also have fallen victim to her appeal. I did not say anything though. No point getting on the wrong side of him. Like his brother, and Holmes' son, he was also susceptible to flattery. It was a flaw in their characters and one Joan obviously knew how to exploit. Of course, I have on occasion exploited this fact as well, when I wanted to bring Holmes around to my way of thinking. I glanced across at my daughter. She gave me a faint smile and appeared to know what I was thinking. It would seem we had certain things in common.

"I thought you might like this opportunity to meet your nephew, Mycroft. It is not a situation that would normally arise, but as they were here," said Holmes.

Mycroft nodded. "Thank you. It is a novelty. And it is reassuring to know that two bachelors such as we will have a son and nephew to carry on our family name."

"No pressure," said Lockie grimacing. "I don't think anyone can live up to your names."

Now both Holmes and Mycroft looked chuffed at that.

"Junior," said Holmes, "Is an extraordinarily gifted musician."

"Really. Perhaps you would play something," said Mycroft.

"Well…" Lockie appeared to be suddenly shy in front of his illustrious uncle.

Holmes solved the problem for him by handing him his violin.

*****

The impromptu concert was interrupted an hour later by Mrs Hudson bringing up our dinner. It proved to be a festive affair with even Mycroft unbending enough to tell our guests about how British intelligence functioned in our day.

"I would love to visit the Diogenes club," said Lockie, looking eager.

"I'm sure that can be arranged," replied Mycroft.

"Me too," added Joan.

"Ah, that I'm afraid is not possible."

"Why?"

"No women allowed."

"But you're the club's founder. Couldn't you make an exception to the rule?"

"I could, but that wouldn't be fair to the other members."

Joan screwed up her nose. "Think how much more fun your club would be if you allowed women in."

Mycroft's eyes twinkled a little as he said, "I'm afraid that if we allowed women in the club, the peace and sanctuary we enjoy would be destroyed. The club is a haven for men to escape their women folk.

"Typical! You mean your club is a place for antisocial misogynistic misfits."

"Even misfits need somewhere to go."

"I could disguise myself as a man," she offered.

He shook his head.

"Is it true that the entrance to the secret underground facility is at the Diogenes club?"

Mycroft looked startled. "How do you know that?"

"Myron told us."

"Hmm. This Myron fellow is not exactly winning my approbation as my clone."

"Not to worry, Uncle. Your secret is safe with us."

"Don't be too hard on him," said Joan. "The Diogenes club gets destroyed during the war and he told us the entrance from there caved in and they never bothered to dig it out. There are shops and things there now."

CHAPTER SIX

The following day, Holmes and his son joined Mycroft for a visit to the Diogenes club. To take my daughter's mind of being excluded I decided to take her shopping for something more suitable to wear than the hideous garment she had on.

"I don't want anything fancy, Dad," she said as we entered a ladies store. There were several fashionable gowns on display but she stared at them in horror. "Look at those tiny waists! There's no way I could squeeze into something like that. It's unnatural."

I smiled. "That's why corsets were invented."

"I'm not wearing a corset!"

"It gives you a good figure."

"I don't care. I'm not going to be strapped up like a Christmas turkey. No wonder women kept fainting in this era. They couldn't breathe properly. Once women stopped wearing corsets they became a lot stronger and weren't prone to the vapors anymore. It's a little hard to function when you can't breathe. I am sure it was a man that invented the corset."

"Possibly. You don't have to wear one. Perhaps rather than a dress, we should look at a skirt and blouse, and a suitable outdoor covering. You can't go about in Mrs Hudson's spare coat. It doesn't suit a girl your age."

Joan nodded, mollified by my acquiescence to her wishes.

After an hour, she finally settled on a dark green woollen skirt, two blouses, a woollen long skirted jacket and an olive colored overcoat, with matching gloves and hat.

"Maybe we should buy Lockie some new clothes," she suggested as we left the store.

I shook my head. "No need. He can continue to borrow what he needs from Holmes."

"I guess."

"I notice you didn't buy any underwear. You are going to be here for a week."

"I brought a spare pair. It's for sure I'm not wearing those bloomers. God, I'd never hear the end of it from Lockie."

I frowned on hearing that. “And how would he know what under garments you are wearing? Surely he is not in the habit of seeing you undressed.”

She must have picked up on my disapproval. “I didn’t mean it like that. Of course he doesn’t see me in my underwear. I just mean that if I’d lifted my skirts or something to get in a carriage and he spotted me wearing bloomers he would tease me mercilessly.”

“Hmm. Then he’s no gentleman.”

“He is for the most part, but he can be a bit of pain some times.”

“You’re very close to him, aren’t you?”

She nodded. “He’s like a brother to me.”

“Nothing more?”

“What do you mean?”

“Well, er, you would like to get married someday would you not?”

“I guess. I haven’t really thought about it.”

“Is there a young man that you are interested in in your time?”

“Nope. I haven’t got time for such nonsense. I want to complete my PhD.”

I stopped walking and turned to her, resting my hand on her arm. “Make time, Joan. Don’t devote your whole life to your work. Make time for love and romance, you’ll be glad you did.”

“I suppose. I’m not twenty-one yet. I’m not in a rush.”

I nodded. “Don’t leave it too late either. I think I would like grandchildren.”

She chuckled. “I guess that’s the beauty of time travel. If I have grandchildren, even if you are long gone, we can still come back and visit you.”

I smiled. “I am sure the machine wasn’t designed for social visits, but I certainly wouldn’t complain.”

She leaned across and kissed my cheek. “I wish I’d known you growing up. I reckon you would have been a wonderful father.”

“Thank you, my dear. That is a lovely thing to say. I wish I had known you existed. I’m glad I do now. You are a credit to your mother, and to me.”

*****

Back at Baker Street, Joan changed into her new clothing and rejoined me in the sitting room, just as Holmes and Lockie returned.

"So, how was it?" asked Joan immediately.

"Dull. There's a whole bunch of men smoking pipes and cigars and what have you, drinking brandy and cocooned in armchairs totally oblivious to everyone around them. They don't even look up when you walk past. Not the slightest bit of curiosity. I mean, it would be a great place to study as you wouldn't have to worry about being distracted, but I wouldn't call it a sociable place."

"Oh, I don't know," said Holmes. "I find it enjoyable."

"Figures," muttered Joan. "Do you like it there, Dad?"

I shook my head. "Not really. I prefer my club where I get to socialize with the other members."

*****

It was the wee hours of Tuesday morning. I was deep in slumber dreaming of playing happy families with Joan and Wiona. So it came as something of a shock to be woken from my dreams to Lockie shaking my shoulder and both he and Joan looking at me anxiously.

I blinked against the light. "Wha...what's wrong?"

"Something has happened to our transponders," said Joan.

I confess my mind was still a little fuzzy with sleep. I had no idea what she was talking about. "Your what?"

"Our transponders. The devices that are supposed to get us home."

Now I was awake. I struggled to sit up. "What has happened?"

Joan, unflatteringly clad in one of my nightshirts, pulled the sleeve up to show me her upper arm, which had a red patch on it. "I could feel the transponder burning and my arm is aching something terrible. I went to check on Lockie. He was awake. Same thing happened to him."

Lockie rolled up his borrowed night shirt sleeve and showed me the red patch on his arm. "I think they had some kind of power surge. Can you remove them?"

"Of course." I thrust my blankets back and got up, pulling on my dressing gown. "My medical bag is in the sitting room."

We three trooped out and while I fetched my bag, Lockie lit several lamps to give me light to work by. "Do Joan first," he said.

I nodded.

Joan sat down by the dining table while I fetched out my scalpel and suture thread. Not wanting to waste time boiling water for sterilization, I used whiskey for that purpose.

"This will hurt," I said.

"Can't hurt any worse than it already is," she replied.

I felt for the small lump that was the transponder and cut into her skin. Brave girl that she is, she said nothing. I used my forceps to remove the tiny chip, cleaned the small wound and put two stitches in to close it.

"Thanks, Dad," she said as she vacated the seat so Lockie could take her place.

I repeated the procedure. When I'd finished I saw that Joan was sitting at Holmes' desk, using his magnifier to study the transponder I'd removed from her arm. Lockie and I joined her there.

"How bad?" asked Lockie worriedly.

She looked up. "Pretty bad. They're completely burned out. It was a power surge all right, but I don't know what caused it. Maybe they turned off the time machine and rebooted it in an effort to override my lockout."

"That means we can't go home."

"I know."

The two youngsters locked eyes. Joan bit her lip and looked away first. "Maybe I can fix them," she said.

"Do you think?" Lockie asked hopefully.

"Anything is possible."

I looked at the tiny chip in front of her. There were strange markings on it. "Where would we find the parts for it?" I asked, and then instantly regretted opening my mouth. Their momentary hope vanished.

"He's right. We can't get parts for them. They're just microchips. We can't even rebuild them from scratch. We just don't have the equipment, the tools or the materials."

"Maybe I could come up with a bigger version," suggested Joan.

Lockie shook his head. "You'd need a computer for that."

"You know there will always be a place for the two of you here," I said.

Joan nodded. "We know, Dad, and we appreciate you saying so, but I'm out of my element here. Lockie could probably fit in. There is always something a good chemist could do, and well, he's male so he wouldn't be subjected to the same restrictions that I'd face. I'm a computer expert. There's not exactly an abundance of computers here."

"That's true, but that doesn't mean there can't be. I am sure Mycroft would be more than happy to make use of your expertise and knowledge. Maybe computers weren't invented in this century, but who is to say that they couldn't be. I am sure the government has technology that we ordinary folk have never heard of and..."

Joan's eyes lit up suddenly. "Of course. They might have more advanced stuff. We might even be able to get suitable parts to make new transponders. Thanks, Dad."

That wasn't exactly the thought I had in mind, but I wasn't about to ruin her second burst of hope. "We'll go see him today. Later, at a more civilized hour. In the meantime you both might as well go back to bed. There is nothing we can do at four o'clock in the morning."

Joan kissed my cheek before she and Lockie returned to their rooms. I cleaned my equipment, took a closer look at the chip and returned to my bed. It took me a while to fall asleep. I didn't think that even our government would have something that she could use to make new chips. They seemed far too advanced for this time. I would be lying if I said I was upset by this turn of events. I rather liked the idea of spending the rest of my life with my daughter as a part of it. Still, it was rather selfish of me to think like that. I know how Holmes and I felt in their time. We were eager to come home. They would not be happy here. For a short while perhaps, but eventually they would miss their old lives and pine for them. I couldn't bear for my daughter to be unhappy and unsatisfied with her life. She was a modern girl, accustomed to the freedoms of her generation. She would be stymied here and unable to live up to her full potential. We had to find a way of getting her—them home.

*****

By the time I got up for a second time, Joan and Lockie were at the dining table having breakfast with Holmes. From his grave expression it was obvious they had told him of their predicament.

"How do your arms feel now?" I asked them as I sat down.

"Better," said Joan. "The redness is gone too."

"We were just discussing the situation," said Holmes. "What would cause a power surge in your transponders?"

Lockie shrugged. "We don't really know. It could be as Joan suggested that they turned off the time machine and turned it back on again in an attempt to reboot and override her lockout. They may not have realized that doing so would damage the transponders."

"Or they may have figured it would and didn't care," added Joan.

"Or it could have been a natural phenomenon," continued Lockie, ignoring Joan's comment. Sun spots have a way of interfering with modern technology. If an extra big sun spot occurred here it might have reacted with the transponders, they being the only modern technology here."

Joan shook her head. "Sun spots are too generalized. This was a localized reaction so it has to be connected to the time machine. It's the only possible explanation."

"I suggested that perhaps Mycroft might be able to help," I said.

Holmes frowned. "I don't see how. He doesn't have a time machine."

"No, but he might have suitable materials that they could use to rebuild the transponders."

"I suppose that is possible. Junior and I will go see him after breakfast."

"But I'm the computer expert," said Joan. "I should be the one to go with you."

"Perhaps you are right. Very well. I'd best send him a telegram first so he can meet us at the Diogenes club. He'd be at work at this time of day."

*****

All four of us were waiting outside the Diogenes club when Mycroft turned up. "This had better be important, Sherlock," he said. "I had to cancel a meeting with the deputy prime minister."

"Sorry. It is. Our offspring are trapped in our time period."

Mycroft's brows knitted. "I thought you said you were due to return on Sunday."

"We were," replied Joan. She held out her hand so he could see the chips on her palm. "Our transponders had some kind of power surge last night and burned out. We are hoping that your intelligence service might have comparable parts so we can repair them. Without them we can't go home."

"We need to have them repaired and functioning by Sunday," added Lockie. "Otherwise we will be stuck here forever."

Mycroft picked one chip up and looked at it. "This doesn't look like anything we've got. Has it occurred to you that perhaps you are meant to stay here?"

"What?" The question was echoed by all four of us.

Mycroft glanced around. "We can't talk here. Come inside. We'll go to the Stranger's room."

Once inside, he led us to the Stranger's room, ignoring the look of disapproval the concierge gave Joan.

"What do you mean, Mycroft?" asked Holmes as soon as the door closed.

"I mean that what if the advance in our technology is actually due to Joan and Lockie. Lockie is an expert in genetics, Joan in computers. How do we know that it isn't Lockie that takes my DNA and stores it for future use? That sort of technology is beyond us at this point. Joan may be the inventor of the first computer. It could be one of those time paradoxes."

"But if that's the case," said Lockie thoughtfully, "wouldn't we leave information for our future selves so as not to make the same mistake again, in which case we wouldn't be here now."

"If you could leave information. What if you are killed during the war and fail to do so."

"You're just full of good cheer, Uncle Mycroft," replied Lockie sourly.

"Sorry, but it is something that should not be ruled out."

"Couldn't you check with your tech people and see if they have anything that we might be able to use to make replacements?" asked Joan.

Mycroft hesitated, clearly considering something. "Very well. Sherlock, Dr. Watson, you will stay here. I'll take these two with me. The less people that know our secret workings the better."

I was rather disappointed by this. I was hoping to see his secret headquarters. After they left, Holmes and I helped ourselves to cigars and made ourselves comfortable. I was hoping to quiz Joan on what transpired while they were with Mycroft, but until then had to reign in my curiosity.

It proved to be a long wait. They did not return for nearly two hours. Joan carried a large brown paper bag, while Lockie hefted a bulky black case that, from the way he was struggling with it, must have been rather heavy.

"Did you get what you needed?" I asked standing up hurriedly as they entered.

"Not sure," said Joan. "I hope so. It's not exactly the right stuff, but I'm hoping to improvise something."

CHAPTER SEVEN

Over the next few days, Joan worked tirelessly on what she called designing micro circuits. The heavy case contained a battery powered soldering iron. She made several drawings of her circuit board, which looked rather artistic to me, but completely incomprehensible. I had no idea how all those squiggly lines could actually function.

On Thursday afternoon, Joan threw off her protective glasses and stood up. "It's no use!" she cried. "The solder is too bulky. The metal for the circuits is not refined enough, and even if I could replicate the pattern I have no way of programming it to match the time machine's signal. It's impossible." She sniffed, appearing close to tears.

I didn't know what to say to reassure her or cheer her up. There really was nothing to say. Lockie got up and went over to her. He wrapped his arms around her protectively.

"It's all right, Joanie. You did your best. You can't work miracles."

"It's my fault. I thought sure my safeguards were foolproof. We're stuck here and it's my fault."

He rubbed her back and soothed her. "Don't be silly. I wanted to come here as much as you, and if our transponders shorted out because of something Myron did, then it is neither of our faults. Try not to fret too much, remember what Mycroft told us. He said if you couldn't fix them, we could come work for him. That scientist fellow that we met was rather impressed by you. I wouldn't be surprised if you aren't the one that actually invents the time machine."

Joan sniffed. "Thanks, Lockie."

I admit I liked young Sherlock, but I warmed to him even more after witnessing his behaviour with my daughter. I could offer comfort and reassurance, but it would be ineffective compared to Lockie's. They had something in common that neither Holmes nor I could share with them: the century of their birth.

*****

The following morning while we were relaxing over breakfast and deciding what entertainment we could provide for our children in an attempt to take their mind of their troubles for the day, we heard Mrs Hudson's voice raised in complaint. It seemed someone had just entered with muddy feet.

Holmes cocked his ear, listening for the footsteps. "Ah," he said. "Junior, be prepared to meet your great great grandfather. He doesn't know anything about our trip to the future and I'd rather keep it that way. It would be too much for him to comprehend."

Lockie nodded.

On Lestrade's knock, Holmes called to him to enter.

"Mr Holmes," cried the little ferret faced inspector bustling into the room. He skidded to a halt when he saw we weren't alone. "Oh! I didn't know you had company." Now he looked curiously at our children.

"Inspector Lestrade, may I introduce you to my nephew Lockland Holmes and Watson's niece, Joan Watson. Joan, Lockie, Inspector Lestrade, one of Scotland Yard's finest."

Lestrade frowned briefly, wondering if Holmes was having him on, then nodded to our guests. "How do."

"You have a problem, Lestrade?" asked Holmes.

He nodded. "Yes, but uh, if you're busy."

"Not at all. In fact I would welcome a knotty problem. My nephew here is considering becoming a consulting detective and I would appreciate the opportunity to see if he has the right mettle."

"Oh. Uh, perhaps the young lady…"

"I'm not squeamish," said Joan.

"She'll be fine, Inspector," I said reassuringly.

"Join us at the table," said Holmes. "Would you like a cup of tea?"

Lestrade pulled over a chair, and we all moved over a little to make room for him.

Holmes poured him a cup. "Tell us all about it."

"Found a body down by the docks. It's the third one."

"Not an uncommon occurrence, surely," said Holmes.

"Not usually. But most of those bodies are from those involved in common brawls or knife fights between the seamen and lascars.'

Lockie and Joan exchanged grins when Lestrade said seamen, I'm not quite sure why. Perhaps the word had a different meaning in their time. The others didn't appear to notice.

"These murders are different," continued Lestrade. "We think they've been done by the same person. Each body was 'orribly mutilated."

"Indeed?" Holmes looked interested. "Do you have a theory, Inspector?"

Lestrade nodded and said in a hushed whisper, "Jack the Ripper is back."

That certainly piqued my interest. "The victims were female?"

"Uh, er no."

Holmes smiled faintly. "Then why do you think it is Jack the Ripper?"

"Well, these corpses are in an 'orrible state. Just like the ripper used to leave 'em."

"Repetitive killers rarely change the sex of their victims. They are usually drawn to killing a particular type. In the case of the Ripper, he preferred easy targets such as streetwalkers. The victims usually went with him unsuspectingly and he easily overpowered them and killed them, taking his time after they were dead to mutilate them. If these victims are male it is unlikely to be the Ripper as I doubt he would change to a more difficult target. I'd like to see the bodies."

"I thought that. I've got the scene of the crime sealed off. That's why I hurried here to fetch you. I know you don't like folks trampling all around a corpse."

"In that case we'd better get going. Will we all fit in your carriage?"

"I don't mind your nephew and the doctor, but I don't think it's a fittin' sight for a young lady."

Joan frowned. It was obvious she didn't like the restrictions on women in this century. "I'm coming," she said and stood up.

"We might not all fit," countered Lestrade.

"Then I'll sit in your lap." Joan glared at him.

I hid a smile behind my hand. She was a rather determined young lady, and clearly poor Lestrade wasn't quite sure what to make of her.

"She will be fine, Lestrade. She's studying to be a doctor," I lied.

"Oh." There was nothing more he could say.

It didn't take us long to rug up for the journey and we soon crammed into Lestrade's carriage. Contrary to her comment, Joan didn't sit in Lestrade's lap, but in Lockie's instead.

Down by the docks, I shivered as we alighted from the carriage. The chill wind that swept across the water seeped through our thick coats and into our bones. There were half a dozen policemen arguing with locals who objected to having a portion of their road cordoned off as they couldn't get past with their carts. I noticed Lestrade had roped off a large square and in the centre was a blanket covered shape.

At the edge of the rope, I caught Joan's hand. "Wait here, Joan."

She glanced at the covered body and nodded. Her bravado had ebbed a little at the sight of an actual corpse.

Holmes went first while Lockie and I stopped just inside the rope.

Joan and Lockie looked on in interest, having this first hand opportunity to see the master sleuth at work.

Holmes studied the ground around the body carefully before moving closer. The body was lying in a puddle of melted snow so the murder must have happened after last night's snow fall. Holmes went down on one knee and pulled the blanket back.

"Watson," he called, and I moved forward.

"Lockie."

Lockie also moved forward at his call.

The victim was a middle aged man with signs of dissipation on his face, what we could see of it. Slightly obese, but with the fine long fingers of a musician or craftsman. At least, I should say he used to have fine long fingers—nearly all were broken.

"He wasn't mutilated," said Lockie. "He was tortured."

Holmes nodded. "Quite brutally too. What's more I know this man."

On hearing that Lestrade hastened forward. "You know 'im?"

"Yes. "It's Fingers McCauly. He specializes in safe cracking, or did." Now Holmes looked up at Lestrade. "Did the other victims look like this?"

Lestrade nodded.

"Have you identified them?"

"One, not sure about the other."

"And the one you identified?"

"Professional burglar name of Lynley Barrows."

"Really?" A thoughtful expression crossed Holmes' face at that. "What do you make of the scene, Lockie?"

Lockie studied the body a little more closely, the blood and gore not seeming to bother him. "He wasn't killed here. His body was dumped. Thrown out of a carriage probably."

Holmes smiled, pleased.

"What?" Lestrade looked surprised. "What do you mean he wasn't killed 'ere?"

"There are muddy footprints here but they belong to your men and perhaps the person that discovered the body. The body is out in the open near a roadway, surrounded by shops and houses. The killer is hardly likely to torture a person out in the open, and he certainly can't do it quietly. For the amount of blood this man has lost, there is very little around him. He was killed elsewhere and his body dumped here. As my nephew said, he was likely thrown out of a carriage."

Holmes stood up. "I'd like to see the other body, the unidentified one."

"Do you want us to come with you, Holmes?" I asked.

Holmes shook his head. "No, take our young guests home. I shouldn't be too long. We'll give you a lift away from here though. It's unlikely you'll find a cab in this neighbourhood," then to Lestrade he added, "You might as well move the body and clear the thoroughfare so these good people can go about their business."

While Lestrade hurriedly set about doing that, we returned to the carriage.

"That's not Jack the Ripper's work," said Lockie.

"Of course not. Lestrade's theories are often farfetched. I have to give him credit for imagination though."

"And to think I'm related to him."

"Fortunately your mother is nothing like him. The name may have passed through the generations unchanged, but it seems each successive generation is more intelligent than the previous one."

"How did he ever make inspector?" asked Lockie.

Holmes smiled. "I may have helped him a little with that."

"Helped him a lot I bet," replied Lockie.

Our conversation ended when Lestrade joined us. Once out of the dockland area, we got out and found another cab to return us to Baker Street.

"Dad already suspects someone, doesn't he?" asked Lockie.

I nodded. "I believe so. There was a certain look on his face when he recognized the dead man. I know that look. It means he's already hatching a theory. The identity of the second victim also obviously fit into that theory. He wants to check on the third man to see if he can confirm it."

"And he'll have the killer caught by sundown."

I smiled. "Perhaps not the killer, but certainly the motive behind the torture and killings. You did well there, Lockie. I must confess I did not connect the lack of blood around the victim with him having been discarded there. I am sure your father is pleased with you."

"Hope so."

Holmes returned two hours later to be greeted with three expectant faces.

"Have you solved it, Dad?" asked Lockie.

Holmes wandered over to the fireplace, took his time selecting a pipe, and then began to stuff it with shag.

"Is he always this annoying?" asked Joan.

I nodded. "Yes."

Holmes puffed on his pipe to get it drawing before seating himself in his favourite chair.

"Oh come on," complained Lockie. "Don't keep us in suspense. Have you solved it?"

"Not quite."

"But you know who did it?"

Holmes shook his head. "No, I don't actually."

Lockie frowned. "But you're Sherlock Holmes. You must know something."

"I know that the young are always impatient."

"He's got a point, Holmes," I added, being as curious as the young ones.

"The third victim is a man called Bull Granger. A strong arm man."

"So all three were criminals," said Lockie.

"Yes."

"And…" his son prodded.

"And all three have been known to work for Professor James Moriarty."

His announcement brought about our immediate silence for a moment.

Joan frowned. "So, did Moriarty kill them?"

"Possibly, but I am not sure why he would torture them first. The other possibility is that someone else tortured them in an effort to find out more about Moriarty, or to try and locate him. He is particularly elusive. Even I do not know where he resides, and I have tried; believe me. The killing is not dissimilar to something Moriarty might do. Torturing a victim for information, dumping the body anonymously in a high crime area, these are in keeping with what I know of the man, so he could be responsible, yet…" Holmes paused, his expression thoughtful, "yet I am not sure it is he. It's just an impression. I could be wrong."

"But you never are," said Lockie admiringly.

"Watson would disagree with you."

"He has been occasionally," I said, "But not often, and even when he is mistaken, he is still fairly close to the truth."

Holmes gave me a faint smile. "If it is not Moriarty it is someone who is very much like him; for all I know it could be an enemy of his."

"In which case you won't have to worry about him," I said. "He'll do your work for you. Anyone so ruthless as to torture and murder to obtain what they want is hardly likely to deal kindly with Moriarty when he finds him."

"There's that," agreed Holmes. "However, how many men must die for this person to achieve his objective. The victims may be criminals, but even so, no man should have to die in such a horrendous way."

"You know," said Lockie, "If this was the 21st century, I'd make the assumption that the killer was a Moriarty clone. It's happened before; it's possible it could happen again. The man that made the first one might have made two of them."

"That would fit Mr Holmes' impression that it's Moriarty but not quite," agreed Joan.

"As you said, Lockie," said Holmes, "if this was your century that would be my first thought. In fact I did consider it a possibility, but only briefly. Moriarty's first clone did not have access to the time machine. One would assume that if there is a second clone, he wouldn't either. Also, there is no reason for him to come back to the past. He can wreck more havoc in the future. I've set some enquiries in motion and hopefully will hear back in the next day or so. In the meantime there is not much more we can do on this so I recommend we take our young guests out to an afternoon concert and then dinner at one of our favourite restaurants. It won't hurt to take our minds of less pleasant thoughts."

"Sounds lovely," said Joan smiling.

CHAPTER EIGHT

The rest of the week seemed to pass rather quickly. Holmes' irregulars had come up with nothing regarding the murders of the three men. The only rumour that they could pick up on was that someone was targeting Moriarty's men and that they were all being doubly vigilant. That was it. Nothing more. Before we knew it, it was Sunday. This was the day Joan and Lockie were supposed to leave us. It was also my daughter's 21st birthday so we decided to have a party for her, if only to distract her from her worries.

Mrs Hudson provided a generous feast for lunch and a rather delectable cake. I noticed that young Lockie didn't share his father's lack of appetite. I am sure he ate at least half of that cake on his own!

"Joan," I said holding out a small package. "This is for you."

Her eyes lit up as she accepted the package. She unwrapped it to find a velvet box. She opened it and I waited, hoping she would like the gift.

"Oh, Dad, it's beautiful!" She lifted the gold finely engraved locket out and held it up by its chain. Then she opened it, and she smiled with delight.

I had placed a picture of myself inside and also one I cut out of her mother from the album she gave me. "I thought it would be nice for you to have the two us together."

"I love it. Thank you so much, Dad. At least now I'll have a picture of mum to remember her by." She came over to me and threw her arms around me in a warm hug.

I responded in kind and kissed her cheek. "I'm sorry, dear. Don't give up hope; you may see her again one day. With all this time travel and what not anything is possible."

"I know. Thanks, Dad."

Holmes cleared his throat to get her attention, and then held out his gift.

She smiled. "Thank you." She unwrapped it. "Oh, how lovely. An antique silver pen set."

"It is not actually antique," said Holmes.

"It will be one of these days." She moved over to him and hugged him as well. "I'll treasure it."

"Your present is under my bed at home," said Lockie hurriedly when she looked at him. "I hadn't forgotten your birthday it's just uh I didn't have any money to buy you something here."

"Well, you still have plenty of time to get me a present after you get a job. We're going to be here for a while."

He nodded. "Happy birthday anyway." He gave her a hug and a kiss on the cheek.

"This is certainly a memorable birthday," she said smiling at us, although it seemed to me that the smile didn't quite reach her eyes. I knew she was thinking of her mother and that she might never see her again. I felt for her.

I was just thinking of suggesting that we all go out and take in a variety show in honour of Joan's birthday when we heard heavy footfalls on the stairs.

"Mycroft," muttered Holmes and Lockie simultaneously. They exchanged brief, companionable smiles.

Holmes got up and opened the door before our caller could knock. It was indeed Mycroft.

"Come in, Brother," greeted Holmes. As he was about to close the door, he stopped and stared. "You're not Mycroft."

"No, I'm Myron."

"Uncle Myron," cried Lockie with delight.

Joan also leaped up from her armchair and threw her arms around him in a heartfelt hug. "You've come for us!"

He endured the hug for a brief moment, and then disengaged her. "No, actually I haven't."

"What?" Lockie looked surprised. "You aren't here for us?"

Myron glared at him, "You and Miss Hudson are in grave trouble. Not only was your stunt a misuse of government property and completely illegal, your actions have had far reaching ramifications and severe consequences. As far as I'm concerned you can both stay in the 19th century!"

Frowning, Holmes moved forward, standing protectively in front of his son. "If that's the case, what are you doing here?" he demanded.

"There has been a serious breach of security and thanks to the lockouts that Miss Hudson put on the time machine we were unable to act upon it immediately."

"Well, you mustn't have very smart people in British Intelligence if you can be stymied by a twenty-one year old girl," I said hotly, defending my daughter.

Myron looked shamefaced for a moment. "It's not our fault she's some kind of computer genius."

Angry as I was at him constantly blaming my daughter, I was still rather pleased to hear that she was smarter than all the experts in Intelligence. I couldn't have been prouder of her than at this very moment. That's one in the eye for those who assume we Watson's aren't as smart as the Holmes' of this world.

"Rather than wasting time assigning blame," said Holmes, "let's find out why you are really here. Obviously you need my help again. Take a load off, Myron and start from the beginning." Holmes seated himself in his favourite armchair and leaned back, while Myron heaved his bulk down onto the settee. I sat down in my favourite chair, and Joan perched on its armrest, her arm draping loosely around my shoulders.

Lockie pulled the chair away from Holmes' desk, flipped it around and sat on it, resting his arms on its back and looking as attentive as Holmes—by that I mean they both looked like they were half asleep.

"Very well," began Myron. "Eight days ago British special forces infiltrated a secret IRA base in the outskirts of London. Once the dissidents were rounded up, a further search of the premises was made and an underground laboratory was discovered." He paused, took a long breath and continued. "Inside there were three men and they all looked like—"

"Moriarty!" Once again Lockie and Holmes spoke as one.

Myron nodded grimly. "Yes, exactly. The laboratory had been set up by Paul Bishop and Moriarty's clone, obviously before Moriarty killed Bishop. Moriarty then proceeded to clone himself—"

"But you can't clone a clone," interrupted Lockie. "If you make a copy from a copy it just degrades over time. There would be too many flaws."

Myron nodded again. "That's what happened in this case. There were three activated Moriarty's and two in stasis chambers. Of the clones in the chambers, one was hideously deformed, while the other, on autopsy, was found to have a brain the size of a walnut. Of the three living clones, one had the mental capacity of a cat; the second was an anxiolytic, obsessive compulsive schizophrenic terrified of his own shadow, and the third was a halfwit."

"Then surely they would pose no threat," I said.

"They don't, no, and have since been terminated. However, after going through the information on the lab's computers and reading Moriarty's workbooks and journals, we discovered that there was a fourth clone. This was the first clone Moriarty made from his genetic material. Apparently each clone cloned himself because that's what they were programmed to do which explains why each successive clone was feebler than the previous one.

"During questioning of the halfwit clone, we learned that Moriarty Clone Two had been put in charge while Moriarty Clone One—"

"Myron, that's a real mouthful," said Lockie. "Why not just call them MC1 and MC2?"

"Yes, all right. While MC1 was trying to hold the world to ransom, MC2 attempted to manufacture an army of Moriarty's with dismal results. However, he must have realized fairly quickly that their genetic material was insufficient for the task, so he turned his attention to something else. That mathematical ability of Moriarty has served him in good stead. When MC1 failed, thanks to your involvement, Sherlock, MC2 invented a machine that could tap into our time machine and access its functions remotely. Six days ago he activated that link and used it to transport himself back to this time period."

"Why?" I asked.

"Because he wants to get new DNA from the original source," replied Holmes. "He wants to meet up with the original James Moriarty."

"Exactly!" declared Myron. "Can you imagine how disastrous such a scenario would be? One Moriarty clone caused enough havoc in our time to have both the Royal Family and the Government on high alert. God help us what an army of fully functioning Moriarty's could do."

"I don't think you have to worry about that," said Holmes dryly. "Moriarty will never make more of himself. That is, he might make a backup copy or two, but he wouldn't activate them while he was alive. It is in his nature to aspire to fortune and power. Any clone he makes will have the same aspirations, which means that an army of Moriartys would be vying with each other to overthrow the one in charge, and then the next one in charge and so forth until there was only one left. They wouldn't be able to help themselves, it's in their genes. No, if Moriarty wanted to make an army, he would clone his top henchman—Colonel Sebastian Moran. He'd be invincible if he had an army of Morans to call on."

"Even if that is the case, we still have a problem on our hands," countered Myron.

Holmes nodded. "Indeed you do. If Moriarty gets his hands on a time travelling device, there will be no stopping him."

"Six days ago?" said Joan, exchanging glances with Lockie.

Myron was quick to pick up on the look. "Do you know something?"

She shook her head. "No, but six days ago the transponders we implanted in our arms fizzled and burned. That's why we couldn't return when the program expired."

"How deep did you implant them?"

"Just under the skin."

"I'm not surprised then. They need to be deeper if you don't want any electromagnetic interference during transports. MC2's transport must have interacted with your transponders."

"Oh."

"At least that explains why you never returned." He cleared his throat noisily and then added. "I had security waiting to arrest you when you materialized."

"Sorry to disappoint you," grinned Lockie.

"Don't get too cocky. I still can you know."

Holmes clapped his hands to get their attention. "Perhaps we can get back to the matter at hand. There is some urgency especially if MC2 arrived here six days ago."

"Yes, indeed," agreed Myron. "He may already have made contact with Moriarty. Thanks to Miss Hudson's lockout, we couldn't come after him until the lockout timed down, which it did half an hour ago, and which is why I am here. I need your help to find him. We cannot, we must not let the real Moriarty get a foothold in the future. Imagine what he could do with our modern technology? His clone was bad enough, but the real Moriarty would be ten times worse. You have to find him, Sherlock, and you have to retrieve the piggyback transporter device. We can't allow it to fall into anyone else's hands."

"You know," said I, as a thought occurred to me. "It's possible that MC2 hasn't found Moriarty yet. After all, he is from the future. This time period is as alien to him as yours was to us. He will be unfamiliar with how things work here and how we find people or make contact. In your time, Myron, a person merely has to do a search on the internet and can find out almost anything they want to know about anyone. It's not so easy here, not if you are not in the know. Many is the time I heard you complain, Holmes, how elusive Moriarty is. If you cannot find him, it will be even harder for someone out of his time to do so."

Holmes smiled. "Excellent point, Watson."

Joan leaned down and kissed me on the top of the head and gave my shoulder a squeeze. "Way to go, Dad."

My moustache bristled in pleasure at their approbation.

Myron looked relieved. "Do you think so?"

Holmes nodded. "I agree with Watson, he hasn't found Moriarty yet, but he's looking."

"The dead men!" exclaimed Lockie suddenly.

A wide smile lit Holmes' face at that. Clearly he was pleased with his son's response. "Exactly," he replied.

"What dead men?" asked Myron looking somewhat confused. I admit I was momentarily puzzled as well.

"Three of Moriarty's men have turned up dead—tortured and killed," explained Lockie.

Myron's eyes widened. "Is this true?"

Holmes nodded. "Yes, Lestrade called me in to advise him on the case. As yet I haven't had much luck. At the time I thought the killings were similar to something Moriarty might do but saw no reason for him to be doing so at this time. My son actuated the premise that if he was home he would suspect a Moriarty clone. That thought also crossed my mind, but to our knowledge Moriarty's clone had no access to the time machine, so I considered it improbable. With this new information it not only becomes probable but highly likely he is behind it. It is obvious he is torturing Moriarty's men in an attempt to ascertain Moriarty's whereabouts."

"But would his men know how to find Moriarty?" asked Myron.

Holmes shook his head. "I don't think so. From what little I've been able to gather on Moriarty's practices, he doesn't associate directly with his minions. He has a brother I believe but does not stay in touch. The only real link to him is Colonel Sebastian Moran. Moran is the go-between when he needs to contact his hirelings or when they need to contact him. He is easier to find in that he frequents clubs and bars and gambling dens, but taking him out would be another issue altogether. Moran is not exactly helpless. He's a big game hunter, a sure shot with a rifle or pistol, strong as three men when it comes to brawling and a formidable foe in his own right. That a man such as he chooses to follow Moriarty says a lot about Moriarty's ability to command."

"Then why doesn't the clone go after Moran?" asked Joan. "That would be the most logical thing to do."

"Good question," agreed Holmes. "I can't really answer that. Perhaps he hasn't studied Watson's writings and doesn't know about Moran, or perhaps he has located Moran but is afraid to approach him. If the clone is a facsimile of the original, he will look like Moriarty, with Moriarty's strength and build. The man is not a fighter. His weapon is his brain. If he needs muscle he uses Moran's. The clone would be no match for Moran. He certainly wouldn't be able to overpower him and torture him for information. It's more likely to be the other way around."

"Here's a thought," said Lockie, "the clone wouldn't be afraid to meet Moran. He looks like Moriarty, so Moran would think he's his boss."

"Not for long. Moriarty couldn't ask his henchman where to find himself, could he," said Joan with a grin. "Think how confused poor old Moran would be. He'd think his boss had gone crazy."

"Actually you both make a good point," said Holmes thoughtfully. "The clone could walk up to Moran, introduce himself as Moriarty's twin brother and tell him he wants to meet him. Maybe Moran would take him to Moriarty, or just get his address and report back to Moriarty. Either way it is for sure the Professor would want to meet his double."

"Then he may already have met him!" wailed Myron, turning ashen.

"Has the time machine only been activated the once?" asked Holmes.

"Yes."

"In that case he probably hasn't found him yet. I would imagine that if someone looking like Moriarty turned up claiming to be from the future, our Moriarty would want proof. The first thing he would do after meeting his clone would be to try out the time machine. If the machine hasn't been activated yet, we may still have time on our side."

"Yes, yes, I agree with you." Myron mopped his clammy brow.

I looked him over closely. He didn't look well. Holmes had once observed that the clones could not handle stress as well as the original. Clearly Myron was under considerable pressure to prevent a major disaster of epic proportions. Moriarty, a time machine and an army of ruthless killer Moran clones was not the stuff of pleasant dreams.

"Couldn't you just deactivate the time machine?" suggested Joan. "If it was turned off, the piggyback device would be useless. Moriarty and his clone would be trapped here and Mr Holmes could take his time about apprehending them."

"It's not quite as simple as that."

Lockie rolled his eyes. "I knew you were going to say that."

Myron frowned at him, and then continued. "If we turn the time machine off, we will destabilize the portal that we use for time travel. When the machine was first designed, it was a fluke that the machine powered up at exactly the same time that a natural time portal was forming. The machine intersected the natural portal, stabilized it and integrated it into its own system. If we turn the machine off, it will sever the connection with the natural portal. As there is no way to predict when or where a natural portal will occur, it would be next to impossible to reestablish a link. Time travel would be lost."

"That wouldn't necessarily be a bad thing," muttered Holmes. "A lot of problems could have been avoided if that were the case."

"We wouldn't exist then," protested Lockie. "Is that what you want, Dad?"

"No. You know that's not what I want. But to put it into perspective, if there was no time travel I would never have met your mother. You wouldn't exist and I would never have met you and I wouldn't know what I was missing."

"And the world would miss out on having another potential super sleuth," added Joan with grin and a wink at Lockie.

"Here is the deal, Myron," continued Holmes. "I will undertake to locate MC2 and retrieve the device; in return you will drop all charges against Joan and my son. If you are smart, you will recruit them when they finish university. You will also take them with you when you return to your own time. If you do not agree to this, you can go find the missing man on your own."

I smiled as I listened to Holmes' demands. He sounded a lot like Morelock when he was blackmailing us into helping him. In this instance though, I agreed with him. If blackmail was what it took to protect our children from the consequences of their endearing but foolhardy actions, then so be it.

Myron scowled.

"You have to admit," I added. "They'd be an asset. After all your experts couldn't crack Joan's codes, but she easily cracked yours to get into the time machine's controls in the first place. Rather than punishing her for that, you should hire her to upgrade all your security systems. It sounds like they are badly in need of an overhaul."

Myron's scowl faded. He nodded and grudgingly conceded the wisdom of my words. "She is very good." He sighed. "I suppose you are right, both of you. We could certainly use people with their talents. Very well, you have a deal; however, I can't take them back with me today, not if their transponders were damaged. I will return in exactly seven days with a couple of spare transponders. Hopefully by then you will have good news for me. And um…" Here he hesitated a moment, "Um, perhaps Mycroft could be present then."

"Why?" I asked.

"Um, well…" Myron flushed, looking suddenly embarrassed.

Holmes smiled. "He wants to meet his father, so to speak."

"Oh." I also smiled. "Now that would be a meeting worth seeing."

Myron looked at his watch. "I will be recalled in exactly fifteen minutes. Perhaps we could have a toast with some of that excellent vintage brandy I see on your mantel?"

I chuckled and stood up. It didn't take me long to do the honors.

Myron raised his glass. "May you once again triumph over evil."

"Screw the bad guys," seconded Lockie.

We clinked glasses and drank. Five minutes later Myron disappeared in a sparkle, his glass falling to the floor as he vanished.

"Well," said Holmes. "It looks like we have our work cut out for us."

"How do we start?" I wondered. To me it seemed like an impossible task.

"In the 21st century, I had you use the internet to help track Moriarty. I will have to use the 19th century equivalent."

"What's that?" asked Joan curiously.

"The Baker Street Irregulars," replied Lockie with a grin. "They go everywhere, see everything and are the first to hear the latest gossip."

"You are quite correct, Junior," said Holmes.

Lockie groaned. "Aw, don't call me that, Dad. I hate it. You know I hate it."

Holmes' grey eyes twinkled. Clearly it amused him to tease his son. "Be that as it may, the irregulars are our best bet. I already have them out trying to get a line on the killer, but now I have a description I can give them. That should help considerably." He walked over to the hat stand and helped himself to his coat and hat.

“Is there anything we can to while you are out, Holmes?” I queried.

He nodded. “Get copies of all the daily papers and check the agony columns. It’s possible MC2 may be trying to communicate with Moriarty through them.”

“We’ll do that.” I was pleased that there was something the rest of us could do to help.

CHAPTER NINE

Over the next few days Wiggins, Holmes' head street urchin reported in with updates. The clone had been sighted several times but as yet his location was still a mystery. We continued to search the agony columns daily to no avail. Perhaps the clone was unfamiliar with the purpose to which the agony columns could be put.

On Tuesday afternoon, Wiggins reported in that they were keeping Colonel Moran under surveillance in case MC2 tried to contact him, along with several others of Moriarty's men. Holmes himself had gone to several of Moran's clubs in disguise to see if the clone had been there. On a couple of these occasions he'd taken his son with him, also in disguise. I know my daughter felt a little left out on these occasions so I tried to keep her busy with scouring the newspapers for possible clues.

That evening as we were relaxing after dinner, Joan wandered over to stand by the fire place. I could see there was something on her mind, but she was hesitant to voice it. She had been here for less than two weeks and already there were signs of repression of her natural exuberance and confidence. In her own time, in her own element, she was supremely confident and not afraid to voice an opinion, but here, now, she was hesitating. As much as I would like her to stay here, I didn't want her turning into the meek and mild women that was so popular in my time. I admired her strength of character and certitude.

"What is it, Joan?" I asked gently.

"Well, I was just thinking. It's obvious that the clone doesn't know about Moran's connection to Moriarty. I guess none of the men he tortured mentioned him. By now the clone must be getting a bit desperate to find Moriarty. He's been here over a week and still nothing. He's not using the agony columns to communicate because like Dad said last week, he's a fish out of water here."

Holmes nodded. "All true. You have an idea?"

"Uh huh. It's probably a silly idea but if I was the clone and I wanted to find Moriarty, I'd do it the easy way."

"Which is?" prodded Holmes.

"Make Moriarty come to me."

"How?"

"I'd get myself noticed. Get my picture in the newspapers. Moriarty would see the picture and know it wasn't him. He'd want to hunt down the imposter and find out who he really was. I mean if that was you, Mr Holmes and you saw a picture of yourself in the newspaper, wouldn't you look him up?"

Holmes smiled. "Indeed I would."

I smiled warmly at my daughter, proud of her as always.

"Good one, Joan," complimented Lockie. "How would he go about it though? There are various ways of getting your picture in the paper. Make a big scene and get arrested, or maybe turn up at some important event where there are sure to be photographers and get photographed there."

"He's unlikely to want to get arrested," I said.

"No," agreed Holmes. "The second alternative is more likely. Of course a photograph isn't necessary. He just needs to get his name mentioned in the newspaper. Naturally he would use Moriarty's name."

"So," I said, "If we can figure out where he is likely to go we can nab him when he shows up."

Holmes shook his head. "No, we would have to follow him back to where he is staying. It is unlikely he would bring his transporter device with him. He'd leave that behind. We need to retrieve both. If we move in on him precipitously all he has to do is remain silent."

"Lord Granville is giving a grand ball this weekend. Everyone and anyone of importance will be there. In fact, I believe you have an invitation Holmes, at least his name is embossed on the envelope," I said.

Joan turned around and looked at the pile of letters on the spike. She pulled them off and flicked through them, picking out the one I'd mentioned. She brought it across to Holmes.

He tore it open and glanced at it. "Yes, it's an invitation for me and a guest."

"There will be reporters there," I pointed out.

"Mmm," murmured Holmes, but he didn't sound convinced.

"There's something else more up his alley," said Joan, her hazel eyes shining brightly. "Hang on." She hurried over to the pile of discarded newspapers and hunted through them for several minutes before finally pulling one out and flicking through it. "Here it is." She waved the paper at us.

Lockie snatched it out of her hand, looked at the main article on the page and read it out loud. "Several renowned mathematicians are holding a forum on the works of other published mathematicians. One of the works to be discussed and possibly debunked is The Dynamics of an Asteroid. Hey now, didn't Professor James Moriarty write that?"

Holmes looked suddenly eager. "He most certainly did."

"So," continued Joan. "What if the clone turns up and claims to be Moriarty and perhaps causes a bit of scene. He's sure to be mentioned then."

Holmes nodded, smiling.

"Er, what if the real Moriarty turns up as well?" I asked. "I mean if colleagues are going to be discussing his work wouldn't he want to be there as well?"

"I am sure he would like to be, unfortunately he would not be welcomed. Once upon a time Moriarty was an esteemed professor of mathematics and highly regarded. He was in his heyday when he wrote The Dynamics of an Asteroid, a book which ascends to such rarefied heights of pure mathematics that it is said that there was no man in the scientific press capable of criticizing it.* He was courted by every major university. He could have had his pick."

"So what happened?" I asked, curious now as I knew that once upon a time Moriarty worked as a lowly tutor to the Holmes children. It was difficult to imagine that he would go from esteemed mathematician to tutor as a career choice.

"He got greedy. He was given large research grants. He squandered them, then falsified his research so he would have something to show the committee when the time came for him to account for his grant. He was discredited and kicked out. After that no university would have him."

"Is that when he came to work for your family?" I asked.

Holmes nodded. "Only for about a year. You know the rest of that story, Watson."

**The Valley of Fear*

"We don't," said Lockie, looking eager.

"And you won't either," replied Holmes. "I've asked Watson not to publish that information."

"But you have got it written down, haven't you, Dad?" asked Joan.

"Well, yes," I admitted, "but it is amongst my private diaries which are not for publication."

"In your lifetime."

"In perpetuity as far as I'm concerned."

"I might have to look around a bit. You'd be amazed how many of your private diaries turn up in the future. Perhaps another author got hold of them and published them."

I frowned. Did I want that? Perhaps I should destroy them. The very thought of destroying those precious memories and untold stories was repugnant to me. Would it really matter if a hundred or a hundred and fifty years from now they came to light? It would let people know just how remarkable a man Holmes was, and perchance my not so little contribution to his fame.

"Getting back to the subject at hand…" said Holmes.

"Not yet," said Lockie. "You don't have to tell us what happened when he worked for you, but how did he end up as the Napoleon of crime as you call him?"

"After he robbed my father, he was a wanted man. He went underground. He turned to crime and using his considerable organizational skills set up a crime network. His fingers are in many pies, and he's making a fortune but he cannot be directly connected with it. I know he is behind it. Many of the crimes committed are out of the league of the men committing them. There is a mastermind behind them all, pulling the strings, giving the orders. That's Moriarty and one day I will prove it."

"That's history, Dad. Of course you'll prove it and you'll beat him as well."

"That's good to know. Can you tell me when?"

Lockie shook his head. "Sorry. If you know in advance you might second guess yourself or get careless and become the victim instead of the victor. I don't want to change history."

Holmes smiled faintly. "No harm in asking. To get back to the matter at hand, Joan is right. That is exactly the sort of place that the clone will go. He will show up as Moriarty. It will be easy enough for him to make a scene and you can guarantee that the reporters will mention his presence. That will arouse Moriarty's interest for sure. Does it say what day the forum is?"

"Friday, two o'clock at St. Peter's College, Oxford," read Lockie.

"Good, then that's where we will go. When the clone turns up we'll follow him home."

"Is that really necessary?" asked Joan. She'd lost her earlier shyness now that her idea hadn't been dismissed.

"How else are we going to know where he lives?" asked Lockie.

"Won't he tell the reporters where he can be found?" she asked. "How else will Moriarty know where to look for him?"

Holmes groaned and slapped his forehead. "Becoming a father has dulled my brains!"

"Hey, don't blame me," countered Lockie immediately.

"What do you mean?" I asked.

"Joan is once again correct. You have a wise and intelligent daughter, Watson. Of course the clone will tell the reporters where he can be found. He will probably issue a challenge to other mathematicians and include his address as part of the challenge just to ensure it gets published. It is not really necessary for us to go there. We can just wait and read it in the paper."

"But wouldn't it be better if we knew before the papers came out? We want to beat Moriarty to him," suggested Lockie.

"And we will. If we are up early on Saturday, we can purchase the early edition of the paper and go straight to the clone. By the time Moriarty learns of it, we will have the clone in captivity and the device in our possession."

"Oh." Lockie looked disappointed. "I was hoping Joan and I could go to Oxford and watch for him. This detective stuff has been pretty boring. I thought I'd be seeing you in action, zipping around with your magnifying glass. Donning disguises left, right and centre, running here there and everywhere. But we've only been to a couple of Moran's clubs and spent the rest of the time here."

"I don't like to exert myself unnecessarily," replied Holmes, amused by his son's complaint. "I only run around and don disguises when necessary. I much prefer to sit in a comfortable chair and smoke my pipe and come up with a solution to the problem in comfort."

"Well, it's not that exciting. I don't think I want to be a detective. I'd rather work in a lab."

"Each to their own. I'm proud of you whatever you choose to do."

Lockie smiled. "Thanks, Dad. I appreciate you saying that."

"I suppose it wouldn't hurt to go to Oxford. The clone doesn't know either of you. Myron will be back on Sunday to take you home. It might be nice for you to visit your alma mater in this century. You can tell me if anything has changed. You and Joan should get out and about a bit and explore this century. It is, after all, an opportunity of a lifetime."

"I was actually going to suggest that myself," I said. "The young ones have been cooped up here long enough. They should go out and enjoy themselves for a bit. It's only Tuesday, the forum isn't until Friday. I think we should go sightseeing tomorrow and the next day. We'll go wherever you like."

Joan and Lockie exchanged pleased grins.

"That's great," said Joan. "I would love to visit a 19th century medium and have my fortune read."

"Oh, yeah, that'd be fun," agreed Lockie. "Better still, how about going to a séance? How cool would that be?"

"I suppose that could be arranged," I said, smiling. It was good to see them looking happy. Their moods had undergone a rather significant change since Myron's arrival on the weekend.

CHAPTER TEN

We spent the next few days taking the children to the lesser known but more interesting places to give them a taste of what it really was like to live in Victorian times. I found the séance fascinating and thought the medium was a most remarkable woman. Holmes of course debunked the whole thing and called her a charlatan, but he couldn't explain how the ectoplasm spewed forth from her mouth during her trance. We supposedly made contact with my deceased father. I am not one hundred percent sure about that. Holmes said she just picked me and made some astute observations. It wasn't a far reach to suggest my father had also been a doctor. Occupations tend to run in the families. Until Holmes made his views known on the subject I truly believed she was genuine, however he succeeded in sowing the seeds of doubt. Joan and Lockie seemed to enjoy themselves though.

We went to a freak fair, to gawk at the oddities of nature—the man with another man growing out of his chest, who had his own head, neck chest and arms, but it was obvious this second creature was mentally deficient. There was the fat lady, an incredibly obese woman that was wheezing like she was about to take her last breath as we looked at her. There was the wolf boy and lizard man and various other unfortunates suffering from birth defects, skin maladies, and birth malformations. This sort of fair was not uncommon in my time. People happily paid to line up and gawk and laugh at these creatures. I suppose we assuaged our guilt for their treatment by reassuring ourselves that it was the only way they could earn a living rather than being incarcerated in asylums or poor houses, which was their only other alternative.

It pleased me to see that the young ones rather than being titillated by these bizarre spectacles became more somber with each new sight, and there was compassion in their eyes. That is one thing I did like about the future. The deformed, the mentally ill, the vulnerable were no longer ostracized or put on display for the entertainment of others. In this our future generation was more civilized.

We took time out to visit the seaside. Lockie and Joan wanted to go to the moors where Holmes tackled the hound tormenting the Baskervilles, but alas we did not have time for that. We did go for a quick trip to Sussex.

On Friday morning Joan and Lockie caught the train to Oxford. I found I was feeling rather nervous about them being out of my sight, but Holmes reassured me that they would be fine and that they were more than capable of looking after themselves. Given that they had infiltrated a top secret facility and over powered the guard and what have you, I suppose he was right. It was just my protective fatherly instincts coming to the fore—belated as they were. Joan promised to give me a blow by blow account of everything that happened and I had to content myself with that.

They returned to Baker Street at six o'clock, looking excited and brimming with news. The following is Joan's narrative of what occurred.

*****

Narrative by Joan Hudson

It was rather fun going on the train, just Lockie and I. Mingling with the masses was such a different experience from the crowded platforms of the underground back home. Everyone was so polite. If they accidentally jostled you in the crowd they apologized, not like in our time. There, you could practically be knocked off your feet and they wouldn't even spare you a glance, and if you made eye contact with someone they'd look away or concentrate more fiercely on their smart phones. Here though, when people made eye contact they'd smile or comment. It really was lovely.

Not so lovely were the gentlemen we shared our compartment with. In this instance, by comparison, the future wins hands down. I am all for the no smoking in public laws. At first they seemed to be rather pleasant and polite. One old fellow would put you to shame, Dad. He had the biggest handlebar moustache I'd ever seen. I didn't think facial hair could grow so luxuriously and so stiff that it stuck out a good twelve inches on either side. The other looked like a well groomed businessman, very fashionably dressed with high collar and cravat and a black pin striped Prince Albert hammer tail coat, spotlessly shiny shoes with pointy toes—ouch! I'm sure they weren't very comfortable, but it is nice to see a man suffering for fashion and not just the women. The third fellow looked the artistic sort, or in my day we'd just call him gay and not the happy kind. He was wearing a bright green velvet overcoat, ruffled shirt front and sleeves and a floppy flamboyant bright red scarf tied around his neck in a bow. They really were an interesting looking trio and I looked forward to chatting to them. They seemed friendly. However, once the train started pulling out of the station big whiskers pulled out a pipe—bigger than Mr Holmes' and proceeded to stuff it with this sticky black looking stuff, even unlit it already had an unpleasant odour.

The businessman whipped out a silver case and took out a cigar, while the colourful chap rolled his own. If I was at home I'd say he was using marijuana. I'm not sure if you can get that in this century, but I guess it was something similar because half hour into the trip he looked pretty chilled out.

My looking pointedly at the no smoking sign above the door had no impact and I didn't want to be rude and ask them not to smoke, but I can tell you I was having trouble breathing, and Lockie was looking a bit green around the gills. We decided to escape to the dining car. People were smoking there too, but it wasn't as enclosed as our compartment had been and they had a couple of windows open. I'll never complain about our public transport ever again—smokeless air to breathe, heaven!

Eventually we got to Oxford. We were early so we took a wander around the town. You know it hasn't really changed all that much. There are still the same old buildings that are around in our time. People really knew how to build solid long lasting structures in the olden days. You wouldn't see many modern buildings lasting a hundred and forty years and looking as good as when it was built. Apart from the clothing, the shop windows and the passing traffic we could easily have been home. It felt a lot like home too: made me feel quite nostalgic.

After lunch (thanks for giving me some money, Dad), we made our way to St. Peter's college. I was surprised to see such a large gathering. I mean, it's a fairly dry as dust subject they were going to discuss, I wouldn't have thought so many would be interested. Saw a couple of reporters there too; one even had an accompanying photographer.

We joined the crowd and found some seats at the back of the auditorium. The mathematics professors were on the stage. One was writing equations on the blackboard. Now I understand mathematical formulas related to computer programming, but I had no idea what they were writing or talking about for that matter. Lockie's pretty good at physics and the like, but he wasn't a hundred per cent sure either. From the looks of the audience I reckon most of the discussion went over their heads as well. Talk about tedious. Things livened up somewhat when our fake Moriarty turned up.

He came in boldly and walked right up to the podium. "How dare you presume to discuss my work! Insects like you have no idea what you are talking about," he said in a booming voice despite his scrawny appearance.

We could hear him from the back of the room. He's not the most attractive looking specimen of manhood is he? Tall and lean, shoulders hunched, massive forehead with receding hair, I couldn't see his eyes from where we sat but his head seemed to move in a reptilian fashion. I have no trouble believing the real Moriarty is the Napoleon of Crime. He looked pretty creepy.

"I am Professor James Moriarty. I am the author and my work has stood the test of time. Even the so called best minds in this field are mere infants when it comes to comprehending the pure mathematics of my text. You cannot debunk something you do not understand. It is like asking a child to explain the universe."

An argument broke out then between clone Moriarty and the professors. They were rather offended by his comments. The journalists though were looking rather happy. He was sure livening up a boring conference. The photographer quickly set up his equipment hoping to capture the scene. The Professors accused Moriarty of being a crook and a charlatan and said he wasn't welcome there.

Moriarty called them a few more names and then issued his challenge. He said if any of them can write a comprehensive treatise explaining the mathematics of his theory they could bring it to him at the Grand Hotel, London, and if they were correct he would pay them five thousand pounds in reward and acknowledge they were his equal in intelligence and mathematical skill.

The photographer called out to him and asked him to pose, which he did. He then turned to leave and was inundated with reporters. He repeated his challenge and the address. By the time he came out we were waiting for him, ready and willing to follow.

MC2 came out and started striding off along the street. We weren't that far behind but he didn't notice us. Suddenly a man stepped out of a side street just as MC2 passed. He pulled up short and stared after him as if he'd seen a ghost, and Lockie and I were just as stunned. The new comer was Moriarty himself. He was sort of in disguise. Mr Holmes doesn't have to fear he has a rival in that department. He's still the king. Moriarty had on an a bulky overcoat that made him look heftier and a black wig that looked rather ridiculous with his big forehead and the fakest looking moustache I'd ever seen. I guess he was coming to the mathematics conference but didn't want anyone to recognize him. I can imagine his shock at seeing himself walk past. Talk about a doppelganger.

He obviously lost interest in the conference and took off after his double. This was the last thing we wanted. We couldn't let Moriarty meet up with the clone, so we in turn headed off after him. The clone was making his way to the train station and Moriarty was fast gaining on him. I guess a train had just arrived as there was a sudden influx of pedestrians emerging from the station. The clone stopped momentarily and Moriarty was only a few feet from him when Lockie suddenly started to run and threw himself onto Moriarty knocking him to the ground.

"You rotten thief!" yelled Lockie, pummeling Moriarty.

MC2 turned around and glanced at them. Luckily Moriarty's wig had stayed on and the clone didn't recognize him. Imagine, he was just two feet away from obtaining his objective and was none the wiser. Mr Holmes was right about Moriarty being physically weak. He couldn't put up much resistance to Lockie. The clone lost interest in the scuffle and entered the train station. Lockie held Moriarty down for a few minutes longer before he let him loose.

Moriarty was livid. For an academic he sure has a potty mouth. He shut up when a constable came over, drawn by the disturbance.

"What's going on here?" he demanded, glaring at Moriarty. "You, sir, there are ladies present. Mind your mouth."

Moriarty glared at Lockie, his beady eyes glittering with malice. It gave me a bit of shiver actually. He's not the sort of fellow who you want to have as an enemy. I imagine he is extremely dangerous.

"This imbecile attacked me," he growled.

Now Lockie looked shamefaced. "Er, I'm sorry," he muttered. "A man bumped into me down the street there and lifted my wallet. From the back he looked like you. Same coat, same hair. I saw you and thought you were him. Honest mistake."

"You were robbed, sir?" asked the policeman of Lockie.

Lockie nodded. "But I see now that it wasn't this gentleman. I guess I just over reacted when I saw him and thought he was the thief. I'm very sorry, sir," he added to Moriarty.

"Well, no harm done then," said the policeman.

"Arrest him for assault," cried Moriarty.

"Do you want to swear out charges?" asked the constable officiously, taking out his notebook and pencil. "And your name, sir?"

The stopped Moriarty. "Forget it," he growled and strode off into the train station.

I gave the policeman a smile. "I guess he changed his mind."

The constable nodded and returned my smile. "Have a good day, Miss. Sir."

As soon as he left us we rushed into the train station. There was Moriarty standing on the platform and a train was pulling out of the station. As it went past us we spotted the clone on it. It just wasn't Moriarty's day. He turned around, saw us, gave us a fierce scowl and stormed past us.

"Whew, that was close," I said. "That was quick thinking, Lockie."

Lockie grinned. "It's not everyone can brag about tackling the real in the flesh evil Professor James Moriarty himself."

After that we caught the next train back to London.

*****

Narrative by Dr. John Watson

At the end of Joan's narrative, I said, "Now Moriarty knows about his double and will go to him."

"He can't," said Lockie. "At least not yet. He was on his way in to the conference so he never heard MC2's challenge. He doesn't know where he lives so we've got until tomorrow before he finds out. We can go take care of the clone tonight before the newspapers come out."

"How fortuitous that the two of you went to Oxford. If you hadn't of been there, Moriarty would have caught up with the clone," said Holmes. "I suggest we go pay him a visit now."

Holmes and I collected our coats and the four of us caught a cab to the Grand Hotel. It seemed our search was over and in two days our children would return home to the future and we would never see them again.

At the hotel Holmes went to the reception desk and asked for Professor Moriarty's room number.

We went up the stairs at a leisurely pace little realizing we had underestimated Moriarty's resourcefulness. Outside the clone's door, Holmes raised his hand to knock, and then noted that the door wasn't closed properly. He pushed it open.

We were rather startled by the sight that met our eyes. The two Moriarty's were there. One was obviously the clone, looking a little scared. The other Moriarty stood there with a gun unerringly pointed at him. The clone was pleading for him to hear him out, that he could explain everything.

"Then I suggest you talk fast," growled Moriarty.

"I'm from the future. Look at me, I'm you! I have a time machine!" cried the clone, and then his eyes shifted slightly as he spotted us in the doorway.

"I'm not falling for that," said Moriarty.

One of us must have made a faint noise.

Moriarty twirled around and glared at us. He obviously recognized Holmes and Lockie. "Sherlock Holmes!"

"Professor," greeted Holmes, unperturbed by the gun now pointed in his direction. "It must have been a bit of a shock to see yourself on the street."

Moriarty frowned. "You know about him? Who is he?"

"He's Professor James Moriarty." Holmes stepped forward through the doorway into the room.

"He is an imposter!"

Holmes shook his head and took another step forward. Lockie and I moved to either side of him, with Joan behind us. "Not at all. He is you, or a close facsimile at any rate.

Now Moriarty's pale blue eyes looked searchingly at Lockie. Clearly he didn't miss his resemblance to Holmes. "You deliberately stopped me today," he said to Lockie.

Lockie smiled. "Didn't want you meeting your double."

Moriarty contemplated Holmes again. "You don't seem old enough to have an adult son. Families create vulnerability."

"Don't think of using that to your advantage, he won't be staying around here much longer and will be well out of your reach," countered Holmes.

"I have a long reach."

"Not that long."

With a nod in the clone's direction, Moriarty added thoughtfully, "He said he was from the future. What did he mean?"

"I'm not here to satisfy your curiosity, Moriarty. My business is with him."

"Well my business takes precedence," countered Moriarty. He waved his gun in Holmes' direction. "This is my guarantee of getting answers to my questions."

"And if you don't like the answers?"

Moriarty smiled; a rather unpleasant smile I thought. It would seem the clone didn't like it either as he began edging backwards. That's when I noticed a small black case on the table.

"He's going for the time machine!" cried Joan suddenly as the clone grabbed up the case and flipped it open. Her mention of the time machine caused Moriarty to look around at the clone. Holmes took advantage of that and leapt forward, going for the gun, while at the same time Lockie sprinted across and tackled the clone. The case fell as Lockie knocked the clone to the floor.

Holmes twisted the gun out of Moriarty's hand and stepped back, holding it loosely. "It would seem your guarantee is now worthless."

Moriarty glared at him, and then glanced back at the clone, still on the floor with Lockie sitting on him.

Joan moved forward, giving Moriarty wide birth and picked up the case. She checked it over. "It's okay," she said. "It's not broken."

"That's a time machine?" Moriarty looked interested. His eyes were gleaming. Clearly he was already thinking of the possibilities that such a thing could provide.

This of course, was the last thing we wanted.

"Time to go, Moriarty," said Holmes.

"You've got nothing on me."

"How about threatening us with a deadly weapon for a current charge? Once the police get here, I can always remind them of the outstanding warrant for your arrest for robbery."

Moriarty snarled an insult and pushed past me as he left the room.

"Why did you let him go, Holmes?" I asked. "You could have had him arrested."

"It wouldn't put him away for long. When I get him I want him to get the death penalty."

Joan smiled at Holmes. "He will. You'll see to that."

Holmes returned her smile. "Good. You might want to get off the clone now, Junior."

Lockie stood up and the clone slowly climbed to his feet, patting at himself to make sure he hadn't been injured.

"It's hard to imagine this feeble creature was able to overpower and torture and kill three men."

"I'm sure he used trickery," said Holmes. "They probably thought he was Moriarty and were lulled into a false sense of security. No doubt he struck them from behind."

"Who are you?" demanded the clone, sounding exactly like the real Moriarty.

"Sherlock Holmes."

"Holmes!" The clone looked positively sick.

Holmes moved over to him and pulled his arms behind his back and handcuffed him. "We'll take him to Mycroft's. He'll organize for him to be put into temporary custody until Myron returns on Sunday."

CHAPTER ELEVEN

Sunday came around rather quickly I thought. I hadn't been looking forward to it as I would be losing Joan forever and I had just started to get to know her over the past two weeks. I kept my feelings to myself though as I didn't want to upset her. She was homesick and needed to go back to her time, but it had been lovely having her here. She gave me a taste of what it felt like to be a father.

At ten o'clock Mycroft turned up with the clone in the company of a rather large surly man. Once inside the flat, Mycroft dismissed him and sent him away, then pushed the clone down into the nearest seat. "What time will my clone be here?"

"Soon," replied Holmes.

Mycroft nodded then fished about inside his coat pocket and pulled out a long black case. "This is for you, young lady," he said to Joan, holding out the case. "It seems I missed your birthday last week."

Joan looked surprised but came forward and accepted the gift. "Thank you, Mr Holmes." She opened the case to reveal a rather lovely gold bracelet studded with rubies. "It's beautiful." She smiled at Mycroft, and then to his surprise and my amusement wrapped her arms around him in a hug. I am sure that is the first time that ever happened.

Mycroft endured her hug for a moment, and then cleared his throat.

She released him and smiled up at him. "I've always been in awe of you, but you know you're a real dear and not half as fearsome."

He took a step back as if fearing she'd hug him again and fished about in his pocket again. "And, as the only nephew I am likely to have, this is for you, Lockie. Consider it a belated twenty-first birthday present."

Lockie came forward and accepted his gift. "I wasn't expecting anything." He opened his jewel case to reveal an elegant pocket watch finely engraved.

"It has the Holmes family crest engraved on it," explained Mycroft.

Lockie smiled proudly. "I'll treasure it. Thank you, Uncle."

The Moriarty clone just scowled at us but we ignored him.

Fifteen minutes later, a faint shimmering appeared in the middle of the room and Myron materialized.

The first thing he saw was the clone. His fat face lit up in a beaming smile. "I see you have him."

"Yes, and the time machine device," said Holmes.

Myron turned around and saw Mycroft for the first time. His mouth dropped open. "Y-y-you're M-My-Mycroft," he stuttered.

"And you are my replica," replied Mycroft studying him with undisguised curiosity. He walked over and started to circle Myron. "You appear somewhat older than I am."

"I was activated twenty-two years ago. Once activated we age like anyone else."

"I see. And how old were you on activation?"

"Twenty-five."

"You didn't look twenty-five," I blurted remembering Myron as I last saw him in the year two thousand.

"They like to mature the clones so they all look alike when activated to prevent confusion."

"Odd that," said Mycroft. "I would have thought they would prefer to activate you as a younger me, when I was thinner and fitter."

"I guess they are comfortable with you as the you everyone knows," replied Myron. "This really is an honour, sir. To meet you in person. I never thought I would ever have such an opportunity." He thrust out his hand to Mycroft.

Mycroft shook his hand gravely.

"He's never going to wash his hand again," murmured Joan softly, causing Lockie to chuckle.

Myron beamed. "Mortimer is going to be green with envy."

Mycroft frowned. "Who's Mortimer?"

"He's clone number three. We had to activate him to help deal with the crisis Joan created with her computer lock out. He's been taking care of routine business while I've been trying to deal with the Moriarty issues."

"I see. Just how many of me is there?"

"There were six. Morelock was killed by Moriarty's first clone."

"I bet you never imagined as a bachelor you'd have so many sons, Uncle Mycroft," said Lockie with a grin.

"Don't be cheeky, Young man. Well, Myron," said Mycroft. "I believe you have a job to do."

Myron nodded. "Yes, yes. Can I see the piggyback time machine?"

Joan fetched it and opened it. "He's put it into a laptop to make it convenient. It's really quite clever. His passwords were about as original as yours, Myron. I've cracked it already and reprogrammed it with a new access password to save you the hassle when we get back."

"Uh, thank you, Joan." He smiled at her. "There really will be a place for you in the organization when you finish university. You too, Lockie."

"Did you get into trouble, Uncle Myron?" asked Lockie.

"No. I said you had infiltrated the complex as part of a security overhaul to look for faults in our system. That the lockout Joan initiated was to test the skill of our programmers, which by the way they failed miserably. Unfortunately Moriarty was an unforeseen glitch which just emphasized what a big issue our poor security was."

"Clever," complimented Mycroft.

I noticed Myron's chest puffed out a little at that. He had it bad where Mycroft was concerned.

"I guess it is time for us to return." Myron took three transponders out of his pocket. They were attached to wrist bands.

Joan and Lockie put one on while Myron attached the other to the clone.

Joan hugged me tightly and kissed me. "I'm going to miss you, Dad, but I am so glad I've had this opportunity to get to know you. I will treasure the locket you gave me."

I hugged her back. "I will also miss you."

Holmes and Lockie shook hands. "Take care of yourself, Junior," said Holmes.

Lockie rolled his eyes at being called Junior. "I'm glad I had the chance to get to know you as well, Dad." He grinned and his eyes twinkled. "Thanks for the violin."

"You're not taking it now," countered Holmes. "You'll get it in a hundred years or so."

Lockie grinned, and then came over to me. "It's been a real pleasure meeting you as well Dr. Watson. I don't think Dad would have been as successful as he is without you. And if it's any consolation, you're as famous as he is. After all, you can't have Holmes without Watson."

I smiled at him and held out my hand to him. "Kind of you to say so, Lockie." We shook hands. "Take care of my daughter, won't you?"

"Always. It goes without saying."

Joan snorted. "You've got that wrong, Dad. I'm the one that has to take care of him." She went over to Holmes and kissed his cheek. "It's a shame I won't be able to brag to everyone back home that I met the Sherlock Holmes."

Holmes smiled at her. "You can brag if you like, but they may think you are mentally ill."

Myron cleared his throat. "It's time."

Lockie pulled Moriarty up off the couch and the four stood together in a group.

I raised my hand to give Joan a final wave as they disappeared. The room felt instantly empty with them gone. "Well," I said. "That's that then."

Holmes nodded.

"I'm having second thoughts about giving my genetic material for the development of future clones," said Mycroft.

"Please don't, Mr Holmes," I said immediately. "If the clones are never developed, we will never travel to the future and I will never have a daughter and your brother will never have a son. Both have unique talents and who knows what they will contribute to the intelligence service of the future. In a time of great crisis, it may fall on them to save our country, just as you do during the Great War."

"I agree," said Holmes. "Some things have happened that I may have preferred they didn't but for the most part I wouldn't change a thing."

"Very well." Mycroft put his hat on. "Until next time."

After he left, I looked across at Holmes. "You haven't really said much on the subject, Holmes, but how did it feel to be a father?"

"Unexpected."

I laughed, and then said, "No, really, Holmes. How did it feel?"

Holmes looked thoughtful for a moment. "After the initial surprise wore off, I must admit I am rather proud of him. He is certainly a credit to me, and I am sure he will be very successful in life. Also, it is rather nice to know that my legacy will live on."

I nodded. "That's how I feel as well. I couldn't be prouder of my daughter. And, I'm actually glad she was born in the future. She has so many more opportunities there than she would here."

"She is certainly a very bright girl. You should be proud of her."

"I am. I truly am."

BOOK THREE

MYCROFTS GALORE

by Joan Watson Hudson

CHAPTER ONE

December 30th 2027

My life and that of those around me has been so interesting, that I decided that it was time to record it. So this then, is the first page of my journal. Of course, it is not for publication now, for the work I do is often top secret, but perhaps one day—in fifty years or so, the things I write about here will be public knowledge and I can share the true facts; so it is with this possible future publication that I have decided to start my journal with this particular case.

To understand the events that occurred in the year 2027, it is necessary to give the reader a bit of background as to myself, and my partner Sherlock Holmes Lestrade, called Lockie for short. He was named after his father, who was none other than Sherlock Holmes, the greatest consulting detective from the 19th century and all time. His mother is Georgina Lestrade, the great granddaughter of Inspector George Lestrade made famous in Dr. Watson's stories. Needless to say that she is also in the force. At this time, she is the Commissioner of Police at Scotland Yard. My own mother's name is Wiona Hudson, and my father was Dr. John Watson—yes, the real one! My name is Joan Watson Hudson. Of course I never use the name Watson, it would raise too many questions, so I usually just sign myself as JW Hudson, and I'm no relation to Mrs Martha Hudson from 221B Baker Street. It's just a coincidence really.

Now you are probably somewhat confused here, wondering how Holmes and Watson ended up in the 21st century. That is a whole story in itself, suffice to say, I will give the abbreviated version. In 1890, Holmes and Watson were brought to the future by the British Government to tackle a clone of Moriarty who was proving to be too much for their forces. The man responsible for bringing them to the future was Morelock, a clone of Sherlock's elder brother – Mycroft.

Morelock was killed during that case and was replaced by the second of six Mycroft clones. This one was called Myron.

Holmes and Watson fit into the times quite well—too well, some would say, and cohabited with our mothers. When they returned to the past after the case was solved, they left behind permanent reminders in the form of Lockie and myself.

I should point out that they weren't aware that our mothers were pregnant when they left; in fact even our mothers weren't aware of this fact. The problem was that even if they had known, they would have had to return as it is part of history that Holmes saves George Lestrade's son's life, who is Georgina's grandfather. (Whew! What a mouthful). Without him, she would never have been born, so he had to go back. It's a bit confusing I know, but that's time travel for you. Anyway, that is how we, Lockie and I, over a century later can claim kinship to two such famous men.

Naturally, our mother's kept us in the dark as to who our biological fathers were. They were sworn to secrecy. Holmes and Watson's presence in the 21st century was top secret. I guess I should point out here that Lockie inherited his father's abilities in music, interest in chemistry and biology and in the field of detection, whilst I have a penchant for computer sciences. In fact, without undue modesty, I'm practically a genius when it comes to computers. There is little I don't know about them. Okay, okay, I'll stop bragging and get back to the story. Samples of Holmes and Watson's DNA was taken when they were here, so it was a small matter for me to type in our own DNA patterns and hack the government DNA database and initiate a search. Imagine my surprise when it turned up a 99.7% compatibility. Proof enough for us to confront our mothers; that's when they told us the above mentioned story. They also introduced us to Myron.

Now Myron, as I said before was a Mycroft Holmes clone, technically he was sort of an uncle to Lockie, genetically, if not biologically. He showed us the time machine. With a bit of team work and cunning we managed to pilfer two transponders, which we implanted in our arms. Then, with trickery and the aid of an advanced computer program designed by yours truly, which could override their protection protocols and send us back to 1892 to meet our fathers. Naturally I put in a safe guard and automated it to retrieve us a week later, with enough inbuilt walls and safeguards to stop them breaking through and bringing us back prematurely.

That was some meeting, I can tell you; Lockie looked so much like a young Sherlock Holmes that the relationship was unmistakable. No one would ever take them for strangers. I ended up with my mother's figure, but my father's eyes and some of his other characteristics. Perhaps that is where I get this urge to put pen to paper from. Literary ambitions flow in my veins. Certainly my father was famous for his ability in this line.

Dr. John Watson wasn't anything like the fuddy-duddy that modern movies make him out to be. He was a warm, friendly and intelligent man, who was far more observant than he was ever given credit for. And his relationship with Sherlock Holmes was one of mutual respect, something that has rarely, if ever been mentioned. Contrary to popular belief, Sherlock Holmes did not look down on my father, instead he valued his opinions. Even if what he said wasn't quite right with regards to his own deductions, they always helped put him on the right track.

Anyway, getting back to the story, we had the shock of our lives when after a few days into our stay our transponders fizzled and burned out leaving us stuck in the past. So much for all my safeguards and everything. To distract us from our gloom, Dad and Mr Holmes threw me a wonderful 21st birthday party (in fact I'm writing this with the pen set that Sherlock Holmes gave me).

Myron turned up once my lockouts expired and we learned that there had been more than one Moriarty clone and that the second Moriarty clone who we dubbed MC2, had invented a transportation device that piggybacked onto the time machine, making use of it to transport himself back to the past so he could get some fresh Moriarty DNA from the original. Sherlock Holmes of course solved the case, with a little help from Lockie and me.

Mr Holmes also convinced Myron that instead of punishing us for our illicit use of the time machine, he should hire us—which he did the following year when we both graduated with honors. That's how Lockie and I came to be working for British Intelligence. We work as a team. He does the leg work and lab work mostly and I do the computer work. I couldn't imagine life without Lockie.

We grew up together, lived together for nearly ten years, as Georgina roomed in my mother's boarding house. We went to the same schools, we just did everything together. We are inseparable. Why, the only time we were separated was when Lockie was sent to summer camp for a month, but he ended up missing me too much, so he smuggled me in disguised as a boy. Of course we were only twelve at the time, so it wasn't too hard. That was some camp! But I digress--again, I'll get back to the story…

It all started on that fateful night of December 30th, 2027. I feel like starting this narrative off with that overworked sentence: 'The night was dark and stormy.' Bit of a cliché but true. It was dark and there was a helluva storm raging. Lightning bolts streaked the sky. One hit the lightning rod on Big Ben, another struck a bus loaded with tourists—seven deaths; and one struck the power lines supplying the laboratory where the clones were stored.

I should point out that there were actually two clones running around now. Myron, who was head of the department and Mortimer (who had been activated from stasis to help with the little crisis Lockie and I created when we went back in time). Once activated however, they couldn't be returned to stasis, hence two clones on duty. Lockie thought it was pretty funny and called them both uncle, much to their disgust.

The mechanism keeping the three remaining clones in stasis had a power surge when the lightning hit and the electricity ran down the wires and zapped each clone. It was only the fact that they were enclosed in nutrient gel that saved them from being fried.

What did happen was that the stasis field shut down and they were activated. Their names were Morlan, Mydas and Mobius—hey, don't look at me. I didn't name them! Anyway, the technician on duty had the fright of his life when they emerged from their stasis chambers naked and covered in goo. They were naturally dazed and more than a little confused, because activation is usually a slow controlled process. Myron was alerted immediately and he had them transferred to the private government hospital for observation.

No one knew if they had suffered any permanent damage. They seemed to recover well, which was fortunate, for if they'd shown any signs of impairment, they would have been terminated immediately. The problem was they all looked alike. We could tell them apart from Myron and Mortimer, as these two had aged, but between the three new ones, there was no difference—they were triplets. Now I like Mycroft, but I must confess I was feeling a little overwhelmed by so many of them. Lockie was too.

This situation put Myron in a bit of pickle. He wasn't sure what to do with them. He was all for terminating them, then sending an agent back a century to get new DNA from Mycroft to propagate new clones. Unfortunately, he discussed this idea with Mortimer within hearing of one of the new clones. So it wasn't all that surprising when they disappeared from hospital the next day, December 31st. This of course was a problem, but Myron assumed it was only a matter of time before they were apprehended or before they turned themselves in. Which was the most logical action that a Mycroft would do. A normal Mycroft that is. It was Lockie that made the discovery that sent the two M's into a flutter—Myron and Mortimer that is.

Lockie was fooling around with DNA structures in the lab. Like his father he liked to dabble in chemistry and with genetics being big in this century he had broadened his field of expertise to include microbiology, biology, genetics and DNA sequencing. I was in the main computer lab with Myron and Mortimer, explaining my latest innovation when he rang us. I joined the two M's as we made our way to the science lab. Lockie looked anxious.

"What is it?" asked Myron.

"I was trying out the new DNA synthesizer. I put in samples of your DNA, Mycroft's, and one of each of the other three clones. Theoretically they should all have come back the same, as all five of you are genetically identical to Mycroft. Well look at this—" He pressed the keypad and brought up the screen on the DNA spectroscope.

"They're different," I said with surprise.

"Uh huh, and they're still changing," stated Lockie flatly.

"What does that mean?" asked Mortimer.

"It means that they were damaged by the lightning strike. Their genes are mutating. No offense, but you guys were cloned from old technology. That means your matrix is not 100% stable, not like the methods used nowadays."

"How will this affect them?" asked Myron, a trifle anxiously.

"I don't know. It may reflect as a change of personality, or it may affect their health, or even their appearance. I really can't say without having them here in the lab to study. Here…" he brought up another screen. "See this strand of DNA, it belongs to Morlan. It has mutated seven times already in just the last half hour.

"I should have terminated them immediately," said Myron, castigating himself.

I put a hand on his shoulder. "I know why you didn't. It's like killing yourself, or your brother, you couldn't do it. Besides, how were you to know this would happen?"

"You don't understand, Joan. There have been people against the Mycroft clone project for years. As we always fill the top job, no one else has chance to get promoted. That generates a lot of resentment. If these clones go berserk or cause mischief, it will be proof that the project is unsuccessful and we could also be terminated. We continually have to prove ourselves. This is one hell of a disaster." Myron was almost beside himself with agitation, wringing his hands repeatedly, while Mortimer looked positively green.

"Okay, settle down a bit fellers. No need to get your knickers in a knot. Joan, can you modify one of these scanners to detect this fluctuating DNA pattern?" asked Lockie.

"I can try, although if I adjust it to do that, it won't pick them up if their DNA stabilizes," I pointed out.

"Good point. I would say we could use two scanners, but we have no idea what they are mutating into so we can't scan for them. The fluctuations are the only thing that sets them apart. We just have to hope their cells don't stabilize before we find them," said Lockie.

"We've had people out looking for them since they left the hospital," said Mortimer.

"Despite the chaos their genes are in, they are still as smart as you are. We're not going to find them using conventional methods," argued Lockie.

"Good point, my boy," agreed Myron. "Sherlock, I want you to take charge of this case. Second anyone you want to help with this. They must be found."

"Just Joan here for starters: the less people who know about this new development the better."

"Agreed."

When the two M's left the lab, Lockie turned to me. "We'll have to keep an eye on them. Do you remember how Dad mentioned that the clones couldn't handle stress as well as the original?"

"Uh huh."

"They could easily crack under the strain of this situation."

I nodded and set about modifying the scanner—programming in the new DNA information.

"What do you really think this is doing to them, the runaway clones I mean?" I asked him as I worked.

He looked grave, and then picked up another slide. "I didn't want to show this to the M brothers in case it freaked them out completely."

He put the slide into the spectroscope and enlarged it. When the DNA strand appeared, he brought up the runaways DNA and compared them.

I looked at it carefully. "Some of the codes match," I observed.

"Yup. Thirty three perfect matches so far. Do you want to guess whose DNA that one is?"

"Why do I have this horrible feeling that it's Moriarty's?"

"Because it is."

"What on earth are we doing with Moriarty DNA around here? Surely they learnt their lesson last time?"

"Yes I know. The scientists have been trying to isolate the genes that determine criminal tendencies, violence and delinquency. They figure that if it can be identified, the gene could be eradicated in infants. There would be no more crime, no more violence."

"Well, it's a noble goal, but keeping things like that around is dangerous. How much do you want to bet that the evil genes are the ones that match our three runaways?"

"No bet. I've been comparing these strands with the other samples here of criminals and there are twenty-seven matching gene codes that are common to all the subjects—the clones and the criminals."

"Three Mycroft brained Moriarty's, oh hell!"

"Think of all the damage one Moriarty inflicted, and Mycroft is ten times smarter than Moriarty ever was."

"We have to find them," I stated.

He nodded soberly.

CHAPTER TWO

It took me about two hours to get the scanner up to scratch and make a copy of the program to be transferred to a portable handheld device.

"Now what?" I asked Lockie, who was still fooling around with the DNA synthesizer.

"Now we go to the hospital and see if we can get a trace," he said.

At the hospital we did pick up a faint trail but lost it in the underground.

"It's like looking for a needle in a haystack," I complained.

"I know. Maybe we should ask the other two what they would do if they wanted to hide," he suggested.

"Wish you thought of that sooner," I grumbled, seeing my plans of attending the New Year's Eve party vanishing.

"At least we know your scanner works," he grinned.

We went back to headquarters and found Mortimer on duty. Myron had gone home for the day.

"Hey, Mortimer," greeted Lockie. "If you were in fear for your life from Government agents and you knew you were being hunted, where would you go?"

"Where would I go?" he repeated in surprise. He looked thoughtful, and then smiled faintly. "Well, if it was me on the run, I'd got to a different timeline. This year is too hot, nowhere is safe. Yes, I'd go back in time."

"But the clones can't go back in time unless they break in here and use the time machine," I pointed out.

"We haven't had any reports of unauthorized entry; and besides, if their DNA is changing the retinal and palm print scanners wouldn't give them access."

"The changes are at the cellular level; their surface appearance may not be altered," cautioned Lockie.

"Well, we can easy check." Mortimer heaved his bulk out of the chair and we made our way to the TM (Time Machine) room. Thanks to Lockie and me, security had been increased, making it almost impossible to access the machine unless authorized to do so. It wasn't easy to override the commands and safeguards I had installed, or so I thought. For even as we entered the room, we heard the familiar hum of the machine as it went through the transport process.

"That's impossible!" gasped Mortimer. "There is no one here, how could it be operating?"

Sherlock frowned, thinking furiously, but I was the one to get it first.

"Oh shit!" I cried and hurried to the main panel. "This is running off the piggyback device!"

"The what?" asked Mortimer.

"The second Moriarty clone's laptop."

"Of course." Lockie understood me perfectly. "Where's the laptop kept?"

"Bioengineering. We've been studying how he made the link work through time to develop new communication devices that the agents can carry. It saves being returned at an inopportune time via the transponders. With the new devices the agent can contact us direct in this time for a beam out," replied Mortimer.

"Ring, Myron. I bet he doesn't answer. They would have had to get his ID to be able to impersonate him and get in here. Joan, head for the lab with the scanner." Lockie activated his wristwatch communicator and sent a call down to the lab. "No answer," he said after a minute.

"No answer from Myron either." Mortimer looked worried.

"Get over there, we'll join you as soon as we've checked out the lab," Lockie ordered.

We raced to the lab and found the night tech tied and gagged and the laptop missing. I scanned the room.

"There was only one of them in here," I said.

"Means the other two are with Myron."

"Were with Myron," I corrected. "Remember the TM was in use. They're going places."

Lockie drove his new Rocket hover car at speeds to match its name. Fortunately we arrived at Myron's in one piece. We found Mortimer looking pale and cradling Myron in his arms. A carving knife protruded from Myron's chest and blood bubbled from his lips.

"I've called an ambulance," said Mortimer, swallowing a lump in his throat.

"Lap top...stole..." Myron gasped.

"We know," soothed Dick, dropping to his knees beside him. "Take it easy, Myron, save your strength. Do you know where they were going?"

"1952...1852...mistake...only one..." Myron tried to say something else but wheezed instead. His eyes glazed over and he slumped in Mortimer's arms. I could feel the tears brimming in my eyes and blinked rapidly to try and disperse them. He would have frowned on tears.

"Joan, the portable is running off the main terminal, do you think you could trace where they went from the main computer at HQ?" asked Lockie.

"Possibly. The trace patterns would be on record, but I...I might not be able to pinpoint it with 100% accuracy, and knowing these guys, they would have installed scramblers, encryptions, safeguards and walls. It could take a while to crack them."

"Get onto it. You might break through faster if you start from 1852," advised Lockie.

"Why 1852? Myron said 1952."

"I think they wanted to go to 1952, but made a mistake and ended up in 1852, and unless I'm mistaken only one clone has gone there. That's what Myron was trying to tell us."

"I agree," said Mortimer, laying Myron's head down gently and pulling the rug off the couch to cover him up. "It sounds like he overheard them talking after one of the clones went. It is the first time they have used the time machine, as they are unfamiliar with it, they could have erred. They would have taken themselves somewhere else."

"Joan and I will go back to HQ, Mortimer. These Mycrofts are dangerous. They have no hesitation in killing. As soon as Joan can pinpoint where in 1852 one of the clones has gone, I'll go after him. What's more, I'll be taking a vaporizer with me."

"Vaporizer?" I raised my eyebrows in query.

"Can't leave a body lying around. Too hard to explain," replied Lockie.

I nodded in understanding. As gruesome as the prospect was, I knew there was no other option. The delinquent clones had to be neutralized fast.

We returned to headquarters. Dick went to the store room and helped himself to suitable clothing. There was a fully equipped dressing room to furnish time traveling agents with the appropriate gear. They could hardly turn up dressed in 21st century clothing.

It was easy to pick up the trace pattern for 1852. The deviant M's had broken through all my safeguards easily, but after doing that they couldn't wait to try it out. One clone was sent back in time—to the wrong time. From what I could gather, when they realized this, they erected walls to make direct tracing impossible and a ninety-three number password with word commands before access could be made. Then I had to search every year for a link as to where the other two had gone. It was fortunate they never thought to do this with the first clone.

I quickly set up the program to send Lockie back to 1852, and because it was so clear, I was able to make it for the same day. When he emerged from the dressing room I whistled.

"Don't you look handsome," I teased.

"I don't know how people wore these," he replied, running a finger around the inside of the high, stiff collar. He wore a black cravat with an Oxford coat of arms on it, a silk floral patterned vest and a frock coat.

Mortimer returned by this time, having seen to Myron's body. He handed Lockie a vaporizer, the modified scanner handset and a cloth purse containing gold coins, and also a communicator linked to the time machine.

"Wish me luck," he said coming over to me.

"Luck," I replied, giving him a smile, although I never felt less like smiling in my entire life. I could still see Myron lying there, bleeding to death . This was the first time we were to be separated since that boy's camp episode. I could feel butterflies in my stomach and I felt just awful. What if something happened to Lockie? I wouldn't be there to back him up.

Lockie looked at me closely, detected my concern and wrapped his arms around me in a quick hug. "I'll be all right, Joanie. You know I'll be back because I want to see what you got me for my birthday."

“What makes you think I got you anything?” I said carelessly.

“Because you’ve never missed one yet,” he smiled at me, his eyes twinkling. He walked over to the platform and took his place. “I’ve got the communicator. I’ll signal you when I’m ready to come back.”

I nodded, not trusting my voice. I was already missing him and he hadn’t even left yet. Lockie threw me a wink and I pulled on the controls before I had second thoughts. He shimmered a moment, and then disappeared. I don’t know why I was feeling so anxious. I knew Sherlock was capable of looking after himself, and he was well versed in self-defense. In recent times my feelings for him had deepened to something more than mere friendship.

Sometimes, when he was bent over some experiment, totally engrossed, I would sit and watch him, and admire him. I liked the way his hair fell over his eyes when he was excited and how his eyes would twinkle when he teased me, even though I hated being teased; and when his long artistic fingers massaged my neck and shoulders after a hard day bent over the computer. I sighed. We were mates, best friends; he never thought of me as anything else. I was sexless to him. I was Joan, his best buddy. He loved me like a sister and I used to love him like a brother, but…lately, just lately I wished that he would notice me…really notice me, as a woman that is.

That’s why I wanted to go to the New Year’s Eve party tonight. That was my resolution. I had bought this stunning new outfit that mum helped me pick. She knew how to display her assets to her best advantage. I didn’t. I was a bit of a tomboy. I always wore jeans and baggy tops and until recently I kept my hair short. I shouldn’t really be surprised that he never noticed me. My only consolation was that he didn’t seem particularly interested in other women either, so at least I didn’t have to worry about competition. Sure we had kissed—on birthdays, at Christmas, things like that, but never on the lips: just the brotherly peck on the cheek and the quick hug. I had it all planned. Tonight I was going to dress to impress and come midnight, give him a kiss that would knock his sox off. So much for my plans. It was nearly midnight now and where were we? He was in 1852 and I was stuck before a computer console with an almost impossible task in front of me. Life sucks!

CHAPTER THREE

Narrative by Sherlock Holmes Lestrade

I have to admit, I was a little apprehensive initially. This was the first time I was going on a case without Joan by my side, still, it was kind of exciting too.

Joan had programmed me to land on Hampstead Heath. That was the thing with time travel; you had to pick places where you knew there were no buildings. A long time back, when Myron's department first started experimenting with time travel, they had the occasional mishap of materializing an agent into a wall. It didn't do much for the agent.

I expected the heath to be deserted, imagine my surprise then to find it packed with people dressed in their Sunday best. It was summer and there was some sort of carnival in progress. Fortunately I materialized behind a tent. People were going about admiring the sideshows, eating rock candy and fairy floss and partaking of the various entertainments on offer. I would have loved to mingle with the crowd and enjoy the festive atmosphere, but I forced myself to concentrate on the task at hand. Surreptitiously I pulled the scanner out of my pocket and did a broad sweep. I picked up a faint trace in a northeasterly direction, so headed that way. It led straight towards the sideshows. There was a bearded lady, a fat lady, a strong man, a dwarf, a wolf man and a two headed tiger, or so the banner claimed.

"Sherlock! Sherlock!" shouted a female voice.

I turned in surprise. I just got here, how could she know my name? The woman was quite an attractive brunette in prim dress. She walked right past me and appeared to be looking around anxiously.

"Sherlock, where are you?"

I stared, open mouthed. What a coincidence. Could she be my paternal grandmother—Violet Holmes?

"He'll show up when he's ready," said a tall bearded man as he moved over to join her. "And when he does the little rascal will feel my belt," he promised grimly.

"Oh, Sigor." Violet Holmes looked even more distressed. "Mycroft, Sherrinford, go look for your brother," she ordered the two boys who had accompanied the man. One was about thirteen, the other fifteen. Mycroft wasn't a bad looking boy. A little sturdy, but not fat. The eldest was rather surly and I noticed he made little effort to look for his errant brother. Mycroft was more diligent.

"I'll try the animal cages, Mother," he offered.

When the Holmes' moved off, I was about to step forward when I felt a tug at my trouser leg. I looked down. There was a cute little boy dressed in a sailor's suit peeking out from under a tent.

"Are they gone, Mister?" he asked.

"Let me guess, you're Sherlock," I said to the six year old who crawled out.

"Sherlock Holmes," said the child offering his hand.

I shook it gravely. What a twist of fate this was! I was meeting my father, yet I was old enough to be his father. Wish I had a camera. Sherlock Holmes in a sailor's suit and short pants, and looking pretty cute in it. I would have loved to have a picture to show mum. She would have laughed her head off.

"So why are you hiding from your folks, Master Sherlock?" I asked.

"I wanted to see the two headed tiger," he stated.

"Did you?"

"Yes."

"Well, were you impressed?"

The boy's face fell. "No. It's fake. The second head is stuffed and stuck on somehow to the live cat."

"Really? How could you tell that?"

"The eyes didn't move." The boy looked me over with interest. "You're not from around here, are you?"

"No. How did you know?" I asked curiously. Who would have thought that he had his deductive and observational skills at so young an age.

"Your shoes…they're un-English."

Spot on, I thought. I had changed my clothes but not my Italian leather shoes. "They're Italian," I said to the boy.

"You're not Italian though," he observed.

"No. Care to guess where I'm from?" I smiled down at him as he studied me with great concentration.

"Oxford," he said finally.

I couldn't hide my surprise. "How on earth?"

The child laughed. "That's an Oxford cravat. Father's got one," he said still grinning.

Of course it was! It's funny how one always goes automatically for the familiar. This was an Oxford cravat from the 19th century. I was used to wearing Oxford ties from the 21st century. Old habits die hard.

I took out my purse and held out a coin to the boy. "I think you've earned this, young Sherlock. And let me just say, you have a bright future ahead of you."

Sherlock took the coin, but instead of pocketing it, he studied it.

"It's Italian too," I said quickly, before he could comment.

He looked up at me with a puzzled expression. "Do I know you?" he asked.

I shook my head. "No, we have never met."

"That's funny. I feel like I know you," he said. He was about to question me further, when Mycroft appeared.

"There you are! Father is furious and mother's nearly in tears. Really, Sherlock, why do you keep running off all the time?" He took his little brother's hand and led him away. Sherlock kept glancing back over his shoulder at me as Mycroft pulled him along. Next moment I heard him telling Mycroft about the two headed tiger. My father was a rather likeable child, if a trifle precocious. It was a real novelty meeting him like this. Oh well, back to work. I turned the scanner on. My signal was stronger. I followed it, dodging pedestrians every now and again as I was hot on the trail

I had almost reached the edge of the fairground when I spotted him. The scanner registered his ID—it was Mobius. He was moving towards the parked carriages, bent on stealing one, no doubt. I quickened my step. The plan was to try and capture him and if that was not possible to vaporize him. When I was almost in arm's length of him, I called out: "Mobius!"

He stopped and spun around. He didn't recognize me as we had never met, but deduced I was from the future because I knew his name. Mycroft's movements were never swift, so I was taken by surprise when he leapt forward. He knocked the vaporizer from my hand and then attempted to throttle the life out of me, his big hands closing around my throat. My karate chops to his neck did nothing to loosen his grip. I was gasping, having trouble breathing as his grip tightened on my windpipe. In desperation, I clenched my hand into a fist, the knuckle of the forefinger extended in jujitsu fashion and aimed a punch at his philtrum—that group of nerves above the upper lip. I struck with all the force I could muster. The pain from such a blow is excruciating. Mobius was not immune.

He screamed and let me go, his hands going up to his face as he staggered back. I dived for the vaporizer. Just as I brought the weapon up to fire, Mobius shimmered and disappeared.

"Damnit!" I cursed. The other two must have retrieved him, which meant they must have stolen some transdermal transponders as well. How else could they have retrieved him? Damn the luck. I had him in my sights, and now he was gone. I had failed. I leant against a carriage, massaging my sore throat. That had been a close one. I was just about to activate my communicator when I noticed people starting to come towards the carriages. They were obviously homeward bound. I decided to return to the fair and find somewhere private to disappear from.

As I walked towards the fairground, I saw the Holmes family moving towards their carriage. Young Sherlock was being pulled along roughly by his father. Sherrinford was grinning spitefully and Mycroft looked worried. Mrs Holmes was almost in tears and pleading for her husband to go easy on the boy. When they reached the carriage, Sigor Holmes pulled off his belt and made to strike Sherlock with it.

I hurried forward and butted in. "Excuse me, sir," I said.

He glared at me. "What do you want, Stranger?" he asked gruffly.

"I don't mean to intrude, but if you are about to strap your son for wandering off, then I beg you, please don't."

"Why? What's it to you how I raise my family?" he demanded.

"It's nothing to me, it's just that it is my fault he was separated from you," I said quickly.

"Your fault? Explain, sir!"

"You see, I asked him directions to the two headed tiger exhibition. I'm new around here. He was kind enough to show me. I didn't realize his family was looking for him until his brother came up."

Young Mycroft looked at me. He knew I was lying. We had been nowhere near the tiger's tent when he found us. However he remained silent.

"Anyway, it would be unfair to punish a child for showing courtesy and kindness to a stranger," I finished off.

Violet Holmes smiled gratefully at me and took young Sherlock into her arms protectively and away from his father.

"Well I suppose…" Sigor said hesitantly.

"The gentleman is right, Sigor. It wouldn't be fair," she said.

I threw Sherlock a wink as I turned to leave.

He grinned impishly at me from behind his mother's skirts. No wonder he didn't like his father, what a brute he was. I made my way to a tent and hid behind it before contacting Joan. I didn't have long to wait before I was beamed back to the present. Within seconds I was back in the TM room at headquarters. Joan looked relieved to see me, and I have to admit, I was relieved to see her, because for a few short moments, I didn't think I ever would.

"Any luck?" she asked.

"I saw him. We had a bit of a fight. Just as I was about to vaporize him, he disappeared."

"Oh, so that's what that was," she said. She came over to me and looked me over. She noticed my torn collar and reached out to pull it off so she could examine my neck better.

"Oh, Lockie!" she gasped.

"I'm all right. It was Mobius, he tried to choke me," I explained.

There was a strange look in her eyes. Sometimes I just couldn't figure Joan out. When we were younger we were always on the same wave length, but the older we got, the less I understood her. I never knew what she was thinking anymore. She was a real mystery.

CHAPTER FOUR

Narrative by Joan Hudson

I was so relieved to see Lockie safe and sound. He grinned at me, trying to distract me from his injuries and said, "You'll never guess who I met?"

"Who?"

"Sherlock Holmes. Actually the whole Holmes family."

"What! You're kidding?"

"No, true. You should have seen my father; he was dressed in a sailor's suit and looked kind of cute."

"You didn't tell him who you were, did you?" I asked in surprise.

"Of course not. He was only about six years old. Met Mycroft and Sherrinford as well. Sigor Holmes was a fearsome type, but his mother was quite nice. I stopped Sherlock from getting a beating.

"A beating—how awful!"

Lockie was smirking like a cat with cream. "Little Sherlock snuck off to see a sideshow. Even at that age he had his observation and deduction skills."

"Wow, that would be weird," I said. "Meeting your own father when he was a child."

Lockie grinned even more widely. "Wouldn't you like to meet a young Watson? Maybe change his nappies?"

"No. That's more than I would want to know about him," I replied, smiling faintly.

"Enough of that," said Mortimer joining us. "You were unsuccessful in eliminating Mobius?"

"Yes. They beamed him away just as I had him in my sights."

"I'm not surprised. Three transponders are missing. I would surmise that they have perfected their use of the time machine and have brought him back to join them wherever they are."

"That's likely," agreed Lockie.

"I just had a thought," I said. "I could probably terminate the link between the laptop and the mainframe."

"No!" Mortimer was adamant. "If you did that we may not be able to reestablish the link. The department has plans for that laptop. Under no circumstances is it to be destroyed or tampered with."

"But if I disconnected the link they would be trapped where they are and it would give us a better chance of catching them," I argued. "I mean, all they have to do now is jump to another time frame whenever we get close."

"Only if they know you are close. They don't know you. They never saw you when they were in hospital. You stayed behind the observation screen."

"Mobius saw Lockie; hell, he tried to strangle him," I pointed out.

"Yes, but the other two haven't. And neither have seen you. On the other hand you both know who you are looking for, so you have an advantage. Lockie can always disguise himself."

"I guess," he agreed.

"Good. Now Joan, how are your investigations coming along?"

"I'm getting there, but I'm so tired I can hardly concentrate. Considering I've been at this all night, Mortimer, I need a break. I have broken through three safeguards, only a few more to go and the digital password. I think I can bypass some of those safeguards though by locking onto Mobius' transport. These clones were pretty cluey. How come they know so much about computers anyway?"

"We were trialing a new program. Subliminal messages were played to them during stasis. Information to keep them up to date, so that when they were activated, they didn't have to spend a week learning everything so they could go into action immediately."

"They went into action all right. You obviously taught them about the time machine. There's no way they could have broken into the system without prior knowledge."

"It was a good idea at the time, Joan. How were we to know they would be struck by lightning and mutate?" said Mortimer dismally."

"Perhaps in the future you should consider an intense data feed technique just before activation, instead of continuous, just in case."

"Well, as there are no more Mycroft clones, I'm the last one, that is not going to be an issue. I doubt if they will want to make any more," replied Mortimer.

"We'll worry about that later. First we have to catch the other three. It would be better not to bring anyone else in on this, just Joan and I," said Lockie. "I have an idea that could save your bacon, but we need to get the others out of the way first, so it's advisable not to tell anyone anything. If they ask, say the clones have taken a turn for the worst and are still in hospital."

Mortimer nodded in agreement, slightly reassured by Lockie's words. "All right, you might as well go home and get some rest, Joan, a day or two won't make much difference. You too, Sherlock."

"Lockie hooked arms with me as we left. "I'll drive you home. You look beat."

"I am," I agreed. "You don't look so hot yourself." I fell asleep in the car as he drove me home and woke to his hand on my shoulder. Lockie stayed at my place, crashing on the couch whilst I went to bed. He often stayed here when we were working. He even stored some of his stuff here in case he needed a toothbrush or a change of clothes, just as I did at his place.

*****

I had a good six hours sleep, ate a late lunch and returned to work. Lockie came with me, although he couldn't help me. He could use a computer but wasn't as proficient with it as I was.

"So much for relaxing on New Year's day," I complained.

"Yeah, sorry about last night, Joan," he said.

"What?" I looked at him, surprised.

"I know you were really looking forward to going to that ball at Albert Hall."

"Yeah, I was. Oh well, there's always next year I guess," I said casually, as if it hadn't been important.

"Mm hmm. If there isn't a plague of Mycroft clones taking over the world," he said with a grin.

"They should have made a few Sherlocks, just for variety," I replied also smiling.

"What do you need with cloned Sherlock's when you have me," he declared immodestly.

The day progressed drearily. It was nearly midnight before I made a breakthrough. Lockie was sprawled out on several chairs. I poked him awake.

"Huh?"

"We're in," I said.

He stood up immediately alert, interest on his face. "So where did they go?"

"Ah, slight problem. I can't pinpoint it exactly. They've installed a scrambler. The nearest I can get is within a six month period meaning they are somewhere between September 1891 and March 1892. I can't narrow it down any further. If I had the lap top itself I could."

"September '91. That's six months before we met our fathers for the first time," said Lockie, a fact which had not escaped me.

"Uh huh."

"Better rouse Mortimer I suppose," murmured Lockie.'

"Already have. He's on his way in."

"You did good, Joan," he said with a grin and a pat on my shoulder. (I wished it was a kiss).

"I've been thinking when would be the best time to go back. If we go back to September, we may be there for the whole six months trying to find them or hanging around waiting for them to appear. I think it would be better to go back at the end of February '92. By that time we have already met our fathers so we would have somewhere to stay and we could enlist their help without having to go into long winded explanations. Your father has numerous resources. If he lets them loose to search for the clones he should get results. Also, it is more likely that the clones are already there and have established themselves, rather than just newly arrived."

"No argument on that. So what date have you picked?"

"The day after we returned home from our last visit," I said.

Lockie grinned. "We haven't seen them in five years. It will be good to meet up with them again."

"It's been five years for us. It will only be a day for them," I reminded him.

"They've hardly had time to miss us."

While we waited for Mortimer to arrive we decided to change into period costume. I couldn't find a decent dress among the collection. It was mostly male agents that got to time travel to the past, simply because they had more freedom in that time period than female operatives did. Lockie was changed before me. I heard Mortimer arrive. I also heard him arguing with Lockie. He wanted Lockie to go alone, but Lockie insisted I came along. He knew I wanted to see my father again, plus we always worked best as a team.

"If Joan doesn't go, then neither will I. You can stew in your own juices, Mortimer. We are a team. I need her." I heard Lockie say adamantly. I smiled: that was loyalty for you. I finally settled on a blue dress that was a little too big for me, but was the best of the lot. I figured the cloak that went with it would hide the horrible dress. There was a bonnet to match.

Lockie hooted with laughter when I emerged.

I felt my face flush. He could be such a pain sometimes. "Oh, shut up," I said crossly, stepping onto the platform.

He joined me, still grinning.

"Now remember, this isn't a social visit," instructed Mortimer. "You have a job to do. Check in once a day via the com link, or sooner if you have any news. There will be someone here twenty-four hours a day. Give my regards to the Holmes brothers."

Lockie gave him a wave as we felt the transporter beam twinkle around us.

CHAPTER FIVE

It was just after sunrise when we materialized in the alley just off Baker Street. The street was starting to come alive as the early morning delivery men made their rounds in the freezing cold. The ground was crisp with fresh snow. We made our way to the familiar address. There was a light on downstairs, so Lockie rapped smartly. The door was opened by a bleary eyed Martha Hudson. She looked surprised to see us.

"Why, if it isn't young Mr Holmes and Miss Watson!"

"Hallo, Mrs Hudson, we're back. I hope you still have our old rooms?" I said.

"Oh aye, but Mr Holmes didna tell me you were coming back. I thought you were going to America," she said.

"We were. We missed our boat," Lockie explained, lying easily.

The landlady let us in. "They're not awake yet," she said.

"We'll be quiet. We'll wait in the siting room." I offered.

She nodded. "I'll send the boy up with a pot of coffee," she offered.

"Thank you," smiled Lockie graciously, causing the old lady to smile back. He was as disarming as his father around her. She was putty in their hands.

We made our way upstairs. "Do you think they'll be pleased to see us?" he asked.

"My dad will be. I'm not sure about yours."

We made ourselves comfortable around the fire and helped ourselves to coffee when Billy brought it up. Half an hour later Holmes wandered out clad in night shirt, slippers and dressing gown. He stopped in surprise, taking in our appearance.

"Hi, Dad," greeted Lockie, a trifle nervously I thought.

"Hallo, Junior, Joan. I see you are back, but you're older so I must assume that while it has only been a day for us, it has been several years for you."

"Five years," I offered.

Holmes nodded sagely and moved forward; selected a pipe and began to fill it with the previous day's dottle. I thought this was a disgusting habit. The fresh tobacco smelled bad enough, the leavings were even worse.

"Is this a social visit or business?" he inquired.

"Business."

"The clones?"

"How'd you guess?" smiled Lockie.

"I never guess," replied Holmes with a faint smile.

Lockie grinned, knowing this to be a lie.

"Those clones seem to be the cause of most of the trouble we've been encountering of late. Don't tell me someone has made another Moriarty?"

"Worse," said Lockie.

"Let's wait for my father to get up before we tell the whole story," I suggested. "It will save us repeating it."

"In that case, you might as well go wake him, Joan. He's not a morning person," advised Holmes. He then wandered back to his own room to get dressed.

I went to my father's room and stood by his bed for a moment watching him sleep. He looked the same as I remembered him. Moustache tinged with grey flecks here and there, twitching slightly as he breathed. I leant down and kissed his cheek. "Dad, wake up. It's Joan."

He continued to slumber.

I shook his shoulder and repeated, "Dad," in a louder voice.

He grunted and grumbled. Opened one eye, saw me, and then opened the other. "Joan!" He sat up. "What on earth?"

"It's all right, Dad. Can you get up?" Dick and I are back. We're working on a case."

"A case. Don't tell me you're a detective too?"

"A secret service agent," I said proudly.

"Good Lord!"

I returned to the sitting room, leaving him to get dressed.

Holmes was out again pouring himself a coffee and Lockie was filling him in on what he'd been doing for the last five years.

"And Joan has been my partner," he finished up.

"I knew you had a lot of potential, Joan," said Holmes, raising his coffee cup to me in a salute.

"What about Lockie – aren't you proud of him?" I asked.

"Of course. But then I expected no less of him."

It was another fifteen minutes before Watson joined us—still a little bleary eyed from being woken before the civilized hour of ten.

Holmes rang the bell for breakfast.

We waited until the table was set and Mrs Hudson had left before telling them about our case. We held nothing back. Holmes was our best bet for tracking down the errant clones.

"Let me get this straight," began Watson. "The lightning strike has affected their genetic structure, mutating it so that although they may look like Mycroft, they do not act like him?"

"Correct," I agreed.

"If what I suspect is true, they'll be Mycroft's opposites," said Lockie earnestly.

"Sort of like Dr. Jekyll and Mr Hyde," I added.

"You mean they're evil?" asked Holmes.

"They killed Myron," said Lockie. "That's evil enough."

"Yeah, and Mobius tried to strangle Lockie," I said.

"Oh." Holmes' eyes roamed over his son, noting the bruise on his neck. "Are you all right?"

"Uh huh." Lockie nodded. "Just miffed that I let him get away."

"So we have three evil Mycrofts running around," mused Watson disbelievingly.

"That's it in a nutshell," I agreed.

"You people from the future cause more trouble than all the villains of our own time," complained Holmes. "Our lives used to be so simple before we got involved with all this."

I felt a little guilty about that. It was true what he said. "Sorry."

Now Lockie looked a little anxious. "Does that mean you're not happy to see us?"

"I'm always happy to see you, Junior, just not the company you keep, nor so soon. You didn't even give me a chance to miss you," said Holmes, but the smile in his eyes belied his words.

Lockie smiled back, too relieved to take offence at being called Junior again.

Watson reached out and gave my hand a squeeze. "Well I'm glad I haven't had a chance to miss you," he said to me.

I smiled. I never had a father growing up, but he sure made up for it now. I wish he had been there, not his fault of course, as I explained earlier, but still it would have been nice, because he was so kind and caring and not afraid to show his affection for me. I guess one was never so old that they didn't need the love of a parent.

Watson looked me over and said, "No offense, dear, but where did you get that awful dress? No daughter of mine is going to run around London dressed in castoffs. I don't care how urgent your business is. Straight after breakfast we're going to go shopping."

I grinned. I certainly wasn't about to argue. I looked atrocious in this dress and knew it, and although I was never particularly fashion conscious I couldn't help wishing I had something decent to wear. "That would be great, Dad."

"Whilst you two are doing that," said Holmes, "Junior and I will visit Mycroft. He'll need to be warned about these clones; they may attempt to impersonate him. Mycroft has access to top secret government files—imagine what a villain could do with those."

We shared a cab to the city centre after breakfast and parted company with Lockie and Holmes. Dad and I went to a dress shop. The last time we went clothes shopping I had opted for something easy and simple. I hadn't been concerned about appearance, just practicality. This time I was hoping to get something more attractive, seeing as how I missed out on making an impression on Lockie on New Year's Eve. We didn't have time to have my clothes custom made, so I had to get an off the rack dress.

The dress maker was rather shocked at my modern underwear and convinced Dad that I needed all the trappings of female finery. It cost him a pretty penny I'm sure, but he didn't complain.

It was late afternoon by the time we arrived home. Holmes and Lockie were already there. I was still wearing the blue dress that I had arrived in.

"Aren't you going to get changed?" asked Lockie curiously.

"After I've had a bath," I said, collecting up my parcels and making use of my father's room and bathroom. After my bath, I unwrapped the packages and attempted to figure out which bit went where. I changed into the underwear—it was the old fashioned sort, but at least it was clean. The saleslady had included a corset. I had got out of wearing one last visit, because everything had happened so fast that I had a good excuse not to bother. Just the thought of wearing a corset put me off—on principle—as the corset symbolized the constrictions enforced on women of this era. I decided to leave it off. I put the dress on, and then found I couldn't do it up because the bulky underwear made it too tight a fit. I had tried this dress on in the shop in my skimpy underwear. As I had just washed my other stuff, I couldn't wear it until it dried and as much as I hated the thought of it, I would have to wear the corset. It was the only way I was going to fit into the dress. This is where I encountered my first difficulty.

I struggled with the beast of a thing for nearly half an hour; there was no way I could do it up. Finally in a fit of temper I stormed out to the sitting room brandishing the offending item. Three stunned faces turned towards me.

Sherlock Holmes' eyebrows went up a notch, my father's jaw dropped, while Lockie pointed at me and hooted.

"Look at you!" he said laughing uproariously. "What an outfit!"

I was clad in a white cotton camisole, a bodice top, and knee length bloomers

"Lockie, it's rude to laugh at a lady," chided Holmes, trying desperately to keep a straight face.

"Good gracious, Joan, cover yourself!" gasped Watson, shocked.

Lockie circled around me. "You're looking very becoming, Joan. You'll be the talk of London," he teased.

"Shut your fat face, Lockie!" I snapped irritably.

"Joan! You don't tell a gentleman to shut his fat face," my father admonished me. "And a lady doesn't parade around in front of three bachelors—two of whom aren't even related—in her underwear."

"She's no la—" Lockie began only to be interrupted by Holmes

"Junior!" he growled. "Manners! And stop looking at Joan in her underwear," he added for good measure.

"Oh, come on, Dad," said Lockie, still grinning. "She's hardly likely to excite unbridled passion in that outfit. Why she's wearing more clothes as underwear than most folks in my time wear on the street."

I flushed at his remark, suddenly embarrassed—so much for making a good impression.

"Well I can't put this goddamned thing on!" I said, trying to hide my hurt.

"That's your department, Watson," said Holmes with a faint smile. "Being a medical man I assume you've encountered female undergarments before. I'm sure you've had more experience with those things than Junior or I."

"As if I'd let you put a corset on my daughter, experienced or otherwise!" Watson said indignantly. "Come on, Joan. I'll help you."

We went back into his room. He closed the door and turned to me. "Are you all right, dear?"

"Yeah."

"Young Sherlock upset you, didn't he?" he asked gently.

Told you he was observant.

"Well he didn't have to laugh at me," I said, feeling tears prick at my eyes.

"No, he shouldn't have laughed at you," agreed Watson. "He's a bit like Holmes in that respect—not always mindful of other people's feelings."

I sat down on his bed. I really wanted to cry like an oversized baby.

Watson came over and sat beside me, putting his arm around my shoulders. "You care for him a lot, don't you dear?"

"It's not returned. He doesn't even notice me. I'm just good old Joan to him. I wanted to impress him and instead I end up a laughing stock."

"If he hasn't noticed you, then he is a fool, but somehow I don't think so. I do believe he does take you for granted. And he may think of you as good old Joan, but have you done anything to make him take notice of you?"

"What?" I was surprised because I hadn't expected this sort of response.

"I remember the way you were dressed last time when you were ready to return to the future. No offense, dear, but it wasn't very feminine—jeans and sweatshirts, I think you called them. If he doesn't notice you as a woman, maybe it's because you have never shown him you were, and a pretty one at that. I know you have to compete with men in your work, but that doesn't mean you have to sacrifice your femininity. Look at Georgina—she has the respect of her male colleagues, yet she always dressed to show of her best features, as did your own mother. It was Georgina's legs that caught Holmes' attention—if she had only worn trousers, he may never have noticed her at all, and Lockie would not exist. Dressing like a woman didn't make them less able, if anything it was more like a statement: that they were successful women in a man's world. You have accomplished so much, Joan. I am so proud of you and you should be proud of yourself. Don't ever be ashamed of being female, you should flaunt it—let those men know what they're up against."

I sniffed and said, "You'd make a great feminist, Dad."

"Perhaps I would." He smiled at me. "Now, shall we get you dressed and wipe that silly grin off Lockie's face."

I turned around and hugged him. He held me tightly, and then kissed me on the top of my head. He helped me into the corset and the dress and then stepped back.

I was surprised to see my reflection in the mirror. "Wow!" I gasped.

"Wow indeed," said Watson, coming over to me and smiling. "Not only is my daughter courageous and intelligent, she's beautiful as well."

I quickly set about fixing my hair, and then when I was ready, said, "Okay, Dad. I want to make a grand entrance, go announce me."

Watson smiled at me, and then went to the door. I heard him say: "Gentlemen, may I present my lovely daughter, Joan Hudson."

I swept out of the room, skirts swishing. Lockie's reaction was worth all the hassle it had taken to get dressed. His jaw dropped and he gaped. And so he should! The corset emphasized my figure which had always been hourglass, and which I had always concealed. This dress accentuated every curve, and the low cut front left no doubt as to my sex. For the first time in my life I really did feel female and I don't care what all the feminists out there say, but I actually liked it. Sure, I wouldn't want to go about in a dress like this all the time, but here now, it was perfect.

"You look very nice, Joan," said Holmes. "Too nice to just sit around here. I think I will take you all out to dinner at Simpsons—just so we can show you off."

"Thank you, Mr Holmes," I responded politely. "Lockie?"

His eyes roamed over me, taking in every curve. "How long have you looked like that?" he asked finally.

A smile twitched at my lips. "I've always looked like this."

He shook his head. "No, I'd have noticed. You're—wow! Stunning! Gorgeous! Why have you been hiding from me?"

"I've been there all the time, Lockie. You just never opened your eyes," I said softly. The two of us were lost in our own world, oblivious of Holmes and Watson.

"Well they're open now, they're more than open, they're practically falling out," he replied, unable to take his wide open, practically falling out grey eyes off me. I had dreamt of a moment like this and could hardly believe it was really happening.

Holmes cleared his throat. "If we are going out to dinner we really should make a start or we won't get a table," he said.

I looked over at him and smiled. "All right, I'll just get my cloak."

"I'll get it," offered Lockie, hurrying to Watson's bedroom for my cloak.

"Joan Watson Hudson, I do believe you have bewitched my son," said Holmes.

"Do you disapprove?"

He shook his head. "On the contrary, I couldn't be more delighted. I can't think of anyone I would rather have as a daughter-in-law than you."

An imp of mischief rose in me and I couldn't resist saying, "What makes you think we will get married. We might just live in sin."

"Not while I'm alive," he declared. "I may have done the wrong thing with his mother, but I don't want that to become a family tradition."

"I concur," added Watson.

Lockie returned at that moment with my cloak and draped it over me gently. "My arm, milady," he said, offering me his arm.

I smiled again and flashed my father a wink.

He understood and smiled back.

Lockie opened the door for me and escorted me downstairs, and, he helped me into the cab. I wasn't quite sure that I knew how to cope with all this attention; it was unexpected to say the least. In the cab, I smiled at him and to my surprise, he blushed.

CHAPTER SIX

We had a lovely dinner. I was fussed over by all three men—Lockie most of all. I'd be a liar if I said I didn't enjoy it. Around nine o'clock, Holmes took Lockie aside. I saw him slip him some notes and tell him something. Then he patted him on the shoulder, before they returned to the table.

"Watson and I are going home now, but no need for you youngsters to come," said Holmes.

"Yes, I am rather tired, I had an early morning," said Watson, standing up hurriedly.

I smiled at his falsehood. He wasn't that tired.

"Seeing we missed the New Year's Eve party, I thought we might go somewhere tonight to make up for it," suggested Lockie.

"We could try out those ballroom dancing lessons we took," I agreed.

"Uh huh."

"Good night, Joan, Sherlock," said Watson. "Don't stay out all night."

Holmes also wished us goodnight and they left.

"Dad suggested a place we can go," said Lockie. We collected our coats and caught a cab to an elegant building called the Palace Dance Hall."

"Wow, this is some place," I said as we entered. Couples were waltzing, most were dressed in formal wear, but some were like me, dressed in clothes suitable for wear anytime of the day, depending on its accessories.

"Shall we?" asked Lockie with a grin, taking me into his arms.

We waltzed out onto the floor to be lost in the crowd. Lockie was a very graceful dancer and I wasn't doing too badly either. It was a fairy tale night. I didn't want it to end, but of course, like all things it eventually had to.

On the ride home, we snuggled into each other.

"I'm sorry, Joan," said Lockie softly.

"For what?" I asked curiously.

"For being blind." He looked into my eyes, his face serious. "You know there has never been anyone else but you, don't you? You have been with me all my life. You are my life. I know I haven't always treated you respectfully, and I've taken you for granted, but I've never really seen you—well, not since you grew up. I never noticed you changing from my mate into a woman…"

"Hey, I'm still your mate," I countered.

"Yes, in every sense of the word," he responded. He leant down and kissed me: really kissed me. No brotherly peck this; and no disappointment.

"Why haven't I done this before," he breathed, a trifle heavily when our lips parted.

"'Coz you're an idiot," I returned affectionately.

"Uh huh," he agreed, leaning forward again. We were still kissing when the cab pulled up in Baker Street. The cabby had to interrupt us with a discreet cough. Lockie paid him and tipped him generously. Holmes had given him his key so we let ourselves in quietly as the house was dark and silent. We were using the two spare rooms downstairs. Lockie escorted me to my door. He kissed me again, tenderly, and then stepped back.

"Um, Lockie," I began, a little hesitantly. "I don't want you to get the wrong idea, but could you…uh…come in and undo me?"

"Undo…?" he was momentarily puzzled, and then grinned with understanding. "Oh—the Victorian's secret, huh? We won't tell your dad."

I smiled. After I took off my dress and he had undone the corset, he slipped his hands around my waist.

"Lockie," I chided.

"It's all right, I'm just checking."

Confused, I turned to him. "Checking what?"

"You don't really need a corset, do you? That figure—that's all your own isn't it?"

"One hundred per cent natural," I agreed with a smile.

"Will I be seeing more of it?"

"Eventually. Goodnight, Lockie."

He looked at me with a woebegone expression. "Can't I…?"

"No."

“Goodnight, Meanie,” he responded dejectedly, giving me a hang dog look.

“That rejected lover look doesn’t suit you,” I said with a grin.

He grinned back. “Can’t blame a fellow for trying, can you?”

“No…but I would if you hadn’t.”

He went out chuckling.

CHAPTER SEVEN

It seems that contrary to returning home after dinner, Holmes had made several calls and put word out on the street, looking for the clones. The trail was too old for us to use the scanner. We first needed to get a trace on where they had last been sighted and take it from there.

We had a late breakfast—it was nearly nine thirty. I was wearing the other dress that my father bought me, one more suited to work.

"I forgot to check in with Mortimer yesterday," said Lockie after we finished breakfast. "I'm afraid something distracted me," he added flashing a brazen wink at me.

"Better do it now then," I advised.

He activated his com link and checked in with Mortimer.

"Glad you called, I was beginning to worry," greeted Mortimer. "We have recorded a further five time jumps since you left. They seem to be visiting different time periods. Don't know why as yet."

"Does that mean they're not in 1892 anymore?" asked Lockie.

"No, they're still there. They seem to have made it their headquarter time period, though I'm not sure why. They are travelling and returning."

"Have there been any changes in history?" asked Holmes.

"No, Mr Holmes, none that I can detect, but if there are changes I would not be aware of them because it would be part of our history and we are none the wiser."

"Of course, my apologies, this time travel business is rather confusing at times."

"To put it mildly," muttered Watson.

"Actually, I think Dad is on the right track, Mortimer. Look through history and check if any valuable artworks have gone missing in the past, or jewelry, gold, whatever. Think how easy it would be to zip back into the past, steal something that you know is valuable, which may not be at the time, and bring it to the future. They could make a fortune."

"Also check for unlisted works that have turned up," added Holmes. "Like an unknown Rembrandt that has suddenly come on the market, for example. Rather than stealing paintings, it would've easier for them to go back and meet the masters and buy the paintings direct."

"Yes, I'll do that. Check in with me again tonight, I should have more information for you then," said Mortimer. "Have you had any luck at your end?"

Not yet. Dad has feelers out though, so we are hoping to hear something sooner or later," Lockie explained.

"All right. Keep looking. Mortimer out."

"That's amazing," said Watson, shaking his head. "To think a device so small allows you to communicate with someone one hundred and thirty-five years into the future."

"Oh, we have all manner of new gadgets," I said with a smile.

"It probably wouldn't be a bad idea if we checked out Sotheby's," suggested Holmes. "After all if the clones are in this century, they have to be able to live—to do that they need money."

"You know, the easiest way to get money would be through gambling," said Watson as an idea came to him.

"Gambling is too chancy," disagreed Lockie.

"Ordinarily. But if you had future knowledge of which horses were racing and who won, it would be a sure thing."

"Good point, Watson. As the turf is your forte, perhaps you can check it out. We all know what Mycroft looks like, so get in touch immediately if you spot one of him."

"All right," agreed Watson.

"Joan and I will go to Sotheby's," offered Lockie.

"I will stay here in case word comes in from my irregulars," said Holmes. "And Lockie, remember, there is a time for work and a time for pleasure. Do not let the latter distract you from the former."

"Don't worry. Joan won't let me." He smiled at me.

"Well, someone has to keep you under control," I replied, causing my father to smile. I think he sometimes had to play that role with Holmes. Protect him from taking undue risks.

"I never asked, Joan. Did you have a good time last night?" he asked.

My answer was a smile and we exchanged significant looks.

*****

We all joined up again late afternoon. Lockie and I had no luck at the auction houses, nor any of the pawn shops that we visited. We were hoping that Watson or Holmes were more successful.

As soon as my father walked in the door, I knew he had news. He was positively beaming. Yes! I thought. It seems his idea paid off. That's one in the eye for those future critics who accused him of being a bumbling idiot compared to Holmes.

"We're all here, so you might as well tell us your good news, Watson," said Holmes from where he was relaxing before the fire.

"A man resembling Mycroft's description is a regular visitor to the track. He bets heavy and always wins. The bookies are leery of him. They don't want his custom, but they daren't refuse. One bookie refused and the clone throttled him within an inch of his life. He dresses flashy, drinks heavily and often has a woman of low repute hanging on his arm."

"Doesn't sound like the Mycroft we know, does it?" mused Holmes. "Still that could be due to the mutation of his genes. When was he last there?"

"Yesterday."

"Did they know when he was likely to come again?"

"Not exactly. But they did say he comes thrice a week…and he's only been once so far this week."

"Well done, Watson. All we need do is keep watch for him. Then we'll follow him home and hopefully he will lead us to where the others are. There is no point in apprehending just the one," said Holmes.

"Lockie and I can go keep watch," I offered.

"No," disagreed Holmes. "If the gambling clone is Mobius, he will recognize Lockie. You and Watson would be a better pair. You can take your scanner with you in case you lose track of him visually. Also, if he likes the ladies, he would be less likely to suspect you. You may even be able to get closer to him."

"No!" Lockie objected forcefully. "That's too dangerous. I won't have Joan taking a risk like that. Mobius almost strangled me and she's…"

"Sherlock!" I stamped my foot down angrily. "I am a trained and qualified agent. I can look after myself. Don't think that the change in our relationship is going to stop me from doing my job. I am not about to quit for you or anyone else, so don't get all highhanded and protective on me."

Holmes looked from me to his son, waiting for his response with interest. He appeared to be rather amused by the whole thing.

Lockie shuffled his feet for a moment, uncomfortably. "It's just that I care about you and I worry…"

"And you think I don't worry whenever you're off on a mission without me? When you are on the scene and I'm stuck in the surveillance van?" I asked a little more gently. "How do you think I felt when you went back to 1852 the other day on your own?"

"1852? That was you, wasn't it, Junior?" said Holmes suddenly, looking at his son with renewed interest. He reached into his pocket and pulled out his watch chain. Attached to the chain was a gold coin. "I believe you gave me this."

Lockie smiled. "Yeah. I was chasing after Mobius. Met you at the fairground. You looked cute, Dad."

"You saved me from a beating. Thank you."

"Anytime."

"What's this?" asked Watson in confusion.

"I'll tell you later, Watson," promised Holmes.

"All right," said Lockie. "I'm sorry, Joan. I don't mean to come on all heavy. I just don't want to lose you. You will be careful, won't you?"

"We know who the reckless one is in this partnership don't we," I returned. "Besides, Dad will be with me and he's saved Holmes' butt on more than one occasion."

"True enough," agreed Holmes, "but I wouldn't have described Watson's help in quite those terms."

CHAPTER EIGHT

The next day Dad and I went to the race track. It was fairly boring waiting around, especially as we couldn't bet. I knew that my father had once had a bit of gambling problem and he wasn't too keen to get started again.

It was perhaps one o'clock when I gripped Dad's arm and said, "Look there!"

He looked. One of the clones was approaching. He was dressed in a maroon frock coat, floral red and white vest, a gaudy yellow cravat, long scarf and top hat, plus draped around his shoulders was an expensive grey woollen cloak with red velvet lining.

"He looks exactly like Mycroft," Watson observed.

I pulled the scanner out of my purse and trained it on the clone. "It's Mydas, not Mobius," I said, feeling a little relieved. After all we knew Mobius was violent, but we weren't sure about the other two as their genes were mutating individually.

For the rest of the day we followed him around discreetly as he wagered large sums of money, and won.

"You know, Dad," I said with a faint smile. "If you want to make some extra money, now is the time—just bet on the same horses as Mydas. He's got future information. You would be guaranteed of a win."

His eyes lit up. "That's a thought isn't it?" Then his face fell as he added, "But that would be cheating."

"So? I'm sure that those bookies have taken enough of your money in the past," I objected.

"True enough. Half my pension at times," he admitted ruefully.

"Well, there then."

He grinned at me. "All right, I'll get in line behind him at the next race."

The next two hours were pleasant. Watson bet on the same horses as Mydas and his pile of cash grew. He was grinning from ear to ear.

"I wish it was always this easy," he said.

It was coming on to the last race of the day. Watson was in line to place a bet, but was held up by a slowpoke of a punter in front of him. Mydas was returning to the members stands. I decided that I would try and make contact and see what happened from there. I moved towards him casually and accidently-purposely bumped into him.

"Oh, I'm so sorry, sir!" I exclaimed.

He stepped back a pace and looked me over avariciously. "Not at all my, dear. Couldn't be bumped by a prettier specimen. What a sight for sore eyes you are, my lovely. Would you care to join me for a drink?"

I smiled at him. "I wouldn't mind, but I'm afraid I am here with someone."

"Oh, who?"

I nodded towards Watson, who was just coming away from the bookie.

"Him? Your father?"

"Oh no! My…er…my benefactor," I replied hesitantly.

"Hmm. I'm sure you could do much better than that, sweet young thing like you." He looked me over calculatingly.

"Oh, like who?" I asked, looking wide eyed at him.

"Like me for instance. I can be very generous."

"Really?" I pretended interest, looking him over as if I was assessing his potential as a new sugar daddy.

Watson was looking around for me. He saw me with Mydas and stopped, unsure of what he should do.

"Is he a big spender?" asked Mydas.

"Not really; he's a bad gambler."

"Not today though. Call him over," he ordered.

I beckoned to Watson who came over, looking suspiciously at Mydas.

"John dear," I said, before he could say anything. "I'd like you to meet…" Here I looked at Mydas inquiringly.

"Mydas Molesh," he introduced, offering his hand to Watson. Molesh! Not very original, I thought. It was just an anagram of Holmes.

"John Watkins," said Watson as they shook hands.

"Your charming companion here has been telling me you like the horses, sir, but are not always so lucky."

"True enough," replied Watson. He wasn't quite sure what was going on, but was willing to go along with it.

"Lucky today though," added Mydas, his grey eyes piercing Watson's.

Watson suddenly felt as though he was in Mycroft's imposing presence. "Uh...yes." He was discomfited by the other's stare.

"You have been following me and betting on the same horses," accused Mydas.

Watson coloured, but stood up straighter and replied, "There's no law against that! I couldn't help noticing that you seem to be picking the winners. I saw no reason why I shouldn't bet on the same horses."

Mydas grinned suddenly. "I can't blame you for that. In fact I congratulate you. I'm surprised no one else has thought of doing that before."

Watson sighed with relief.

Me too. For a moment there I thought Mydas would take exception to being copied. At that moment there came a faint beeping from Mydas' pocket.

"Excuse me a moment," he said hurriedly and moved away from us, taking something out of his pocket as he walked.

"Looks like he's got a mobile," I said.

"A telephone?"

"Yes. Though I wonder how it works here in this time period."

"Don't ask me, you're the techno wizard of the family."

I smiled at him. "Techno wizard—that's a pretty impressive word, Dad."

"I did learn a few things in the 21st century," he returned, also smiling.

"Perhaps it's more like a walkie-talkie than a phone. They wouldn't be dependent on phone networks and such."

"Perhaps," agreed Watson, although I could see he had no idea what I was talking about.

"When he comes back I'm going to lead him on a bit," I said. "By the way, Dad, he thinks I'm your floozy." I couldn't help grinning at Watson's surprised expression in response to that. "Maybe he'll invite us home."

Mydas returned. "It seems I have to leave."

"Oh!" I tried to look disappointed.

“A pleasure meeting you both.” He bowed and took my hand in his to kiss. When he let it go, I felt a card in my hand and quickly concealed it, as if I didn’t want Watson to know. He smiled at me, shook Watson’s hand, and then hurried away.

“Quick, let’s follow him!” cried Watson, starting after him. As we moved, a crowd surged in front of us on their way to the payout booth. They obstructed us for a few crucial moments; long enough for us to lose sight of Mydas. With effort, we cleared the crowd.

“I’ll use the scanner,” I suggested, putting words to action. Within minutes we had picked up his trail and were moving forward again. I was so intent on watching the scanner that I never noticed the two drunks having an altercation ahead and to the left of me.

Suddenly, I was sent reeling as one of the drunks crashed into me. The scanner went flying and hit the ground, breaking into pieces. As if that wasn’t enough, some fool also stepped on it in an attempt to help me up. I looked at it in dismay. Watson checked quickly to see if I was all right, before deserting me to hurry through the crowd in search of Mydas. I was crawling around on hands and knees picking up the scattered pieces of the scanner by the time he returned.

“I lost him,” said Watson miserably.

“You think that’s bad, look at the scanner.”

He helped me pick up the pieces; we were both thinking the same thing. We had stuffed up bad. If it had been Holmes or Lockie, they’d probably be right on his tail.

“I’m sorry, Joan,” said my father.

I shook my head. “Don’t be silly. It’s not your fault. I’m the trained agent here.”

“Now who is the one being silly? It’s not your fault either,” he replied, trying to console me. As I dropped the broken pieces into my purse I saw the card that Mydas had given me. In the excitement I had forgotten about it. I quickly took it out. On its back was scribbled in pencil:

THE RIALTO – 5 PM SATURDAY

I grinned and waved the card under Watson’s nose. “We haven’t lost him. He wants to meet me tomorrow.”

Now Watson also smiled.

"Excellent. We can follow him home tomorrow. Well done, Joan, dear."

I felt better now.

Back at Baker Street, as we made our way upstairs, we could hear a violin playing. On entering, we found it was Lockie who was the musician whilst Holmes sat by listening intently.

Lockie looked across at us as we entered. "Hey, guys. How did it go?"

"Adequately," I replied, causing him to narrow his eyes. He put the rare Stradivarius violin down and stepped in front of me. "Okay, what went wrong?"

"Hold out your hands and close your eyes," I instructed. He did and I emptied my purse into his hands.

He opened his eyes and his mouth fell open with surprise. "The scanner?"

"Slight mishap."

"What about the clone," asked Holmes. "Did he turn up?"

"Yes. It was Mydas," I said. I calmly took off my coat and made myself comfortable in front of the fire.

Watson smiled faintly, but said nothing, also keeping the two Holmes' in suspense.

"Well?" prodded Lockie finally, impatiently.

"He wants me to meet him for a clandestine rendezvous tomorrow," I said.

"What! No way!" objected Lockie.

"Not so fast, Lockie," interrupted Holmes. "I take it you were not able to follow him home."

Watson shook his head. "We got caught in a crowd. A couple of fighting drunks knocked Joan over; that's when she dropped the scanner. By the time we managed to get free, we had lost him."

"However," I continued, 'before leaving us, Mydas slipped me his card with the invitation written on it. I'll meet him tomorrow. You can follow him home from the Rialto. It will be easier."

Holmes nodded. "What was he like?" he asked.

"Lecherous. Nothing at all like Mycroft in character. He's the spitting image in looks though, although quite a dandy."

Mycroft will be pleased to hear that," returned Holmes with a faint smile tugging at his lips. I knew that he was joking. Mycroft would be mortified if anyone who knew him saw Mydas and assumed it was him.

"You did well, Joan," complimented Holmes.

I smiled and poked my tongue out at Lockie: He merely put his thumb to his nose and waggled his fingers at me.

CHAPTER NINE

The next day I put my best dress on (the one that got Lockie a little excited), and made ready to go to the Rialto. Lockie and Holmes were coming in with me, whilst Watson was going to wait outside with the hired carriage. He couldn't come in because Mydas would recognize him from the day before.

"Don't worry, Watson. Junior and I will look after her," promised Holmes.

At the Rialto, we separated. Holmes and Lockie wandered over to the bar, whilst I sat in the foyer. I could see them through the open doorway and vice versa. I only had to wait about ten minutes before Mydas turned up. He was dressed in a khaki green coat with red silk edged lapels. Very colourful and dapper. He really was nothing like Mycroft, who always dressed so conservatively. This clone considered himself a ladies man.

I smiled at him when I saw him and he came over smiling effusively. He sat down beside me and draped an arm familiarly around me. He certainly didn't waste any time. Over his shoulder I could see Lockie's indignant face. He was half off his bar stood and had Holmes' restraining hand on his shoulder.

"What a pleasure it is to see you, my dear," greeted Mydas.

"The pleasure is mine, Mr Molesh," I returned demurely.

"Mr Molesh makes me feel old, call me Mydas. I wasn't sure if you would come."

"Let us say that I am open to better offers," I said.

He smiled, understanding me completely. "And Mr Watkins?"

"He always has his wife to turn to if he gets lonely."

Mydas stood up and held out his hand to me. "I believe I offered you a drink yesterday."

We strolled into the lounge room just off the bar, where respectable ladies were welcome. Mydas ordered champagne for me and a straight whiskey for himself. We sat down on a settee in a secluded corner. He sat close to me, one arm around my waist, which he squeezed, often. He leaned close and slobbered a bit, kissing my neck. Lockie's face was a study. I must confess, I did not find Mydas' attention particularly appealing; actually it was nauseating, but it was almost worth putting up with it just to see Lockie's face. Who would have thought that in just two short days he could go from disinterest to jealousy?

"So, Mydas, dear, why don't you tell me about yourself?" I said, moving away from him a little. He proceeded to tell me he was an entrepreneur that had, like his name, the Midas touch. I laughed at his pun, feeling it was expected.

"Do you live in London?"

"Of course. I have a house on Kensington Park Road."

"Really? Ooh, there are all those lovely nice posh houses along there. You must be rich, Mydas," I cooed. "I'm envious. I've always wanted to live in a house like one of those." I smiled invitingly at him.

As we chatted, I managed to pour my champagne out into the large potted plant beside the settee.

He polished off his whiskey and ordered refills.

Holmes and Lockie had moved closer and taken arm chairs nearby where they could watch us discreetly.

I continued to encourage him to drink and pump him for information. The more alcohol he drank, the more voluble he became, and unfortunately for me, the more active his hands became.

Lockie was looking more thunderous by the moment.

I snuggled up to Mydas and said, "What's your house number, Mydas, honey? Is it twenty-six? That's my favourite number…"

He grinned foolishly at me. "I'm not going to tell you that. I will tell you the house used to belong to Lord Gerald Vosper."

"Ooh, really?" I pretended awe.

"Uh huh. He lost it over a card game," bragged Mydas.

"To you—ooh, you're so smart, Mydas." I nuzzled him, then leant back and offered him his refilled glass. He gulped it down, so I poured him a refill.

"Do you live alone?"

"No, my two brothers live with me. But don't worry, sweetheart, we'll practically have a whole wing to ourselves. Enough privacy for you?"

"I'm sure it is. Have another drink, Honey," I offered him. I could see it wasn't' long until the drink won.

He gulped it down.

I noticed Holmes signaling me. "Mydas," I said, pushing his hands away as they groped at me. "It's not very private here. Why don't we go to your place?"

"All right," he agreed quickly. He stood up and almost overbalanced and fell on me on.

I pushed myself away quickly. I didn't fancy him landing on me. Standing up he put his arms around me and I around him to steady him enough to get him outside. Holmes and Lockie could help me once we were out.

The cold air hit him and he reeled. He would have fallen but for Holmes coming up and catching him.

"Thank you, my good man," said Mydas, his voice a little thick with drink.

"Let me help you into a cab, sir," offered Holmes.

"Thank you, thank you," was the merry reply.

Holmes led him towards the waiting carriage.

I moved ahead and opened the door.

When they reached it, Mydas made another grab for me just as Lockie came up. I evaded his hand and he looked around at Lockie in surprise. "Wha—?"

Lockie's right fist shot out and landed on his jaw. He slumped against the carriage.

"Junior!" growled Holmes, "what did you do that for?"

"He was mauling Joan, and…uh…he was starting to get suspicious."

"You could have waited until we had him in the carriage," Holmes chided. "Now we have to lift him!"

"Oh. Sorry, Dad."

With lots of huffing and puffing they managed, with Watson's help, to get Mydas into the carriage. When Watson climbed back up to the driver's seat, Holmes rubbed at his back.

"I'm getting too old for this."

Lockie grinned, whilst I looked at him and said sweetly:

"I wouldn't have thought you were the jealous type, Lockie."

"Jealous? Who me?"

"Yes. I saw your face in there."

"I wasn't jealous. I just didn't like the way you were behaving, why it was positively disgusting. I could have thrown up."

"I am sure it wasn't very pleasant for you, Joan, but how did you do?" asked Holmes.

"He wouldn't tell me the address. Just said it was a house that belonged to Lord Gerald Vosper who lost the house to him in a card game. It's situated on Kensington Park Road. Is that any help? The other two clones live with him."

"It's a big help," replied Holmes smiling. "I know the place. There is a lot to be said for the use of female operatives. No man would have been able to entice so much information out of him."

"Then he looked up at Watson. "Watson, drive to Mycroft's house, I have an idea."

"You're going to substitute Mydas with Mycroft," guessed Lockie.

Holmes nodded. "Yes. Mycroft can go in and get hold of the laptop. Once we have that we can round up the other two. You can contact Mortimer from Mycroft's and have him retrieve Mydas."

Watson pulled up in front of Mycroft's lodgings. Mydas was coming round, much to Holmes' relief. I'm sure he wasn't relishing the idea of carrying him up a flight of stairs.

"Joan, we'll take Mydas in. Can you go across and fetch Mycroft from the Diogenes club? That's where he will be at this time of the day."

"Sure." I hopped out and went across the street to the club, whilst Holmes, Lockie and Watson let themselves into Mycroft's building. Holmes had a key to his brother's flat.

At the Diogenes club, I stopped at the concierge's desk. "Could you please ask Mr Mycroft Holmes to return to his lodgings immediately?" Then I went out and waited for him outside. Less than a minute passed before Mycroft emerged.

"Mr Holmes," I called.

He turned. "Joan, what's going on?"

We've got one of the clones."

"At my place?" He sighed. "Why didn't you take him back to Baker Street...No, don't answer that. I have a feeling I am not going to like the answer. Sherlock's behind it, isn't he?"

I smiled innocently at him. There was something about the real Mycroft that was missing in the clones. They may have had the same brain capacity but he seemed to have a more imposing presence than Mortimer. He also seemed more confident and self-assured. I guess nothing beats the original.

He sighed again.

We walked across the road to his place. Upstairs in his rooms, Mydas was slumped on the settee, snoring softly.

"What an appalling taste in clothing," said Mycroft looking at him.

"Mycroft, we need your assistance," began Holmes.

"You want me to impersonate him," replied Mycroft, starting to undo his coat.

"Joan, be so kind as to wait in the other room while we change these two," ordered Holmes.

With a bit of effort they managed to undress Mydas, and then instead of dressing him, they wrapped him Mycroft's dressing gown, whilst Mycroft donned his finery.

"You can come out, Joan," called Lockie.

"Don't you look dashing, Mr Holmes," I said to Mycroft, smiling at him.

"I look ridiculous," returned Mycroft, after he buttoned up the green coat.

Lockie activated his communicator and got hold of Mortimer. "We've got one to beam back, Mortimer," he said.

"You've caught one of the clones?" asked Mortimer, his voice coming across clearly.

"Mydas. He's pretty harmless. Just likes the ladies. Mycroft is going to impersonate him and get hold of the laptop. We will apprehend the other two after we have retrieved the computer."

"Excellent, good work, Lockie, oh and the rest of you also. Is Mycroft there?"

Lockie held the com link out to Mycroft. "He wants to talk to you."

"Mycroft here. Sorry to hear about Myron."

"Yes, it was quite a shock. How are you, Mycroft?"

"Fine. I can't say I am too impressed with these clones though."

"Er…yes…" Mortimer sounded hesitant.

"Oh, don't be too hard on him, Uncle Mycroft," said Lockie. "He had a rough trot, what with Myron being killed and copping the blame for the storm and the errant clones. It wasn't his fault you know."

"Mortimer," interrupted Watson, who had been examining the unconscious clone. "When you get Mydas back do a complete examination. I don't think he is well. His pulse is slow and thready, his breathing is quite laboured, and I don't like his colour."

"Will do, Doctor. Lockie can you attach a transponder to him?"

"Done."

"Ready to transport now, please stand back," advised Mortimer.

We all moved as far away from Mydas as we could. He shimmered a moment and then disappeared.

CHAPTER TEN

With Mydas gone and Mycroft ready, we headed to number thirty-nine Kensington park Road.

"Mycroft, when we get there, go in, find the lap top—you know what it looks like and come out. As soon as you're out, we'll move in and apprehend the other two."

"Why can't we just apprehend the two clones first?" asked Watson.

"They're tricky. They will only need a moment to get hold of the laptop and zoom away to another time period and beyond our reach. If we get hold of the time machine first, they'll have nowhere to go," explained Holmes.

Watson pulled up in front of the address and Mycroft got out. We stayed down low, so that if anyone was looking out the windows they wouldn't see us.

"Good luck, Mycroft," said Holmes softly.

Mycroft let himself into the house using Mydas' key. Watson drove the carriage away further down the street and we disembarked. We all made our way back towards the house, finding cover in the garden of the home opposite.

We waited. After what seemed an interminable time, Holmes glanced at his watch. "Something's wrong," he said.

"Let's barge in," suggested Watson, all for action.

"No," disagreed Lockie. "Maybe they're not at home and Mycroft is searching for the laptop. Give him more time."

"But if no one was home, Mycroft would have signaled us," I added.

Holmes looked a little anxious as he stared towards the house. It was one thing for him to take risks with his own safety, another to put someone else at risk. "I'll go across and check it out," he decided. As he was about to stand up, a hansom turned the corner and pulled up in front of the house.

"It's only one of them," I said.

"I'm going over." Holmes stood up. At that moment we all sighted the two struggling figures as they staggered in front of a window. As the other clone had just entered, we knew it wasn't him as there hadn't been enough time, which meant that the second clone was in the house fighting with Mycroft.

"Hurry!" cried Holmes as he leapt over the three foot high bush. Lockie followed. Watson and I ran around. The two Holmes' put their shoulders to the front door and it gave way under their force. They staggered over the threshold, regained their balance and ran towards the room where the fighting was. Holmes and Watson had drawn their revolvers, and Lockie his vaporizer.

Mycroft was struggling in the grasp of his double, whose grey eyes gleamed with unholy savagery. Despite the situation, or perhaps because of it, I noticed that the clone's clothing was heavily stained with fresh blood. To my relief, I also noticed that Mycroft wasn't bleeding, so it wasn't his blood.

"Mobius, let him go!" cried Lockie, raising the vaporizer, only he dared not fire for fear of hitting Mycroft.

The second clone, which had to be Morlan, was also screaming at Mobius to release Mycroft, but Mobius was in a violent, uncontrollable rage. Morlan held the laptop. I saw him activate it, run forward and grab Mycroft's arm, jerking him away from Mobius. Then the two of them disappeared in a flash, leaving Mobius behind in a spitting, snarling fury. Three guns came up but none had the chance to fire.

Mobius was hurtling towards them at full speed. One fist struck Watson, another Holmes, sending them reeling, whilst he bowled right into Lockie, causing him to reel back.

Lockie hit the wall with a thump and collapsed.

I leapt out of the way to avoid being run down by Mobius as he charged like a mad bull. As soon as he was past, I took off in pursuit. I was unarmed but thought that the least I could do was keep track of him. Holmes and Watson followed, but Mobius had a head start on us and he was quick; moving with a speed that belied his bulk.

He spotted our empty carriage and leapt aboard, whipping the horses into movement instantly. Holmes ran after the carriage for a short way then stopped as Mobius turned the carriage and came charging down the street, no doubt intending to run him down.

There was a young constable crossing the street just ahead of us. Holmes leapt forward yelling to him to run. The man did not hear, he seemed to be totally unaware, until Holmes threw himself bodily at him, knocking him out of the path of the speeding carriage. They crashed to the ground. The carriage missed them by mere inches.

Holmes stood up and held out a hand to help the policeman up.

The young man was shaken and pale. "Y-you saved my life, sir!" he gasped.

"That's all right, why didn't you watch where you were going?" demanded Holmes.

"I was thinking about my girl," the other answered sheepishly. "May I have the honour of knowing your name, sir?"

"Sherlock Holmes."

"Sherlock Holmes! Why, you know my father, George Lestrade. I'm Simon." (Georgina's great grandfather and the man who Holmes saved to go on and have children, one of whom sired her).

Holmes nodded to him. "Nice to meet you. Just pay attention when you are crossing the street in the future. You may not be so lucky next time."

"Thank you, sir," he replied, and was about to say more when I interrupted, saying, "Where's Lockie?" I had only just noticed his absence.

"Back at the house," said Watson.

Holmes said a quick goodbye to Constable Simon Lestrade and as one, we all trooped back to the house.

Lockie lay where he had fallen.

I hurried over, all at once anxious. "Lockie!" I dropped to my knees beside him. "Oh God, Lockie don't be dead!"

His eyes fluttered, but remained closed.

"Please, Lockie, I can't live without you. I love you, please wake up," I sobbed, losing it totally.

Homes hovered anxiously, as Watson moved over. He was about to bend down to examine him, when Lockie opened his eyes and to my utmost surprise, grinned at me.

"So you love me do you, Joan honey?" He sat up, still grinning.

Watson stepped back, relieved, as I stared down at him, speechless at his chicanery.

"Ooh! Ooh!" I gave him a whack on the arm. "Ooh—how could you scare me like that? You...you beast!"

Holmes heaved an audible sigh of relief and said to Watson resignedly, "Children."

Watson smiled faintly and replied, "Inappropriate sense of humour. Reminds me of you."

Holmes' lips twitched in response to that, but he remained silent.

Lockie stood up, feeling at the back of his head. "Got a bump the size of an egg." He looked mischievously at me. "How long have you felt that way about me, Joan?" he asked.

"I take it back. Words uttered under duress or false pretenses don't count," I countered.

"Do too."

"Don't!"

"Do."

"They don't. Who could love a fool like you?" I sniffed.

He smiled at me and slipped an arm around my waist. "I know one girl," he whispered.

Before I could reply, his communicator beeped.

"Lockie here," he responded.

"Have you got them?" asked Mortimer.

The four of us exchanged glances. We had been distracted for a moment from the worsening situation.

"Uh…no. Mobius tried to kill Mycroft and Morlan abducted him via the time machine to get him away from Mobius, who was quite berserk."

"But you did get Mobius?"

"Uh…not quite. He's quick on his feet and strong as three men. He got away."

There was silence for a long moment, before Mortimer replied. "What's this about Mycroft? Is he all right?"

Homes moved forward. "I believe he will be. Morlan knows that he cannot kill Mycroft. If he does, he will cease to exist. That's why he abducted him—to save his life. Can you track where they've gone?"

"No. We picked up the transport signal, it's the second in the last fifteen minutes, but it has some kind of additional security coding attached."

"That will be their getaway time," I said.

"Their what?" asked Mortimer.

"Mycroft surmised that they would have a preprogrammed time period in the laptop in case of an emergency for a quick getaway," Lockie explained.

"It seems he was right."

"What about the transport prior to that, Mortimer?" asked Holmes.

"From 1888 to your time," replied Mortimer.

"I wonder what Mobius was doing in '88?" queried Watson, frowning.

"This situation is going from bad to worse," complained Mortimer.

"In which case it can only get better," said Holmes. "We will concentrate on finding Mobius; he appears to be the most dangerous of the three. Wherever he is, Mycroft is relatively safe. How is Mydas? Maybe you can ask him what the escape time was and the code."

"Mydas is in a coma, he's dying."

"What?" gasped Lockie with surprise.

"The multiple and frequent time traveling that he has been doing has destabilized his already erratic genetic matrix. He is deteriorating by the hour and hasn't very long to go," explained Mortimer.

"Then the other two could be affected as well," said Watson. "We might not have to worry about catching them. They may die of their own accord."

"That's a possibility, Doctor. It depends on the stability of their genetic matrix and how often they use the time machine. Mydas told me he was jumping forward each week, collecting back issues of the sporting pages, and then returning, so that he could be guaranteed a win on the horses. He has lived a rather decadent lifestyle since going back in time. Rich food, excess drink…and women of course," replied Mortimer.

"Keep us posted, Mortimer," said Holmes. "See if you can track down Mycroft. I have an idea about where Mobius will go next."

"Good luck." Mortimer signed off.

"What sort of an idea, Dad?" asked Lockie.

Holmes looked at him. Instead of answering he asked, "If you developed a bloodlust and were satisfying it in the past and then escaping to the future, and you no longer had a time machine, what would you do?"

Lockie thought for a moment, and then said, "I'd be looking for new victims in the present."

"Exactly." Holmes smiled approvingly at his son's grasp of the situation.

"Hang on," I interrupted, frowning slightly. "What makes you think Mobius has developed a bloodlust or that he's going into the past to commit murders?"

"You saw him, Joan. He was covered in blood. Unless he spends his free time in a slaughter house, which I doubt, then that was human blood on his clothes. From what I can gather from the signs around here, Mycroft came in and found the place empty. He began searching for the computer. Mobius appeared from the past. Perhaps the two conversed and Mycroft must have given himself away somehow. After all the clones are very different people from Mycroft. Mobius attacked him and well, we saw the rest."

"Mortimer said the transport had come from 1888, do you think—" Watson stopped mid-sentence and a look of horror crossed his face.

I saw what he was getting at. "He's Jack the Ripper!" I gasped.

Holmes nodded. "It is not implausible. In fact, it is highly probable. The Ripper always disappeared without a trace. Watson and I were on that case, but even we could find no clue as to his identity, or his whereabouts. Mobius zaps into the past, murders a woman and returns here straight after the deed."

"The man is demented," stated Watson.

"Very demented. I'm afraid his genes have mutated him into something wholly evil. He will not want to give up his hobby so easily. It is only a matter of time before he kills again, before he must kill again."

CHAPTER ELEVEN

Watson, Lockie and I returned to Baker Street. Holmes left us to meet with the street urchins that made up his band of irregulars. He wanted to get them looking for Mobius.

Meantime, I had to put up with Lockie's teasing on the way home. He sat next to me, wriggled up close and slipped both arms around me saying, "So, Joan honey, do you want to tell me how much you love me?"

"Shut up, Lockie," I replied, feeling a little embarrassed.

Watson smiled tolerantly, eyeing us with amusement. I knew he wasn't averse to Lockie as a prospective son-in-law. He had a great deal of respect and admiration for Holmes. I think he liked the idea of Holmes' son and his daughter getting together. The fact that he was an incurable romantic at heart also had something to do with his pleasure at seeing us together. He also knew how I felt about Lockie and that his current attentive behaviour was not exactly abhorrent to me, despite what I said.

"Shut up? Is that any way to talk to the love of your life?"

"It's the only way. Don't be a pain."

Lockie smiled at me, his eyes twinkling, he could be such a tease.

"You're a lot like your father, Lockie," observed Watson. "Perhaps a little more open with regards to revealing your emotions, but a lot like him nevertheless."

"I wish I'd known him growing up," replied Lockie, a trifle wistfully.

"He feels the same. As do I. I would have loved to have been there for all your milestones, Joan. I've always wanted children. I wasn't blessed in this century, but in your own, fate was kinder."

"You would have been a great dad." I smiled at him. "In fact, you are."

His eyes lit up at my compliment. "I've enjoyed spending time with you, with both of you. You know you are welcome to visit me anytime you are able."

"Thanks, Dad. I don't know how often we'll be able to do that once this clone business is sorted out. It wouldn't surprise me if they crack down a bit on time travel—it causes a lot of trouble."

At 221B, Lockie checked in with Mortimer and learnt that Mydas was not expected to see the day out. Also, they had been unable to override the security lockout on Mycroft and Morlan's location. Lockie asked him to check how many jumps to 1888 were recorded—seven so far—this coincided with the number of Ripper victims. It supported Holmes' theory.

After Lockie signed off, I said, "I guess that proves that we are going to stop Mobius. There were only seven ripper victims, he doesn't commit anymore."

"It could mean that, or it could simply mean that he starts killing in this time period instead."

What a depressing thought!

Holmes returned several hours later. He was hungry and looked rather tired. It had been a hectic day and God only knows how much ground he'd covered since he left us. Rather than bother Mrs Hudson, I went down to the kitchen and made him some sandwiches and brought them up. He was just lighting his pipe when I returned with the tray.

"For you, Mr Holmes," I said, putting the tray on the table.

He looked surprised, but pleased. "Thank you, Joan dear, that's very kind of you." He sat down and ate with gusto. When he'd finished, he pushed the empty plate away with satisfaction and relight his pipe. Lockie had been hovering—he was an impatient son-of-a-gun at times.

"Well, anything happening?"

"There's a great deal happening," returned Holmes placidly. "I'm having Mycroft's office, lodgings and the Diogenes club watched around the clock in case Mobius decides to impersonate him. The best place to hide is often in the open. We will be notified the minute he is sighted. Also I have scouts out scouring the Whitechapel district for him and the lower East End."

"Why there?" I asked.

"Bloodlust is like a disease. He feeds on it. The craving may strike him again and he will need to satisfy it. If he is bent on murder he will go somewhere familiar. He has terrorized

Whitechapel in 1888, it is logical to assume he will return there in '92."

"So what can we do in the meantime?" asked Lockie. "I hate waiting around."

"I'm afraid waiting is all we can do. So, for the moment we rest. It's late, we might as well sleep. Mobius was in a panic when he ran. It's possible he will lay low for a day or two, perhaps hoping that Morlan will come back for him."

"Do you think he will?" asked Lockie.

Holmes shrugged. "Who can say. He looked rather frightened when he took off with Mycroft. He might consider this an ideal opportunity to be rid of him."

Watson shook his head and said, "Who would have thought that the lightning would affect the clones in such a diverse manner. One violent, one lecherous and one, well, I don't know what Morlan is like."

"For Mycroft's sake, I hope he's the decent one of the three," said Holmes, rubbing tiredly at his eyes.

"At least he won't kill him," reassured Lockie.

"Unless he has suicidal tendencies. I've been thinking…Mydas is dying from the time travel, what if Morlan is also suffering? What if he is also dying and doesn't want to go on anymore. He may blame Mycroft for his unstable matrix. What if he decides to kill Mycroft to change history so that he never exists in the first place?"

Lockie and Holmes exchanged a private glance. Lockie put his hand on his father's shoulder. "Dad…I…"

Holmes placed his own hand over his son's in an open gesture of affection. "It's all right, Junior. It wasn't your fault. There was nothing you could have done to prevent him taking Mycroft. Anyway, Mycroft is not exactly helpless; he can look after himself in a sticky situation. Believe it or not, when he could be bothered, he could out box me. He always beat me when we were children. The clones may have his brains, but they do not have his experience or his composure under pressure."

"And besides," I added, "If he hasn't returned by the time we have to go back, I'll get to work on trying to break through the security lockout or maybe we can get Morlan alive and he'll tell us."

"Joan's right," agreed Watson. If anyone can break through a code, it is she. They'll bring Mycroft home again, Holmes, count on it."

Holmes gave him a weak smile. "Thank you, Watson. Now, on that note of cheer, let's call it a night."

I kissed Dad goodnight and on an impulse, as I passed Holmes, I leant down and kissed his cheek. He looked up at me and to my surprise, gave me a wink and a smile. I realized with a start that Dad had been right. Lockie was very much like his father, and not only in looks, but in sense of humour and character as well. It made me wonder if Holmes had been as carefree as Lockie in his younger years and why he chose to live the celibate life in this century.

The fact that he was attracted to Georgina proved he wasn't totally against dalliance with the opposite sex. What was it that made a man shun personal happiness for the sake of his work? I wondered if he ever got lonely. Maybe that's why he liked Dad's company. Watson filled the void, and was there in the role of companion and confidant. I felt a sudden rush of sympathy for Holmes, but turned away quickly lest he see it in my eyes. There was no room in his life for maudlin sympathy. But he had been happy with Georgina and he hadn't wanted to return. Only his duty and obligation to maintain the conformity of the time line sent him back.

CHAPTER TWELVE

The next two days were uneventful. Holmes and Watson appeared patient and unconcerned, but Lockie was chaffing at the bit.

"I hate all this waiting around," he complained. "My brain is bursting with things I want to do and I can't do any of it. How do you stand this inactivity, Dad?"

Holmes looked up from where he sat updating his commonplace books. "I meditate, now. I used to be like you, still am at times. My cure for inactivity and boredom was drugs. I wouldn't recommend it. It nearly killed me. But for Watson, it probably would have."

"No, I don't want to take drugs," said Lockie, frowning. "How did you get hooked on that habit anyhow?"

"I was in University. I was bored. Some fellows were going to visit the opium dens in China town and invited me along. I wasn't particularly keen on opium, but a fellow there offered me cocaine. I tried it. It took away my boredom. Foolishly I thought I could take it or leave it. By the time I met, Watson, I took it whether I was bored or not. It was just a good excuse."

"Not that good," countered Watson.

Holmes flashed him a smile and the two men exchanged companionable glances of times shared and past.

"IV drug use in your day, I mean now, wasn't that common. Not like in our times," said Lockie. "I see junkies and they gross me out. No, I don't ever want to take drugs. Anyway," Lockie looked across at me and added, "Joan wouldn't let me get started on something like that. She keeps me from mischief. She's always been able to cheer me up when I've got the dumps."

"It must be a generational occupation," teased Holmes. "The Watsons are bound by fate to look after us in each and every century."

Lockie chuckled. "Are you pleased, Dr. Watson…that Joan is carrying on the family tradition?"

"Someone has to. I am sure she will be much sterner with you than I have been with Holmes."

"Oh yeah, she's a bossy old thing."

"Liar! I am not." I protested.

"It must be a female thing," continued Lockie. "Mum can be bossy too."

The other two bachelors murmured in agreement.

"Well!" I said, pretending to be insulted. "It is obvious I'm outnumbered here by male chauvinists. I'm going downstairs to keep Mrs Hudson—the only other intelligent person in the house—company." I left, with their chuckles sounding at my back.

That evening Mortimer contacted us to tell us that Mydas was dead. The autopsy showed complete intracellular breakdown. He also mentioned that he died horribly and in incredible pain that no narcotic could ease.

"It was a blessing to see him go finally," he said. "It was like he was being tortured from the inside out. It was really awful to watch."

Next day, as we sat down to breakfast, Holmes flipped open his morning paper. Large black headlines glared at us:

JACK IS BACK!

"The Ripper!" I gasped.

Holmes quickly read the story and then summarized it for our benefit. "A prostitute named Mavis Allsop was found in a back alley in Whitechapel. She had been mutilated and disemboweled, similar to the Ripper murders of '88."

"Mobius," stated Lockie.

Holmes nodded. "This changes things. We cannot sit around and wait for him to come to us. We have to find him and stop him before he kills again."

"You were afraid this was going to happen, weren't you, Holmes," said Watson.

Holmes nodded again. "I'm surprised none of my scouts have reported in. Surely he has been seen by someone."

"So what are we going to do?" asked Lockie eager for action.

Holmes frowned, thinking, but I interrupted his thoughts.

"I'll dress up as a prostitute and lure him out," I said.

"No!" came the vehement reply from the three men simultaneously.

"Not on your life," added Lockie.

"Out of the question," declared Watson.

"No, Joan, it is far too dangerous," stated Holmes.

I stood, hands on hips. "Look here you guys. I'm not some weak helpless female. I can take care of myself you know."

"We're not saying you can't," Watson placated me. "It's just…"

"It's just that Mobius is too dangerous," continued Holmes when I faltered. "You saw him at the house. He's no match for a man. Mycroft was getting the worst of it and they were both equal in size, height and weight. How could any woman contend with him, no matter how competent she is?" He glanced across at Lockie and added, "I like your idea though. We'll dress Junior up."

"What!" gasped Lockie in shock. "Dress me in drag—no way! Never in a million years!"

His reaction brought grins to our faces. I was annoyed at their attitude towards me, although I will admit I wasn't too keen to tackle Mobius on my own, but it was almost worth it to see Lockie dressed up as a prostitute.

"It's either you Junior, or Joan," replied Holmes, using the one argument guaranteed to win him over.

"Not Joan. What about you, Dad? You've disguised yourself as a female before."

"We want it to be a young attractive female. I'm too long in the tooth for that. I can only dress as an old crone nowadays."

"I'm not attractive," said Lockie stubbornly.

"Yes you are, Lockie. Not out and out handsome, but there is something about you that attracts," I said.

"Yes, but you're biased," he argued.

"Shut up, Lockie, said Holmes copying my favourite phrase. "It's settled. We'll dress you up. You can trot about down in Whitechapel and try to attract Mobius. The rest of us will stay hidden, but keep you in our sights. When he appears, we'll corner him."

"Sounds easy enough, but this is Mobius we're talking about," Watson reminded Holmes.

"Lockie will have his vaporizer and we will be armed, Joan too."

I smiled at that. At least Holmes wasn't planning on leaving me at home while they staked out Whitechapel. Obviously he knew me better than that.

Holmes went out after breakfast to purchase a suitable disguise for Lockie and returned with several packages.

That evening, Lockie disappeared into Holmes' room with his father. Every now and again we could hear Lockie's voice raised in protest, at some comment from Holmes. An hour later, Holmes emerged and mimicked Watson from the other day, when he introduced me in my new dress.

"Allow me to present my lovely daughter—Shirley Holmes." He performed a theatrical gesture towards the door and was smiling broadly. Lockie did not appear, so Holmes added. "Be kind, she's a little shy."

I sniggered at that.

Finally, Lockie appeared—his face as red as his dress. The gown was a gaudy red and orange affair, high necked and figure hugging. He had a full bosom and long dark brown hair. Holmes had applied his makeup carefully, accentuating Lockie's eyes and lips.

Watson whistled and I clapped, grinning broadly.

I circled him, and pinched his backside, causing him to jump, and said in a southern American accent, "Now ain't you a purty lil' thing."

"Shut up, Joan!" he growled, face flushing in embarrassment.

"Oh, don't frown, Shirl, it will give you lines," I teased.

"Dr. Watson, tell her to shut up," Lockie entreated.

Watson smiled, "I would, but I'm too busy admiring you. Holmes, it's a shame you never had a daughter as well. Sherlock Junior makes a lovely girl."

"You're on her side," accused Lockie.

"Stop this nonsense, Lockie," chided Holmes, then as an aside to Watson he said, "I wouldn't let a daughter of mine dress like a tart."

"Dad!"

"No—just your son," grinned Watson.

Holmes chuckled. It was nice to see Lockie on the receiving end of the teasing for a change, and from his own father at that.

Holmes went to his desk and unearthed a colt .45 1873 civilian model Peacemaker, with a four and a half inch barrel. "This should suit you, Joan. It's not as big and heavy as some of the other guns around," he said, offering it to me. He also passed over a box of bullets. I set about loading it.

"Is that a new gun, Holmes?" Watson asked, curiously.

"Er, actually I bought it for you. It's your birthday present. I thought it was time you replaced that old thumb buster of a service revolver with something more efficient."

"Really? Why thank you, Holmes." Watson was as delighted as a child with a new toy. He came over and examined the gun with relish.

"The colt peacemaker is one of the best handguns ever made," added Holmes.

Lockie was having trouble finding a hiding place for his vaporizer.

Holmes went back into his room and returned with a rather large lady's bag, which he tossed to Lockie.

"If you don't have time to draw a gun, you can always clout him with your purse," I suggested.

"I'm starting to reconsider—maybe you should play this part," growled Lockie.

"Don't pout," I chided with a grin. "It's unbecoming in a lady."

"I'm not a lady!"

"Not dressed like that you're not."

Holmes draped a bright green cloak around Lockie's shoulders and put a dark seafaring man's coat on himself and a peaked cap.

"Let's go," he said opening the door.

CHAPTER THIRTEEN

We caught a cab to Whitechapel. In the cab, Holmes attached a beard and moustache and ran his fingers through his hair, combing it to the opposite direction. He looked immediately different.

"Go into a pub, Junior and make yourself seen. I'll be there as well to keep my eye on you and watch for any sign of Mobius. Stay for an hour, then exit. Walk around the streets for a bit. If you get no takers after half an hour, we will repeat the whole thing at another pub."

Lockie nodded.

"Watson and Joan will take up position outside to keep watch for Mobius and to follow you when you leave. I won't be far behind you. You are not to try and tackle Mobius on your own. If he's too dangerous for Joan, he's too dangerous for you." He clapped a hand to Lockie's shoulder. "We won't let anything happen to you."

"Oh, I'm not worried about that," said Lockie. "I just hate the thought of being caught dead dressed like this."

Holmes' lips twitched. "In that case I will make sure that you are not caught dead."

*****

I looked around the dark streets after the cab dropped us off, and shuddered. It was creepy down here in the slums. I could imagine the Ripper lurking in the shadows, looking for his next victim.

"I'll go in there," said Lockie, pointing to a dingy placed labelled as Dirty Nellies. Lockie moved ahead, whilst Dad and I found a hiding place behind a pile of lumber. Holmes waited a few moments, and then followed Lockie in.

The place stank of unwashed bodies and was noisy with laughter and cursing. Lockie circulated among the crowd, smiling at customers. Looking for all the world like a working girl, a successful one, as he had quite a few offers. He declined them on one pretext or another.

Outside, Watson and I watched the customers that entered. None fit Mobius' description or size. An hour and fifteen minutes passed before Lockie emerged alone. He looked about him, gathered his cloak in and started to walk slowly down the street. We kept him in sight.

Then a man emerged from a dark alley and also started up the street. I heard Watson hiss. The man passed a street lamp and his face had been briefly reflected. It was Mobius.

At that moment, Holmes joined us. "See him?" he whispered.

"Yes, he's after Lockie," I said, sounding a little anxious.

"Not for long," replied Holmes and started off after them rapidly. We kept to the shadows. Lockie stopped under a street lamp for a moment before moving on. I noticed he was clutching his bag tightly. I guess his nerves were jumpy, mine sure as hell were.

We watched as Mobius approached Lockie and saw him hold out some money. They exchanged a few words and Lockie agreed to accompany him. They started to move away towards a dark alleyway. We hurried forward. Mobius must have heard our footfalls for he whirled around. We ducked into cover. Lockie was trying to extricate the vaporizer from the purse, but it caught in the purse strings. He swung it at Mobius, and not a moment too soon. The moon glinted on the blade of a long knife in Mobius' hand. The bag hit him across the face, causing him to curse luridly.

Holmes leapt out of concealment with his gun raised. "Surrender, Mobius!"

Mobius snarled; he whipped off his cloak and threw it at Holmes. And as before, he ran. Holmes became entangled in the cloak and Watson tripped over the edge of it as he attempted to pursue Mobius.

I was the only one free to go, so I took off after him.

Lockie came after me, hampered somewhat by his dress.

I ran after Mobius as he turned down an alley and came to a sudden halt. It was a dead end! The hair stood up on my neck. Mobius had come down here, so where was he? I heard a soft footstep and turned, coming face to face with him. Mycroft was an imposing man. But a Mycroft with his grey eyes glinting wildly and red rimmed, lips coated with saliva as he drooled in anticipation of a bloodbath, was bloodcurdling. I saw the knife come up. I froze for a vital moment when I should have acted. He looked like the devil himself.

"Mobius!" called Lockie from the mouth of the alley, bringing the vaporizer up.

With a snarl and a quick movement, Mobius leapt forward and grabbed me. Using me for a shield and holding the knife to my throat, he turned to face Lockie. I'm not ashamed to admit I was absolutely terrified.

"Drop the gun or I'll slit her throat," said Mobius.

I felt the knife pricking my neck and warm blood trickle down.

Lockie's face was ashen.

It's funny what the mind thinks of at such a time. For me, all I could think of was that Lockie was in exactly the same position as Holmes had been when a crazed Moriarty had used Georgina for a shield. Of course, I could hardly advise Lockie to shoot me, as Georgina had of Holmes. A vaporizer didn't merely injure. It destroyed completely, no matter what part of the body was hit. Besides which, Mobius was just as likely to slit my throat just for the hell of it.

"Drop the gun," snarled Mobius, moving forward slowly. I was helpless in his grasp. At that moment, Holmes and Watson caught up and stopped in shock, no doubt reliving the scene. I heard my father growl a curse, but he was as helpless as Lockie.

"Back up," ordered Mobius, continuing to move forward gradually. None of the men could shoot for fear of hitting me.

That's when the idea struck me. My hands were free, so I reached my right hand down and slipped it into my coat pocket. I was wearing trousers and jacket for tonight's outing. I grasped the gun and carefully cocked the hammer back. I pointed the gun backwards in the pocket, said a silent prayer and pulled the trigger.

The explosion was loud in the silence. Mobius yelped and leapt back. I threw myself to the left. Holmes, Watson and Lockie all fired simultaneously. Mobius glared for a moment, then disintegrated into a clump of ashes.

I shivered and could feel reaction setting in. My neck was bleeding where the knife had cut it, but the cut was shallow. It was just the shock of my close call.

Lockie hurried forward and took me into his arms.

I hugged him closely. For a while there, I thought I would never get the chance again.

"I don't know what I'd do if I lost you, Joan," he murmured.

I cuddled and kissed him.

"If you two are done smooching," said Holmes, "We should return home." Despite his words, there was a hint of relief in his voice.

"Are you all right, Joan?" asked Watson anxiously.

"I will be," I replied. "He was too close for comfort."

We had to walk quite a few blocks before we found a cab. Lockie held onto me the whole time, not wanting to let me go. As for myself, I didn't want him to. We rode in silence.

Back at Baker Street, Watson treated my cut and then poured four brandies, neat, and handed them around. I wasn't much of a drinker, but the brandy put colour back in my cheeks. I hadn't realized I was looking so white.

Lockie quickly changed back to his male clothes and contacted Mortimer. "Mobius is dead," he reported flatly, when Mortimer answered.

"Good, good. The time machine was used again. I think Morlan has returned, or it could be Mycroft. Has he turned up?"

"No. We haven't seen either." Lockie logged off.

Holmes looked at us. "Why don't we call it a night," he suggested. "You could both use some rest."

I nodded.

Lockie slipped his arm around my waist as we went downstairs. Outside my door, he took me fully into his arms and said seriously, "For a while there tonight I thought I was going to lose you. I couldn't bear that. All teasing aside, I do love you, Joan. I always have. I want us to be together forever—will you stay with me?"

"Sherlock Holmes Lestrade, is that a proposal," I asked looking up into his intense eyes.

"Yes, I believe it is." He smiled tentatively.

I reached up and kissed him. “I can’t think of anyone I’d rather be with,” I breathed. It was a good ten minutes before we parted. I didn’t really want to, but I was an old fashioned sort of girl. The loose morals of our mother’s time had reverted back to more Victorian values. More young couples were now waiting until they were married before they got intimate. I liked this idea and Lockie was the supreme gentleman. We finally parted and said goodnight.

I had such a lovely dream that night and spared not a single thought for Mobius or my ordeal.

CHAPTER FOURTEEN

Next morning, Lockie asked me to wait downstairs while he formally asked my father for my hand. I agreed, but activated my com link so that I could eavesdrop. Shameless, I know, but what the heck.

I heard Holmes and Watson greet him.

"Er...Dr. Watson, I wonder if I may have a word with you, sir," began Lockie formally.

"Certainly. What about?" asked Watson, although from the tone of his voice I deduced that he had a pretty fair idea.

"Uh..."

I could picture, Lockie hesitating, suddenly nervous. Holmes nearby, no doubt puffing on his abominable pipe and trying to keep his face expressionless.

"Well, Dr. Watson, sir. I'd...um...like to have your permission for Joan's hand in marriage...and...uh...the rest of her too."

"I see," replied Watson. "Marriage is a big step, young man. Are you ready for such a commitment?"

"Sure," Lockie replied casually.

I could imagine Watson frowning at that.

"I mean...um...well...we've grown up together. Done everything together. I can't imagine life without Joan. I...I guess I don't feel complete without Joan by my side." This sort of expression of feelings was not something Lockie practiced much. I thought he wasn't doing too bad, after all I knew it didn't come easy to him. He, like his father was a very private individual that liked to keep his secret feelings bottled up inside. "An...and besides, we Holmes' are a loyal breed. Once we love a woman we stay faithful for the rest of our lives, right, Dad?"

"Something like that," agreed Holmes.

"Well, I do believe that," said Watson. "Just promise me you will never take her for granted."

"After yesterday when we came so close to losing her, there's no fear of that; that will never happen."

"In that case, welcome to the family...Son," replied Watson, smiling and offering his hand.

Lockie heaved a sigh of relief. "Whew! Thanks, Doc...Dad?"

"I'm happy for you, Son," approved Holmes. "It is a pleasure to me to know that you will never be alone. I doubt if you could ever find a finer girl than Joan."

"I wish I could come to the wedding," murmured Watson wistfully.

"We might be able to arrange something," grinned Lockie, and then he added into his communicator. "You can come upstairs now, Joan."

The dog! How did he know I was eavesdropping? I went upstairs and Dad hugged me. Over breakfast he smiled at Holmes and said, "You know Holmes, this means we are going to be related."

"True. It also means you are going to be related to Lestrade as well."

"Oh!" Watson's face fell at the thought, while the rest of us laughed. It was a merry meal. After breakfast however, Holmes brought us back to business.

"I've been thinking about Morlan. As Mycroft hasn't reported in, that transport yesterday must have been the clones. He is unlikely to return to the house, but we never really searched it properly. I think we should. We may find some clue as to his whereabouts."

"Joan and I can do that," offered Lockie. "You and Dr. Watson have done most of the work on the case, when it's supposed to be ours. We really should start to earn our keep, besides I don't think there will be any danger."

"All right. But if you do find a clue, come back here first. I would like to have the opportunity to interrogate Morlan—find out where he sent Mycroft."

"Count on it."

*****

At the house, Lockie and I searched it from top to bottom. In what we took to be Morlan's room, we found a receipt for warehouse rental, and not much else.

"What does he need with a warehouse?" I queried.

"Who knows, but I'd bet money that's where he is."

"No bet."

We returned to Baker Street and collected the other two, before heading out to the warehouse. Holmes picked the lock easily and we entered. We could hear faint music playing somewhere at the back. We followed the sound. Neither of us thought to draw a weapon and as it turned out, we didn't need to.

The warehouse was stacked high with art treasures and antiquities of all sorts—paintings, furniture, Egyptian relics, all sorts of rare and valuable goods. There was even a taxadermied dinosaur! It seems Morlan was a collector, a hoarder of antiquities. He must have used the time machine to go back into the past and pick up the items, then return here. God knows what he planned on doing with it all.

Lockie put a finger to his lips as we approached the door; the music was louder now. He opened the door cautiously. With a quick movement he jumped inside and we followed, only to stop in surprise. The room's occupant was a large woman. She whirled at our entrance, her face coated heavily with powder and rogue. I think four jaws dropped synchronously—for this was no female. It was Morlan! He looked so utterly ridiculous that we were too stunned for words.

When he saw us, his face crumpled and he looked down at his feet sadly. "I knew you would come," he said.

"Morlan, I presume," said Holmes, stepping forward.

"Yes, and you're Sherlock."

Holmes nodded. "Where's Mycroft?" he asked.

Morlan's face flushed and he looked suddenly guilty. "I only took him to stop Mobius from killing him. I didn't want to hurt him—truly I didn't."

Holmes' eyes narrowed. "What did you do to him?"

Now Morlan began to cry and all of a sudden I felt sorry for him. He wept as a woman might, and he looked ludicrous; yet his sobs were so pathetic that my heart went out to him.

I moved over and patted his shoulder. "There, there, Morlan, don't cry. We're not going to hurt you. Just tell us what happened?"

"It was an accident. I didn't mean to hurt him!"

"Morlan, stop blubbering and tell us what happened," demanded Holmes sharply.

Morlan turned a tear stained face up to him. His makeup had run leaving streaks down his chubby cheeks. "I…I activated the escape route. Mycroft thanked me for saving his life…th…then…h-he tried to take possession of the laptop. We were t-tugging at it…an…and he pulled extra hard. I let go. He fell backwards and hit his head. I saw bl-blood." Here he started to cry again.

"Pull yourself together man!" growled Holmes with disgust. "Was he alive? Did you check for a pulse?"

"N-no…I was so scared, so much blood! I grabbed the lap top and ran…" gasped Morlan, and then continued to wail.

Holmes grimaced. "In other words, you left him there to bleed to death."

"Mycroft can't be dead," said Lockie suddenly. "If he was it would have changed history and the clones wouldn't exist. Mycroft doesn't donate his genes until 1915. So he has to be alive."

Morlan stopped sobbing and looked up hopefully. "Yes! You're right!"

"I know I am," stated Lockie firmly.

"Why are you wearing that ridiculous dress?" asked Holmes, being both disgusted and curious. Obviously he was irritated at finding his brother's replica looking so foolish.

"I…I…like to dress this way. I think I should have been a female."

It was hard to hold down a smile at that. It was lucky Mycroft couldn't see him dressed like that, he would have been mortified. He had been disgusted enough at Mydas' garb.

"Morlan, where did you take Mycroft?" I asked gently."

"I'm not sure. I didn't stay long enough to get my bearings."

"Well, what is the lockout code? We'll be able to trace him ourselves if you tell us that," I said.

"I…uh…don't know it. It was Mobius who programmed the escape route in. All I did was activate it. We didn't need the code for our end; that was just for your benefit."

From the expression that crossed Holmes' face, I guessed that if I hadn't been with them, he would have started cursing fit to blister Morlan's ears. Always the gentleman, he refrained.

Instead, he just glared at Morlan, who looked like he was about to break into tears again at any minute.

"What were you going to do with all this stuff?" asked Lockie, indicating the treasures which surrounded us.

"Nothing. Just keep them. I like them."

"Look, Morlan, we know you didn't mean to hurt Mycroft, and you did save his life. Is there any way we can find out where you took him?" asked Lockie, keeping his voice level and calm, so as not to agitate the clone any more than was necessary. It was obvious that he was emotionally unstable.

Morlan was silent for a moment, then his face brightened. "It's still in the computer. If I activated it, we could all beam there."

"Good, good. Where's the laptop?" Lockie smiled encouragingly at him.

"I'll get it." Morlan jumped up and to my horror clambered onto a rickety chair to retrieve the laptop from the top of a cupboard. Though why in God's name he thought to hide it up there in the first place is beyond me. It was in his hand when one leg of the chair broke. Morlan fell, yelling in fear. He hit the ground with a crash and a thud.

The laptop fell from his hand and went sliding along the floor.

Lockie leapt forward and made a grab for it, but missed.

I winced as it hit the brick wall with a tinkling, crashing noise.

We turned our horror stricken faces towards it. No one moved. Finally, I bestirred myself and approached, dreading what I would find when I opened it. I picked it up and slowly opened the case. It was as bad as I feared. Slivers of glass fell out—the remains of the LED display. I pressed the on button, which caused sparks to fly and electricity to run along it.

"Ouch!" I yelped as I was zapped. The computer fell from my hands and crashed to the floor, several more pieces breaking off.

Lockie came over and looked down at it. He draped an arm around my shoulders and said, "Oops. We haven't exactly distinguished ourselves on this case, have we, Joan?"

"Scanner broken, laptop broken, Mycroft lost, not to mention Mobius escaping and killing another woman down in Whitechapel, and Mortimer's instruction to retrieve the laptop at all cost…yes, I think we can safely say we have stuffed up badly," I replied a trifle sarcastically I regret to say.

"Uh…what are you going to do with me?" asked Morlan.

"We'll have to take you back…" began Lockie.

"No! Mortimer will kill me!"

"No he won't. But if you don't go back you're going to die," Lockie said, and explained how the time travel was affecting the clones.

Morlan looked as if he was about to start crying again but a glare from Holmes silenced him.

"That could explain this pain I feel—all over, sort of an ache," he said.

"Probably. We need to get you back to see if they can help you before it is too late." Lockie then told him about the death of the other two clones.

"I'm sorry about Mydas. He was okay," said Morlan, "but I'm glad about Mobius. He scared me…he was so vicious. He killed Myron for no reason. We just wanted to tie him up and leave him, only before we could do that he stabbed him."

"Yes, it's strange how all three of you are so different," said Watson.

"Oh, not that strange," replied Morlan, appearing more confident for the first time. "You see when the lightning hit, we were each affected. All of us are like split personalities of Mycroft. We each represent a different aspect of his individuality. In small doses, these characteristics make up the man that Mycroft is. In every person some characteristics are more dominant and this defines their outward personality, but there are many hidden ones inside. With us, it's these hidden characteristics that dominated and became amplified. Mobius was Mycroft's temper. It is something he has always kept under control, but you know, Sherlock that your brother is a dangerous man when crossed; he is not to be trifled with. This characteristic came out in Mobius as his dominant feature. This anger, not tempered by other, kinder characteristics manifested itself as uncontrollable violence. Mycroft's more flamboyant side, which he has, but usually keeps repressed, came out in Mydas. He was a Mycroft with no self-control for the excesses of life."

"What about you?" asked Holmes with almost a sneer. "Mycroft has never had a fetish for women's clothes."

"No of course not, but I represent his feminine side."

At Holmes' look of disbelief, he went on.

"You can sneer, Sherlock, but we all have it—all men I mean. We have a feminine side which manifests itself as kindness and gentleness, and tempers our aggression; without it we would be like Mobius. All decent men have this side to them. In me it has come out as the overwhelming characteristic. I should have been a female, then it would have suited me. I can't help being the way I am, it's not of my choosing. If there had been more clones, each one would represent a different aspect of Mycroft's personality."

"Perhaps," said Holmes, "meantime we have no way of tracing Mycroft's whereabouts. He's as good as dead, unless we can find him and bring him home."

"I'm sorry, truly I am," said Morlan, looking like he was about to start crying again.

CHAPTER FIFTEEN

Holmes didn't want to return home with Morlan dressed the way he was so Lockie contacted Mortimer.

"We have Morlan," he said.

"Excellent! Can he tell us where Mycroft is?" asked Mortimer excitedly.

"Uh…no. he doesn't know and he doesn't know the security code."

"Oh?"

"Mortimer, there's one other thing."

"What?"

"The…uh…the laptop is broken."

"Can you fix it?"

Lockie looked down at the multiple pieces and said, "I don't think so. You see it wasn't our fault. Morlan dropped it and…"

"Lockie, you haven't exactly distinguished yourself…"

"Lay off the boy, Mortimer," interrupted Holmes. "You haven't exactly distinguished yourself either. All your so called computer experts can't break the security lockout. What kind of experts are they? What kind of feeble organization are you running anyway?"

"All right all right, just take it easy, Sherlock. I can understand you are upset," muttered Mortimer. "This whole case has been a nightmare from beginning to end. But I promise you, we will continue to search for Mycroft. He's the number one priority around here. Lockie, you and Joan gather around Morlan, and I'll bring you back."

"No," argued Holmes. "Take Morlan, but Lockie has left some things behind at Baker Street. We have to return there first. They will notify you later, when they're ready."

"Well…I don't know…" began Mortimer.

"Mortimer!" growled Holmes in his sternest voice. "It's the least you owe me."

"Yes, all right, but don't be too long. They have to come home today. We need Joan. If anyone can break through the lockout, it is she."

"They'll be there," replied Holmes.

I attached a transponder to Morlan's sleeve and said. "One to go, Mortimer." A moment later Morlan vanished.

"What about all this stuff?" I asked, looking around me.

"I'll contact the British museum and donate it to them. It's not stolen; he picked them up from the source. I'll say it belonged to a relative of mine, which is sort of true," said Holmes. "They'll be happy to take it off my hands."

I found a sack and picked up the pieces of the laptop. The machine was broken but it was possible I might be able to salvage the hard drive."

On the way back to Baker Street, Lockie asked curiously. "What sort of things have I left behind?"

"You'll see," was all that Holmes would say.

Back at Baker Street, I went to see Mrs Hudson to tell her we were leaving again and that Lockie and I were engaged. She was delighted, but not overly surprised. She said she always knew we would get together.

Upstairs, Holmes went to his desk and removed a small jewellery box. He opened it and handed it to Lockie. "This was my mother's. I want you to give it to Joan."

Lockie looked at the ring. "It's beautiful, Dad. Are you sure…?"

"My mother wanted me to give it to my wife, but as I am not likely to get married, it is only fair that it should go to my son. It's a family tradition."

Watson came over. "That is lovely, Holmes. Joan will treasure it."

"I'm sure she will," agreed Holmes."

"What will I treasure?" I asked, entering the room.

"You'll find out," said Lockie, hurriedly concealing the jewelry box in his pocket. Father and son faced each other.

"I don't know when I'll be able to see you again, Dad. I'll try and talk Mortimer into letting you come for our wedding, but I can't promise anything. Unless I'm greatly mistaken, there is going to be a ban on time travel in the future. There have been too many problems of late."

"It's all right, Junior, I understand," replied Holmes.

"Can't you call me Lockie instead of junior?"

"Very well, but calling you Junior denotes you as my son, Lockie does not."

"Oh. Well…uh, I just want to say it's been a real honour having this opportunity to work with you and get to know you better. Growing up I'd often wondered what my father was like. I used to imagine all sorts of things, but you are more than I ever imagined. I'll try and live up to your standards and make you proud of me," promised Lockie solemnly.

Holmes held out his hand to his son. "I already am."

Lockie shook his hand, and then took Holmes by surprise by hugging him. Despite his astonishment, I could see that the gesture moved him far more than he would ever admit.

I also hugged and kissed my father.

He held me tightly. "I wish you all the best, my dear sweet girl," he whispered to me.

I looked up at him, feeling suddenly close to tears.

"I don't care what Mortimer says, I am going to have my father give me away at my wedding."

"Knowing you, Joan, I will consider that a definite date," he replied.

I smiled at him.

Lockie came across and shook Watson's hand. "I'll look after her, sir. I promise I won't let anything happen to her. And who knows, in a few years' time we'll probably be sending hordes of grandchildren back in time for you to babysit." This last was said with a grin.

"I don't know about hordes," I disagreed. I moved over to Holmes and smiled up at him.

"Go on," he said, reading my mind.

My smiled broadened and I hugged him too.

"Take care of my boy, won't you? If he's anything like me, he'll need firm handling."

"Count on it." My smile faded. I looked seriously at him and made a solemn promise. "I'll find Mycroft. I won't stop working on it until I find him and send him home. The laptop is broken but I still have the hard drive. If I can access the information on that it will help to narrow down the search."

"If anyone can find him, it will be you," agreed Holmes. "Thank you, Joan. I already know you will be successful because Mortimer still exists. If Mycroft were dead, Mortimer wouldn't be here. I'll let his employers know that he is ill. When you return him, perhaps make it a week from this date to support the story."

I nodded.

With our goodbyes said, I stepped back. Lockie put his arm around me and activated the com link. "We're ready, Mortimer."

We waved to them as we shimmered and faded from their view. Our next was of Mortimer behind the controls back at HQ."

CHAPTER SIXTEEN

We changed out of our period clothes and I went to the computer to begin trying to crack the code and find Mycroft. I hooked up the hard drive. The files were badly corrupted but I was hoping I could salvage them enough to get a clue as to Mycroft's whereabouts.

Morlan was in hospital. Scans had shown he was also deteriorating, but at a much slower rate than Mydas. Mortimer hadn't told him there was no treatment for the condition. The damage was irreversible.

"When we find Mycroft, Mortimer, you can get some new genetic material and make new clones," suggested Lockie.

"No. I'm the last. It will end with me. It is time other people took on the responsibility. It was a good idea when it was first introduced, but we cannot keep looking to people from the past to solve the future's problems. Mycroft was indispensable at the time, but that doesn't apply anymore. I am not indispensable, nor were the other clones." He smiled weakly at us and added, "Who knows, you and Joan may be the next heads of this organization."

*****

Finding Mycroft was not going to be an easy task. I couldn't break through the code, so I went about it in a roundabout way, checking every year back two hundred years and forward two hundred years. It was time consuming and tedious. I would work twelve to fifteen hours a day. Sometimes I felt like giving up in frustration but just the fact that Mortimer was still alive proved that we eventually succeeded in finding Mycroft. That was my incentive, only time sure passed slowly. It was all of six months before we had a break, and it was Lockie that came up with it.

It was Saturday. Lockie had been working down in the lab in the morning and came up to the time machine room to drag me away for lunch. I was in one of my frustrated moods.

"I have checked everywhere for two hundred years, future and past, and I can't pick up a single trace. It's like he's disappeared off the planet!" I complained.

"I think Morlan would have told us if they went to another planet. What date are you taking the search from?"

"The day he disappeared," I replied. "Why?"

"I just had a funny thought. You've checked the past and the future, but have you searched the present?"

I stared at him. "Well, no. I mean, what was the point. If Mycroft was in the present, he'd have got in contact with us, Mortimer or Georgina at Scotland Yard."

"That's what you would expect him to do. But what if he was injured, or lost his memory. Morlan said he hit his head. What if he has been wandering around with amnesia?"

"Oh my God! I never even thought of that. Poor Mycroft. Anything could have happened to him!" I quickly turned to the controls and set the date of his disappearance six months ago, but this time set the tuner to the present. The familiar transport spike appeared on the screen.

"There!" I grinned delightedly.

"Let's go to the main operations room," said Lockie, as excited as I.

We went to the operations room. There was only minimum staff on duty. I reprogrammed the search satellite with Mycroft's genetic coding and set it to scan. We then sat back and waited anxiously.

"Two hits," Lockie said.

"Two?"

"One is Mortimer, the other must be Mycroft."

"Shouldn't there be three, counting Morlan?"

"No, his genetic structure is too chaotic for it to register." Lockie looked intently at the pinpoints on the map of Britain. "This will be Mortimer. He lives in this area. Can you narrow the search?"

I manipulated a few controls, until the map highlighted a single address.

"Yes!" Lockie quickly wrote it down and we hurried out. Mortimer was at home, but we decided not to report in. We thought it would be a nice to surprise him.

"I wonder what Mycroft is doing in Cambridge," I said, as we drove out of London.

"Who knows; I hope he's all right."

"What if he has lost his memory?"

"Maybe seeing us will jog it for him," suggested Lockie.

My relief at knowing Mycroft was alive was tempered with the concern that he may have suffered brain damage. What if he had permanent damage? It was just too awful to contemplate. I just couldn't think of any other reason why he would not have reported in once he realized what century he was in.

CHAPTER SEVENTEEN

It was late afternoon by the time we reached Cambridge and it took another half hour to find the address. It proved to be a neat single story red brick cottage with an exquisite garden surrounding it.

At the front door, Lockie rang the bell. Moments later the door was opened by a tall, stately woman in her early forties. She had brown hair and brown eyes. She wasn't beautiful, but there was a gracefulness and a presence about her that caught the eye.

"Yes?" she queried, looking at us with curiosity.

"Sorry to bother you," said Lockie politely. "We are looking for Mr Mycroft Holmes."

"Mycroft…Holmes?" recognition for the name, the Christian name, flashed in her eyes which she quickly covered up before replying. "I'm sorry, there is no Mr Holmes living at this address."

Just as I was about to flash my government badge at her, we heard a door open and a man's voice say: "Who's that, Rachel?" Then he came into view. It was Mycroft—a thinner, more healthy looking Mycroft, but nevertheless it was he. He saw and recognized us. For an instant it looked as if he was about to flee. Then he shrugged and came forward. There was no welcome in his eyes.

"I should have known you would find me. I'm just surprised it took you so long," he said.

"Mycroft," greeted Lockie. "You know why we're here?"

Mycroft nodded.

"Mycroft, do you know these people? They called you Holmes," said the woman turning to him.

"Yes, Rachel. This is my nephew, Sherlock Lestrade and his fiancée Joan Hudson."

A stab of relief went through me at that. Whatever reason Mycroft had for not reporting in, it wasn't brain damage. His observation skills were as acute as always. He had spotted my engagement ring and drew the correct conclusion from it.

"Well, I suppose you had better come in and not loiter on the doorstep," he said, a little ungraciously.

We entered. I noticed the woman was giving him puzzled glances and wondered who she was. He led us into the sitting room.

"We need to talk, Mycroft," said Lockie was we entered the room.

"Yes. May I present my wife, Rachel Sherrinford."

Wife! Whew! No wonder he hadn't reported in. He had gotten married instead. Talk about surprises.

"Mrs Sherrinford," I greeted. "We're pleased to meet you."

"Miss Hudson," she returned, and then looked at Mycroft. "Why did they call you Holmes, Mycroft?"

"It's a long story, my dear."

"Mycroft, that's classified," warned Lockie urgently.

Mycroft drew himself up to his full imposing six foot two inch height and glared coldly at Lockie.

Lockie back stepped a pace, feeling suddenly intimidated.

"Firstly, young man, you will address me as Uncle Mycroft. Secondly, as I founded and developed the organization I have the right to decide who is and who isn't privy to this information."

"Er, yes sir, Uncle Mycroft, sir." Lockie sat down hurriedly.

"Rachel has every right to know, especially if you are here to take me back."

"Take you back? Mycroft, what's going on?" asked his bewildered wife.

Mycroft took her hands in his and looked at her with warmth, an expression sadly lacking when he looked at us. "Rachel, my dear. I owe you a thousand apologies. I had hoped to live the rest of my life out with you. If I kept you in the dark it was for your own safety. Now that these two are here, things have changed. I cannot conceal my identity any longer."

"You're not a criminal, are you?"

Mycroft smiled. "Hardly."

"Is your name Holmes?"

"Yes. Mycroft Holmes. I've been using my mother's maiden name, which was Sherrinford. Do you remember when I told you that my parents named me after the Mycroft Holmes from the Sherlock Holmes stories by Dr. Watson?"

"Yes."

"Well, I wasn't named after him. I am him."

"What!" she looked startled. "But that is impossible. It would make you—"

"One hundred and eighty years old...yes, under normal circumstances, but my arrival here was anything but normal." He led her to an armchair and seated her. "I'll begin at the beginning." For the next twenty minutes he described everything that had happened up until he entered the house at Kensington Park Road.

She was looking rather stunned by all this information. "You devised and founded the British Secret Service?" she asked.

"Yes, invented it, ran it, and continue to run it to this day via clones."

"I had no idea," her eyes lit on her husband and she sat up straighter. There was wonderment there, but also pride and respect in her gaze.

"So, Uncle Mycroft, what happened at Kensington Park? Why did Mobius attack you?"

"When I entered the house it was empty. I searched around but could find no sign of the laptop. I had probably only been there five minutes when Mobius appeared. He stank of filth and sweat and was covered in blood. At first he mistook me for Mydas, but then I made a mistake. I assumed all the clones would have my proclivities. I poured myself a brandy and offered one to Mobius. How was I to know that he didn't drink? Of course Mydas knew this; he also knew that to offer him alcohol was enough to set him off. He suspected me immediately and well, you saw the rest. He tried to strangle me, almost succeeded too. He was brutally strong. Morlan arrived, pulled me free and brought me to this time to get away from Mobius. I hope you have stopped him?"

"Yes. He was Jack the Ripper," I said.

"Ah, I inferred something of the sort when I saw him. Anyway, Morlan and I arrived here in Cambridge. I was grateful to Morlan for saving my life. Then I urged him to turn himself in. He refused and was about to use the time machine again. I tried to grab it from him. We fought. I gave an extra strong tug and he let go at the same time. I lost my balance and fell, hitting my head. When I came to, Morlan was gone and I was dazed and confused. I didn't know where I was, or even, for a short while, who I was.

"I staggered away and wandered the streets until I crawled into Rachel's shed and fell asleep in sheer exhaustion." Here Mycroft flashed her a smile. "Next morning Rachel found me. I was covered in blood, as the head wound had bled rather profusely, although it was not that deep. She wanted to take me to hospital, but confused as I was, I had a dim memory of Mobius trying to throttle me and fighting with Morlan. So I begged her not to, saying that it was dangerous. Instead, sweet angel that she is, she brought me inside and tended my wound. As the days passed I got to know Rachel during my periods of lucidity. Then, finally one morning I woke up and it was all clear to me. I remembered everything."

"Why didn't' you contact us then?" asked Lockie.

"By that time I had fallen in love with Rachel and I didn't want to leave her. You know, Lockie, Sherlock has told me how much he wanted to stay with Georgina. How much he regretted returning, and that the days he spent with her were the happiest of his life. So I thought why should I go back? I have devoted my whole life to Queen and country. I have lived for my job, sacrificed all personal happiness for my work. Why shouldn't I be selfish for once? With Rachel I learned to live—really live—as a normal man, and what's more, these past six months have been the most wonderful time of my life. I have done my bit. In fact, I have done more than my share. Let someone else take up the mantle of responsibility. I'm staying here."

We were silent for a moment. "Mr Holmes, sir," I began. "It's not quite that simple as you well know. If you stay here you will change the time line. The clones will never be developed. Lockie and I will cease to exist and, well, you actually won't be here either. After all, if there is no clone to kidnap you, you can't end up in the future. And whilst I might say okay, you can sacrifice Lockie and me for your personal happiness, but can you in good conscience sacrifice the whole of Britain?"

"The whole of Britain is not dependent on me," argued Mycroft.

"Actually it is," countered Lockie. "Have you ever wondered why they cloned you in the first place, and not a famous statesman like Winston Churchill?"

"The thought did cross my mind."

"You were the major player in WWI. Everyone assumes that it was the battlefield generals that gave the orders and made the decisions of the war, but this is not true. I've read the top secret documents from the time. The orders came from you. All the intelligence reports came to you and you based your decisions on them. You were the only person in the British Government and British military that had all the facts at your fingertips with instant recall of these facts. Your brain is like a computer, Mycroft—one not subject to power failures. But for your leadership and direction during that time, we would have lost the war. The battles that recorded the largest loss of life took place when battlefield generals made their own decisions, and also during the month that you were laid up in hospital recovering from a serious bullet wound. A German assassin tried to kill you, but luckily for us, he failed.

"You worked night and day nonstop during the crisis periods and only your quick thinking saved the day on numerous occasions. It was you that invented the cat nap. A short one hour nap every ten. My father played an important part as one of your spies, but he was dispensable, you were not. When scientists came up with the cloning project, the Government declared that they needed a Mycroft to run the British Intelligence department. With you at the helm they thought, nothing would ever go wrong. That's why you and only you were cloned and that is also why they made six backups."

"It's also why," I added, "That the head of MI6 is always called M, no matter what their real name is. It's in honor of you."

Mycroft was silent for a moment. "I had no idea," he said softly.

His wife placed her hand over his, feeling a little awed at the enormity and importance of her husband to the history of her nation.

"If you don't go back, Uncle Mycroft, you will change history. You will doom England to German rule. That could mean that during World War II, the British will become Nazi's. Do you really want that? It's not just Joan and me whose lives are at stake here, but millions of people over a century and a half. You have always been responsible, Uncle Mycroft, can you really live with that on your conscience?"

"You know how to rub it in, don't you?" sighed Mycroft. "What if I stay and Mortimer goes back in my place. I could take over for him…"

Lockie shook his head. "You can't clone a clone and what's more, the clones can't handle stress and believe me, you were under a helluva lot of stress during the war. Mortimer would crumple."

"What year did you come from, Mycroft?" asked Rachel suddenly.

"1892."

"And these young people are here to return you to that time?"

"Yes."

"I always knew there was something special about you, that you were above the average man. I also knew that there was something different about you. I fell in love with you for your old fashioned ways and mannerisms. Sometimes I think that I was born in the wrong era."

"Rachel!" Mycroft moved closer to her and looked down at her. "You're not suggesting…?"

"Why not? I'm your wife, Mycroft. Until death do us part, in this, in any century, but only if you want me to be."

I felt a lump rising in my throat at this touching scene.

"You would give this all up? All the modern conveniences just to come back with me?"

"Only if you want me," she repeated.

"Want you…," Mycroft went down on his knees before her. "My dearest Rachel." He took her hands in his and kissed them. "I would be the happiest man in the world." They beamed at each other, oblivious of Lockie and me.

Who would have thought that Mycroft would find himself a wife, and even more importantly be such a devoted husband? It occurred to me that he probably never really had the opportunity to meet women before because he never varied his lifestyle. Just work, his lodgings and the Diogenes club. I grinned suddenly as a thought struck me.

"Mr Holmes, does this mean that you won't be spending all your free time at the Diogenes club?"

Mycroft glanced around. "Who would want to hang around with a group of unsociable men when I can have the pleasure of a fair lady's company?"

Rachel smiled at him.

He stood up. "You will have to give us four weeks to settle our affairs in this century. I teach politics and accounting at Cambridge, Rachel teaches English history. Come back in four weeks and we will return with you. Don't tell Mortimer where I am, he'll only irritate me."

Lockie stood up and offered his hand. "All right, we'll give you the four weeks."

I shook Mrs Sherrinford/Holmes' hand and said, "I think you're awfully brave. Having visited the past a couple of times, I can't say that I'd want to live there. Those corsets are hell."

Lockie caught the last part of my sentence and grinned. "They may be hell, but you should have seen her—she looked great. Women in those days really knew how to get a man's attention." He rolled his eyes and smacked his lips in an exaggerated motion.

"Don't be disgusting," I said, giving him a slap on the arm.

He just grinned and shook hands with Rachel, adding. "It's a pleasure meeting you Aunt Rachel. Uncle Mycroft here will no doubt give you more of our background later on. When you go back you'll meet my father as well."

"Your father is Sherlock Holmes then?"

"Yes."

Rachel smiled. "I'll look forward to it. I never thought I would be joining such a distinguished family."

"You'll meet my father, too," I added. "He's Dr. Watson."

"That will also be a pleasure as I am a big fan of his."

We said our goodbyes and promised to return in four weeks and not a day before. I had a momentary misgiving that they would flee, but it passed. Mycroft knew he couldn't hide from us. We could track him down wherever he went. Besides, he didn't have to. Unlike Georgina and Wiona, this lady was willing to give up her modern lifestyle and return with him to the past. I was pleased for Mycroft, considering how much he contributed to his country, he deserved this happiness.

CHAPTER EIGHTEEN

It was four weeks to the day that we returned to Cambridge to pick up Mycroft and his wife. They only had two suitcases, containing things that they wanted to take with them.

Rachel locked the door on her house and then turned to me, holding out the keys. "Joan, this is for you and Lockie."

I looked at the keys in surprise as Mycroft came up. "We want the two of you to have the house, as a wedding present. It is of no use to us."

"I…I don't know what to say," I gasped.

"Uncle Mycroft, Aunt Rachel, this is too much…" began Lockie.

"Nonsense. We considered selling it, but what good is future money in the past? No, when you want to get away from the hustle and bustle of London, you will have a country place to retreat to."

I was delighted. It was a quaint cottage and I loved the garden. I could already picture myself retiring to it. "It's a wonderful present. We will treasure it," I said, smiling warmly.

Mycroft handed Lockie the deeds. "It's all fixed up."

Before long we were on our way to London. Several hours later, Lockie drove to the underground car park beneath headquarters. We noticed as we climbed out of the car and started to walk towards the elevators that there was a code red emergency in place. A red light was flashing above the lift."

"Is it a fire?" asked Mycroft.

"No, a security breech. Something is going on." Lockie and I exchanged glances.

"Perhaps we should wait here until the situation is under control," suggested Mycroft.

"Good idea. You two wait here, Joan and I will check it out." Lockie pulled his gun from his shoulder holster and we approached the lifts. Before we could touch any of the controls, the door slid open and Morlan—a crazy-eyed, ill looking Morlan stood there.

He saw us and screamed. That's when I noticed he was armed. He fired before any of us could react, shooting Lockie through the shoulder.

Lockie fell, dropping his gun.

"Help me!" screamed Morlan, crazed with pain.

Mortimer had told us that Mydas had suffered the agonies of the damned before he died: That no amount of narcotics could relieve the pain which was occurring at the cellular level. Morlan was at the same stage of intense unrelenting pain. He saw Mycroft and despite his dementia realized a way out.

"I don't want to exist!" he cried and raised the gun, firing at Mycroft.

It all happened in mere seconds, but to me it felt like an eternity. I watched as Rachel threw herself in front of Mycroft.

The bullet hit.

It was like seeing it in slow motion. Rachel fell backwards against Mycroft, blood staining her chest.

The sight galvanized me into action. I dropped to Lockie's side and grabbed his gun up. I emptied chamber after chamber into Morlan as he tried to raise his weapon for another shot at Mycroft.

Mycroft was oblivious to it all. He cradled Rachel in his arms and dropped down to his knees, clutching her tightly.

Security guards came up in the lift and took in the scene.

"Get Mortimer," I ordered. I pulled my scarf off and made a wad and pressed it against Lockie's shoulder to try and stem the bleeding.

Rachel opened her eyes and looked up at Mycroft. "I couldn't let him kill you, you're too important," she said weakly.

"I will die a thousand deaths without you by my side," replied Mycroft shakily.

"Love you," she whispered, her eyes closing for the final time.

Mycroft had never struck me as the sort of man that was capable of tears, but he wept now as he held his first and last love in his arms.

I felt my own tears well up. Life was so unfair!

Mortimer arrived along with some medics. We had briefed him about Rachel and he understood at a glance what happened. One of the medics treated Lockie's shoulder temporarily. He would need an operation to remove the bullet.

After nearly twenty minutes, Mortimer moved over and dropped a hand to Mycroft's shoulder. "Mycroft," he said gently.

Mycroft did not respond.

"Mycroft, there is nothing you can do for her," said Mortimer.

Finally, Mycroft turned a tear stained face up to him and said coldly, tonelessly, "I never want to see another god damned clone for as long as I live."

Mortimer looked hurt. Mycroft was like a father figure to the clones. He stepped back, saying nothing.

I helped Lockie stand up.

Mycroft looked down at the lifeless woman on the ground. He wiped his eyes, and then slipped out of his coat. He balled it up and placed it under her head as a pillow. He straightened up. I knew words were useless at such a time, but my heart went out to him. As he started to turn away from Rachel, I moved over to him and slipped my arms around him, giving him a warm embrace. He held me for a long moment, and then let me go.

"Send me home, Joan, Sherlock," he said, ignoring Mortimer and not looking back at Rachel as he strode to the lift.

We joined him and took him down to the time machine room. He walked silently over to the platform as I took the controls. Today should have been one of the happiest days of his life, instead…

"Mycroft. Dad has told your work that you are ill, so you are not expected back yet. Take all the time you need. Don't rush it. We will return you one week past the date you were kidnapped," said Lockie.

Mycroft nodded, but remained silent.

"Goodbye Mr Holmes," I said, knowing in my heart that we would never see him again. If ever we had to travel to the past, he would avoid us as painful reminders of what could have been. Poor Mycroft! I manipulated the controls and he shimmered from view.

Lockie was looking pale.

"Come on, let's get you to the medical centre," I said, taking his good arm and leading him along.

"Joan," he said, stopping abruptly.

I looked at him.

He was looking at me with a curious expression on his face. "I don't know that I should marry you."

"What? Why not?"

"We Holmes men don't seem to have a very good track record with women. Look at Dad. Look at poor Mycroft. I would never forgive myself if anything happened to you."

I looked up at him. "Nothing will happen to me. I promise that I won't jump in front of you if someone tries to shoot you," I said, trying to lighten the mood, but he remained serious. "Well, it's not like Sherlock lost Georgina. She's alive and well," I added.

"No, but he lost her all the same. You remember what Mycroft said about how he'd told him that he wished he'd stayed. That he was at his happiest when he was with mum."

"He didn't belong in our time, Lockie," I said gently. "Neither did Mycroft. Maybe Rachel was never meant to go back. All we can do is honour her memory; she sacrificed herself to save Mycroft because she knew how important he was. She did it willingly. In time Mycroft will come to understand that, and time will heal his grief."

"Perhaps, but not his loneliness."

"So because Sherlock and Mycroft Holmes are lonely men, you want to doom yourself to the same fate?"

Lockie looked at me, his eyes wide. "I don't want to be lonely."

"You don't have to be," I said, moving closer to him.

"I love you, Joan."

"I love you, Sherlock Lestrade."

The End

☺

15183222R00186

Printed in Poland
by Amazon Fulfillment
Poland Sp. z o.o., Wrocław